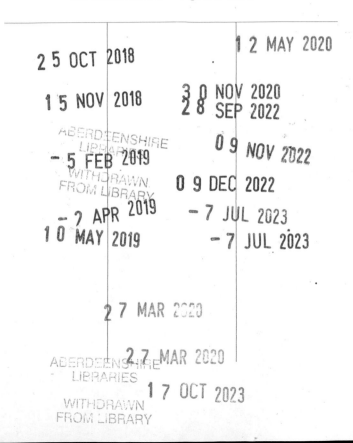

Praise for Bear Grylls

'Unputdownable! Bear has made the leap into fiction with great ferocity'   Sir Ranulph Fiennes

'This debut thriller by the adventurer Bear Grylls is enthralling. Grylls excels in describing the trials and tribulations of tramping through uncharted Amazon rainforests'   *The Times*

'[A] fast and furious debut novel'   *Press Association*

'An impressively strong fiction debut from one of the best known TV faces of survival and outdoor adventure, Bear Grylls makes full use of his military and survivalist background to deliver a rip-roaring and vividly colourful *Boy's Own*-style thriller'
Irish Independent

'A modern-day conspiracy to raise Hitler's Third Reich from the ashes'   *Mail on Sunday*

'*Ghost Flight* is a great adventure story: huge spiders, deadly piranhas, unforgiving terrains, evil Nazis, and death at every turn. What's not to like? Jason Bourne meets Ben Hope with a dash of Indiana Jones in an adventure series set to continue'
Buzz Magazine

Bear Grylls has become known around the world as one of the most recognised faces of survival and outdoor adventure. His journey to this acclaim started in the UK, where his late father taught him adventure and how to climb.

Trained from a young age in martial arts, Bear went on to spend three years as a soldier in the British Special Forces, serving with 21 SAS. It was here that he perfected many of the skills that his fans all over the world enjoy, watching him pit himself against Mother Nature.

His TV Emmy nominated show *Man Vs Wild / Born Survivor* became one of the most watched programmes on the planet with an estimated audience of 1.2 billion. He then progressed to US Network TV, hosting the hit adventure show *Running Wild* on NBC, where he takes some of the world's best known movie stars on incredible adventures, including the likes of President Barack Obama, Ben Stiller, Kate Winslet, Zac Efron and Channing Tatum.

Bear co-owns and hosts the BAFTA award winning *The Island with Bear Grylls* on Channel 4, which has sold as a format all around the world. In addition, Bear also co-owns and hosts ITV & CITV's *Bear Grylls Survival School* as well as *Survivor Games* and *Absolute Wild* for Chinese TV.

Bear is currently the youngest ever Chief Scout to the UK Scout Association and is an honorary Colonel to the Royal Marines Commandos.

He has authored twenty books, including the number one bestselling autobiography *Mud, Sweat & Tears*. Bear's latest live project brings the adventure to our doorsteps with the live arena spectacular **Endeavour** which sees Bear recreate some of the greatest ever moments of human exploration.

Find out more at www.beargrylls.com or follow Bear on Twitter @BearGrylls or Instagram @beargrylls

BEAR GRYLLS

BURNING ANGELS

An Orion paperback

First published in Great Britain in 2016
by Orion
This paperback edition published in 2017
by Orion Books,
an imprint of The Orion Publishing Group Ltd,
Carmelite House, 50 Victoria Embankment
London EC4Y 0DZ

An Hachette UK company

3 5 7 9 10 8 6 4

A CIP catalogue record for this book
is available from the British Library.

ISBN 978 1 4091 5687 1

Typeset by Input Data Services Ltd, Somerset

Printed in Great Britain by Clays Ltd, St Ives plc

www.orionbooks.co.uk

For Roger Gower, killed by poachers while flying conservation patrols over East Africa, and for the Roger Gower Memorial Fund and Tusk Trust, two foremost conservation charities.

ACKNOWLEDGEMENTS

Special thanks to the following: literary agents at PFD Caroline Michel, Annabel Merullo and Laura Williams, for their hard work and effort to support the publication of this book; Jon Wood and Jemima Forrester, and all at Orion – Malcolm Edwards, Mark Rusher and Leanne Oliver – who make up 'Team Grylls'. Thanks also to all at BGV, for making the movie side of the Will Jaeger thriller series such an exciting reality.

Thanks also to the following: Hamish de Bretton-Gordon, Ollie Morton and Iain Thompson of Avon Protection, for their invaluable insight, advice and expertise on all things CBRN, and their input into the chemical, biological and nuclear aspects of this book, including the defence and protection measures. Chris Daniels and all at Hybrid Air Vehicles, for their unique insight and expertise on all things Airlander, and for pushing the envelope in terms of what is possible with such an airship; to Paul and Anne Sherratt, for such potent insight into Cold War relations immediately following World War Two; to Bob Lowndes, of Autism Wessex, for advice on all things autism and regarding those on the spectrum; to Peter Message, for a youthful critique of the early stages of the manuscript for this book; and to Ash Alexander-Cooper OBE for your technical military advice.

And a final special thank you to Damien Lewis, for helping to build upon what we discovered together in my grandfather's war chest marked 'Top Secret'. Bringing those World War Two documents, memorabilia and artefacts to life, in such a modern context, is pure brilliance.

AUTHOR'S NOTE

This book is inspired by the true life exploits of my grandfather, Brigadier William Edward Harvey Grylls, OBE, 15/19th King's Royal Hussars and Commanding Officer of Target Force, the covert unit established at Winston Churchill's behest at the end of World War Two. The unit was one of the most clandestine bands of operators ever assembled by the War Office, and its mission was to track down and protect secret technologies, weaponry, scientists and high-ranking Nazi officials to serve the West's cause against the world's new superpower, the Soviet Union.

No one in our family had any idea of his covert role as Commanding Officer T Force – 'T' standing for 'Target' – until many years after his death and the release of information under the Official Secrets Act seventy-year rule – a process of discovery that inspired the writing of this book.

My grandfather was a man of few words, but I remember him so fondly from when I was a child growing up. Pipe-smoking, enigmatic, dry-humoured and loved by those he led.

To me, though, he was always just Grandpa Ted.

BURNING ANGELS

Daily Mail, August 2015

Nazi Gold Train is FOUND: deathbed confession leads treasure hunters to secret location as Polish officials claim they have seen proof on radar.

A Nazi gold train has been found in Poland after the man who helped hide it at the end of the Second World War revealed its location in a deathbed confession. Two men, a German and a Pole, last week claimed they had found the train – believed to contain treasure – close to the small town of Walbrzych in south-west Poland.

Piotr Zuchowski, Poland's National Heritage and Conservation Officer, said: 'We do not know what is inside the train. Probably military equipment, but also jewellery, works of art and archive documents. Armoured trains from this period were used to carry extremely valuable items, and this is an armoured train.'

Local lore says Nazi Germany ordered the vast underground rail network, which snakes around the massive Ksiaz Castle, be built to hide Third Reich valuables. Concentration camp inmates were used to build the huge tunnels – code-named Riese (Giant) – to use as production spaces for strategic weapons, as the site was safe from Allied air raids.

. . . .

Sun, October 2015

History tells us that the Special Air Service regiment created in 1942 was disbanded in 1945 . . . But a new book by acclaimed historian Damien Lewis has revealed that in fact one lone, top secret 30-man SAS unit fought on. This group 'went dark' at the end of the war to go on an unofficial mission to hunt down Nazi war criminals.

Their aim was to find the SS and Gestapo monsters who had murdered their captured comrades, as well as hundreds of French civilians who had tried to help them. By 1948 the band had captured more than 100 of the war's worst killers – many of whom had avoided facing justice at Nuremberg in 1945 and 1946 – and brought them to trial.

This tiny SAS unit, dubbed 'the Secret Hunters' was run from a shadow HQ based in the Hyde Park Hotel in London. It was funded off the books by an exiled Russian aristocrat working for the British War Office, Prince Yuri Galitzine.

And it was members of this group who were the earliest to uncover the full horror of the Nazi extermination camps . . . The Natzweiler concentration camp near Strasbourg had been the scene of horrific experiments by the Nazis. It was there that commandant Josef Kramer experimented with the technique of using gas to murder Jewish prisoners.

....

BBC, January 2016

OETZI THE ICEMAN HAD A STOMACH BUG, RESEARCHERS SAY.

Microbes extracted from the insides of a 5,300-year-old mummy have shown he was suffering from a stomach bug before he died, scientists have discovered. Oetzi the Iceman, the name given to the frozen body discovered in the Alps in 1991, had a bacterial infection that is common today, researchers said.

A genetic analysis of the bacteria – *Helicobacter pylori* – was carried out, helping to trace the history of the microbe, which is closely linked to the history of human migration.

Professor Albert Zink, head of the Institute for Mummies and the Iceman, at the European Academy in Bolzano, said: 'One of the first challenges was to obtain samples from the stomach without doing damage to the mummy. Therefore we had to completely defrost the mummy, and could finally get access by an opening . . .'

16 October 1942, Helheim Glacier, Greenland

SS Lieutenant Herman Wirth brushed aside the flakes of swirling snow that obscured his vision. He forced himself closer, so that his face and hers were barely a foot apart. As he stared through the intervening mass of ice he let out a strangled gasp.

The woman's eyes were wide open, even in her death throes. Sure enough, they were sky blue – just as he'd known they would be. But there his hopes came to a sudden, crashing end.

Her eyes drilled into his. Crazed. Glazed. Zombie-like. A pair of red-hot gun barrels boring into him from out of the translucent block of ice that held her.

Unbelievably, when this woman had fallen to her death to be entombed within the glacier, she had been crying tears of blood. Wirth could see where the oozing, frothy redness had streamed from her eye sockets, only to be frozen into immortality.

He forced himself to break eye contact and flicked his gaze lower, towards her mouth. It was one that he had spent countless nights fantasising about, as he shivered in the Arctic cold that penetrated even his thick goose-down sleeping bag.

He had envisaged her lips in his mind. He'd dreamed about them ceaselessly. They would be full and pouting and gorgeously pink, he'd told himself; the mouth of a perfect Germanic maid who had waited five thousand years for a kiss to revive her.

His kiss.

But the more he looked, the more he felt a wave of revulsion rise within his guts. He turned and dry-retched into the icy blast of wind that seared and howled through the crevasse.

In truth, hers would be the kiss of death; the embrace of a she-devil.

The woman's mouth was encrusted with a deep red mass – a frozen bolus of engorged blood. It thrust into the ice before her like a ghastly swirling funeral shroud. And above the mouth, her nose too had been voiding a tidal wave of crimson fluid, a gruesome haemorrhage.

He swung his gaze lower and to left and right, letting his eyes rove across her frozen, naked flesh. For some reason this woman of the Ancients had torn off her clothes, before crawling across the ice sheet and stumbling blindly into this crevasse that cut through the glacier. She had come to rest on an ice shelf, becoming frozen solid within a matter of hours.

Perfectly preserved . . . but far from perfect.

Wirth could barely believe it, but even the ice woman's armpits were streaked with thick, stringy beads of crimson fluid. Before she had died – *as* she had died – this so-called Nordic ancestor goddess had been sweating out her very lifeblood.

He let his gaze creep lower still, dreading what he would find there. He was not mistaken. A thick frozen smear of red surrounded her nether regions. Even as she had lain there, her heart pounding its last, thick gouts of putrid blood had flowed from her loins.

Wirth turned and vomited.

He heaved the contents of his stomach through the wire mesh of the cage, seeing the watery liquid splatter deep into the shadows far below. He retched until there was nothing left, the dry heaving subsiding into short, stabbing, painful gasps.

Hands clawing at the mesh, he hauled himself off his knees. He glanced upwards at the glaring floodlights, which threw a fierce, unforgiving blaze into the shadowed ice chasm, reflecting all around him in a crazy kaleidoscope of frozen colour.

Kammler's so-called Var – his beloved ancient Nordic princess: well, the General was welcome to her!

SS General Hans Kammler: what in the name of God was Wirth going to tell – and show – him? The famed SS commander had flown all this way to witness her glorious liberation from the ice, and the promise of her resurrection, so that he could deliver the news in person to the Führer.

Hitler's dream, finally brought to fruition.

And now this.

Wirth forced his gaze back to the corpse. The longer he studied it, the more horrified he became. It was as if the ice maiden's body had been at war with itself; as if it had rejected its own innards, disgorging them from every orifice. If she had died like this, her blood and guts becoming frozen within the ice, she must have been alive and bleeding for some considerable time.

Wirth didn't believe any more that it was the fall into the crevasse that had killed her. Or the cold. It was whatever ancient, devilish sickness had held her in its grasp as she stumbled and crawled her way across the glacier.

But weeping blood?

Vomiting blood?

Sweating blood?

Urinating blood, even?

What in the name of God would cause that?

What in the name of God had killed her?

This was far from being the ancestral Aryan mother figure they had all hoped for. This wasn't the Nordic warrior goddess he had dreamed of for countless nights – proving a glorious Aryan lineage stretching back five thousand years. This was no ancient mother to the Nazi *Übermensch* – a perfect blonde, blue-eyed Norse woman rescued from far before the reach of recorded history.

Hitler had thirsted for so long for such proof.

And now this – a devil woman.

As Wirth gazed into her tortured features – those empty, bulging, blood-encrusted eyes, full of the terrifying glaze of the walking dead – he was struck by a sudden blinding realisation.

Somehow he knew that he was staring through a doorway into the very gates of hell.

He stumbled backwards from the ice corpse, reaching above his head and tugging violently on the signal rope. 'Up! Get me up! Up! Start the winch!'

Above him an engine roared into life. Wirth felt the cage lurch into motion. As it began to lift, the horrifying, bloodied block of ice retreated from his view.

The dawn sun was throwing a faint blush across the wind- and ice-whipped snow as Wirth's hunched figure rose above the surface. He climbed exhaustedly from the cage and stepped on to the hard-packed, frozen whiteness, the sentries to either side attempting to click their heels as he passed. Their massive fur-lined boots made a dull clump, their rubber soles caked in a thick layer of ice.

Wirth snapped up a half-hearted salute, his mind lost in tortured thoughts. Setting his shoulders into the howling wind, he pulled his thick smock closer around his numb features and pushed onwards towards the nearby tent.

A savage blast whipped the black smoke away from the chimney that protruded through the roof. The stove had been stoked, no doubt in readiness for a hearty breakfast.

Wirth figured his three SS colleagues were already awake. They were early risers, and with today being the day the ice maiden would rise from her tomb, they would be doubly eager to face the dawn.

Originally there had been two fellow SS officers with him – First Lieutenant Otto Rahn and General Richard Darre. Then, with no warning, SS General Hans Kammler had flown in on an aircraft equipped with ice skids, to witness the final stages of this epic operation.

As the overall commander of the expedition, General Darre

was supposedly in charge, but no one was pretending that General Kammler didn't wield the real power. Kammler was Hitler's man. He had the Führer's ear. And in truth, Wirth had thrilled to the fact that the General had come to witness in person his moment of greatest triumph.

Back then, barely forty-eight hours earlier, things had been looking golden; the perfect ending to an impossibly ambitious undertaking. Yet this morning . . . Well, Wirth had little appetite to face the dawn, his breakfast, or his SS brethren.

Why was he even here? he wondered. Wirth styled himself as a scholar of ancient cultures and religions, which was what had first brought him to Himmler and Hitler's attention. He'd been awarded his Nazi party number by the Führer himself – a rare honour indeed.

In 1936 he had founded the Deutsche Ahnenerbe, the name meaning 'inherited from the forefathers'. Its mission was to prove that a mythical Nordic population had once ruled the world – the original Aryan race. Legend had it that a blonde, blue-eyed people had inhabited Hyperboria, a fabled frozen land of the north, which in turn had suggested the Arctic Circle.

Expeditions to Finland, Sweden and the Arctic had followed, but all without any great or earth-shattering revelations. Then a group of soldiers had been sent to Greenland to establish a weather station, and there they had heard tantalising reports that an ancient woman had been discovered entombed within the Greenland ice.

And so the present, fateful mission had been born.

In short, Wirth was an archaeological enthusiast and opportunist. He was no diehard Nazi, that was for sure. But as the Deutsche Ahnenerbe's president, he was forced to rub shoulders with the darkest fanatics of Hitler's regime – two of whom were in the tent before him right now.

He knew this would not end well for him. Too much had been promised – some of it directly to the Führer. Too many lofty expectations, too many impossible hopes and ambitions hinged upon this moment.

Yet Wirth had seen her face, and the lady of the ice had the features of a monster.

2

Wirth ducked his head and thrust it through the double layer of thick canvas: one layer to keep out the murderous cold and the storm-whipped snow; the second, inner layer to keep in the heat thrown off by live human bodies and the roaring stove.

The smell of freshly brewed coffee hit him. Three pairs of eyes looked at him expectantly.

'My dear Wirth, why the long face?' General Kammler quipped. 'Today is the day!'

'You didn't drop our lovely *Frau* into the bottom of the crevasse?' Otto Rahn added, a wry grin twisting his features. 'Or try to kiss her awake, only to get slapped around the face for your troubles?'

Rahn and Kammler guffawed.

The diehard SS general and the somewhat effeminate palaeontologist seemed to share a peculiar brand of camaraderie. Like so much in the Reich, it made no sense to Wirth. As to the third seated figure – SS General Richard Walter Darre – he just scowled into his coffee, dark eyes smouldering under hooded brows, thin lips clamped tight shut as always.

'So, our ice maiden?' Kammler prompted. 'Is she ready for us?' He swept his hand across the breakfast spread. 'Or do we have our celebratory feast first?'

Wirth shuddered. He was still feeling nauseous. He figured it might be better if the three men got to see the Lady of the Ice before they ate.

'It's perhaps best, Herr General, to do this before your breakfast.'

'You seem downhearted, Herr Lieutenant,' Kammler prompted. 'Is she not all we were expecting? A blonde-haired, blue-eyed angel of the north?'

'You have freed her from the ice?' General Darre cut in. 'Her features are visible? What do they tell you about our Freyja?' Darre had borrowed the name of an ancient Norse goddess – meaning 'the lady' – for the woman entombed within the ice.

'Surely she is our Hariasa,' Rahn countered. 'Our Hariasa of the ancient north.' Hariasa was another Nordic deity; her name meant 'the goddess with the long hair'. Three days earlier, it had seemed entirely fitting.

For weeks the team had been carefully chipping away at the ice so as to enable a closer look. When finally they managed it, the ice maiden proved to be turned into the wall of the crevasse, with only her back showing. But it was enough. She had revealed herself to possess glorious tresses of long golden hair, plaited into thick braids.

At that discovery, Wirth, Rahn and Darre had felt a bolt of excitement burn through them. If her facial features likewise matched the Aryan racial model, they were home and dry. Hitler would shower his blessings upon them. All they needed to do was free her from the wall of the crevasse, turn the block of ice around and get a proper look at her.

Well, Wirth had had that look ... and it was utterly stomach-churning.

'She's not quite what we were expecting, Herr Generals,' he stammered. 'It's best you come see for yourselves.'

Kammler was the first to his feet, a faint frown creasing his forehead. The SS General had appropriated the name of a third Nordic goddess for the frozen corpse. 'She will be cherished by all who set eyes upon her,' he had declared. 'That is why I have told the Führer that we have named her Var – "the beloved".'

Well, it would take a true saint to love that bloody, corrupted

8

corpse. And of one thing Wirth was certain: there were few saints in that tent right now.

He led the men across the ice, feeling as if he were heading his own funeral cortège. They entered the cage and were lowered, the floodlights flaring to life as they sank beneath the surface. Wirth had ordered the lights kept extinguished, unless someone was working on or inspecting the corpse. He didn't want the heat thrown off by the powerful illumination melting the ice and thawing out their lady-in-waiting. She would need to remain utterly deep-frozen for safe transport back to the Deutsche Ahnenerbe's headquarters in Berlin.

He glanced across the cage at Rahn. His face lay in dark shadow. No matter where he might be, Rahn wore a wide-brimmed black felt fedora hat. A self-styled bone-hunter and archaeological adventurer, he had adopted it as his trademark.

Wirth felt a certain camaraderie with the flamboyant Rahn. They shared the same hopes, passions and beliefs. And, of course, the same fears.

The cage came to a lurching halt. It swung back and forth for an instant like a crazed pendulum, before the chain holding it brought it to some kind of standstill.

Four sets of eyes stared into the face of the corpse entombed within the block of ice; ice that was streaked with hideous swirls of dark red. Wirth could sense the impact the apparition was having upon his SS colleagues. There was a stunned, disbelieving silence.

It was General Kammler who finally broke the quiet. He turned his gaze on Wirth. His face was inscrutable as ever, a cold reptilian look flaring behind his eyes.

'The Führer expects,' he announced quietly. 'We do not disappoint the Führer.' A pause. 'Make her a figure worthy of her name: of Var.'

Wirth shook his head disbelievingly. 'We go ahead as planned? But Herr General, the risks . . .'

'What risks, Herr Lieutenant?'

'We have no idea what killed her . . .' Wirth gestured at the corpse. 'What caused all—'

'There is no risk,' Kammler cut in. 'She came to grief on the ice cap five millennia ago. That's five thousand years. You will clean her up. Make her beautiful. Make her Nordic, Aryan . . . perfect. Make her fit for the Führer.'

'But how, Herr General?' Wirth queried. 'You have seen—'

'Unfreeze her, for God's sake,' Kammler cut in. He gestured at the block of ice. 'You Deutsche Ahnenerbe people have been experimenting on live humans – freezing and unfreezing them – for years, have you not?'

'We have, Herr General,' Wirth conceded. 'Not myself personally, but there have been human freezing experiments, plus the salt-water—'

'Spare me the details.' Kammler jabbed a gloved finger at the bloodied corpse. 'Breathe life into her. Whatever it takes, wipe that death's-head smile off her face. Banish that . . . look from her eyes. Make her suit the Führer's prettiest dreams.'

Wirth forced out a reply. 'Yes, Herr General.'

Kammler glanced from Wirth to Rahn. 'If you do not – if you fail in this task – on your heads be it.'

He yelled an order for the cage to be lifted skywards. They rose together in silence. When they reached the surface, Kammler turned to face the Deutsche Ahnenerbe men.

'I have little stomach for breakfast any more.' He clicked his heels together and gave the Nazi salute. '*Heil Hitler!*'

'*Heil Hitler,*' his SS colleagues echoed.

And with that, General Hans Kammler stalked across the ice, heading for his aircraft – and Germany.

3

Present day

The pilot of the C-130 Hercules cargo aircraft turned to eye Will Jaeger. 'Kinda overkill, buddy, hiring a whole C-130 for just you guys, eh?' He had a strong southern drawl, most likely Texas. 'There's just three of you, right?'

Through the doorway into the hold Jaeger eyed his two fellow warriors, seated on the fold-down canvas seats. 'Yeah. Just the three.'

'Bit over the top, wouldn't you say?'

Jaeger had boarded the aircraft as if ready to do a high-altitude parachute jump – decked out in full-face helmet, oxygen mask and bulky jumpsuit. The pilot had not the slightest hope of recognising him.

Not yet, anyway.

Jaeger shrugged. 'Yeah, well we were expecting more. You know how it is: some couldn't make it.' A pause. 'They got trapped in the Amazon.'

He let the last words hang in the air for a good few seconds.

'The Amazon?' the pilot queried. 'The jungle, right? What was it? Jump that went wrong?'

'Worse than that.' Jaeger loosened the straps that held his jump helmet tight, as if he needed to get some air. 'They didn't make it . . . because they died.'

The pilot did a double take. 'They died? Died like how? Some kinda skydiving accident?'

Jaeger spoke slowly now, emphasising every word. 'No. Not an accident. Not from where I was standing. More like very planned, very deliberate murder.'

'Murder? Shoot.' The pilot reached forward and eased off on the aircraft's throttles. 'We're nearing our cruise altitude . . . One-twenty minutes to the jump.' A pause. 'Murder? So who was murdered? And – heck – why?'

In answer, Jaeger removed his helmet completely. He still had his silk balaclava tight around his face, for warmth. He always wore one when leaping from thirty thousand feet. It could be colder than Everest at that kind of altitude.

The pilot still wouldn't be able to recognise him, but he would be able to see the look in Jaeger's eyes. And right now, it was one that could kill.

'I figure it was murder,' Jaeger repeated. 'Cold-blooded murder. Funny thing is – it all happened after a jump from a C-130.' He glanced around the cockpit. 'In fact, an aircraft pretty similar to this one . . .'

The pilot shook his head, nervousness creeping in. 'Buddy, you lost me . . . But hey, your voice sounds kinda familiar. That's the thing with you Brits – you all sound the goddam same, if you don't mind me sayin'.'

'I don't mind you saying.' Jaeger smiled. His eyes didn't. The look in them could have frozen blood. 'So, I figure you must've served with the SOAR. That's before you went private.'

'The SOAR?' The pilot sounded surprised. 'Yeah, as a matter of fact, I did. But how . . . Do I know you from somewhere?'

Jaeger's eyes hardened. 'Once a Night Stalker, always a Night Stalker – isn't that what they say?'

'Yeah, that's what they say.' The pilot sounded spooked now. 'But like I said, buddy, do I know you from somewhere?'

'Matter of fact, you do. Though I figure you're gonna wish you'd never met me. 'Cause right now, *buddy*, I'm your worst nightmare. Once upon a time, you flew me and my team into

12

the Amazon, and unfortunately no one got to live happily ever after . . .'

Three months earlier, Jaeger had led a ten-person team on an expedition into the Amazon, searching for a lost Second World War aircraft. They'd hired the same private air charter firm as now. En route the pilot had mentioned how he had served with the American military's Special Operations Aviation Regiment, also known as the Night Stalkers.

The SOAR was a unit that Jaeger knew well. Several times when he'd been serving in special forces, it was SOAR pilots who'd pulled him and his men out of the crap. The SOAR's motto was 'Death waits in the dark', but Jaeger had never once imagined that he and his team would end up being the target of it.

Jaeger reached up and ripped off his balaclava. 'Death waits in the dark . . . It sure did, especially when you helped guide in the hit. Very nearly got the whole lot of us killed.'

For an instant the pilot stared, eyes wide with disbelief. Then he turned to the figure seated beside him.

'Your aircraft, Dan,' he announced quietly, relinquishing the controls to his co-pilot. 'I need to have words with our . . . English friend here. And Dan, radio Dallas/Fort Worth. Abort the flight. We need them to route us—'

'I wouldn't do that,' Jaeger cut in. 'Not if I were you.'

The move had been so swift that the pilot had barely noticed, let alone had any chance to resist. Jaeger had whipped out a compact SIG Sauer P228 pistol from where it was concealed within his jumpsuit. It was the weapon of choice for elite operators, and he had the blunt-ended barrel pressed hard against the back of the pilot's head.

The colour had drained completely from the man's face. 'What . . . what the hell? You hijacking my aircraft?'

Jaeger smiled. 'You better believe it.' He addressed his next words to the co-pilot. 'You a former Night Stalker too? Or just another traitorous scumbag like your buddy here?'

'What do I tell him, Jim?' the co-pilot muttered. 'How do I answer this son of a—'

'I'll tell you how you answer,' Jaeger cut in, releasing the pilot's seat from its locked position, and swinging it violently around until the guy was facing him. He levelled the 9mm at the pilot's forehead. 'Swiftly, and truthfully, without deviation, or the first bullet blows his brains out.'

The pilot's eyes bulged. 'Freakin' tell him, Dan. This guy's crazy enough to do it.'

'Yeah, we were both SOAR,' the co-pilot rasped. 'Same unit.'

'Right, so why don't you show me what the SOAR can do. I knew you as the best. We all did in British special forces. Prove it. Set a course for Cuba. When we're across the US coastline and out of American airspace, drop down to wave-top level. I don't want anyone to know we're on our way.'

The co-pilot glanced at the pilot, who nodded. 'Just do it.'

'Setting a course for Cuba,' he confirmed, through gritted teeth. 'You got a specific destination in mind? 'Cause there's several thousand miles of Cuban coastline to choose from, if you know what I mean.'

'You're going to release us over a small island via parachute drop. You'll get the exact coordinates as we close in. I need us over that island immediately after sundown – so under cover of darkness. Set your airspeed to make that happen.'

'You don't want much,' the co-pilot growled.

'Keep us on course due south-east and steady. Meantime, I've got a few questions to ask your buddy here.'

Jaeger folded down the navigator's seat, positioned to the rear of the cockpit, and settled himself into it, lowering the SIG's barrel until it menaced the pilot's manhood.

'So. Questions,' he mused. 'Lots of questions.'

The pilot shrugged. 'Okay. Whatever. Shoot.'

Jaeger eyed the pistol for a brief moment, then smiled, evilly. 'You really want me to?'

The pilot scowled. 'Figure of speech.'

'Question one. Why did you send my team to their deaths in the Amazon?'

'Hey, I didn't know. No one said anything about any killin'.'

Jaeger's grip on the pistol tightened. 'Answer the question.'

'Money,' the pilot muttered. 'Ain't it always thus. But hell, I didn't know they were gonna try and kill you all.'

Jaeger ignored the man's protestations. 'How much?'

'Enough.'

'How much?'

'One hundred and forty thousand dollars.'

'Okay, let's do the maths. We lost seven. Twenty thousand dollars a life. I'd say you sold us cheap.'

The pilot threw up his hands. 'Hey, I had no freakin' idea! They tried to wipe you out? The hell was I supposed to know!'

'Who paid you?'

The pilot hesitated. 'Some Brazilian guy. Local. Met him in a bar.'

Jaeger snorted. He didn't believe a word, but he had to keep pressing. He needed details. Some actionable intelligence. Something to help him hunt down his real enemies. 'You got a name?'

'Yeah. Andrei.'

'Andrei. A Brazilian named Andrei you met in a bar?'

'Yeah, well maybe he didn't sound too Brazilian. More like Russian.'

'Good. It's healthy to remember. Especially when you've got a 9mm pointed at your balls.'

'I ain't forgettin'.'

'So, this Andrei the Russian you met in a bar – got any sense who he might have worked for?'

'Only thing I knew was some guy named Vladimir was the boss.' He paused. 'Whoever killed your people, he's the guy giving the orders.'

Vladimir. Jaeger had heard his name before. He'd figured he was the gang leader, though there were certain to be other, more powerful people above him.

'You ever met this Vladimir? Got a look at him?'

The pilot shook his head. 'No.'

'But you took the money anyway.'

'Yeah. I took the money.'

'Twenty thousand dollars for each of my guys. What did you do – throw a pool party? Take the kids to Disney?'

The pilot didn't answer. His jaw jutted defiantly. Jaeger was tempted to smash the butt of the pistol into the guy's head, but he needed him conscious and compos mentis.

He needed him to fly this aircraft as never before, and get them over their fast-approaching target.

4

'Right, now that we've established how cheaply you sold my guys, let's agree on your route to redemption. Or at least part way there.'

The pilot grunted. 'What you got in mind?'

'Here's the thing. Vladimir and his lot kidnapped one of my expedition team. Leticia Santos. Brazilian. Former military. Young divorcee mother with a daughter to care for. I liked her.' A pause. 'They're holding her on a remote island off the Cuban mainland. You don't need to know how we found her. You do need to know we're flying in to rescue her.'

The pilot forced a laugh. 'And who the hell are you? James freakin' Bond? You're three. A three-person team. And what? You think the likes of Vladimir won't have company?'

Jaeger levelled his grey-blue eyes at the pilot. There was a calm but burning intensity about them. 'Vladimir has thirty well-armed men under his command. We're outnumbered ten-to-one. We're still going in. And we need you to ensure that we hit that island with maximum stealth and surprise.'

With his dark hair worn longish, and his slightly gaunt, wolf-ish features, Jaeger seemed younger than his thirty-eight years. But he had the look of a man who had seen much, and who wasn't to be messed with, especially when his hand was gripping a weapon, as now.

The look wasn't lost on the C-130 pilot. 'Assault force hitting a well-defended target: in US spec ops circles we always figured on three-to-one odds in our favour.'

Jaeger delved into his rucksack, pulling out an odd-looking object: it resembled a large baked bean tin with the label removed, and with a lever clipped to one end. He held it out in front of him.

'Ah, but we have this.' His fingers traced the lettering stamped around one side of the canister: *Kolokol-1*.

The pilot shrugged. 'Never heard of it.'

'You wouldn't. Russian. Soviet-era. But put it this way: if I pull the pin and let fly, this aircraft gets pumped full of toxic gas, and it's going down like a stone.'

The pilot eyed Jaeger, tension knotting his shoulders. 'You do that, we're all dead.'

Jaeger wanted to push this guy, but not too far. 'I'm not about to pull the pin.' He dropped the canister back into his rucksack. 'But trust me, you don't want to mess with Kolokol-1.'

'Okay, I got it.'

Three years back, Jaeger himself had had a nightmarish encounter with the gas. He'd been camping with his wife and son in the Welsh mountains. The bad guys – the same group as were holding Leticia Santos now – had come in the depths of the night and struck using Kolokol-1, leaving Jaeger unconscious and fighting for his life.

That was the last he had seen of his wife and eight-year-old son – Ruth and Luke.

Whatever mystery force had taken them had proceeded to torment Jaeger with the fact of their abduction. In fact, he didn't doubt any more that he'd been left alive just so they *could* torture him.

Every man has his breaking point. After scouring the earth for his missing family, Jaeger had finally been forced to accept the horrific truth: they were gone, seemingly without trace, and he had been powerless to protect them.

He had pretty much cracked up, seeking solace in drink and oblivion. It had taken a very special friend – and the re-emergence of evidence that his wife and son were still alive – to draw him back to life. To himself.

But he'd come back a very different person.

Darker. Wiser. More cynical. Less trusting.

Content with his own company: a loner, even.

Plus the new Will Jaeger had proved far more willing to break every rule in the book to hunt down those who had torn his life to pieces. Hence the present mission. And he wasn't averse to learning a few dark arts from the enemy along the way.

Sun Tzu, the ancient Chinese master of war, had had a saying: 'Know your enemy'. It was the simplest message of all, yet during Jaeger's time in the military he'd come to treat it like a mantra. *Know your enemy:* it was the first rule of any mission.

And these days he figured the second rule of any mission was *learn from your enemy*.

In the Royal Marines and the SAS – the two units in which Jaeger had served – they'd stressed the need to think laterally. To keep an open mind. To do the unexpected. Learning from the enemy was the zenith of all that.

Jaeger figured the last thing the force on that Cuban island would be expecting was to be hit in the depths of night by the same gas they themselves had used.

The enemy had done that to him.

He had learned the lesson.

It was payback time.

Kolokol-1 was an agent that the Russians kept swathed in secrecy. No one knew its exact make-up, but in 2002 it had taken a sudden leap into the public consciousness when a bunch of terrorists had taken control of a Moscow theatre, holding hundreds hostage.

The Russians hadn't messed around. Their special forces – the Spetsnaz – had pumped the theatre full of Kolokol-1. Then they'd hit the place like a whirlwind, breaking the siege and killing all the terrorists. Unfortunately, by that time many of the hostages had also been affected by the gas.

The Russians had never admitted to what exactly they had used, but Jaeger's friends in Britain's secret defence laboratories had got hold of some samples and confirmed that it was Kolokol-1. The gas was supposedly an incapacitating agent, but prolonged exposure to it had proved lethal for some in that Moscow theatre.

In short, it was well suited to Jaeger's purposes.

Jaeger wanted some of Vladimir's men to survive. Maybe all of them. If he wiped them out, he'd very likely end up with the entire Cuban police, army and air force on his tail. And right now he and his team were winging it; they needed to slip in and out without being noticed.

Even for those who survived, Kolokol-1 was a knockout agent. It would take them weeks to recover, by which time Jaeger and his people – plus Leticia Santos – would be long gone.

There was one other reason why Jaeger wanted Vladimir, at least, alive. Jaeger had questions to ask. Vladimir would be providing the answers.

'So this is how we're going to do it,' he told the pilot. 'We need to be over a six-figure grid at 0200 hours. That grid is a patch of ocean just to the west of the target island, two hundred metres off shore. You're to fly in at treetop height, then blip up to three hundred feet to release us in an LLP.'

The pilot stared. 'LLP? It's your funeral.'

The LLP – low-level parachute drop – was an ultra-stealthy elite forces technique rarely used in combat, due to the risks involved.

'Once we're gone, you drop down as low as possible,' Jaeger continued. 'Give the island a wide a berth. Shield your aircraft – and the noise – from any watching—'

'Hell, I'm a Night Stalker,' the pilot cut in. 'I know what I'm doin'. I don't need telling.'

'Glad to hear it. You pull away from the island and set a course for home. At which stage, we're done. You're free of us.' Jaeger paused. 'Are we clear?'

The pilot shrugged. 'Kind of. Thing is, yours is one shitty kind of a plan.'

'Try me.'

'Simple. There are any number of ways I can double-cross you. I can drop you over the wrong coordinates – how about the middle of the goddam ocean? – and leave you to swim for it. Or I pull up high and buzz the island. Hey, Vladimir! Wake up! The cavalry's comin' – all three of 'em! Hell, your plan's got more holes than a freakin' sieve.'

Jaeger nodded. 'I hear you. But the thing is, you won't do any of those things. And here's the reason why. You're guilty as hell about my seven dead men. You need a shot at redemption, or it'll torture you for the rest of your days.'

'You figure I got a conscience,' the pilot growled. 'You figure wrong.'

'You've got one all right,' Jaeger countered. 'But just in case, there's a second reason. You shit on us, you'll end up in a whole world of hurt.'

'Says who? Like how?'

'Thing is, you'll have just completed an unsanctioned flight to Cuba at below radar level. You'll be routing back to DFW, as you got nowhere else to go. We have good friends in Cuba. They're awaiting a one-word signal from me: SUCCESS. If they don't get that signal by 0500 hours, they'll contact US Customs with a tip-off that your aircraft has been flying shuttle runs stuffed full of drugs.'

The pilot's eyes blazed. 'I never touch the stuff! It's an evil business. Plus the guys at DFW – they know us. They'll never buy it.'

'I think they will. At the very least they'll have to check. They can't ignore a tip-off from the director of Cuban Customs. And when the DEA bring their sniffer dogs aboard, they'll go crazy. You see, I've made sure to scatter some white powder around the rear of your aircraft. Lots of hiding places in a C-130's hold for a few grams of cocaine.'

Jaeger could see the pilot's jaw cramping with tension. He eyed the pistol in Jaeger's hand. He was desperate to jump him, but he knew for sure he'd take a bullet.

Every man has his breaking point.

You could push a guy too far.

'It's carrot and stick, Jim. The carrot is your redemption. Leaves us just about even. The stick is life imprisonment in a US penitentiary for running drugs. You fly this mission, you're home and dry. You're clean. Your life goes back to normal, only you've got a little less on your conscience. So every which way you look at it, it makes sense to fly the mission.'

The pilot levelled his gaze at Jaeger. 'I'll get you to your drop zone.'

Jaeger smiled. 'I'll go tell my guys to get ready for the jump.'

5

The C-130 roared in low and fast, skimming the night-dark wave crests.

Jaeger and his team were poised at the open ramp, the fierce blasts of the aircraft's slipstream howling around their ears. Outside was a sea of raging darkness.

Here and there Jaeger could see a flash of seething white as the aircraft passed low over a reef, the waves breaking wild across its surface. The target island was also ringed with jagged coral – terrain that they would do best to avoid. Water would provide a relatively soft landing, coral a leg-shattering one. All being well, Jaeger's intended jump point would get them into the ocean inside the innermost reef, and just a short distance from the shoreline.

Once the C-130 pilot had been persuaded that he had no option but to fly the mission, he'd signed up to it more or less wholeheartedly. And right now Jaeger could tell that these guys truly were what they claimed to be – former Night Stalkers.

The chill night air swirled into the hold as the four hook-bladed propellers hammered away to either side. The pilot was flying at close to wave-top height, throwing the massive machine around as if it was a Formula 1 racing car.

The effect in the dark and echoing hold would have been puke-inducing were Jaeger and his team not so used to such a ride.

He turned to his two fellow operators. Takavesi 'Raff' Raffara was a massive hunk of a man – a rock-hard Maori and one of

Jaeger's closest friends from their years in the SAS. A totally bulletproof operator, Raff was the man Jaeger would choose to fight back-to-back with if ever the shit went down. He would trust Raff – who wore his long hair braided, traditional Maori style – with his life. He'd done so many a time when they'd soldiered together over the years, and again more recently, when Raff had come to rescue Jaeger from drink and ruin at the ends of the earth.

The second operator was a quiet, sylph-like figure, blonde hair whipping around her fine features in the tearing slipstream. A former Russian special forces operator, Irina Narov was striking-looking and unflappable, and she had proved herself many times during their expedition to the Amazon. But that didn't mean Jaeger had got the measure of her, or found her any the less troublesome.

Oddly, though, he'd almost come to trust her; to rely upon her. Despite her awkward and sometimes downright maddening manner, in her own way she was as bulletproof reliable as Raff. And at times she'd proved herself just as deadly – a cold, calculating killer without equal.

Nowadays Narov lived in New York and had taken American citizenship. She'd explained to Jaeger that she operated off-grid, working with some international outfit whose identity he had yet to fully get to grips with. It stank of shady, but it was that outfit – Narov's people – who had bankrolled the present undertaking: rescuing Leticia Santos. And right now that was all Jaeger cared about.

Then there were Narov's mysterious links to Jaeger's family, and in particular to his late lamented grandfather, William Edward 'Ted' Jaeger. Grandpa Ted had served with British special forces during the Second World War, inspiring Jaeger to go into the military. Narov claimed to have regarded Grandpa Ted as her own grandfather, and to be working in his name and memory today.

It made little sense to Jaeger. He'd never heard anyone in

his family make the barest mention of Narov, Grandpa Ted included. At the end of their Amazon expedition, he'd vowed to get some answers from her; to break the enigma she embodied. Yet the present rescue mission had had to take priority.

Via Narov's people and their contacts in the Cuban underworld, Jaeger's team had been able to monitor the location where Leticia Santos was being held. They'd been fed useful intelligence, and as a bonus they'd been passed a detailed description of Vladimir himself.

But worryingly, in the last few days Leticia had been moved, from a relatively low-security villa to the remote offshore island. The guard had been doubled, and Jaeger was worried that if they moved her again he might lose her completely.

There was a fourth figure in the C-130's hold. The loadmaster was roped tight to the aircraft's side, so he could perch on the ramp without being torn out by the raging slipstream. He pressed his headphones closer as he listened to a message from the pilot. Nodding his understanding, he got to his feet and flashed five fingers in front of their faces: five minutes to the jump.

Jaeger, Raff and Narov levered themselves to their feet. The success of the coming mission would rely on three things: speed, aggression and surprise – 'SAS' for short, the unofficial slogan of special forces operators. For that reason it was vital that they were light on their feet and could move swiftly and silently across the island. Accordingly, their kit had been kept to the absolute minimum.

Apart from their LLP parachute, each team member carried a backpack containing Kolokol-1 grenades, explosives, water, emergency rations, a medical kit and a small, sharp-bladed axe. The rest of the space was taken up by their CBRN protective suits and respirators.

When Jaeger had first served in the military, the emphasis had all been on NBC: nuclear, biological and chemical. Now it was CBRN – chemical, biological, radiological and nuclear – the new terminology reflecting the new world order. When the Soviet Union had been the enemy of the West, the top threat was nuclear. But in a fractured world rife with rogue states and terrorist groups, chemical and biological warfare – or more likely terrorism – was the new priority threat.

Jaeger, Raff and Narov each carried a SIG P228, with an extended twenty-round magazine, plus six mags of spare ammo. And each had their blade. Narov's was a Fairbairn-Sykes fighting knife, a razor-sharp weapon for up-close killing. It was a highly distinctive weapon that had had been issued to British commandos during the war. Her attachment to that blade was another of the mysteries that so intrigued Jaeger.

But tonight, no one was intending to use bullets or blades to take care of the enemy. The quieter and cleaner they could keep this, the better. Let the Kolokol-1 do its silent work.

Jaeger checked his watch: three minutes out from the drop. 'You ready?' he yelled. 'Remember, give the gas time to take hold.'

He got a nod and a thumbs up. Raff and Narov were absolute pros – the best – and he didn't detect the slightest hint of nerves. Sure, they were outnumbered ten-to-one, but he figured the Kolokol-1 evened up the odds a little. Of course, no one was exactly relishing using the gas. But sometimes, as Narov argued, you used a lesser evil to fight a greater one.

As he psyched himself up for the jump Jaeger felt a niggling worry, though: there were never any guarantees when doing an LLP.

When serving in the SAS, he'd spent a great deal of time trialling cutting-edge, space-age equipment. Working with the Joint Air Transport Establishment (the JATE) – a secretive outfit overseeing James Bond-like air-insertion techniques – he'd leapt from the very highest altitudes possible.

But recently the British military had developed a very different kind of concept. Instead of jumping from the edge of the earth's atmosphere, the LLP was designed to enable a paratrooper to leap at near-zero altitude and still survive.

In theory, it allowed a jump height of some 250 feet, so keeping the aircraft well below radar level. In short, it enabled a force to fly into hostile territory with little risk of detection – hence why they were using it on tonight's mission.

With split seconds in which to deploy, the LLP chute was designed to have a flat and wide profile, to catch the maximum air. But even so, it still required a rocket-assisted pack to get the chute to fully deploy before the jumper splashed down. And even with that rocket pack – in essence, a release mechanism that blasted your parachute high into the air – you still had barely five seconds in which to slow your descent and make landfall.

That allowed no time for messing up.

But likewise, it gave zero time for the enemy to spot you, or to prevent you from reaching the ground – or the water – alive.

6

The jump light flashed green for go.

In one continuous stream lasting bare milliseconds, Jaeger, Raff and Narov dived out of the C-130's open ramp. Their stick-like figures were sucked into the howling void. Jaeger felt himself buffeted like a ragdoll in a giant wind tunnel. Below him, he could just make out the seething ocean rushing ever closer: impact had to be just seconds away.

Not a moment too soon he triggered his rocket-assisted chute, and suddenly he felt as if he was being blasted into the heavens on the tail of some roaring missile. Moments later the rocket motor died, and the chute's canopy bloomed high in the darkness above him.

It inflated with a sharp snap, catching the air just seconds after the rocket pack reached the apex of its climb. Jaeger's stomach did a series of sickening somersaults . . . and the next instant he found himself drifting gently downwards towards the heaving sea.

As his feet hit the water, Jaeger punched his quick-release mechanism, discarding his bulky parachute rig. The prevailing ocean current was south-easterly, so it would carry the chutes towards the open waters of the Atlantic, which meant they'd very likely never be seen again.

That was just as Jaeger wanted it: they needed to get in and out leaving no sign that they had ever been here.

Very quickly the Hercules disappeared, its ghostly form being swallowed up by the empty night. Roaring darkness was all around Jaeger now. All he could hear was the growl of the ocean surf; all he could feel was the warm punch and drag of the Caribbean Sea, its salty tang strong in his mouth and nostrils.

Each of their rucksacks was lined with a waterproof canoe bag. The tough black sacks transformed the heavy packs into makeshift flotation devices. Holding these before them, the three figures began to kick out for the ragged fringe of palm trees that marked the shoreline. They began surfing inwards on the powerful breakers. Barely minutes after hitting the water they made landfall, crawling on to the sand and dragging their sodden forms into the nearest patch of cover.

For five minutes they waited and listened in the shadows, scanning their surroundings with eagle eyes.

If someone had spotted the C-130 making the drop, it was now that they were most likely to put in an appearance. But Jaeger could detect nothing. No unusual noise. No surprise movement. Seemingly no life out there at all. Apart from the rhythmic pounding of the waves on the pristine white sand, all around was utter stillness.

Jaeger could feel the adrenalin of the coming attack kicking into his veins now. It was time to get moving.

He pulled out a compact Garmin GPS unit to check his position. It wasn't unknown for aircrew to put troops down on the wrong grid, and tonight's pilot would have had more excuse than most to do so.

Grid confirmed, Jaeger grabbed a tiny, luminous compass, took a bearing and signalled the way forward. Narov and Raff moved in behind him and they set off noiselessly into the forest. No words were necessary between such battle-hardened professionals.

Thirty minutes later, they'd traversed the largely deserted landmass. The island was cloaked in thick groves of palm trees, interspersed with swathes of shoulder-high elephant grass, which meant they'd been able to move like wraiths through its cover, unseen and undetected.

Jaeger signalled a halt. By his calculations they should be one hundred metres short of the villa complex in which Leticia Santos was being held.

He crouched low, and Raff and Narov closed in.

'Suit up,' he whispered.

The threat from an agent like Kolokol-1 was twofold: one, breathing it in; two, absorbing it via a living, porous membrane like the skin. They were using Raptor 2 protective suits, a special forces variant made of an ultra-lightweight material, but with an inner layer of activated carbon microspheres to soak up any droplets of agent that might be sloshing around in the atmosphere.

The Raptor suits would prove hot and claustrophobic, and Jaeger was glad they were going in during the dead of night, when the Cuban air was at its coolest.

They also had state-of-the-art Avon FM54 gas masks, to shield face, eyes and lungs. They were superlative pieces of kit, having a flame-hardened exterior, a single visor and an ultra-flexible, close-fitting design.

Even so, Jaeger loathed donning these respirators. He was a man who thrilled to the open and the wild. He detested being locked up, entrapped or unnaturally constrained.

He steeled himself and threw his head forward, dragging the respirator over his face, making sure that the rubber formed an airtight seal with his skin. He tightened the retaining straps, and felt the mask pull in close around his features.

They'd each selected a mask personally tailored to fit their own face size, but had had to bring a looser-fitting escape hood for Leticia Santos. The hoods were universal in size, yet still provided a decent period of protection in high concentrations of toxic gas.

Jaeger placed his hand over the respirator's filter and breathed in hard, drawing the mask tighter on to his face, doing a 'confidence check' to make sure the seal was good. He dragged in a few gasps of air, hearing the alien suck and blow of his own breathing roaring in his ears.

Mask checked, he stepped into the cumbersome rubber overboots, and dragged the hood of his CBRN smock over his head, the elastic sealing around the front of the mask. Finally he pulled on the thin cotton under-gloves, plus the heavy rubber over-gloves, to doubly protect his hands.

His world was now reduced to the view provided by the eyepiece of the mask. The bulky filter was attached to the front left-hand side, so as to prevent it from blocking his vision, but already he could feel the claustrophobia starting to build.

It was all the more reason to get in there fast and get this done.

'Mic check,' he announced, speaking into the tiny microphone embedded within the rubber of the mask. There was no need to press any buttons to talk; they were all permanently on send. His voice sounded weirdly muted and nasal, but at least the short-range radio intercom would mean they were able to communicate during the coming action.

'Check,' Raff responded.

'Check . . . Hunter,' Narov added.

Jaeger allowed himself a smile. 'The Hunter' was the nickname he'd earned during their mission to the Amazon.

On Jaeger's signal, they moved ahead into the darkness. Shortly, they spotted the lights of the target building glimmering through the trees. They crossed a patch of waste ground until they were directly opposite the rear of the villa. All that separated them from it was a narrow dirt track.

From the cover of the trees they studied the target. It was bathed in a halo of intense illumination from the security lighting. Right now, there was no point trying to use night vision equipment. The harsh light would overload any such kit, rendering their surroundings into a blinding whiteout.

In spite of the night-time chill, it was proving hot and sticky inside the suits and masks. Jaeger could feel drops of sweat trickling down his forehead. He thrust a gloved hand across the eyepiece of his respirator, in an effort to clear it.

Windows were lit up on the villa's second floor, which was all that was visible above the high perimeter wall. Every now and then Jaeger spotted a silhouette passing back and forth. As expected, Vladimir's men were keeping careful watch.

He noted a couple of 4x4s parked next to the perimeter wall. They would need immobilising, just in case anyone tried to give chase. He flicked his eyes up to the flat roof of the building. It was the obvious place to post sentries, but there was no movement that he could detect. It looked to be deserted. Yet if there was access on to it, the roof was the one point they would have problems keeping covered.

Jaeger spoke into his throat mic. 'We're a go. But be wary of the roof. Plus we immobilise those vehicles.'

There were replies in the affirmative.

Jaeger led them in a dash across the open track. They paused at the vehicles, using grenades rigged to motion-sensitive triggers to booby-trap them. If anyone tried to pull away in either vehicle, the movement alone would detonate the explosives.

Raff veered off alone now, heading for the main power line. He would use a compact sabotage device to send a powerful surge of current through the villa's electrics, blowing the fuses and light fittings. Vladimir was sure to have an emergency generator, but it would be of little use, for the circuitry would have been fried.

Jaeger glanced at Narov. He placed the palm of his hand on the crown of his head – the signal for 'on me'. Then he rose to his feet and hurried across to the villa's front entrance, his pulse pounding in his ears as he went.

If there was a moment when they were most likely to be spotted, it was now, as they prepared to scale the high wall. Jaeger inched his way around the corner and took up position to one side of the front gate. A split second later, Narov was beside him.

'In position,' he breathed into his radio mic.

'Affirmative,' came Raff's whispered reply. 'Going dark.'

A split second later there was a fizzing and a popping from the villa's interior.

In a shower of sparks the entire complex went suddenly very dark.

7

Jaeger hoisted Narov by her legs, and propelled her upwards. She reached for the top of the wall and hauled herself on to it. Then she leant down and helped him to scramble up. Seconds later they dropped on to the far side.

All was pitch darkness.

It had taken only seconds to scale the wall, but already Jaeger could hear muffled shouts coming from the building.

The front door swung open and a figure stumbled out, flashlight sweeping the darkened compound and glinting off the assault rifle gripped in his hand. Jaeger froze. He watched the figure make his way to a shed set in one corner – very likely the backup generator house.

As the figure disappeared inside, Jaeger dashed forward, Narov bang on his shoulder. He flattened himself to one side of the villa's doorway, Narov doing the same on the other. Jaeger whipped out a canister from one of his pouches, unhooking a small hand-axe at the same time.

He glanced across at Narov.

She gave a thumbs up.

Eyes cool like ice.

Jaeger grabbed the pin holding the retainer clip. Once he pulled it, the grenade was primed to pump out its gas. They were on the point of no return now.

Gently he eased the pin free, his fingers holding the fly-off lever closed. If he relaxed his grip, the clip would spring free, and the grenade would start gushing.

'In position,' he breathed into his radio.

'In position,' Raff echoed. Having killed the villa's power, the big Maori had made his way to the rear, the only other way in or out of the building.

Jaeger steeled himself. 'Going in.'

He swung the axe through the window. The sound of breaking glass was drowned out by those inside crashing about in the darkness. He dragged the axe out again and heaved the canister in, letting the fly-off lever ping free.

Opposite him, Narov mirrored his movements, hurling her canister through the window that she'd just smashed.

Jaeger mouthed off the seconds. *Three. Four. Five* . . .

Through the broken glass he could hear a fierce hissing, as the grenades gushed out their choking contents. It was followed by a gasping and retching, as the Kolokol-1 began to take effect, and panicked bodies stumbled into unseen obstructions.

Suddenly there was a cough and a roar at Jaeger's back as the generator kicked into life. The figure emerged to check if the power had come back on, but all remained pitch black. He swung his flashlight this way and that, trying to identify the reason for the blackout.

Jaeger had a split second in which to deal with him. He dragged his SIG Sauer from its chest holster. The silhouette of the pistol was different now: longer, and more barrel-heavy. He, Raff and Narov had each fitted an SWR Trident silencer to the business end of the P228s. They'd also loaded the magazines with subsonic rounds – ones that travelled slower than the speed of sound, so avoiding the crack that a bullet makes when going through the sound barrier.

To compensate for the lack of velocity, the rounds were heavier in weight, the combined effect rendering the weapon almost silent but no less lethal for it.

Jaeger raised the P228, but before he could open fire, a familiar figure emerged from the shadows and squeezed off a double tap – *pzzzt, pzzzt*; re-aim; *pzzzt*. Raff had been a split second faster than Jaeger, and one step ahead in taking the shot.

Ten. Eleven. Twelve . . . The voice in Jaeger's head continued counting out the seconds, as the Kolokol-1 did its work.

Momentarily, he was struck by a sense of what it must be like inside the building. Pitch darkness. Utter confusion. Then the first chilling caress of the Kolokol-1. A moment's panic as each man tried to make sense of what was happening, before the terror hit, the gas searing down windpipes and flaming into lungs.

Jaeger knew from personal experience what such a gas did to people; what a horrible way it was to go under. You might well survive, but it was something you would never forget.

For a terrible moment he was back on that Welsh mountain-side, as a knife sliced through the thin canvas of his tent and a nozzle was thrust inside, disgorging a cloud of choking gas. He saw hands reach in and grab his wife and child, dragging them out into the darkness. He tried to raise himself to fight, to save them, but the Kolokol-1 seared into his eyes, freezing his limbs completely.

And then a gloved fist grabbed him savagely by the hair, forcing his face upwards, until he was staring into the hate-filled eyes behind the mask.

'Get this moment burned into your brain,' a voice hissed. 'Your wife and child – they're ours. Don't ever forget: you failed to protect your loved ones.'

Though distorted by the mask, Jaeger had figured he'd recognised the man's vicious, hate-filled tones, but he couldn't for the life of him put a name to the voice of his tormentor. He knew him, and yet he didn't know him, and that had proved to be a torture from which it had been impossible to hide.

Jaeger forced the images from his mind, He reminded himself just who they were gassing here. He'd witnessed the murderous horrors visited on his team in the Amazon, not to mention on poor Leticia Santos herself. And of course there was a part of him that hoped to discover here something that might lead him to his wife and child.

Every second was precious now. *Seventeen. Eighteen. Nineteen. Twenty!*

Jaeger stepped back, raised his leg and smashed his boot savagely into the door. The rich tropical hardwood hardly gave an inch, but the frame was made of cheap plywood and it splintered, the door cannoning inwards on its hinges.

Jaeger fought his way into the dark interior, SIG at the ready. He swept the room with the beam of the torch attached to the underside of the barrel. The air was thick with an oily white fog that danced in the light. Bodies writhed on the floor, clawing at their faces as if they wanted to rip their own throats out.

No one even noticed that he was there. Their eyes were blinded by the gas, their bodies on fire.

Jaeger moved deeper into the room. He vaulted over a figure heaving and writhing underfoot. He used his boot to roll another over, taking a good look at faces as he passed.

None was Leticia Santos.

Momentarily his torch beam caught in a slurry of vomit, a body writhing in the shadows. The stench would have been sickening, but no smell could make it through Jaeger's respirator.

He forced himself to keep pressing ahead, to blank out the horror. He had to remain focused on the job: *find Leticia.*

As he moved through the eerie, disorientating cloud of gas, his flashlight picked out a ghostly white fountain – a Kolokol-1 canister gushing out the last of its contents – and then he was at the rear of the room. A set of stairs lay ahead: one flight up, the other down. Instinct told him that Leticia would be held underground.

He fished inside his smock and pulled out a second canister. But as he ripped out the pin, ready to hurl the grenade down the stairwell, a spike of blinding claustrophobia hit him like a punch to the stomach. He felt himself freeze, his mind locked in that dark moment on the mountainside, which seemed to play through his head on a continuous loop.

It was crucial to keep the momentum going on an assault such as this. But waves of nausea swept up from the pit of Jaeger's stomach, doubling him over in their vice-like grip. He felt as if he was back in that tent, drowning in the sea of his own failure, unable even to defend his own wife and child.

His limbs seemed utterly frozen.

He couldn't hurl the canister.

8

'Throw it!' Narov screamed. 'THROW IT! Santos is in there somewhere! Throw the goddam canister!'

Her words ripped through Jaeger's paralysis. It took a stupendous effort of will, but somehow he managed to regain his grip on his senses and let fly, launching the grenade far into the darkness below. Seconds later, he was pounding down the steps, sweeping the area before him with his weapon, Narov right behind him.

During the years he'd served with elite units, clearing buildings was one of the most heavily rehearsed of all of their drills. It was fast, natural and instinctive.

Two doors led off the staircase, one to either side. Jaeger went right, Narov left. He let fly the retainer clip on a third canister of Kolokol-1. His boot hit the door, crashing through the wood and shunting it wide open, and he tossed the canister inside.

As the gas began to pump, a figure stumbled towards him, choking and cursing in some language that Jaeger didn't understand. The figure opened fire, spraying wildly with his weapon, but he was blinded by the gas. An instant later he keeled over, his hands grasping at his throat as he gasped for air.

Jaeger advanced into the room, expended brass bullet casings crunching under the soles of his overboots. He did a rapid scan for Leticia Santos. Not seeing her anywhere, he was about to leave when he was struck by a blinding realisation: *he recognised this place.*

Somehow, somewhere, he had seen it before.

And then it hit him. In an effort to torture him remotely, Santos's captors had emailed Jaeger images of her captivity. One had shown her bruised, bound and kneeling before a torn and dirtied bed sheet, on which had been scrawled the words:

> Return to us what is ours.
> Wir sind die Zukunft.

Wir sind die Zukunft: we are the future.

The words had been crudely daubed in what appeared to be blood.

Jaeger could see that very sheet before him now, pinned to one of the walls. Below it on the floor was the detritus of captivity: a dirty mattress, a toilet bucket, lengths of frayed rope, and a few dog-eared magazines; plus a baseball bat, no doubt used to beat Santos into submission.

It wasn't the room that Jaeger had recognised; it was the instruments of Leticia Santos's incarceration and torture.

He whipped around. Narov had cleared the room opposite, and still there was no sign of Santos. *Where had they taken her?*

The two of them paused for a second at the bottom of the stairs. They were soaked in sweat and their breath was coming in heaving gasps. Each grabbed a canister and prepared to press on. They had to keep the momentum going.

They hammered up the flights of stairs leading towards the roof, hurling more canisters, then spreading out to search, but the entire floor appeared empty. After a few seconds Jaeger heard a burst of static in his earpiece, and Raff's voice came over the radio.

'Stairway at rear leads to the roof.'

Jaeger turned and sprinted in that direction, fighting his way through the thick swirling gas. Raff was standing at the bottom of a flight of worn metal rungs; above him a trapdoor was open to the sky.

Jaeger barely hesitated before he started to climb. Leticia had to be up there. He could feel it in his bones.

As his head neared the opening, he flicked off the torch beam on his pistol. There would be enough moonlight to see by, and the flashlight would simply make him an obvious target. With one hand he eased his way up the ladder, the other keeping his gun at the ready. No point unleashing the gas up here. It was little use in the open.

He stole his way up the last few inches, sensing Narov on the rungs below him, then eased his head and shoulders above the opening, scanning all around for the enemy. For several seconds he stayed utterly still, watching and listening.

Finally, in one swift move, he vaulted on to the roof. As he did so, he heard a crash. It sounded deafening in the comparative silence. A battered television set had been dumped in the centre of the roof, a pile of old furniture heaped up behind it.

A broken chair had tumbled over as a figure raised a weapon from behind the patch of cover.

A moment later there was a savage burst of fire.

Jaeger came to his feet, keeping low, his pistol in the aim. All around him, bullets were ricocheting off the slick concrete of the roof. Either he dealt with this pronto, or he was a dead man.

He took aim on the muzzle flash, and squeezed off three rounds in quick succession: *pzzzt, pzzzt, pzzzt!* In this game it was all about being able to unleash rapid but deadly accurate fire.

This was life and death in the kill zone. Here, the dividing line was measured in fractions of an inch and milliseconds. And Jaeger's aim had been that much faster and better.

He moved position and went into a crouch, scanning all around him. As Narov and Raff leapt out of the stairwell to either side of him, Jaeger crept forward, perfectly balanced on the balls of his feet, a cat stalking its prey. He swept the heap of broken furniture with his weapon. More of the enemy were hiding there, he just knew it.

All of a sudden a figure broke cover and began to run. Jaeger pinned the runner in his sights, but as he tensed to fire, his finger bone-white on the trigger, he realised it was a woman; a dark-haired woman. *Leticia Santos, it had to be!*

He saw a second figure sprint after her, the silhouette of a pistol gripped in his hand. It was her captor and would-be killer, but they were too close for Jaeger to open fire.

'Drop the gun!' he snarled. 'Drop the gun!'

The FM54 mask had an inbuilt voice-projection system, which acted like a megaphone, making his words sound weirdly metallic and robotic.

'Drop your weapon!'

In response the gunman snaked a powerful arm around the woman's neck, forcing her towards the edge of the roof. Jaeger advanced, keeping them covered.

In his respirator and suit he looked twice as large as normal. He figured Leticia would have little idea who was behind the mask, and his steely, voice-projected tones would be equally unrecognisable.

Was he friend or foe?

She would have no way of telling.

She took a fearful step backwards, the bad guy fighting to keep her under control. The edge of the roof was right at their backs. There was nowhere to retreat or to run.

'Drop your weapon!' Jaeger repeated. 'Drop the bloody gun!'

He held the SIG before him double-handed and tight to his body: the silencer tended to force the gases from the barrel back into the shooter's face, so it was crucial to keep as firm a stance as possible in order to dampen the kickback. He had the bad guy pinned in his sights, the pistol's hammer was back and his index finger was on the trigger – yet still he couldn't take the shot. In the faint light he couldn't be certain of his aim, the bulky gloves making the shot doubly difficult.

The bad guy had his own pistol jammed in Leticia's throat.

Stalemate.

Jaeger felt Narov move up on his shoulder. She too had her

long-barrelled P228 in the aim. Her hands remained rock solid: steady and ice cool as always. She moved a step ahead of him, and he flicked his gaze across to her. No response. Not the hint of a reaction. She didn't break eye contact with the iron sights of the SIG.

But there was something very different about her profile now.

Narov had ripped off her respirator, leaving it hanging on its straps, and slipped on a pair of AN/PVS-21 night vision goggles. They lit up her features with a fluorescent green alien glow, and she had also pulled off her gloves.

For a horrible moment Jaeger knew exactly what she was about to do.

He reached out a hand to try to stop her. He was too late.

Pzzzt, pzzzt, pzzzt!

Narov had pulled the trigger.

She'd taken the shot.

9

The standard military round for the 9mm P228 weighs in at 7.5 grams. The three subsonic bullets that Narov had unleashed were each two grams heavier. Travelling one hundred metres per second slower, it still took them only a fraction of an instant to bite.

They tore into the gunman's face, driving him backwards and over the edge of the roof in a death plunge. It was incredible shooting. But as he fell, his arm remained locked around the woman's neck.

With a piercing scream, both figures disappeared from view.

The drop from the roof was a good fifteen metres. Jaeger let out a savage curse. *Bloody Narov!*

He turned and raced for the trapdoor. As he thundered down the ladder, the Kolokol-1 swirled around his knees like a ghostly fog. He dropped down the last of the metal rungs, tore along the corridor, then hammered down the stairway, vaulting bodies as he went. He raced out through the shattered doorway, turned right and sprinted around the corner of the building, coming to a breathless halt where two figures lay in a crumpled heap.

The gunman had perished instantly as a result of three shots to the head, and it looked as if Leticia's neck had been broken by the fall.

Jaeger cursed again. How could it all have gone so wrong so quickly? He knew the answer pretty much instantly: *it was Narov's trigger-happy, dumb-ass attitude.*

He bent over Leticia's crumpled form. She lay face down, unmoving. He placed a hand on her neck, checking for a pulse. Nothing. He shuddered. He could barely believe it: the body was still warm, but she was dead, just as he had feared.

Narov appeared beside him. Jaeger glanced up, eyes blazing. 'Nice bastard work. You just—'

'Take a closer look,' Narov's voice cut in. It had the characteristic cold, flat, emotionless ring to it – the one that Jaeger found so disconcerting. 'A proper look.'

She reached forward, grabbed the fallen figure by the hair and jerked the head roughly backwards. *No respect, not even for the dead.*

Jaeger stared at the ashen features. It was a Latino woman all right, but it wasn't Leticia Santos.

'How the—' he began.

'I am a woman,' Narov cut in. 'I recognise another woman's posture. Her gait. This one – it wasn't Leticia's.'

For a moment Jaeger wondered whether Narov felt even the slightest remorse for having killed this mystery captive, or at least for taking the shot that had sent her plunging to her doom.

'One more thing,' Narov added. She reached inside the woman's jacket and fished out a pistol, holding it up to Jaeger. 'She was a member of their gang.'

Jaeger gawped. 'Jesus. The drama on the roof. It was all an act.'

'It was. To draw us in.'

'How did you know?'

Narov turned her blank gaze upon Jaeger. 'I saw a bulge. A gun-shaped bulge. But mostly – instinct and intuition. A soldier's sixth sense.'

Jaeger shook his head to clear it. 'But then – where the hell's Leticia?'

With a sudden flash of inspiration he yelled into his radio:

'Raff!' The big Maori had remained in the target house, checking the survivors and looking for clues. 'Raff! You got Vladimir?'

'Yeah. Got him.'

'Can he talk?'

'Yeah. Just.'

'Right. Bring him here.'

Thirty seconds later Raff emerged from the building with a figure thrown across his massive shoulders. He dumped the man at Jaeger's feet.

'Vladimir – or so he claims.'

The leader of the kidnap gang showed the unmistakable symptoms of a Kolokol-1 attack. His heart rate had slowed to a perilously low level, as had his breathing, his muscles going strangely slack. His skin was clammy and his mouth dry.

He'd just been hit by the first waves of dizziness, which meant that vomiting and seizures would quickly follow. Jaeger needed to get some answers, before the guy was rendered beyond any use. He whipped a syringe out of his breast pouch and held it before the man's eyes.

'Listen good,' he announced, his voice reverberating through the mask's voice-projection system. 'You've been hit by sarin,' he lied. 'Know much about nerve agents? Horrible way to die. You've only got a few minutes left.'

The man's eyes rolled in terror. Clearly he understood enough English to get the gist of what Jaeger was saying.

Jaeger waved the syringe. 'You see this? Compoden. The antidote. You get this, you live.'

The man thrashed about, trying to reach for the syringe.

Jaeger shoved him with his foot. 'Right, answer the following question. Where is the hostage, Leticia Santos? You get the injection in exchange for an answer. If not, you're dead.'

The man was twitching violently now, saliva dribbling from his nose and mouth. Yet somehow he raised a shaking hand and pointed back into the villa.

'Basement. Under rug. In there.'

Jaeger raised the needle and plunged it into the man's arm. Kolokol-1 requires no antidote and the syringe contained a harmless shot of saline solution. A few minutes in the open air would be enough to ensure his survival, though it would take him many more weeks to fully recover.

Narov and Jaeger headed inside, leaving Raff to keep tabs on Vladimir. Back in the basement, Jaeger's torch revealed a bright Latino-style rug laid across the bare concrete floor. He scuffed it aside, uncovering a heavy steel trapdoor. He tugged at the handle, but it didn't budge. It had to be locked from the inside.

He dug out a shaped explosive charge from his rucksack and unrolled it, exposing the sticky strip, then chose a spot at the back of the trapdoor and taped the charge along the crack.

'Soon as the charge blows, get the gas in,' he announced.

Narov nodded and readied a Kolokol-1 grenade.

They took cover. Jaeger triggered the fuse, and instantaneously there was a sharp explosion, a thick cloud of smoke and debris billowing through the air. The trapdoor was now a blasted ruin.

Narov lobbed the gas canister into the smoke-filled interior. Jaeger counted down the seconds, allowing the gas to take hold before lowering his frame through and letting himself drop. He hit the deck, taking the impact on his knees, and immediately had his gun in the aim, sweeping the room with the flashlight attached to the weapon. Through the thick fog of gas in the air he could see two figures lying on the floor, comatose.

Narov dropped in next to him and Jaeger swept his torch over the two unconscious men. 'Check them.'

As Narov went to do so, he slid around the wall towards the back of the room, where there was a small alcove containing a heavy wooden chest. He reached out with his gloved hand and pulled at the handle, but the chest was locked.

Screw searching for the key.

He placed both hands on the handle and a foot against the front, tensed his shoulder muscles and yanked with all his might. With a snapping of wood the lid came away from its hinges. Jaeger threw it to one side and flashed his torch inside.

In the depths of the chest lay a large formless bundle wrapped in an old sheet. He reached in and heaved it up, feeling the distinctive weight of a human body inside, then lowered it gently to the floor. When he peeled away the sheet, he found himself gazing into Leticia Santos's face.

They'd found her. She was unconscious, and by the looks of her ravaged features Vladimir and his crew had put her through hell these past few days. Jaeger didn't even want to think what they had done to her. But at least she was alive.

Behind him, Narov was checking the second body, just to make sure he was dead to the world. Like many of Vladimir's gunmen, this one was wearing body armour; no doubt about it, they had been a serious bunch of operators.

But as she rolled the cumbersome figure on to his back, her flashlight glinted on something that had been left lying beneath him on the floor. It was spherical and metallic, about the size of a man's fist, its outer surface segmented into scores of tiny squares.

'GRENADE!'

Jaeger whirled about, taking in the threat in a matter of instants. The gunman had set a trap. Believing himself to be dying, he'd pulled the pin on a grenade and lain himself on top of it, keeping the clip in place with his own body weight.

'TAKE COVER!' Jaeger yelled, scooping Leticia up and diving for the shelter of the alcove.

Ignoring him completely, Narov slammed the figure back down on to the grenade, throwing herself on top of him to shield herself from the explosion.

There was a massive, searing detonation. Narov was catapulted into the air by the blast, the force of which hurled Jaeger further into the alcove, his head smashing against the wall.

A bolt of agony shot through him . . . and seconds later his whole world went black.

10

Jaeger turned left, taking the exit leading into London's Harley Street, one of the city's most exclusive districts. Three weeks had passed since their Cuban mission, and he was still stiff and in pain from the injuries he'd suffered in the villa, but his blackout had been only momentary: his mask had saved his head from worse injury.

It was Narov who had taken the real pounding. In the enclosed environment of the cellar, she'd had no option but to dive on the grenade. She'd used the gunman's bulk, plus his body armour, to shield them from the blast, allowing Jaeger an instant to get Leticia into some cover.

Jaeger came to a halt opposite the Biowell Clinic, tucking his Triumph Tiger Explorer into one of the free parking places reserved for motorcycles. The Explorer was fast through the traffic, and he rarely failed to find a vacant parking space. It was one of the joys of navigating the city on two wheels. He shrugged off his battered Belstaff jacket, stripping down to his shirtsleeves.

Spring was in the air, the leafy plane trees that lined London's streets bursting into leaf. If he had to be in the city – as opposed to the open wild of the countryside – this was about his favourite time of year to be here.

He'd just got news that Narov was conscious again and had eaten her first solid meal. In fact the surgeon had even mentioned the possibility of releasing her from his care sometime soon.

No doubt about it, Narov was tough.

Getting off that Cuban island had proved something of a challenge. Having come to after the grenade blast, Jaeger had stumbled to his feet and hoisted both Narov and Leticia Santos out of the cellar. Then he and Raff had carried the two women out of the gas-choked building, making their getaway through the villa grounds.

The assault had turned very noisy very fast, and Jaeger didn't know who else on that island might have heard the gunfire. The alarm had most likely been raised, and their priority was to get the hell out of there. Vladimir and his lot would be left to explain it all to the Cuban authorities.

They'd headed for the nearby dock, where the kidnappers kept an ocean-going rigid inflatable boat. They'd loaded Narov and Santos aboard, fired up the RIB's powerful twin 350-horsepower engines and headed east towards the British territory of the Turks and Caicos Islands, a 180-kilometre ride across the intervening stretch of ocean. Jaeger knew the governor of the islands personally, and he'd be expecting them.

Once they hit the open sea, Jaeger and Raff had stabilised Narov, stemming her bleeding. They'd laid her in the recovery position, making her and Leticia comfortable at the back of the RIB, cushioned by a pile of lifejackets.

That done, they'd gone about ditching the bulk of their kit. Weapons, CBRN suits, respirators, explosives, Kolokol-1 canisters – anything that might link back to the mission – had all been dumped overboard.

By the time they'd made landfall, there was little left to associate them with any military action. They had the appearance of four civilian pleasure-boaters who had run into a little trouble at sea.

They'd made sure they'd left no trail to follow back on the island, gathering up the used Kolokol-1 canisters. All that was left behind was a few dozen untraceable 9mm casings. Even their footprints had been masked by their CBRN overboots.

There had been CCTV cameras in the villa, but once Raff had fried the electric circuitry, there had been no power. In any case, Jaeger would challenge anyone to ID him and his team through their respirators.

All that remained was their three parachutes, and even they should drift out to sea with the prevailing tides.

Any way Jaeger looked at it, they were clean.

As they'd powered across the calm, night-dark ocean, he'd spared a thought for the fact that he was still alive; that all his team were. He'd felt that warm buzz – that incredible rush – of entering a deadly kill zone and surviving.

Life never seemed more real than in the moments after it had very nearly been taken away from you.

Perhaps because of that, an image had come unbidden into his mind. Of Ruth – dark-haired, green-eyed, with fine, almost delicate features, an air of Celtic mystery about her; of Luke – eight years of age and even then the spitting image of his father.

Luke would be eleven now, his twelfth birthday just a few months away. He was a July baby, and they'd always managed to celebrate his birthday somewhere magical, for it fell midway through the summer holidays.

Jaeger spooled through the birthday memories in his mind: carrying a two-year-old Luke across the Giant's Causeway on Ireland's wild west coast; surfing off the Portuguese beaches when Luke was six; trekking through the snowy wastes of Mont Blanc when he was eight.

But after that there was just a sudden, empty blackness . . . a chilling loss that had lasted for three long years. Each of those missing birthdays had been sheer hell, and doubly so since whoever had kidnapped his wife and son had started to torture Jaeger remotely with images of their captivity.

He had been emailed photos of Ruth and Luke in chains, kneeling at the feet of their captors, their faces gaunt and haunted, their gazes red-rimmed and plagued by nightmares.

To know that they were alive and being held somewhere in

utter, abject misery and despair had driven Jaeger to the edge of madness. It was only the hunt – the promise of their rescue – that had brought him back from the brink.

With Raff manning the RIB's engines, Jaeger had navigated across the night-dark ocean using a portable GPS unit. With his free hand he'd unlaced one boot and removed something from beneath the insole.

He'd flashed his head-torch across it briefly, his eyes lingering on the faces that stared back at him from the tiny, battered photo – one that he carried on every mission, no matter what or where it might be. It had been taken on their last family holiday – a safari trip to Africa – and showed Ruth wrapped in a bright Kenyan sarong, a suntanned Luke in shorts and a *SAVE THE RHINO* T-shirt standing proudly at her side.

As the RIB had cut through the night sea, Jaeger had said a short prayer for them, wherever they might be. In his heart he knew they were still alive, and that the Cuban mission had brought him one step closer to finding them. While searching the villa, Raff had grabbed an iPad and some computer drives, stuffing them into his backpack. Jaeger hoped they might yield vital clues.

When the RIB had made landfall at the Turks and Caicos capital, Cockburn Town, calls had been made from the governor's residence; strings pulled. Leticia and Narov had been airlifted out of there direct to the UK, on a private jet equipped with state-of-the-art medical facilities.

The Biowell Clinic was an exclusive private hospital. Patients tended to have few questions asked of them, which was convenient when you had two young women suffering from Kolokol-1 poisoning, and one peppered with fragments of shrapnel.

When the grenade had exploded a scattering of steel splinters had struck Narov, piercing her suit, hence the Kolokol-1 poisoning. But the long ride in the RIB and the fresh sea air had helped to blow the worst of the toxins away.

Jaeger found Narov in her hospital room, propped against a

pile of spotless pillows. Sunlight streamed in through the partially open window.

All things considered, she was looking remarkably well. A little pinched and pale, perhaps. Heavy rings around the eyes. She still sported the odd bandage where the shrapnel had hit her. But just three weeks after the attack, she was well on the road to recovery.

Jaeger took the seat beside her bed. Narov didn't say anything.

'How are you feeling?' he prompted.

She didn't so much as glance at him. 'Alive.'

'Gives a lot away,' Jaeger grumbled.

'Okay, how is this? My head hurts, I'm bored shitless, and I'm desperate to get out of here.'

In spite of himself, Jaeger had to smile. It never ceased to amaze him how exasperating this woman could be. Her flat, expressionless, overly formal tones lent her words just a hint of menace, yet there was no doubting her self-sacrifice or her bravery. By diving on that body and smothering the grenade, she had saved the lot of them. They owed Narov their lives,

And Jaeger didn't like being so in debt to someone who was such an enigma.

11

'The doctors say you're not going anywhere fast,' Jaeger volunteered., 'Not until they've run some more tests.'

'The doctors can go screw themselves. No one is keeping me here against my will.'

While Jaeger felt a driving sense of urgency to get on the case again, he needed Narov fit and capable.

'Softly softly catchee monkey,' he told her. She looked at him quizzically. More haste, less speed was his basic meaning. 'Take the time to get well.' He paused. 'And *then* we get busy.'

Narov snorted. 'But we do not have time. After our Amazon mission, those who came after us vowed to hunt us down. And now they will be triply determined. Yet still there is all the time in the world for me to lie here and get pampered?'

'You're no use to anyone half-dead.'

She glared. 'I am very much alive. And time is running out, or have you forgotten? Those papers we discovered. In that warplane. *Aktion Werewolf.* Blueprint for the Fourth Reich.'

Jaeger hadn't forgotten.

At the end of their epic Amazon expedition, they'd stumbled across a giant Second World War-era warplane secreted in the jungle, on an airstrip hewn out of the bush. It turned out that it had carried Hitler's foremost scientists, plus the Reich's *Wunderwaffe* – its top-secret, cutting-edge weaponry – to a place where such fearsome weapons could be developed long after the war was over.

Finding the aircraft had been a mind-blowing discovery. But

for Jaeger and his team, the real shocker had been the revelation that it was the Allied powers – chiefly America and Britain – that had sponsored those ultra-secret Nazi relocation flights.

In the closing stages of the war, the Allies had cut deals with a raft of top Nazis to ensure they would escape justice. By that point, Germany was no longer the real enemy: Stalin's Russia was. The West faced a new threat: the rise of communism, and the Cold War. Working to the old rule that my enemy's enemy is my friend, the Allied powers had bent over backwards to safeguard the foremost architects of Hitler's Reich.

In short, key Nazis and their technologies had been flown halfway around the world to secrecy and safety. The British and Americans had referred to this deep-black programme by various codenames: it was Operation Darwin to the British, and Project Safe Haven to the Americans. But the Nazis had had their own operational codename, and it beat all the others by a country mile: *Aktion Werewolf* – Operation Werewolf.

Aktion Werewolf had a seventy-year timescale, and was designed to deliver the ultimate revenge against the Allies. It was a blueprint to bring about the rise of a Fourth Reich by working top Nazis into positions of world power, while at the same time harnessing the most fearsome of the *Wunderwaffe* to their ends.

That much had been revealed in documents recovered from the aircraft in the Amazon. And in undertaking that expedition, Jaeger had realised that another, frighteningly powerful force was also searching for the warplane, intent on burying its secrets for ever.

Vladimir and his people had hunted Jaeger's team across the Amazon. Of their captives, only Leticia Santos had been spared, and that so as to coerce and entrap Jaeger and his fellow operators. But then Narov had turned up trumps, discovering the location of Santos's prison – hence the rescue mission they had just undertaken, a mission that had thrown up new and vital evidence.

'There's been a development,' Jaeger announced. Over time, he'd learnt that it was best to ignore the worst of Narov's crabbiness. 'We broke the passwords. Got into their computer; their drives.'

He handed her a sheet of paper. It had a few words scrawled across it.

Kammler H.
BV222
Katavi
Choma Malaika

'These are the keywords we've picked up from their email chatter,' Jaeger explained. 'Vladimir – if that's his real name – was communicating with someone higher up. The guy who calls the shots. Those words came up repeatedly in their comms.'

Narov read them over a few times. 'Interesting.' Her tone had softened slightly. 'Kammler H. That is SS General Hans Kammler, presumably, though we all thought of him as long dead.

'BV222,' she continued. 'The Blohm and Voss BV222 *Wiking* – has to be. A Second World War flying boat – a real beast of a machine that could land just about anywhere there was water.'

'*Wiking* meaning Viking, presumably?' Jaeger queried.

Narov snorted. 'Well done.'

'And the rest?' he prompted, not rising to the provocation.

Narov shrugged. 'Katavi. Choma Malaika. Sounds almost African.'

'It does,' Jaeger confirmed.

'So, have you checked?'

'I have.'

'Well?' she demanded irritably.

Jaeger smiled. 'Want to know what I discovered?'

Narov scowled. She knew that Jaeger was playing with her now. 'How do you say – does the bear shit in the woods?'

Jaeger smiled. 'Choma Malaika is Swahili for "Burning Angels", Swahili being the language of East Africa. I learned some while on operations there. Plus get this. Katavi translates into English as . . . "the Hunter".'

Narov flashed him a look. The significance of that name certainly wasn't lost on her.

Ever since childhood, Jaeger had believed in portents. He was superstitious, and especially when things seemed to signify something to him personally. 'The Hunter' was the nickname he'd been given during their expedition into the Amazon, and it wasn't one he had adopted lightly.

An Amazon Indian tribe – the Amahuaca – had helped them in their quest for that hidden warplane. They had proved the most constant and loyal of companions. One of the tribal chief's sons, Gwaihutiga, had coined that name – The Hunter – for Jaeger, after he had saved them from all-but-certain annihilation. And when Gwaihutiga had lost his life at the hands of Vladimir and his murderous crew, the name had become even more precious. Jaeger cherished it, lest he forget.

And now, another hunter on another ancient continent – Africa – seemed to be calling to him.

12

Narov gestured at the scribbled list. 'We need to get this to my people. Those last words – Katavi; Choma Malaika – they are sure to signify something more to them.'

'You've got a lot of confidence in them – your people. A lot of trust in their abilities.'

'They are the best. In every sense of the word they are the best.'

'Which reminds me – just who are your people? I'm long overdue an explanation, don't you think?'

Narov shrugged. 'I agree. To that end my people have invited you to come and meet with them.'

'With a view to what exactly?'

'Being recruited. Joining us. That is, if you can prove you are truly . . . ready.'

Jaeger's face hardened. 'You almost said *worthy*, didn't you?'

'It doesn't matter. It doesn't matter what I think. It is not my decision either way.'

'And what makes you think I'd want to join you? Join *them*?'

'Simple.' Narov glanced at him. 'Your wife and child: right now my people offer the best chance you'll ever have of finding them.'

Jaeger felt a surge of emotion well up inside him. Three terrible years – it was one hell of a long time to be searching for your loved ones, especially when all evidence suggested they were being held captive by a merciless enemy.

Before he could think of a suitable response, he felt his phone vibrate. Message incoming. Leticia Santos's surgeon was keeping him updated by text, and he figured it was maybe news of how she was doing.

He glanced at the cheap mobile's screen. These pay-as-you-go phones were often the most secure. If you kept the battery removed, only powering up briefly to check for messages, they were pretty much untraceable. Otherwise your phone would betray your location every time.

The message was from Raff – normally a man of few words. Jaeger clicked and opened it.

Urgent. Meet me at the usual place. And read this.

Jaeger scrolled down and clicked on a link embedded in the message. A news headline appeared: 'London edit suite fire-bombed – suspected terrorism spectacular'. Below was a photo of a building engulfed in a cloud of billowing smoke.

The image hit Jaeger like a punch to the guts. He knew that place well. It was The Joint, the edit suite where the final touches were being put to a TV film telling the story of their expedition into the Amazon.

'Oh my God . . .' He reached across and presented the screen to Narov. 'It's started. They've hit Dale.'

Narov stared for an instant, betraying little visible reaction. Mike Dale had been their Amazon expedition film-maker. A young Aussie cameraman-cum-expeditioner, he'd filmed their epic journey for a number of TV channels.

'I warned you,' she said. 'I told you this would happen. Unless we finish this, they will hunt every one of us down. And after Cuba, even more so.'

Jaeger slipped the phone into his pocket, grabbing his Belstaff and bike helmet. 'I'm meeting Raff. Don't go anywhere. I'll be back with an update . . . and an answer.'

As much as he felt like burning some rubber to work off his pent-up anger, Jaeger forced himself to take the ride easy. The last thing he needed right now was to smash himself up, and especially as they might well have lost another of their team.

At first, Jaeger and Dale had had a fractious, troubled relationship. But over the weeks spent in the jungle, Jaeger had come to respect and value the cameraman's craft, and to cherish the man's company. By the end, Dale had become someone he counted as a close friend.

By the 'usual place' Raff meant the Crusting Pipe, an ancient bar set in the former cellars of a central London town house. With its low, vaulted brick ceiling stained yellow with tobacco smoke and a layer of sawdust scattered underfoot, it had an air about it of a meeting place of pirates, desperadoes and gentleman thieves.

It was just the kind of venue that suited Raff, Jaeger and their ilk.

Jaeger parked the bike on the cobbled square and made his way through the crowds, taking the stone steps to the lower level two at a time. He found Raff in their usual cubbyhole, a place about as private and conspiratorial as you could ever wish for.

There was a bottle of wine on the ancient, battered table. By the glow of the candle beside it, Jaeger could tell that it was already half empty.

Wordlessly, Raff placed a glass in front of Jaeger and poured. Then he raised his own, darkly, and they drank. Each man had seen enough bloodshed – and lost a good many friends and fellow fighters – to know that death was a constant companion. It came with the territory.

'Tell me,' Jaeger prompted.

In answer, Raff slid a sheet of paper across the table. 'A summary from one of the coppers. A guy I know. I got it about an hour ago.'

Jaeger skimmed the text.

'The hit happened sometime after midnight,' Raff continued, his face darkening. 'The Joint's got tight security – packed full of expensive editing gear, it's got to. Well, the guy got in and out without triggering any of the alarms. IED planted in the online suite where Dale and team were doing their final edit, hidden amongst the bank of hard drives.'

Raff took a long pull on his glass. 'The explosion seems to have been triggered by someone entering the room. Most likely a pressure-plate IED. Either way the blast served two purposes: one, it obliterated all film of the expedition. Two, it turned half a dozen steel hard drives into a storm of shrapnel.'

Jaeger asked the obvious question. 'Dale?'

Raff shook his head. 'Nope. Dale turned back at the edit suite to fetch a bunch of coffees. Getting one for everyone on the team. His fiancée, Hannah, was the first in. Her and a young runner.' A heavy pause. 'Neither survived.'

Jaeger shook his head in horror. Over the weeks that Dale had spent cutting together his film, Jaeger had got to know Hannah pretty well. They'd enjoyed a few nights out, and he'd warmed to her sparky, spirited company, plus that of the runner/edit assistant, Chrissy.

Both of them dead. Blown to pieces by an IED. It was a nightmare.

'How's Dale taking it?' Jaeger ventured.

Raff glanced at him. 'Have a guess. Him and Hannah – they were set to get married this summer. He's a complete mess.'

'Any CCTV images?' Jaeger asked.

'The word is they were wiped clean. The guy who did this is a pro. We're getting access to the drive and we may have someone who can recover something. But don't hold your breath.'

Jaeger refilled their glasses. For several seconds the two men sat in sombre silence. Finally, Raff reached across the table and grabbed Jaeger's arm.

'You know what this means? The hunt is on. Us for them. Them for us. It's kill or be killed now. There's no other way.'

'There is some good news,' Jaeger ventured. 'Narov's back. Awake. Hungry. Seems pretty much recovered. Plus Santos is crawling her way back to consciousness. I figure they're both going to pull through okay.'

Raff signalled, ordering more wine. No matter what, they would drink to the dead. The barman arrived with a second bottle and showed the label to Raff, who nodded his assent. He pulled the cork and offered it so Raff could check whether the bottle was good. Raff waved it away. This was the Crusting Pipe. They took proper care of their wine.

'Frank, just pour, okay. We're drinking to absent friends.' He turned his attention back to Jaeger. 'Tell me: how is the ice queen anyway?'

'Narov? Antsy. Feisty as ever.' A pause. 'She's invited me to go meet her people.' Jaeger glanced at the sheet of paper lying on the table. 'After this, I think we need to be there.'

Raff nodded. 'If they can get us access to whoever did this, we should all go.'

'Narov seems to believe in them. She's got every confidence.'

'And you? You sure of her? Of her people? No more doubts, like you had in the Amazon?'

Jaeger shrugged. 'She's difficult. Cagey. Doesn't trust anyone. But I figure right now her people are the only option we've got. And we need to know what they know.'

Raff grunted. 'Good enough for me.'

'Right. Send a message. Alert everyone. Warn them we are being hunted. And tell them to prepare to meet – timescale and destination to be decided.'

'Got it.'

'Plus warn them to watch their backs. The people who did this . . . One moment's carelessness, we're all dead.'

13

The spring rain felt soft and chill on Jaeger's exposed skin. A damp, grey caress, one that suited his state of mind perfectly.

He stood in some pine woods set well back from the playing field, his dark biking trousers and Belstaff jacket merging with the dripping, dank wetness of the scene.

A cry echoed across to him. 'Back him up! Go with him, Alex! Back him up!'

It was the voice of a parent, one that Jaeger didn't recognise. The guy must be new to the school, but as Jaeger had been absent a good three years, most of the faces seemed unfamiliar to him now.

As his face must be to them.

An awkward, distant figure half hidden amongst the trees, watching a schoolboy rugby match in which he seemingly had no interest; no child to cheer for.

A worrying stranger. Gaunt-faced. Reserved. Troubled.

It was a wonder no one had called the police on him.

Jaeger raised his eyes to the clouds. Low-lying, glowering; scudding with a swiftness that mocked the tiny but determined figures making a push for the try line, as their proud fathers yelled encouragement, scenting a hard-fought victory.

Jaeger wondered why he'd come.

He guessed he'd wanted to remember, before the next chapter of the mission opened – meeting Narov's people, whoever they might be. He'd come here – to these rain-lashed playing fields – as it was the last place he had seen his son happy and free, before the darkness took him. Took them.

He'd come here to try to recapture some of that – some of that pure, glittering, priceless magic.

His eyes roamed around the scene, coming to rest upon the squat but imposing form of Sherborne Abbey. For well over thirteen centuries the Saxon cathedral and then Benedictine abbey had stood sentinel over this historic town, and the school where his son had been nurtured and thrived.

All that fine education and tradition crystallised here, so potently, on the rugby field.

'KA MATE? KA MATE? KA ORA? KA ORA?' *Will I die? Will I die? Will I live? Will I live?* Jaeger could hear the words even now, echoing across the pitch and reverberating through his memories. That iconic chant.

Together with Raff, Jaeger had been a stalwart in the SAS rugby team, as they'd pounded rival units half to death. Raff had always led the Haka – the traditional pre-match Maori war dance – the rest of the team flanking him, fearless and unstoppable. There were more than a few Maoris in the SAS, so it had seemed peculiarly appropriate.

Childless and not the marrying type, Raff had more or less adopted Luke as his surrogate son. He had come to be a regular visitor at the school, and an honorary coach to the rugby team. Officially, the school hadn't permitted them to do the Haka before matches. But unofficially the other coaches had turned a blind eye – especially when it had set the boys on a winning streak.

And that was how an ancient Maori war chant had come to echo across Sherborne's hallowed fields.

'KA MATE! KA MATE! KA ORA! KA ORA!'

Jaeger eyed the match. The opposing team were rucking the Sherborne boys back again. No try. Jaeger doubted the Haka was still an opener to their matches, with him and Raff being absent now for three long years.

He was about to turn and leave, making for the Triumph parked discreetly beneath the trees, when he felt a presence at his side. He glanced round.

'Jesus, William. I thought it must be you. But what . . .? Hell. It's been a long time.' The figure thrust out a hand. 'How the devil are you?'

Jaeger would have recognised the guy anywhere. Overweight, snaggle-toothed, with somewhat bulging eyes and greying hair held back in a ponytail, Jules Holland was better known to all as the Ratcatcher. Or the Rat for short.

The two men shook hands. 'I've been . . . Well, I've been . . . alive.'

Holland grimaced. 'Doesn't sound too hot.' A pause. 'You just kind of disappeared. There was that Christmas rugby sevens tournament: you, Luke and Ruth a big presence at the school. By the New Year – gone. Not a word.'

His tone was bordering on hurt. Jaeger could understand why. To some they were the most unlikely of friends, but over time Jaeger had warmed to the Rat's unconventional, maverick ways, plus his complete lack of pretentiousness.

With the Rat, what you saw was what you got – always.

That Christmas had been one of the few occasions on which Jaeger had got Ruth to really buy in to the rugby thing. Prior to that, she'd been loath to watch matches, for she couldn't bear to see Luke getting 'so beaten up', as she put it.

Jaeger understood, but even at eight years of age Luke had been obsessed by the game. Blessed with natural protective instincts and a fierce loyalty, he'd proven a stalwart in defence. A rock. A lion.

His tackling was fearsome, and few were the opposition players who managed to get past him. And in spite of his mother's worries, he wore his bruises and cuts as badges of honour. He seemed to have a natural appreciation of the saying – 'What doesn't break you makes you stronger'.

That Christmas's sport – Rugby Sevens; seven-a-side – tended to be more fast-flowing and less bogged down by the brutal attrition of the regular game. Jaeger had lured Ruth to that first sevens match, and once she had seen her son running like the wind and scoring a fine try, she'd been hooked.

From then on she and Jaeger had stood arm in arm on the sidelines, screaming out their support for Luke and his team. It had been one of those precious moments when Jaeger had felt the simple joy of being a family.

He had videoed one of the toughest matches, so they could play the tape to the boys and analyse how best to improve their game. Lessons learned. But now, those were some of the last images he had of his missing son.

And he had replayed those scenes over and over during the three dark years since losing him.

14

On the spur of the moment, they'd driven north that Christmas, to Wales, to do some winter camping, the car stuffed full of gear and presents. Ruth was a lover of all things nature, and a diehard conservationist, and her son had inherited those same interests. As a threesome, they loved nothing more than to head out into the wild.

But it was there on the Welsh mountains that Ruth and Luke had been ripped away from him. Jaeger – traumatised and driven wild by grief – had cut off all links to the world they had once inhabited, Jules Holland and his son Daniel included.

Daniel – who had Asperger's, a form of autism – had been Luke's best friend at school. Jaeger could only imagine how suddenly losing his battle buddy had affected him.

Holland waved a hand vaguely towards the match. 'As you'll have noticed, Dan's still blessed with two flat feet. Takes after his dad, a cack-handed monster at any sport. At least with rugby you can bumble through with a bit of fat and muscle.' He glanced at his paunch. 'More the former, when you're talking about a son of mine.'

'I'm sorry,' Jaeger offered. 'About the disappearance. The silence. Stuff happened.' He glanced around at the rain-swept scene. 'I guess maybe you heard.'

'A little.' Holland shrugged. 'I feel for you. No need to apologise. No need to say anything at all.'

A silence lay between them. Companionable. Understated.

Accepting. The thud of boots on wet turf and the yells of the parents punctuated their thoughts.

'So how is Daniel?' Jaeger asked eventually. 'It must've been hard for him. Losing Luke. Those two were utterly inseparable.'

Holland smiled. 'Kindred spirits, that's how I always thought of them.' He glanced at Jaeger. 'Dan's made some new friends. But he never stops asking, "When's Luke coming back?" That kind of thing.'

Jaeger felt a lump in his throat. Maybe it had been a mistake coming here. It was twisting him up inside. He tried changing the subject. 'You busy? Still up to the same old monkey business?'

'Busier than ever. Once you earn a certain reputation, every agency and their mother comes knocking. I'm freelance still. For hire to the highest bidder. The more competitors, the more my rates keep rising.'

Holland had earned his reputation – and his nickname – in a decidedly uncertain field: computer and internet piracy. He'd started in his teens, by hacking into the school portal and re-placing the photos of the teachers he didn't like with donkeys.

He'd gone on to hijack the A-level examination board web-site, awarding himself and his school mates straight A's. A natural-born social activist and rebel, he'd graduated to hack-ing a wealth of criminal and gang-related groups, taking money from their bank accounts and transferring it direct to their opponents.

As just one example, he'd hacked the bank account of a Brazil-ian mafioso outfit that traded illegal narcotics and timber out of the Amazon, transferring several million dollars to Greenpeace.

Of course, the environmental activists hadn't been able to keep the cash. They couldn't be seen to profit from the very thing they fought against, not to mention the illegality. But the resulting press coverage had dragged the mafioso group into the limelight, speeding their demise. And it had been one more step in earning the Ratcatcher his notoriety.

With each success, Holland left the same message: *Hacked by the Rat.* And so it was that his unique skills had come to the attention of those who make it their business to know.

At that stage, he had found himself at a crossroads: either go to court facing a plethora of hacking charges, or start working quietly for the good guys. Accordingly, he was now a much-sought-after consultant to an alphabet soup of intelligence agencies, with an enviable security clearance.

'Glad to hear you're busy,' Jaeger told him. 'Just don't ever take a contract with the bad guys. The day the Rat starts working for the wrong side, we're finished.'

Holland brushed back his straggly hair and snorted. 'Fat chance.' He swivelled his gaze from the rugby field to Jaeger. 'You know something: you and Raff – you were the only ones ever to take Dan seriously on the sports field. You gave him self-belief. You gave him a bloody chance. He still misses you. Enormously.'

Jaeger grimaced apologetically. 'I'm sorry. My world was a mess. For a long while I couldn't even be there for myself, if you know what I mean.'

Holland pointed at his son, as the young, gangly lad stepped forward for a scrum. 'Will, take a look at him. He's still crappy, but at least he's *playing*. He's one of the boys. That's your doing. Your legacy.' He glanced at his feet, then up at Jaeger again. 'So, like I said, no apologies asked for or required. Quite the reverse, in fact. I owe you. You ever need my . . . unique services, you only have to ask.'

Jaeger smiled. 'Thanks. I appreciate it.'

'I mean it. I'd drop everything.' Holland grinned. 'And for you I'd even waive my obscenely expensive fees. It'd be all at no charge.'

15

'S o, what exactly is this place?' Jaeger ventured.

A few days after his visit to the school, he found himself in a vast concrete edifice set deep within the heavily forested countryside to the east of Berlin. The team from his Amazon expedition was filtering in from various scattered locations, and he was the first to arrive. When all had reached here they would be seven in number – Jaeger, Raff and Narov included.

Jaeger's guide, a silver-haired man with a neatly trimmed beard, gestured at the dull-green walls. They rose to a good twelve feet on either side, the oblong windowless tunnel having an even greater breadth. Massive steel doors branched off to either side, and overhead ran a squat duct. The place was clearly military in design, and there was something sinister about its empty, echoing passageways that put Jaeger's nerves on edge.

'The identity of this place depends upon your nationality,' the elderly man began. 'If you are German, this is the Falken-hagen Bunker – after the nearby town of the same name. It was here, in this vast complex – most of which is underground and was thus immune to bombing – that Hitler ordered the creation of a weapon to finally defeat the Allies.'

He glanced at Jaeger from under silvery brows. His transat-lantic accent made it difficult to place his nationality. He could be British, or American, or a citizen of any number of Euro-pean nations. But somehow a simple, basic decency and honesty shone out of him.

There was a calm compassion about his gaze, but Jaeger didn't doubt that it masked a core of inner steel. This man – Peter Miles as he'd introduced himself – was one of Narov's top people, which meant that he was bound to share some of her unique killer instincts.

'You have heard perhaps of *N-stoff*?' Miles queried.

'Afraid not.'

'Very few have. Chlorine trifluoride: *N-stoff* – or Substance-N as it would be in English. Imagine a fearsome dual agent: napalm crossed with sarin nerve gas. That was *N-stoff*. So volatile was it that it would ignite even when tipped into water, and as it burned it would also gas you to death.

'According to Hitler's *Chemicplan*, six hundred tonnes were to be manufactured here every month.' He let out a gentle laugh. 'Thankfully, Stalin rolled in with his armour long before more than a fraction of that amount could ever be produced.'

'And then?' Jaeger prompted.

'Post-war, this place was transformed into one of the Soviet regime's foremost Cold War defensive sites. It was where the Soviet leaders would sit out nuclear Armageddon, safely en-sconced one hundred feet below ground and encased in an impregnable steel and concrete sarcophagus.'

Jaeger glanced at the ceiling. 'Those ducts; they're for piping in clean, filtered air, right? Which means the entire complex could be sealed off from the outside.'

The elderly man's eyes twinkled. 'Indeed. Young but smart, I see.'

Young. Jaeger smiled, his own eyes crinkling with laughter lines. He couldn't remember the last time anyone had called him that. He was warming to Peter Miles.

'So how did we – you – end up here?' he queried.

Miles turned a corner, ushering Jaeger down another inter-minable passageway. 'In 1990, East and West Germany were reunified. The Soviets were forced to hand back such bases to the German authorities.' He smiled. 'We were offered it by the German government. Very discreetly, but for as long as we might need. Despite its dark history, it suits our purposes admirably. It is utterly secure. And very, very discreet. Plus, you know how the English saying goes: beggars can't be choosers.'

Jaeger laughed. He appreciated the guy's humility, not to mention his turn of phrase. 'The German government offering up a former Nazi bunker? How does that work?'

The old man shrugged his shoulders. 'We feel it is somewhat fitting. There is a certain delicious irony about it all. And you know something: if there is one nation that will never forget the horrors of the war, it is Germany. They are driven and empowered by their guilt – still, to this day.'

'I guess I've never really thought about it,' Jaeger confessed.

'Well perhaps you should,' the old man chided, gently. 'If we are safe anywhere, we are perhaps most safe hiding in a former Nazi bunker in Germany, where all of this began. But . . . I get ahead of myself. These are discussions best to be had when the rest of your team is here.'

Jaeger was shown to his sparse room. He'd eaten on the flight, and in truth he was dog-tired. After the whirlwind of the past three weeks – the Cuban mission, the edit suite bombing, and now mustering his team – he was looking forward to a long sleep secreted deep below ground.

Peter Miles bade him goodnight. Once the massive steel door had swung shut, Jaeger became aware of a deafening silence. This far underground, and encased in several feet of reinforced concrete, not the slightest sound could be heard.

It felt utterly unearthly.

He lay down and focused on his breathing. It was a trick he'd learned during his time in the military. A deep breath in, hold it for several seconds, followed by a long breath out again. Repeat. Focus on the act of breathing, and all other worries would dissolve from your mind.

His last conscious thought was that, lying here beneath the ground and in utter darkness, it felt as if he had been consigned to his own grave.

But he was exhausted, and it wasn't long before he drifted into a deep sleep.

16

'OUT! GET OUT! OUT!' a voice screamed. 'OUT! BAS-
TARD MOVE!'

Jaeger felt the vehicle's door being ripped open as a horde of
dark figures wearing balaclavas swarmed around, weapons held
at the ready. Hands reached in and dragged him out violently, as
Peter Miles was likewise hauled from the driver's side.

After a solid fourteen hours' sleep, Jaeger had joined Miles on
a ride to the airport, to collect two of the others from his team.
But as they'd wound their way along the narrow forest track
leading out of Falkenhagen, they'd found their way blocked
by a fallen tree. Miles had slowed to a halt, clearly suspecting
nothing. Moments later, a crowd of balaclava-clad gunmen had
swarmed out of the trees.

Jaeger was thrown to the ground, his face forced into the
sodden dirt.

'KEEP DOWN! FUCKING DOWN!'

He felt powerful arms pinioning him. His face was driven so
hard into the earth that he couldn't breathe. As he choked and
spluttered on the smell of rot and decay, he was gripped by a
rising sense of panic.

They were suffocating him.

He tried to lift his head to grab a gasp of air, but a series of
savage kicks and punches rained down.

'GET DOWN!' the voice screamed. 'Get your ugly, shitty
face down into the dirt!'

Jaeger tried to break away, flailing at his attackers and

screaming curses. All it earned him was a fusillade of vicious blows, this time from a rifle butt. As he went down under the beating, he felt his hands being wrenched violently backwards, as if his arms were about to be ripped out of their sockets, and then his wrists were lashed vice-tight with gaffer tape.

The next moment the forest chill was rent by gunshots. *Bang! Bang! Bang!* Wild shots, echoing deafeningly amongst the shadows beneath the thick cover. Shots that made Jaeger's heart skip a beat.

This is bad. Real bad.

He managed to force his head up enough to grab a quick peek. He saw that Peter Miles had managed to make a break for it and was weaving through the trees.

More shots were unleashed. Jaeger saw Miles falter and stumble, and then he tumbled on to his front and lay still. One of the gunmen rushed across to him. He levelled a pistol at the fallen man, pulling the trigger three times in quick succession.

Jaeger felt himself shaking. They'd executed Peter Miles – that gentle old man – in cold blood. *Who in the name of God was behind this?*

An instant later, someone grabbed Jaeger's hair and yanked his head backwards. Before he could say a word, he felt a strip of gaffer tape being slapped across his mouth, then a black cloth bag was dragged over his head and tied around his neck.

Everything went very dark.

Stumbling blindly, Jaeger was yanked to his feet and propelled forward helter-skelter through the woodland. He tripped over a fallen branch and fell hard.

Wild screams: 'GET UP! UP! UP!'

He was dragged onwards across a patch of boggy ground, the smell of rotten leaf matter assailing his senses. The frantic forced march went on and on, until Jaeger felt totally disorientated. Finally he detected a new noise up ahead: the rhythmic throb of an engine. They were taking him to some kind of vehicle.

Through the bag he could just make out two bright spots piercing the thick shadows.

Headlamps.

With two guys gripping him by the armpits, he was thrust towards the lights, his feet dragging uselessly. The next moment he was slammed face-first into the front grille of the vehicle, pain shooting through his forehead.

'BASTARD KNEEL! ON YOUR KNEES! *KNEEL!*'

He was thrust into a kneeling position. He could feel the headlamps playing across his face, the blinding light bleeding through the bag. Without a word of warning it was torn away. He tried to turn his head from the glare, but he was held by his hair in a savage grip, eyes forced into the light.

'NAME!' the voice snarled. It was right beside his ear now. 'Let's hear your bastard name!'

The speaker was hidden from Jaeger, but the voice sounded foreign, and thick with some Eastern European accent. For a terrible moment Jaeger had visions of the gang who'd suffered the Kolokol-1 attack – Vladimir and his lot – taking him captive. But surely it couldn't be them, for how in God's name would they have found him?

Think, Jaeger. Fast.

'NAME!' the voice yelled again. '*NAME!*'

Jaeger's throat was dry with shock and fear. He managed to rasp out the one word: 'Jaeger.'

The men holding him slammed his face into the nearest headlamp, leaving his features scrunched up tight against the glass.

'Both names. *Both bastard names!*'

'Will. William Jaeger.' He coughed out the words through a mouthful of blood.

'So, this is better, William Jaeger.' The same voice, sinister and predatory, but a fraction calmer now. 'Now you tell me: what are names of the rest of your crew?'

Jaeger said nothing. No way would he answer. But he could sense the anger and aggression rising again.

'One more time: what are the names of the rest of your crew?'

From somewhere Jaeger found his voice. 'I've no idea what you're talking about.'

He felt his head being wrenched backwards, then his face was rammed into the forest dirt, deeper than it had been before. He tried to hold his breath as the insults and curses began again, punctuated by expertly aimed kicks and blows. Whoever his captors were, they sure knew how to hurt someone.

Finally he was pulled upright and the bag was yanked over his head once more.

The voice spat out a command. 'Lose him. He's no use if he won't talk. You know what to do.'

Jaeger was dragged around to what had to be the rear of the vehicle. He was lifted up and hurled aboard. Hands forced him into a sitting position – legs out straight, arms linked behind his back.

Then silence. Just the rasp of his own laboured breathing.

The minutes dragged on. Jaeger could sense – taste – the metallic tang of his own fear. Eventually he had to try to shift position, in an effort to ease his aching limbs.

Slam! Someone booted him in the stomach. Not a word had been spoken. He was forced back into the same seated pose. He knew now that in spite of the spikes of pain, he was not permitted to move. He'd been put into a stress position, one designed to deliver a relentless and unendurable torture.

Without warning, the vehicle gave a sudden lurch and began to move. The unexpected motion threw Jaeger on to his front. Instantly he was booted around the head. He dragged himself into position again, but moments later the truck hit a ditch and he was catapulted on to his back. Again, elbows and fists rained down, driving his head into the cold metal skin of the vehicle.

Finally one of his tormentors dragged him back into the same stress position as before. The pain was intense. His head throbbed, his lungs were bursting and he was still winded from the beating. He felt as if his heart was about to explode out of his chest. Fear and panic gripped him.

Jaeger knew he'd been captured by utter professionals. The question was, who were they exactly?

And where in God's name were they taking him?

17

The truck ride seemed to take forever, jolting along rutted tracks and rattling over rough ground. In spite of the pain he was in, at least it gave Jaeger time to think. Someone must have betrayed them. No one could have found them in the Falkenhagen Bunker otherwise, that was for certain.

Was it Narov? If not, who else had known where they were meeting? None of the team had been informed of their end destination. All they'd been told was that they would be collected from the airport.

But why? After all they'd been through, why would Narov have sold him out? And to whom?

All of a sudden the truck slowed to a stop. Jaeger heard the rear door being hinged open. He tensed. Hands grabbed him by the legs and hauled him out, letting him drop. He tried to use his arms to break the fall, but still his head cannoned into the ground.

Jesus, that hurt.

He was dragged away, pulled along by his feet like an animal carcass, his head and torso ploughing through the dirt. From the brightness filtering in through the bag, he could tell that it was daylight. Otherwise, he had lost all sense of time.

He heard a door being wrenched open and he was booted inside some kind of building. It went suddenly dark again. A terrifying sense of total blackness. Then he heard the familiar whir of a lift motor and felt the floor beneath him drop away. He was in an elevator, going deep.

Finally, the movement stopped. Jaeger was dragged out and propelled through a series of sharp right-angled turns – some kind of twisting corridor, he figured. Then a door opened, unleashing a tsunami of deafening sound. It was as if a TV had been left on tuned to nothing, blasting out electronic interference – so-called white noise – at top volume.

He was gripped beneath the armpits and dragged backwards into the white-noise room. His hands were cut free and his clothes were torn away from him with such force that the buttons flew off. He was left in nothing but his boxers; even his shoes were gone.

He was manoeuvred into a position facing the wall, his hands against the cold brickwork but balanced only on the tips of his fingers. His captors kicked his legs further and further backwards until he was suspended at what felt like a sixty-degree angle on fingertips and toes.

Footsteps stomped away. Utter silence, apart from his own pained and laboured breathing.

Was there anyone but him here any more?

Did he have company?

There was no way of telling.

Years back, Jaeger had been put through simulated resistance-to-interrogation training, as part of the selection process when joining the SAS. It was designed to test your resolve under pressure, and to train you how to cope with captivity. It had been thirty-six hours of hell, but he'd always known it was only an exercise.

This, by contrast, was very real and terrifying.

His shoulder muscles started to burn, his fingers cramping, as all the while the deafening white noise pounded into his skull. He wanted to cry out with the pain, but his mouth was still taped shut. All he could do was scream and yell inside his own head.

Eventually it was the finger cramps that got too much for him. The pain seared through his hands, the muscles tensing so hard it felt as if his fingers would be ripped from their very sockets. For an instant he relaxed, pressing his palms against the wall. It was blissful relief to allow them to take his full weight. But the next moment he doubled over as a jabbing bolt of pain shot up his spine.

Jaeger screamed, but it came out as a muffled yelp. He was far from alone in here, and someone had just applied an electrode – a cattle prod? – to the small of his back.

With brute savagery he was kicked back into his former position. Not a word had been said, but there was no misunderstanding the situation: if he tried to move or relax, they'd jab him with the electrode.

It wasn't long before his arms and legs began to shake uncontrollably. At the very moment when he felt he couldn't go on, his feet were booted out from under him, and he collapsed to the floor like a dead man. There was absolutely no let-up. Hands grabbed him like a lump of meat, forcing him into the sitting position he'd adopted in the truck, but this time with his arms folded in front of him.

His captors were faceless, voiceless tormentors. But their message was crystal clear: movement equals pain.

All that assailed Jaeger now was the screaming blast of white noise. Time became meaningless. When he lost consciousness and keeled over, they wrestled him into a new stress position, and on and on and on.

Eventually something seemed to change.

Without a hint of warning, Jaeger felt himself dragged to his feet. His hands were whipped behind his back, wrists taped together, and he was propelled towards the door. He was dragged along the corridors again, swinging left-right-left-right around the sharp series of turns.

He heard another door open and he was thrust into a room. A sharp edge was rammed into the back of his knees. It was a bare wooden chair, and it forced him to sit. He hunched there in silence.

Wherever he was now, there was an extra chill to the atmosphere, plus a faint smell of airlessness and damp. In one way this was the most terrifying moment yet. Jaeger had understood the white-noise room; its purpose and its rules. His captors had been trying to exhaust him, to break him down and force him to crack.

But this? This unknown. This total lack of noise or any sense of a human presence other than his own – it was utterly chilling.

Jaeger felt a spike of fear. Real, visceral fear. He had no idea where he had been brought to, but he sensed there was nothing good about this place. Plus he had little sense who might have captured him, or what they intended to do with him now.

All of a sudden, light flooded in, blinding him. The bag had been ripped off, and at the same instant a powerful beam switched on. It seemed to be shining directly into his face.

Gradually his eyes started to adjust and he began to figure out detail.

There was a stark metal desk before him, with a glass surface. Sitting on the desk was a bland-looking white china mug.

Nothing else: just a mug of steaming liquid.

Behind the desk was seated a portly, bearded, balding man. He looked to be in his mid-sixties. He was dressed in a threadbare tweed jacket and fraying shirt. With his dated dress and spectacles, he had the demeanour of a jaded university lecturer or an underpaid museum curator. A bachelor who did his own cleaning, overcooked his vegetables and was fond of collecting butterflies.

He looked utterly unremarkable: he'd be forgotten in an instant and would never turn heads in a crowd. The archetypal grey man. And the very last thing that Jaeger had been expecting to encounter right now.

He'd expected a gang of shaven-headed Eastern European thugs, each wielding a pickaxe handle or baseball bat. This was just so weird. It was way out left field, and it was messing with his head.

The grey man stared at Jaeger without saying a word. His expression almost gave the impression that he was . . . uninterested; bored; studying some unedifying museum specimen.

He nodded at the mug. 'Tea, white, one sugar. A cuppa. Isn't that what you say in England?'

He spoke quietly, with just a hint of a foreign accent, but to Jaeger it was untraceable. He didn't sound particularly aggressive or unfriendly. In fact he gave the impression of being slightly weary – as if he had done this a thousand times before.

'A nice cuppa. You must be thirsty. Have some tea.'

In the military, Jaeger had been taught to always take a drink or food if ever he were offered. Yes, it could be poisoned, but why would anyone bother? It was much easier to beat a captive to a pulp, or shoot him dead.

He stared at the white china mug. Faint wisps of steam curled into the chill air.

'A cup of tea,' the man repeated quietly. 'White with one. Have a drink.'

Jaeger flicked his eyes up to the grey man's face and back to the mug again. Then he reached out and grabbed it. From the smell, it just seemed to be hot, sweet, milky tea. He raised it to his lips and gulped it down.

There was no adverse reaction. He didn't collapse or puke or go into convulsions.

He placed the mug back down.

Silence descended once more.

Jaeger took a momentary glance at his surroundings. The room was a stark, utterly featureless cube devoid of any windows. He felt the grey man's eyes upon him, staring intently. He returned his own gaze to the floor.

'You are cold, I think? You must be. Cold. Would you like to be warm?'

Jaeger's mind raced. What was this – a trick question? Maybe. But Jaeger needed to buy himself some time. And in truth he was sitting there in his boxers freezing his nuts off. 'I've been warmer, sir. Sir, yes – I'm cold.'

The 'sir' bit was another lesson ingrained during Jaeger's military training: treat your captors as if they warranted some respect. There was just a chance that it might be repaid; it might persuade them to view you as a fellow human.

Yet right now Jaeger held out little hope. All that he had experienced here was designed to reduce him to the level of a defenceless animal.

'I think you would like to be warm,' the grey man continued. 'Look beside you. Open the bag. Inside, you will find dry clothes.'

Jaeger glanced down. A cheap-looking sports bag had appeared beside his chair. He reached for it and did as instructed, unzipping it. He half feared he would find the severed, bloodied head of one of his Amazon team lying inside. Instead, he discovered a set of faded orange work overalls and a pair of threadbare socks, plus some battered plimsolls.

'But what were you expecting?' the grey man asked, a faint smile playing across his features. 'First, a nice cup of tea. Now, clothes. Clothes to make you warm. Get dressed. Put them on.'

Jaeger slid into the overalls and buttoned up the front, then slipped on the shoes and sat back down again.

'Warmer? Does that feel better?'

Jaeger nodded.

'So now I think you understand. I have the power to help you. I can truly help. But I need something in return: I need *you* to help *me*.' The grey man left a weighty pause. 'I just need to know when your friends will be arriving, who we are to expect, and how we are to recognise them.'

'I cannot answer that question, sir.' It was the standard response that Jaeger had been trained to give: a negative, but as polite and respectful as he could make it in the circumstances. 'I don't know what you're on about either,' he added. He knew he had to stall.

The interrogator sighed, as if he had been expecting that response. 'It does not matter. We have found your . . . equipment. Your laptop. Your cell phone. We will crack your security codes and passwords and soon these things will reveal to us your secrets.'

Jaeger's mind was whirling. He was certain he'd not brought a laptop with him. And as for his cheap pay-as-you-go mobile, that would reveal nothing of any great import.

'If you cannot answer my question, at least tell me this: what are you doing here? Why are you in my country?'

Jaeger's mind reeled. *His country*. But this was Germany. Surely he hadn't been in the truck long enough for them to have crossed into some eastern European state? Who in God's name had he been taken by? Was it some rogue arm of the German intelligence services?

'I don't know what you're talking—' he began, but the grey man cut him off.

'This is very sad. I helped you, Mr Will Jaeger, but you are not trying to help me. And if you cannot help, then you will be returned to the room with the noise and the pain.'

The grey man had barely finished speaking when unseen hands whipped the bag over Jaeger's head again. The shock of it made his heart skip a beat.

Then he was hauled to his feet, spun around, and without another word he was marched away.

18

Jaeger found himself back in the white-noise room, leaning at a crazy angle against the brick wall. During SAS selection, they'd referred to such a place as 'the softener' – the room where grown men became weak. All he could hear was the empty, meaningless howl tearing through the darkness. All he could smell was his own sweat, cold and clammy against his skin. And in his throat he could taste the acid tang of bile.

He felt battered and exhausted and utterly alone, and his body was hurting like it had rarely hurt before. His head was throbbing; his mind screaming.

He started to murmur songs in his head. Snatches of favoured tunes remembered from his youth. If he could sing those songs, maybe he could block out the white noise, the agony and the fear.

Waves of fatigue washed over him. He was close to his limit and he knew it.

When the songs faded, he told himself stories of his childhood. Tales of his heroes that his father used to read to him. The feats of those who had inspired him and driven him on when he had faced his hardest tests; both as a kid, and later during his worst trials in the military.

He relived the story of Douglas Mawson, an Australian explorer who went through hell and back, starved and alone in Antarctica, yet somehow managed to haul himself to safety. Of George Mallory, very possibly the first person ever to climb Mount Everest, a man who knew for certain that he was sacrificing his life to conquer the world's highest peak. Mallory never made it down alive, perishing on those ice-bound slopes. But that was the sacrifice of his choosing.

Jaeger knew that humankind was capable of achieving the seemingly impossible. When the body was screaming that it could take no more, the mind could force it to go on. An individual could go way beyond the possible.

Likewise, if Jaeger believed strongly enough, he could beat the odds. He could get through this.

The power of the will.

He began to repeat the same mantra over and over: *Stay alert to the chance to escape. Stay alert . . .*

He lost all track of time; all sense of day and night. At one moment the bag was lifted to free his mouth, and a cup was thrust to his lips. He felt his head being forced backwards as they poured its contents down his throat.

Tea. Just like before.

It was followed by a stale biscuit. Then another and another. They rammed them in, pulled down the bag, and shoved him back into position.

Like an animal.

But at least for now they seemed to want to keep him alive.

Sometime later his head must have dropped, jerking downwards into sleep and slumping on to his chest. He felt himself torn into savage wakefulness as he was forced into a new stress position.

This time he was made to kneel on a patch of gravel. As the minutes passed, the sharp, jagged stones dug deeper into his flesh, cutting off the circulation, causing bolts of pain to shoot up into his brain. He was in agony, but he told himself he could get through this.

The power of the will.

How long had it been? he wondered. Days? Two or three, or more? It felt like an eternity.

At some point the white noise died abruptly, and the insanely inappropriate tones of the Barney the Dinosaur theme tune began to blast out at full volume. Jaeger had heard about such techniques: playing kids' cartoon tunes over and over to break a man's sanity and his will. It was known as 'psyops' – psychological operations. But for Jaeger, it had something of the opposite effect.

Barney had been one of Luke's favourite TV characters when he was an infant. The song served to bring the memories flooding back. Happy moments. Ones to grasp hold of; a rock upon which to tether his storm-lashed soul.

He reminded himself that this was what had brought him here. Chief amongst his motives, he was here on the trail of his missing wife and child. If he let his captors break him, he was abandoning that mission and giving up on those he loved.

He would not betray Ruth and Luke.

He had to hold on and hold firm.

Eventually he felt himself propelled into motion again. He was barely able to walk now, so they half carried him, out of the door, along the switchback corridor and into what he figured was the same room as before.

He was slammed into the chair, the bag was ripped off and the light flooded in.

Seated before him was the grey man. From where Jaeger was sitting, he could smell the stale sweat on the guy's clothes. He kept his eyes glued to the floor as the grey man did the bored staring act.

'This time, sadly, we do not have any tea.' The grey man shrugged. 'Things will only get better for you if you can be helpful. I think you understand that now. So can you? Can you be helpful to us?'

Jaeger tried to muster his muddled thoughts. He felt confused. He didn't know what to say. Helpful like how exactly?

'I wonder, Mr Jaeger,' the grey man raised one eyebrow questioningly, 'are you willing to be helpful? If not, we have no further use for you.'

Jaeger didn't say a word. Confused and exhausted though he might be, still he sensed a trap.

'So tell me, what is the time? Tell me the time. Surely that is not too much to ask. Are you willing to help me by simply telling me the time?'

For an instant Jaeger went to check his watch, but it had been ripped off him just moments after his capture. He had no idea what day it was, let alone the hour.

'What is the time?' the grey man repeated. 'You can easily help me. I just want to know the time.'

Jaeger didn't have a clue how he was supposed to respond.

All of a sudden a voice was screaming in his ear: 'ANSWER THE BASTARD QUESTION!'

A fist made contact with the side of his head, punching him out of the chair. He landed awkwardly. He'd not even known there was anyone else in the room. The shock of it set his pulse hammering like a machine gun.

He caught a glimpse of three muscular, crew-cut guys in dark tracksuits reaching down to grab him. They slammed him back into his seat before melting back into the silence.

The grey man remained utterly inscrutable. He gestured to one of the muscle-bound thugs and they exchanged a few words in a guttural-sounding language, one that Jaeger didn't understand. Then the chief enforcer pulled out a radio and spoke into it briefly.

The grey man turned back to Jaeger. He sounded almost apologetic. 'There is really no need for any of this . . . unpleasantness. You will realise shortly that we are not to be resisted, because we hold every card – every single one – in our hand. Helping us will only mean helping yourself, and also your family.'

Jaeger felt his heart miss a beat.

What in God's name did he mean – *his family*?

19

Jaeger felt a surge of vomit rising from within his guts. By sheer strength of will he forced it back down again. If these were the people who were holding Ruth and Luke, they were going to have to kill him. Otherwise he would get free and rip every last one of their throats out.

There was a click from behind him as the door opened. Jaeger heard someone enter the room and walk past. His eyes bulged disbelievingly. He'd feared as much, but still, surely to God this had to be a dream. He felt like smashing his head against the cold grey wall in an effort to wake himself from the nightmare.

Irina Narov came to a halt with her back to him. She handed something across the desk to the grey man. Wordlessly she turned. She went to hurry past, but as she did so, Jaeger managed to catch a glimpse of the consternation – and the guilt – burning in her eyes.

'Thank you, Irina,' the grey man said quietly. He turned his empty, bored eyes on Jaeger. 'The lovely Irina Narov. You know her, of course.'

Jaeger didn't respond. There was no point. He sensed there was worse – much worse – to come.

Narov had left a bundle lying on the table. Something about it struck Jaeger as familiar. The grey man pushed it across to him.

'Take a look. You need to see this. You need to see this to understand why you have no choice but to help us.'

Jaeger reached out, but even as he did so, he sensed with

chilling certainty what lay before him. It was Luke's *SAVE THE RHINO* T-shirt, the one he had got during their family safari to East Africa a few years back. The three of them had trekked across the moonlit savannah amongst herds of giraffe, wildebeest and, best of all, rhinos – their favourite animal. It had been utterly magical. The perfect family holiday. The T-shirts some of their most precious mementoes.

And now this.

Jaeger's aching, bloodied fingers grasped at the thin cotton. He lifted it up and held it close to his face, his pulse pounding in his ears. He felt as if his heart was going to burst. Tears pricked his eyes.

They had his family – the murderous, merciless, sick bastards.

'You must understand – there is no need for any of this.' The grey man's words cut through Jaeger's tortured thoughts. 'All we need is some answers. You give me the answers we seek, and we reunite you with your loved ones. That is all I ask. What could be easier?'

Jaeger felt his teeth grinding against each other. His jaw locked solid. His muscles were taut with tension as he fought against the blind urge to lash out; to strike back. He knew where it would get him. His hands had been bound with duct tape again, and he could feel the thugs' eyes upon him, willing him to make the first move.

He had to await his chance. Sooner or later they would make a mistake and then he would strike.

The grey man spread his hands invitingly. 'So, Mr Jaeger, in an effort to help your family, please tell me: when will your friends be arriving? Who exactly are we to expect? And how are we to recognise them?'

Jaeger felt a war explode within his head. He was being torn in opposite directions. Was he to sell out his closest friends? Betray his fellow warriors? Or lose the only chance he had of seeing Ruth and Luke again?

Screw it, he told himself. Narov had betrayed him. She was

supposedly on the side of the angels, but it had all been an act. She had sold him out as no one ever had before.

Who was there left that he could trust?

Jaeger's mouth opened. At the last moment, he choked back the words. If he let them break him, he was betraying his loved ones.

He would never betray his wife and child.

He had to hold firm.

'I don't know what you're talking about.'

The grey man raised both eyebrows. It was the nearest that Jaeger had seen him come to any kind of spontaneous reaction. Clearly he was surprised.

'I am a reasonable, patient man,' he breathed. 'I will give you another chance. I will offer *your family* another chance.' A pause. 'Tell me, when will your friends be arriving? Who exactly are we to expect? And how are we to recognise them?'

'I cannot answer—'

'Look, if you will not cooperate, things will become very difficult for you. For your family. So it is very simple. Give me the answers. When will your friends arrive? Who exactly are they? How will we know them?'

'I cannot—'

The grey man cut Jaeger off with a snap of the fingers. He glanced in the direction of his thugs. 'Enough. It is over. Take him away.'

The black bag was whipped over Jaeger's head; he felt his chin slammed on to his chest and his arms jammed together.

An instant later he was on his feet, being dragged from the room like a broken rag doll.

20

B ehind the glass partition, Narov shuddered. She watched in horrified fascination as Jaeger's hooded form was dragged from the room. The two-way mirror offered her a perfect view of proceedings.

'You are not enjoying this, I think?' a voice ventured.

It was Peter Miles, the elderly man whom Jaeger had presumed had been shot dead in the woods.

'I am not,' Narov muttered. 'I thought it was necessary, but . . . Does it have to go on? To the bitter end?'

The old man spread his hands. 'You are the one who told us he needed to be tested. This blockage he has over his wife and child . . . this utter desperation; this guilt. It can drive a man to contemplate what he would never normally do. Love is a powerful emotion; love of a child perhaps the most powerful of all.'

Narov slumped lower in her seat.

'It is not for too much longer,' Peter Miles offered. 'The biggest test – he is surely through it. If he had failed that, he would not be joining us.'

Narov nodded morosely, her mind lost in a swirl of dark thoughts.

There was a knock at the door. A much older, wizened figure entered. He planted his walking stick firmly inside the doorway, concern etched in his gaze. He looked to be in his nineties, but under his thick, bushy brows his eyes remained beady and alert.

'You are done here, I think?'

Peter Miles massaged his forehead exhaustedly. 'Almost. Thank God. Just a short while and we will know for certain.'

'But was this all really necessary?' the old man queried. 'I mean, remember who his grandfather was.'

Miles glanced at Narov. 'Irina seemed to believe it was. Remember, she has served with him in high-stress situations – in the heat of combat – and has witnessed how his nerve can sometimes appear to falter.'

A flash of anger blazed through the old man's eyes. 'He has been through so much! He may falter, but he'll never break. Never! He is my nephew, and a Jaeger.'

'I know,' Miles conceded. 'But I think you understand my meaning.'

The old man shook his head. 'No man should have to suffer what he has been put through these past few years.'

'And we're unsure what effect that has had upon him long-term. Hence Narov's concerns. Hence the present ... procedures.'

The old man glanced at Narov. Surprisingly, there was a kindly look in his eyes. 'My dear – cheer yourself. What will be will be.'

'I'm sorry, Uncle Joe,' she murmured. 'Perhaps my fears are misplaced. Unfounded.'

The old man's face softened. 'He comes from good stock, my dear.'

Narov glanced at the silvery-haired man. 'He has not placed a foot wrong, Uncle. He has not let anyone down, all through the testing. I fear I was mistaken.'

'What will be will be,' the old man echoed. 'And perhaps Peter is right. It is perhaps best we are absolutely certain.'

He turned to leave, pausing in the doorway. 'But if he does fall at the final hurdle, promise me one thing. Do not tell him. Let him leave this place without ever knowing that it was we who tested him, and that he ... failed us.'

The old man stepped out of the observation room, leaving a final comment hanging in the air.

'After all he has been through, that knowledge – it would break him.'

21

Jaeger expected to be dragged back into the stress room. Instead he was steered left for several seconds, before being brought to a sudden halt. There was a different smell in the air now: disinfectant, and the unmistakable reek of stale urine.

'Toilet,' his captor barked. 'Use the toilet.'

Ever since his ordeal had started, Jaeger had been forced to piss wherever he stood or squatted. Now he unbuttoned his overalls with his bound hands, leant against the wall and relieved himself in the direction of the urinal. The black bag had still not been removed, so he had to pee blind.

There was a sudden conspiratorial whisper. 'You look like I feel, mate. Bastards in here, aren't they?'

It sounded close, as if the speaker was standing right beside him. It sounded friendly; trustworthy almost.

'The name's Dave. Dave Horricks. You lost all track of time? Yeah, me too. Feels like forever, eh, mate?'

Jaeger didn't answer. He sensed a trap. Another mind game. He finished his business and went to button up his overalls.

'Mate, I hear they got your family. Holding them nearby. You got a message – I can pass it across to them.'

By a massive force of will, Jaeger managed to remain silent. But what if there really was a chance here to get a message to Ruth and Luke?

'Quick, mate, before the guard returns. Let me know what you want me to tell 'em – your wife and kid. And if you've got a message for your friends, I can get one to them 'n' all. How many are there? Quick now.'

Jaeger leant towards the man, as if he wanted to whisper something in his ear. He could sense the guy moving closer.

'Here's the message, Dave,' he croaked. 'Go screw yourself.'

Moments later his head was rammed down and he was whipped around and marched out of the urinal. A few twists and turns and he heard a door open. He was shoved into another room and steered into a chair. The hood was pulled off; light flooded in.

Before him sat two figures.

His mind could barely take it in.

It was Takavesi Raffara, plus the youthful figure of Mike Dale, though right now the latter's long hair was straggly and unkempt, his eyes deep-set and dark – no doubt the result of the recent loss he'd suffered.

Raff tried a smile. 'Mate, you got a face that looks like it's been hit by a bloody truck. I've seen you looking worse, after an all-nighter in the Crusting Pipe watching the All Blacks hammer your guys. But still . . .'

Jaeger said nothing.

'Listen, mate,' Raff tried again, realising that humour wasn't going to cut it. 'Listen to me. You've not been taken captive by anyone. You're still in the Falkenhagen Bunker. Those guys who threw you in that truck – they drove around in circles.'

Jaeger remained silent. If he could only get his hands free, he'd murder the both of them.

Raff sighed. 'Mate, you have to listen. I don't want to be here. Neither does Dale. We're not in on this shit. We only learned what they'd done when we got here. They asked us to sit in and be the first people you got to see. They asked because they figured you would trust us. Believe me. It's over, mate. It's finished.'

Jaeger shook his head. *Why the hell should he trust these bastards; trust anyone?*

'It's me. Raff. I am not trying to trick you. It's over. It's done.'

Jaeger shook his head again: *Screw you.*

Silence.

Mike Dale leaned forward, placing his elbows on the desk. It struck Jaeger that he looked like a washed-out heap of shit. Even during their worst moments in the Amazon, Jaeger had never once seen Dale looking anything close to this.

Dale glanced at Jaeger with tired, puffy eyes. 'As you can probably tell, I've not been sleeping. I just lost the woman I loved. You think I'd be here, dumping this kind of crap on you, after losing Hannah? You think I'm capable of that?'

Jaeger shuddered. A bare whisper: 'I figure anyone's capable of just about anything right now.' He didn't have a clue what or who to believe any more.

From behind him, he heard a faint knock at the door. Raff and Dale eyed each other. *What the hell now?*

Unbidden, the door swung open and an aged, stooped figure entered, stick held firmly in his grasp. He stopped beside Jaeger, placing a wizened hand on his shoulder. He winced as he eyed the beaten and bloodied figure sitting in the chair.

'Will, my boy. I trust you don't resent the intrusion of an old man into these . . . proceedings?'

Jaeger stared up at him through swollen, bloodshot eyes. 'Uncle Joe?' he croaked disbelievingly. 'Uncle Joe?'

'Will, my boy, I'm here. And as I'm sure your friends have told you, it's over. It really is over. Not that any of this should ever have been necessary.'

Jaeger reached up with his bound hands and clasped the old man's arm tightly.

Uncle Joe squeezed his shoulder. 'It's over, my boy. Trust me. But now the real work begins.'

22

The President sniffed the air appreciatively. Washington in springtime. Very soon the cherry trees would be in bloom, the city streets lined with pink blossoms and the air thick with their heady scent.

It was a favourite time of year for President Joseph Byrne; a time when the bleak winter's chill lifted from the eastern seaboard, ushering in the long, balmy months of summer. But of course, for those who knew their history, those cherry trees also embodied a dark and inconvenient truth.

The commonest were a strain called the Yoshino cherry – descendants of some three thousand saplings shipped to the USA in the 1920s, as a gift of eternal friendship from Japan. In 1927, the city had hosted its first ever Cherry Blossom Festival, which quickly became a regular date on the Washington DC calendar.

And then, in 1942, the massed ranks of Japanese warplanes had descended on Pearl Harbor, and overnight the Cherry Blossom Festival had come to an end. Sadly the Japanese promise of friendship hadn't turned out to be quite as eternal as had been first suggested.

For three years the USA and Japan had been locked in the bitterest of conflicts. But post-war, the two nations had rekindled their friendship. Necessity certainly made for strange bedfellows. By 1947, the Cherry Blossom Festival had been resurrected, and the rest, as the President was fond of saying, was history.

He turned to the two figures beside him, gesturing at the sweeping view, the first touch of pink lighting up the distant treetops, those closest to the waters of the city's tidal basin.

'A fine sight, gentlemen. Each year I worry that the blooms might fail to materialise. Each year they prove me wrong.'

Daniel Brooks, the director of the CIA, uttered a few suitably appreciative remarks. He knew that the President hadn't summoned them here to admire the view, striking though it might be. He'd prefer to get down to the business of the day.

Beside him, the Agency's deputy director, Hank Kammler, shielded his eyes from the sunlight. It was clear from their body language that the two CIA men couldn't bear each other's presence. Other than a presidential summons like this, they endeavoured to spend as little time as humanly possible in each other's company.

The fact that Hank Kammler was slated to be the next director of the Agency – once Brooks was forced to stand down – made the older man shudder. He could think of no worse a figure to take over command of the world's most powerful intelligence agency.

The trouble was, for some inexplicable reason, the President seemed to trust Kammler; to put his faith in his dubious abilities. Brooks couldn't understand it. Kammler seemed to have a peculiar hold over Byrne; an unfathomable hold.

'So, gentlemen, to business.' The President waved them towards some comfy chairs. 'It seems there has been some trouble in what I like to think of as our backyard. South America. Brazil. The Amazon, to be specific.'

'What's it concerning, Mr President?' Brooks asked.

'Two months ago, seven individuals were killed in the Amazon. Mixed nationals, but mostly Brazilians; none were American citizens.' Byrne spread his hands. 'Why does it concern us? Well, the Brazilians seem convinced that those doing the killing were Americans, or at least under the control of an American agency. When I shake hands with the Brazilian president and get asked about this, I don't like feeling I don't know what the hell she's talking about.'

The President left a weighty pause. 'Those seven individuals were part of an international expedition, the purpose of which was to recover a Second World War warplane. It seems that when they got close to their objective, a mystery force started to hunt them down. It's the make-up of that force that has brought this to my office.'

Byrne eyed the two CIA men. 'That hunter force had significant assets at its command, assets that only an American agency could bring to bear – or so the Brazilian president argues. They included Predator UAVs, Black Hawk stealth helicopters, and a fairly impressive array of weaponry.

'So, gentlemen, is this something that either of you might be aware of? Is there any way it could be the work of a US agency, as the Brazilians seem to be suggesting?'

Brooks shrugged. 'It's not beyond the realms of possibility, Mr President. But put it this way, sir: it's not something I have any knowledge of. I can check and we can reload in forty-eight hours, but I know nothing about it right now. I can't speak for my colleague.' He turned to the figure beside him.

'Sir, as it happens, I do know something.' Kammler threw a withering glance at Brooks. 'I make it my business to know. That warplane was part of a project known back then by various codenames. Point is, Mr President, it was top secret then and it is entirely in our best interests for it to remain that way.'

The President frowned. 'Go on. I'm listening.'

'Sir, it's an election year. As always, securing the support of the Jewish lobby is crucial. Back in 1945, that warplane carried some of the top Nazi leaders to a secret South American safe haven. But of chief concern to you, Mr President, was that it was also loaded with Nazi loot. Inevitably, of course, that included a great deal of Jewish gold.'

The President shrugged. 'I don't get the reason for the concern. The looted Jewish gold story – it's been around for years.'

'Yes, sir, it has. But this time it's different. What isn't known is that we – the American government – sponsored this specific relocation flight. We did so in strictest secret, of course.' Kammler cast a shrewd glance in the President's direction. 'And I would respectfully suggest that it should stay a strict secret.'

The President sighed deeply. 'A deal with the proverbial devil. It could be embarrassing in an election year – is that what you're saying?'

'Yes, sir, it could. Very embarrassing and very damaging. It didn't happen on your watch. It happened in the late spring of 1945. But that doesn't mean the media wouldn't have a feeding frenzy.'

The President glanced from Kammler to Brooks. 'Dan? What's your take on this?'

A frown creased the CIA director's brow. 'Not for the first time, sir, where my deputy director is concerned, I am in the dark. If true, sure – it could prove embarrassing. Conversely, it could be a whole crock of horseshit.'

Kammler stiffened. Something in him seemed to snap. 'I would have thought you should make it your business to know all that happens within the Agency!'

Brooks pounced. 'So, it *was* CIA-related? It *was* Agency business! The goddam Brazilians have you bang to rights!'

'Gentlemen, please.' The President held up his hands for silence. 'I have a very persistent Brazilian ambassador demanding answers. At present it is a private government-to-government affair. But there's no guarantee that it will stay that way.' He eyed Brooks and Kammler. 'And if you're right, and this is an American-sponsored Nazi Jewish gold conspiracy . . . well, it looks bad.'

Brooks remained silent. Much as he hated it, the President – and Kammler – was right. If this hit the press, it wouldn't be the greatest ever launch pad for the President's re-election. And while he knew Byrne was weak, right now he was about the best they had.

The President addressed his next words directly to Kammler. 'If, as the Brazilians claim, there is a rogue US outfit involved, things could get very messy. So is there, Hank? Was any of this at the behest of people under our command or control?'

'Sir, your predecessor signed an EXORD,' Kammler offered, by way of an answer. 'A presidential executive order. It green-lit the mounting of certain operations without any need for clearance. In other words, with no presidential oversight. That's because in certain circumstances it's better for you not to know. That way, you can always deny knowledge if things get . . . messy.'

President Byrne looked troubled. 'Hank, I understand that. I know all about deniability. But right now I'm asking to to be briefed as fully as you are able.'

Kammler's expression hardened. 'Sir, let me put it this way: sometimes things cannot remain a secret unless there are agencies striving to ensure they preserve that secrecy.'

Byrne massaged his temples. 'Hank, make no mistake – if the Agency's fingerprints are on this, it's best we know the worst as early as possible. I need to know the fallout potential.'

'Sir, it wasn't CIA business.' Kammler threw a daggers look at Brooks. 'I can say that categorically. But I am glad you recognise the pressing need for secrecy, and might I suggest that's in *all* our best interests.'

'I'll let the Brazilians know it was none of our doing,' President Byrne announced with relief. 'And Hank, I appreciate the need for secrecy.' He glanced at Brooks. 'We all appreciate it. We really do.'

Five minutes later, Brooks drew away from the White House, his driver at the wheel. He'd made his excuses to the President – his schedule didn't allow him to stay for lunch. Kammler had remained behind, of course. That little creep was never one to turn down an opportunity to schmooze.

Brooks's driver turned on to the main drag heading south out of downtown Washington. Brooks pulled out his cell phone and dialled.

'Bucky? Yeah, Brooks here. It's been a while. How you doing?'

He listed to the response, then laughed.

'You got me. It's not just a social call. How d'you fancy a short spell out of retirement? You bored of shooting spuds across Chesapeake Bay? You are? Perfect. What say I drive down to your place, you get Nancy to fix me a bowl of clam chowder, and you and I shoot the breeze for a while?'

He glanced out of the window at the passing cherry blossoms. Kammler and his black operations: at best the guy was a loose cannon; at worst, he and his people were overstepping their controls big time.

With Kammler, the deeper Brooks seemed to dig, the more he uncovered. But sometimes you just had to dig and keep digging, until you found the truth.

And sometimes the truth was very ugly.

23

The impenetrable woodland surrounding the Falkenhagen complex lent a certain raw wildness to the setting. It really was the kind of place where no one would ever hear you scream.

'How long was I in there for?' Jaeger asked, as he tried to massage some life back into his hands.

He was standing outside the nearest bunker, feeling exhausted from his brutal testing and desperate for fresh air. He was also burning up with anger. Seething.

Raff checked his watch. 'It's 0700 on the eighth of March. You were in there for seventy-two hours.'

Three days. *The bastards.*

'So whose idea was it anyway?' Jaeger probed.

Raff was about to answer when Uncle Joe appeared at their side. 'A quiet word, my boy.' He took Jaeger gently but firmly by the arm. 'Some things are best explained by family.'

After Jaeger's grandfather's premature death two decades ago, Great-Uncle Joe had taken on the role of honorary grandpa. Having no children of his own, he'd grown uncommonly close to Jaeger, and susequently to Ruth and Luke.

They'd been regular summer vacationers at Uncle Joe's cabin, on remote Buccleuch Fell, in the Scottish Borders. After his family's abduction, Jaeger had seen very little of 'Uncle Joe', as they called him, yet in spite of that they remained incredibly close.

Uncle Joe and Jaeger's grandfather had soldiered together in the earliest years of the SAS, and Jaeger was fascinated by the derring-do of their exploits.

Now the old man led him off to where the woods shaded a patch of flat concrete, no doubt the roof of one of the countless subterranean buildings – maybe even the very room in which Jaeger had suffered his interrogations.

'You'll want to know who's responsible,' Uncle Joe began, 'and of course, you have every right to answers.'

'I can guess,' Jaeger ventured darkly. 'Narov played her part to perfection. It's got her signature all over it.'

Uncle Joe shook his head gently. 'Actually, she wasn't overly keen. As time went on, she tried to get it stopped.' A pause. 'You know, I think – in fact I'm absolutely certain – that Irina has something of a soft spot for you.'

Jaeger ignored the gentle teasing. 'So who, then?'

'You have met Peter Miles? He plays a far more important role in this set-up than perhaps you might imagine.'

Jaeger's eyes blazed. 'What the hell was he trying to prove?'

'He was worried that the loss of your family might have de-stabilised you somewhat; that the trauma and guilt might have pushed you to breaking point. He was determined to test you. To prove his – and Narov's – fears either right or wrong.'

Jaeger's anger flared. 'And what gives him – *them* – the right?'

'Actually, I would suggest he has every right.' Uncle Joe paused. 'Have you ever heard of the *Kindertransport*? In 1938, British diplomat Nicholas Winton managed to save hundreds of Jewish children, by organising trains to ship them to Britain. Peter Miles wasn't called by that name back then. He was an eleven-year-old boy called Pieter Friedman, a German Jewish name.

'Pieter had an older brother, Oscar, whom he idolised. But only those aged sixteen or under were allowed to board Winton's trains. Pieter made it. His brother did not. Neither did his father, his mother, his aunts, uncles or grandparents. All were murdered in the death camps. Pieter was the only one of his family to survive, and to this day he believes that his life is a miracle; a gift from God.' Uncle Joe steadied his voice. 'So you see, if anyone knows what it is like to lose a family, Peter does. He knows how it can break a man. He knows what it can do to your mind.'

Jaeger's anger seemed to have dissipated somewhat. Hearing such a tale put everything into perspective.

'So did I pass?' he asked, quietly. 'Did I prove their worries wrong? It's all such a blur. I can barely remember what happened.'

'Did you pass the test?' Uncle Joe reached out to embrace him. 'Yes, my boy. Of course. As I told them you would, you passed with flying colours.' A pause. 'Indeed, there are few who could have endured what you did. And whatever comes next, it is clear now why you must take the lead.'

Jaeger glanced at him. 'There is one other thing. The T-shirt. Luke's shirt. Where did it come from?'

A shadow crept across the old man's features. 'Lord knows, people have done things they should not have. In your apartment in Wardour, there is a closet. It is filled with your family's clothes, awaiting, I presume, their return.'

Jaeger's anger flared again. 'They burgled my apartment?'

The old man sighed. 'They did. Extreme times do not justify extreme measures, but perhaps you will find it in your heart to forgive them.'

Jaeger shrugged. Most likely in time he would.

'Luke and Ruth: they will return,' Uncle Joe whispered, with an intensity bordering on ferocity. 'Reclaim that T-shirt, Will. Replace it carefully in your closet.'

He gripped Jaeger's arm with surprising strength. 'Ruth and Luke – they will be coming home.'

24

P eter Miles – Pieter Friedman as once was – stood before them in the former Soviet command bunker of the Falkenhagen complex. It made a curious setting for the coming briefing.

The bunker was massive and set impossibly deep underground: to reach it, Jaeger had had to descend six flights of switchback steps. It had a high, domed ceiling, criss-crossed by a latticework of massive steel girders, like some kind of giant robotic bird's nest sunk far into the earth.

To left and right were bolted steel ladders, which in turn led to hatchways recessed into the walls. Where those led was anyone's guess, for off the main rooms lay a labyrinth of tunnels, pipes, vertical shafts, tubes and ducts, plus ranks of enormous steel cylinders – presumably where the stocks of *N-stoff* had been produced by the Nazis.

There were few creature comforts in the bare, echoing chamber. Jaeger and his team were seated on cheap plastic chairs arranged in a semicircle, around a bare wooden table. Raff and Dale were there, along with the rest of Jaeger's Amazon team. He eyed each in turn.

Nearest was Lewis Alonzo, a black American and former US Navy SEAL. During their Amazon expedition, Jaeger had got the measure of the man. He liked to play an act – big, muscled and indestructible, but not the sharpest tool in the box.

In actual fact, quite the reverse was true. He had a mind almost as imposing as his massive physique. In short, Alonzo combined Mike Tyson's stature with Will Smith's looks and sharp, incisive wit. He was also genuine, fearless and possessed of a very generous heart.

Jaeger trusted him.

Next was the comparatively diminutive figure of Hiro Kamishi, a former member of Japan's special forces – the Tokusha Sakusen Gun. Kamishi was something of a modern-day samurai; a soldier of the higher path. A man steeped in the mystic warrior creed of the East – of bushido – he and Jaeger had developed a deep affinity during their time in the Amazon.

Third was Joe James, a giant bear of a man and arguably the most unforgettable of Jaeger's former Amazon team. With his long, straggly hair and massive beard, he looked like a cross between a homeless bum and a Hell's Angels biker.

In reality, he was a former member of the New Zealand SAS – perhaps the toughest and most renowned of the Special Air Service family. A natural-born bushman and tracker, he was part-Maori, which made him a natural running mate to Taka-vesi Raffara.

Having undertaken countless SAS combat missions, James had struggled to come to terms with losing so many mates along the way. But over the years Jaeger had learned to never judge a book by its cover. James had a can-do attitude second to none. Equally as important, he possessed an unrivalled think-outside-the box mentality.

Jaeger respected him greatly as an operator.

Plus there was Irina Narov, of course, though she and Jaeger had spoken barely a word since he had faced his brutal testing.

In the intervening twenty-four hours, Jaeger had largely come to terms with what had happened, recognising it for what it was: a classic case of resistance-to-interrogation training – what they called 'R2I' in the trade.

Every SAS hopeful was subjected to R2I as the culmination of the murderous selection course. It came complete with much of what Jaeger had suffered here: shock, surprise, disorientation, plus horrific mind games.

Throughout the days of simulated physical and psychological testing, they were studied minutely for anything that might betray a propensity to crack or to sell out their fellow operators. If they answered any of the questions thrown at them – answers that would betray their mission – they were thrown off the selection course.

Hence the answer learned as if it were a lifesaving mantra: *I cannot answer that question, sir.*

Here at Falkenhagen, it had all come so utterly out of the blue, and was executed so mercilessly, that it had never occurred to Jaeger that it might be a dark and vicious game. And with Narov playing her part to perfection, he had been convinced that he had suffered the ultimate betrayal.

He'd been tricked, beaten and taken to the edge, but he was alive, and he was one step closer to finding Ruth and Luke. And right now that was all he cared about.

'Gentlemen, Irina, thank you for coming.' Peter Miles's words served to drag Jaeger's mind back to the present. The elderly man glanced around at the concrete and steel edifice. 'Much of what we are here for is rooted in this place. In its terrifying history. In these dark walls.'

He turned his attention fully on his audience. There was an intensity about the man's gaze that Jaeger hadn't seen before. It demanded attention.

'Germany. Spring 1945,' he announced. 'The Fatherland had been overrun by the Allies, German resistance crumbling fast. Many of the key Nazis were already in Allied hands.

'The top commanders were taken to an interrogation centre near Frankfurt, codenamed Dustbin. There, they tried to deny point blank that the Reich had ever possessed weapons of mass killing, or planned to use them to win the war. But, one of the captives eventually broke, and confessed to what at first seemed to be a series of incredible revelations.

'Under intense questioning he revealed that the Nazis had developed three fearsome chemical agents: tabun and sarin nerve gases, and the fabled *Kampfsoffe* – poison gas – called *N-stoff*, or Substance N. He also confessed to the full extent of Hitler's *Chemicplan* – his project to manufacture thousands of tonnes of chemical agents to crush the Allies. What was extraordinary is that this was utterly unknown to the Allies, and consequently we possessed no defence against such agents.

'How could this have come to pass? First, as you'll have noticed, the Falkenhagen complex is set deep underground. From the air, it is more or less invisible. And it was in places like this that the most fearsome agents were manufactured. Second, Hitler contracted out his chemical weapons programme to a civilian company: the massive industrial complex I. G. Farben.

'They masterminded the building of these factories of death. It would have been an entirely daunting task were it not for the fact that the Nazis possessed a seemingly limitless supply of slave labour. Underground facilities like Falkenhagen were built by the millions of hapless souls sent to the Nazi concentration camps. Even better, the hazardous production lines were also staffed by concentration camp inmates – for of course, they were all destined for death anyway.'

Miles let his words hang in the air, portentously. Jaeger shifted about uncomfortably in his chair.

He felt as if a strange and ghostly presence had crept into the room, its icy fingers clutching at his fast-beating heart.

25

'Massive stockpiles of weaponised agents were found by the Allies,' Miles continued speaking, 'including at this place, Falkenhagen. There was even talk of a long-range V weapon – the V-4, a sequel to the V-2 rocket – that could drop nerve agents on Washington and New York.

'The general feeling was that we had won the war by the skin of our teeth. To some it made sense to harness the Nazi scientists' expertise in preparation for the coming war with the Russians – the Cold War. Most of the Nazi V-weapon scientists were shipped off to the USA to design missiles to combat the Soviet threat.

'But then the Russians dropped their bombshell. In the midst of the Nuremberg war crimes trials, they called a surprise witness: Brigadier General Walter Schreiber, of the Wehrmacht's medical service. Schreiber stated that a little-known SS doctor named Kurt Blome had run a beyond-top-secret Nazi project whose focus had been biological – *germ* – warfare.'

Miles's eyes narrowed. 'Now, as you all know, germ weapons are the ultimate mass killers. A nuclear bomb dropped on New York might kill everyone in the city. A sarin warhead might do likewise. But a single missile carrying bubonic plague could kill everyone in America, for the simple reason that a germ agent is self-replicating. Once delivered, it breeds in the human host and spreads, so killing all.'

'Hitler's germ warfare project was codenamed *Blitzableiter* – lightning rod. It was disguised as a cancer-research programme, to hide it from the Allies. The agents so developed were to be used under the Führer's direct orders to achieve the final victory. But perhaps the most shocking of Schreiber's revelations was that at war's end, Kurt Blome was recruited by the Americans to re-create his germ warfare programme – only this time for the West.

'Certainly, during the war Blome had developed a fearsome array of agents: plague, typhoid, cholera, anthrax and more. He had worked closely with the Japanese Unit 731, which had unleashed germ agents that killed half a million Chinese.'

'Unit 731 is a dark stain upon our history,' a quiet voice cut in. It was Hiro Kamishi, the Japanese member of Jaeger's team. 'Our government has never truly said sorry. It has been left to individuals to try to make their peace with the victims.'

From what Jaeger knew of Kamishi, it would be entirely in keeping with his nature to have reached out to the victims of Unit 731, to seek peace.

'Blome was the undisputed grandmaster of germ warfare.' Miles eyed his audience, his eyes gleaming. 'But there were certain things he would *never* reveal, not even to the Americans. The *Blitzableiter* weapons weren't used against the Allies for one simple reason: the Nazis were perfecting a super-agent, one to truly conquer the world. Hitler had ordered it to be made ready, but the sheer speed of the Allied advance had taken everyone by surprise. Blome and his team were defeated, but only by time.'

Miles glanced across at a seated figure clutching a slender walking cane. 'Now I'd like to hand over to someone who was actually there. In 1945, I was but an eighteen-year-old youth. Joe Jaeger can better relate this darkest episode of history.'

As Miles went to help Uncle Joe to his feet, Jaeger felt his heart start to pound. Deep in his being he knew that fate had led him to this moment. He had a wife and child to save, but by the sound of what he was hearing, there was far more at stake than simply their lives alone.

Uncle Joe stepped forward, leaning heavily on his walking stick. 'I will need to ask you all to bear with me, for I'd wager I am thrice the age of some of you in this room.' He glanced around the bunker thoughtfully. 'Now, where should I begin? I think perhaps with Operation Loyton.'

His eyes came to rest upon Jaeger. 'For most of the war I served with this young man's grandfather in the SAS. Perhaps it goes without saying, but that man, Ted Jaeger, was my brother. In late 1944 we were sent into north-eastern France on a mission codenamed Loyton. Its aim was simple. Hitler had ordered his forces to make a last stand, to halt the Allied advance. We were to frustrate them.

'We parachuted in and caused a good deal of havoc and chaos behind enemy lines, blowing up railway tracks and killing the top Nazi commanders. But in return, the enemy hunted us relentlessly. At mission's end, thirty-one of our force had been captured. We were determined to find out what had happened to them. Trouble was, the SAS was disbanded shortly after the war. No one thought we were needed any more. Well, we felt differently. Not for the first time, we disobeyed our orders.

'We set up a totally off-the-books unit, charged to search for our missing men. It didn't take us long to discover that they had been tortured and murdered horrifically by their Nazi captors. And so we set about hunting down the killers. We gave ourselves a grand-sounding title – the SAS War Crimes Investigation Team. Informally, we were known as the Secret Hunters.'

Joe Jaeger smiled wistfully. 'It's amazing what you can achieve with a little bluff. Because we were hiding in plain sight, everyone presumed we were a bona fide outfit. We were not. In truth, we were an unsanctioned, illegal unit doing what we believed was right, and sod the bloody consequences. Such were the times. And they were good times.'

The old man seemed choked with emotion, yet he steeled himself to go on. 'Over the next few years we tracked down every single one of the Nazi killers. In the process of doing so, we discovered that several of our men had ended up in a place of utter horror – a Nazi concentration camp called Natzweiler.'

For a moment Uncle Joe's eyes sought out Irina Narov. Jaeger knew already that they shared a special bond. It was one of the many things that he been meaning to get Narov to fully explain to him.

'Natzweiler possessed a gas chamber,' Uncle Joe continued. 'Its foremost role was to test Nazi weapons on live humans – the inmates of the camp. A senior SS doctor oversaw such tests. His name was August Hirt. We decided we needed to talk to him.

'Hirt had disappeared, but few could hide from the Secret Hunters. We discovered that he too was working secretly for the Americans. During the war he had tested nerve gas on innocent women and children. Torture, brutality and death were his hallmarks. But the Americans were more than happy to shield him, and we knew they would never let him stand trial. In the circumstances we took an executive decision: Hirt had to die. But when he realised what we intended, he offered an extraordinary trade: the Nazi's greatest secret in exchange for his life.'

The old man braced his shoulders. 'Hirt revealed to us the Nazis' plan for *Weltplagverwustung* – world plague devastation. He claimed it was to be achieved using a wholly new breed of germ agent. No one seemed to know where that agent had come from, but its lethality was off the scale. When Hirt tested it in Natzweiler, it proved to have a 99.999 per cent kill rate. No human seemed to have any natural resistance. It was almost as if the agent was not of this earth; or at least not of our time.

'Before we killed him – because believe me, we would never

have let him live – Hirt told us the name of the agent, a name given to it by Hitler himself.'

Uncle Joe's haunted gaze came to rest upon Jaeger. 'It was called the *Gottvirus* – the God virus.'

26

U ncle Joe asked for a glass of water. Peter Miles handed him one. No one else stirred. Everyone in that echoing bunker was gripped by his tale.

'We reported our discovery up the chain of command, but there was little real interest. What did we have? We knew a name – the *Gottvirus* – but other than that . . .' Uncle Joe lifted and lowered his shoulders resignedly. 'The world was at peace. The public were tired of war. Gradually the whole thing was forgotten. For twenty years it was forgotten. And then . . . Marburg.'

He stared into the distance, his gaze lost in far-off memories. 'In central Germany lies the small, pretty town of Marburg. In the spring of 1967, there was an unexplained outbreak of disease in the town's *Behringwerke* laboratory. Thirty-one lab workers were infected. Seven died. Somehow, a new and unknown pathogen had broken out: it was named the Marburg virus, or *Filoviridae*, because its form was thread-like; like a filament. Nothing like it had ever been seen before.'

Uncle Joe drained his glass of water. 'Apparently the virus had escaped into the laboratory from a shipment of monkeys from Africa. That, at least, was the official story. Teams of virus-hunters were sent to Africa to track down the source of the virus. They were searching for its natural reservoir – its home in the wild. They couldn't find it. Not only that, they couldn't find its natural host either – the animal that normally carries it. In short, there was no sign of the virus in the African rainforest from where the monkeys had come.

'Now, monkeys are used widely in laboratory experiments,' he continued. 'Trialling new medicines, that kind of thing. But they are also used for testing biological and chemical weapons, for the simple reason that if an agent kills a monkey, it is also likely to kill a human.'

Uncle Joe sought out Jaeger again. 'Your grandfather, Brigadier Ted Jaeger, began to investigate. As with so many of us, the work of the Secret Hunters was on-going. A chilling picture emerged. It turned out that during the war, the Behringwerke laboratory was an I. G. Farben factory. Not only that, but by 1967 the chief scientist at the lab was none other than Kurt Blome, Hitler's former grandmaster of germ warfare.'

Uncle Joe glanced at his audience, a fire burning in his eyes. 'In the early 1960s, Blome had been contacted by a man we had long suspected dead: former SS General Hans Kammler. Kammler had been one of the most powerful men in the Reich, and one of Hitler's closest confidantes. But at war's end, he had disappeared off the face of the earth. For years Ted Jaeger hunted him. Eventually he discovered that Kammler had been recruited into a CIA-sponsored intelligence outfit, tasked to spy on the Russians.

'Due to his notoriety, the CIA made Kammler operate under various assumed names: Harold Krauthammer, Hal Kramer and Horace Konig amongst others. By the 1960s, he had worked his way into a very senior post at the CIA and he went about recruiting Blome to his hidden cause.'

Uncle Joe paused, a shadow passing across his craggy features. 'By certain means we broke into Kurt Blome's Marburg apartment and found his private papers. His journal revealed an utterly extraordinary story. It would have been unbelievable in any other context. As it was, a lot of things started to make sense to us. Horrible, chilling sense.

'In the summer of 1943, Blome had been ordered by the Führer to concentrate on one germ agent exclusively. That agent had already killed. Two men, both SS lieutenants, had died as a result of exposure to it. They perished in an utterly horrifying way. Their bodies had started to collapse from the inside. Their organs – liver, kidneys, lungs – had disintegrated, putrefying even as the outer being still lived. They died voiding streams of thick, black blood – the remains of their rotten, liquefied organs – and with a ghastly zombified expression on their features. Their brains had been transformed into mush by the time death took them.'

The old man raised his eyes to his audience. 'What, you might wonder, were two SS lieutenants doing meddling with such an agent? Each had served with an SS agency charged with dabbling in ancient history. Remember, Hitler's twisted ideology was that the "true Germans" were a mythical northern race – tall, blonde-haired, blue-eyed Aryans. Bizarre, when you consider that Hitler was a short little man with black hair and brown eyes.'

Uncle Joe shook his head, in vexation. 'Those two SS Lieutenants – amateur archaeologists and myth hunters – had been tasked to "prove" that the so-called Aryan master race had ruled the earth since time immemorial. Needless to say, their mission was an impossible one, but in the process of their work they had somehow stumbled upon the *Gottvirus*.

'Blome was ordered to isolate and culture this mystery pathogen. This he did, and it proved utterly devastating. It was perfect; a God-given germ agent. The ultimate *Gottvirus*. He wrote about it in his journal: "It is as if this pathogen has not originated on this planet; or at least has come from a time of ancient prehistory, long before modern man walked the earth".'

Uncle Joe steadied himself. 'There were two challenges to unleashing the *Gottvirus*. One, the Nazis needed a cure: an inoculation that could be mass-produced to safeguard the German population. Two, they needed to alter the virus's means of infection, from fluid-to-fluid contact to airborne means. It needed to act like the flu virus: one sneeze, and it would burn through a population in a matter of days.

'Blome worked feverishly. His was a race against time. Fortunately for us, it was one that he lost. His lab was overrun by the Allies before he could either perfect a vaccine or re-engineer the virus's method of infection. The *Gottvirus* was categorised *Kriegsentscheidend*, the highest security classification ever assigned by the Nazis. At war's end, SS General Hans Kammler was determined it would remain the Reich's topmost secret.'

Uncle Joe braced himself against his walking stick; an old soldier coming to the end of a long tale. 'That is where the story pretty much ends. Blome's journal made it clear that he and Kammler had safeguarded the *Gottvirus*, which they began developing again in the late sixties. There is one final thing: in his journal, Blome repeated the same phrase over and over again. *Jedem das Seine*. Over and over he wrote: *Jedem das Seine* . . . It is German for "everyone gets what they deserve".'

He ran his eyes around the room. There was a look in them that Jaeger had rarely if ever seen before: fear.

27

'Excellent work – the London job. I understand there was little left of anything. And not a trace as to who was responsible.'

Hank Kammler had addressed the remark to an absolute monster of a man who was seated on the bench beside him. Shaven-headed, with a goatee beard and a fearsome cut to his hunched shoulders, Steve Jones reeked of menace.

He and Kammler were in Washington's West Potomac Park. All around, the cherry trees were in full bloom, but there was nothing remotely joyful about the look on the big man's scarred features. Younger – maybe half Kammler's sixty-three years – Jones had a stone-cold expression and the eyes of a dead man.

'London?' Jones snorted. 'Could've done it with my eyes closed. So what's next?'

As far as Kammler was concerned, Jones's fearsome physicality and his killer instincts were useful, but he still doubted whether he should make him a truly trusted part of his team. He suspected Jones was the kind of man best kept in a steel cage and only brought out at a time of war . . . or to blow to pieces a London edit suite, which had been his last contract.

'I'm curious. Why do you hate him so much?'

'Who?' Jones queried. 'Jaeger?'

'Yes. William Edward Jaeger. Why the all-consuming hatred?'

Jones leaned forward, resting his elbows on his knees. ''Cause I'm good at hating. That's all.'

Kammler lifted his face, enjoying the feel of the warm spring sunshine on his skin. 'I would still like to know why. It would help me bring you into my . . . innermost confidence.'

'Put it this way,' Jones replied darkly. 'If you hadn't ordered me to keep him alive, Jaeger would be dead by now. I'd have killed him when I ripped his wife and child away from him. You should have let me finish this when I had the chance.'

'Perhaps. But I prefer to torture him for as long as possible.' Kammler smiled. 'Revenge, as they say, is a dish best served cold . . . And with his family in my hands, I have every means to deliver it. Slowly. Painfully. Oh so satisfyingly.'

The big man gave a cruel bark of a laugh. 'Makes sense.'

'So back to my question: why the all-consuming hatred?'

Jones turned his gaze on Kammler. It was like looking into the eyes of a man without a soul. 'You really want to know?'

'I do. It would be helpful.' Kammler paused. 'I have lost practically all confidence in my . . . Eastern European operators. They were occupied with business of mine on a small island off the coast of Cuba. A few weeks back Jaeger hit them hard. He and his team were three, my people thirty. You can understand why I've lost trust in them; why I may want to use you more.'

'Amateurs.'

Kammler nodded. 'My conclusion also. But the hatred for Jaeger. Why?'

The big man's gaze turned inwards. 'A few years back, I was on SAS selection. So too was an officer name of Captain William Jaeger of the Royal Marines. He saw me supplementing my supplies and took it upon himself to impose his misjudged morals on my personal business.

'I was flying selection. No one could touch me. Then we came to the final test. Endurance. Sixty-four kilometres over piss-wet mountains. At the penultimate checkpoint I was pulled aside by the directing staff, stripped and searched. And I knew it was Jaeger who had dobbed me in.'

'It doesn't sound enough for a lifetime's hatred,' Kammler remarked. 'What kind of supplies are we talking about?'

'I was popping pills – the kind athletes use to up their speed and endurance. The SAS claims to encourage lateral thinking. To value a maverick, outside-the-box mindset. What a load of horseshit. If that wasn't lateral thinking, I don't know what is. They didn't just bin me from selection. They reported me to my parent unit, which meant I got thrown out of the military for good.'

Kammler inclined his head. 'You were caught using performance-enhancing drugs? And it was Jaeger who shopped you?'

'For sure. He's a snake.' Jones paused. 'Ever tried getting work when your record shows you've been thrown out of the army for doing drugs? Let me tell you something: I hate snakes, and Jaeger's the most self-righteous and venomous of the lot.'

'It's fortunate then that we have found each other.' Kammler ran his gaze eye along the ranks of cherry trees. 'Mr Jones, I think I may have work for you. In Africa. On certain business I have under way there.'

'Where in Africa? Generally I bloody hate the place.'

'I run a game ranch in East Africa. Big game is my passion. The locals are slaughtering my wildlife at such a rate it is heart-breaking. The elephants in particular, for ivory. The rhinos too. Gram for gram, rhino horn is now more valuable than gold. I'm looking for a man to go out there and keep a careful eye on things.'

'Careful ain't my hallmark,' Jones replied. He turned over his massive, gnarled hands, balling them into fists like cannon balls. 'Using these is. Or better still, a blade, some plastic explosives and a Glock. Kill to live; live to kill.'

'I'm sure there'll be ample need for those where you'll be going. I'm looking for a spy, an enforcer and very likely an assassin, all rolled into one. So what do you say?'

'In that case – and the money being right – I'm on.'

Kammler stood. He didn't offer Steve Jones his hand. He didn't exactly like the man. After his father's tales about the English from the war years, he was loath to put his trust in any Englishman. Hitler had wanted Britain to side with Germany during the war; to cut a deal once France had fallen and unite against the common enemy: Russia and communism. But the English – stubborn and wilful to the last – had refused.

Under Churchill's blind, mulish leadership, they had refused to see sense; to understand that sooner or later, Russia was going to become the enemy of all free-thinking people. If it weren't for the English – and their Scots and Welsh brethren – Hitler's Reich would have triumphed, and the rest would be history.

Instead, some seven decades later, the world was awash with deviants and misfits: socialists, homosexuals, Jews, the disabled, Muslims and foreigners of all types. How Kammler despised them. How he hated them. Yet somehow these *Untermenschen* – sub-humans – had worked their way into the highest echelons of society.

And it was up to Kammler – and a few good men like him – to bring about an end to all this madness.

No, Hank Kammler would be reluctant to put his faith in any Englishman. But if he could use Jones, then use him he would – and on that level he decided to throw him an extra bone.

'If all goes well, you may get to have a final crack at Jaeger. To see your thirst for revenge finally quenched.'

For the first time since they'd started talking, Steve Jones smiled, but there was no warmth in his eyes. 'In that case, I'm your man. Bring it on.'

Kammler rose to leave. Jones held out a hand to stop him.

'One question. Why do you hate him?'

Kammler frowned. 'In my position, I get to ask the questions, Mr Jones.'

Jones wasn't a man to scare easily. 'I told you my reasons. I figure I deserve to hear yours.'

Kammler gave a thin smile. 'If you must know, I hate Jaeger because his grandfather killed my father.'

28

They'd broken off the Falkenhagen briefing for food and rest. But Jaeger never had been one for a lot of sleep. The past six years he could count on the fingers of one hand the nights he had enjoyed a full, unbroken seven hours' kip.

It had proved just as difficult to sleep now, for his mind was stuffed to bursting with all that Uncle Joe had told them.

They reconvened in the bunker, Peter Miles taking up the thread. 'We now believe the 1967 outbreak in Marburg was Blome's attempt to test the *Gottvirus* on monkeys. We think he had succeeded in making the virus airborne – hence the lab workers becoming infected – but in so doing he had vastly reduced its potency.

'We watched Blome closely,' Miles continued. 'He had several collaborators – former Nazis who'd worked with him under the Führer. But after the Marburg outbreak, their cover was at risk of being blown. They needed somewhere remote to brew up their cocktails of death, somewhere they would never be found.

'For a decade we lost track of them.' Miles paused. 'Then, in 1976, the world said hello to a new horror: Ebola. Ebola was the second of the *Filoviridae*. Like Marburg, it was said to be carried by monkeys and to have somehow jumped species, to humans. Like Marburg, it emerged in central Africa, near the Ebola River – hence its name.'

Miles's eyes sought out Jaeger. They drilled into him. 'To be certain of an agent's potency, you have to test it on humans. We are not identical to primates. A pathogen that kills a monkey may have no effect on a human. We believe Ebola was a deliberate release by Blome, as a live human test. It proved to have a 90 per cent lethality. Nine out of ten of those infected died. This was deadly, but it still wasn't the original *Gottvirus*. Clearly Blome and his team were getting close. We presumed they were working somewhere out of Africa, but it is a vast continent with many a wild and uncharted place.' Miles spread his hands. 'And that's pretty much where the trail went cold.'

'Why didn't you question Kammler?' Jaeger interjected. 'Drag him into a place like this and find out what he knew.'

'Two reasons. One, he'd attained a position of real power within the CIA, just as many former Nazis had in American military and intelligence circles. And two, your grandfather had no choice but to kill him. Kammler had learnt of his interest in the *Gottvirus*. The hunt was on. There was a fight to the death. Kammler lost, I'm glad to say.'

'So that's why they pursued my grandfather in turn?' Jaeger pressed.

'It is,' Miles confirmed. 'The official verdict was suicide, but we have always believed that Brigadier Ted Jaeger was killed by those loyal to Kammler.'

Jaeger nodded. 'He'd never have taken his own life. He had far too much to live for.'

When Jaeger was still in his teens, his grandfather had been found dead in his vehicle, a hosepipe through the window. The verdict was that he'd gassed himself, due to the cumulative trauma of the war years. But few in the family had ever believed it.

'When all seems lost, it often makes sense to follow the money,' Miles continued. 'We began to trace that trail, and one path did indeed lead us to Africa. Other than Nazism, former SS General Kammler claimed to have one major passion in life: wildlife conservation. At some stage he had purchased a massive private game ranch, using what we believe was money looted by the Nazis during the war.

'After your grandfather killed General Kammler, his son, Hank Kammler, inherited that game ranch. We feared he was carrying on his father's secret work there. For years we watched, monitoring the reserve for any sign of a hidden germ laboratory. We detected nothing. Nothing at all.'

Miles eyed his audience, his gaze coming to rest upon Irina Narov. 'And then we heard about a lost Second World War plane lying in the Amazon. As soon as we learned of the type of aircraft, we knew this had to be one of the original Nazi Safe Haven flights. And so Ms Narov joined your Amazon team, in the hope that that warplane might reveal something – a clue to lead us to the *Gottvirus*.

'It did indeed yield clues. But almost of more importance, your search flushed out the enemy; it forced them to show their hand. We suspect that the force that hunted you – the force that still hunts you – is under the command of Hank Kammler, SS General Kammler's son. He is presently the deputy director of the CIA, and we fear he has inherited his father's mission – to resurrect the *Gottvirus*.'

Miles paused. 'That was our state of knowledge as of a few weeks ago. Since then, you have rescued Leticia Santos, who was being held by Kammler's people, and in rescuing her you seized her captor's computers.'

Click. Flash. Miles threw up an image on to the bunker's wall.

Kammler H.
BV222
Katavi
Choma Malaika

'Keywords retrieved from the Cuban island kidnap gang's emails,' he continued. 'We've analysed the chatter, and we believe the messages flow between the boss of the kidnap gang – Vladimir – and Hank Kammler himself.'

Miles waved a hand towards the image. 'I'll start with the

third word on the list. Amongst the documents you discovered in that Amazon warplane, there was one that revealed a Nazi flight routed to a place called Katavi. Kammler's game ranch is situated on the western fringes of the African nation of Tanzania, near a certain Lake Katavi.'

'Now, why would a Nazi-era Safe Haven flight be routed to a stretch of water? Consider that second item on the list: BV222. During the war, the Nazis had a secret seaplane research centre at Travemunde, on the German coast. There they developed the Blohm and Voss BV222, the largest aircraft operated during the war.

'This is what we now believe happened. At war's end, Tanzania was a British colony. Kammler promised the British a wealth of Nazi secrets in return for their protection. So they greenlit a flight to the ultimate Safe Haven – Lake Katavi – using a BV222. SS General Hans Kammler was on that flight, as was his precious virus – either frozen, or in a kind of desiccated powder form – though of course that was one secret he would never reveal to the Allies.

'When the British decolonised East Africa, Kammler lost his sponsors – hence his decision to purchase a vast expanse of land around Lake Katavi. And there he set up his laboratory – somewhere to develop the *Gottvirus* in absolute secret.

'Of course, we have no proof that this germ laboratory exists,' Miles continued. 'If it does, it has perfect cover. Hank Kammler runs a bona fide game reserve. It has all the trappings: game guards, a top conservation team, a plush safari lodge, plus an airstrip for flying clients in and out. But the last item on our list offers a final clue.

'Choma Malaika is Swahili – the language of East Africa. It means "Burning Angels". Within Kammler's game ranch there happens to be a Burning Angels Peak. It sits in the Mbizi mountain range, to the south of Lake Katavi. The Mbizi mountains are densely forested and almost completely unexplored.'

Miles flicked up another image. It showed a jagged-rimmed

mountain towering above the savannah. 'Now of course, the existence of those keywords in the email chatter and the existence of a mountain of the same name could just be a bizarre coincidence. But your grandfather taught me never to believe in coincidences.'

He stabbed a finger at the image. 'If Kammler has a germ warfare lab, we believe it's hidden deep beneath Burning Angels mountain.'

29

Peter Miles ended his briefing by calling for a brainstorming session, utilising the vast military expertise in the room.

'Stupid question,' Lewis Alonzo began, 'but what's the worst that can happen?'

Miles eyed him quizzically. 'The Armageddon scenario? If we're faced with a madman?'

Alonzo flashed his signature smile. 'Yeah, a real nutter. A fruitcake. Not pulling any punches – tell us.'

'We fear we are facing a germ agent that just about no one would survive,' Miles replied darkly. 'But only if Kammler and his people have worked out how to weaponise it. That's the nightmare scenario: a worldwide release of the virus, with enough simultaneous outbreaks so no government has the time to develop a cure. It would be a pandemic of unprecedented lethality. A world-changing – a world-*ending* – event.'

He paused, letting the chilling import of those words sink in. 'But what Kammler and his cronies may be *intending* to do with it – that's another guess entirely. An agent like that would be priceless, obviously. Would they sell it to the highest bidder? Or somehow blackmail world leaders? We just don't know.'

'Couple of years back, we war-gamed some key scenarios,' Alonzo remarked. 'Had the top guys in from US intelligence. They listed the three foremost threats to world security. The absolute numero uno was a terror group acquiring a fully func- tioning weapon of mass destruction. There are three ways they could do that. One, buy a nuclear device off a rogue state – most likely a former Soviet bloc country gone to rack and ruin. Two, intercept a chemical weapon being moved from one state to another; so maybe sarin gas from Syria, en route to disposal. Three, acquire the necessary technology to build their own nuclear or chemical device.'

He eyed Peter Miles. 'Those guys sure knew their stuff, and no one ever mentioned some crazed son-of-a-bitch offering a ready-made germ weapon to the highest bidder.'

Miles nodded. 'And for good reason. The real challenge is to deliver it. Presuming they've perfected an airborne version, it's easy enough to board an aircraft and wave around a handkerchief liberally sprinkled with the dry virus. And remember, one hundred million crystallised viruses – that's the populations of England and Spain put together – would cover the full stop at the end of your average sentence.

'Once our man's shaken out his handkerchief, he can rely on the aircraft's air-conditioning system to do the rest. By the end of the flight – let's say it's an Airbus A380 – you've got some five hundred people infected, and the beauty is that not a soul amongst them will know it. Hours later, they disembark at London Heathrow. Big airport, crammed with people. They board buses, trains or tubes, spreading the virus via their breath. Some are in transit to New York, Rio, Moscow, Tokyo, Sydney or Berlin. In forty-eight hours, the virus has spread across all cities, nations and continents . . . And that, Mr Alonzo, is your Armageddon scenario.'

'How long's the incubation period? How long before people realise something's wrong?'

'We don't know. But if it's similar to Ebola, then it's twenty-one days.'

Alonzo whistled. 'That's real badass shit. You couldn't design a more fearsome agent.'

'Exactly.' Peter Miles smiled. 'But there's one catch. Remember the man who boarded the Airbus A380 with a handkerchief spiked with one hundred million viruses? He's got to be some kind of a guy. In infecting the people on that aircraft, he's also infecting himself.' He paused. 'But of course, in certain terror groups there is an abundance of young men ready to die for the cause.'

'Islamic State; al-Qaeda; AQIM; Boko Haram.' Jaeger listed the usual suspects. 'There's any number of similarly minded crazies out there.'

Miles nodded. 'Which is why we fear Kammler may sell the agent to the highest bidder. Some of those groups have a practically unlimited war chest, and they certainly do have the means – the suicidal human means – to deliver the agent.'

A new voice cut in. 'There is one problem with all that. One flaw.' It was Narov. 'No one sells such an agent to anyone without possessing the antidote. Otherwise they'll be signing their own death warrant. And if you have the antidote, the man waving the handkerchief would be immune. He would survive.'

'Maybe,' Miles conceded. 'But would you like to be that person? Would you want to rely on that vaccine – one that in all probability has only ever been tested on mice, rats, monkeys? And where is Kammler going to get live humans on whom to try out his vaccines?'

At the mention of human testing, Miles's gaze flicked across to Jaeger, as if drawn to him irresistibly. Almost guiltily. What was it about human testing that kept forcing the man's attention his way? Jaeger wondered.

His habit of doing so was starting to get Jaeger seriously spooked.

30

Jaeger figured he'd tackle Miles on the human testing issue later. 'Right, let's cut to the chase,' he announced. 'Whatever Kammler's planning to do with his *Gottvirus*, this Katavi ranch is the most likely location to nail it down, right?'

'That's our understanding,' Miles confirmed.

'So what's the plan?'

Miles glanced at Uncle Joe. 'Let's just say we're open to all suggestions.'

'Why not simply go to the authorities?' volunteered Alonzo. 'Send in SEAL Team Six to bust Kammler's ass?'

Miles spread his hands. 'We have tantalising clues, but we don't have anything like proof. Plus there is no one we can absolutely trust. Power has been infiltrated at the highest echelons. Certainly the present director of the CIA, Dan Brooks, has reached out to us, and he is a good man. But he has concerns, even up to the level of his own President. In short, we can only rely on ourselves; on our network.'

'Just who is that network?' Jaeger queried. 'Who exactly is this *we* you keep referring to?'

'The Secret Hunters,' Miles replied. 'As formed after the Second World War and kept alive until today.' He gestured in Uncle Joe's direction. 'Sadly, the only one of the originals left is Joe Jaeger. We are blessed that he is still with us. Others have taken up the reins. Irina Narov is one.' He smiled. 'And we are hoping for six new recruits in this room today.'

'What about funding? Backup? Top cover?' Jaeger pressed.

Peter Miles grimaced. 'Good questions ... You'll all have heard about this Nazi gold train that's recently been discovered by a bunch of treasure hunters, hidden beneath a Polish mountain. Well, there were a lot more such trains, most from the looting of the Berlin Reichsbank.'

'Hitler's treasury?' Jaeger prompted.

'The treasury for his Thousand-Year Reich. At war's end, its wealth was staggering. As Berlin descended into chaos, the gold was loaded on to trains and dispersed into hiding. One such train came to the attention of the Secret Hunters. Much of its cargo was ill-gotten loot, but once melted down, gold is untraceable. We figured it was best if we kept hold of it, as working capital.' He shrugged. 'Beggars can't be choosers.

'As for top cover, we have some. Originally the Secret Hunters were formed under the Ministry for Economic Warfare. Churchill established the ministry to run his most secret wartime operations. At the end of the war it was supposedly shut down. In fact, there's a small executive branch still in existence, operating out of an unremarkable Georgian town house in London's Eaton Square. They are our benefactors. They oversee and support our activities.'

'I thought you said it was the German government who loaned you this place?'

'The Eaton Square people are very good networkers. At the highest levels only, of course.'

'So who are you specifically?' Jaeger pressed. 'Who are the Secret Hunters? Numbers? Staff? Operators?'

'We are all volunteers. We are called on only when needed. Even this place is only operational when we are. Otherwise, it's in mothballs.'

'Okay, let's say we're in,' Jaeger declared. 'What next?'

Click. Flash. Miles pulled up a slide showing an aerial view of Burning Angels mountain.

'Choma Malaika, photographed from the air. It's part of Kammler's game reserve, but it's totally off limits. It's designated as an elephant and rhino breeding sanctuary, one closed to all but the senior reserve staff. There's a shoot-to-kill policy for anyone else who tries to enter.

'Of chief concern to us is what lies *beneath* the mountain. There are a series of massive caves – originally water-worn, but enlarged in more recent times by the action of animals. Apparently, all large mammals need salt. Elephants enter the caves in search of it, and use their tusks to gouge it out. They've extended the caves to mammoth proportions – if you'll forgive the pun.

'You'll notice the main geological structure is a caldera – a collapsed former volcano. It's left a ragged ring of walls around a massive central crater, where the former cone of the volcano blew itself apart. Mostly the bowl of the crater is awash with seasonal water, so forming a shallow lake. The caves lie off the water, and crucially all are within Kammler's shoot-to-kill zone.'

Miles ran his gaze around the room. 'We have no proof that anything sinister is hidden in those caves. We need to go in and find that proof. And that's where you guys come in. After all, you're the professionals.'

Jaeger eyed the aerial photo for a good few seconds. 'Crater walls look around eight hundred metres high. We could HALO into the crater itself, pulling our chutes within the cover of the walls. Drift to ground unseen and head into the caves . . . The problem is remaining undetected once we're there. They're sure to have motion sensors positioned in the cave entrances. If it was me, I'd have video surveillance, infrared cameras, security lighting, trip flares – the works. That's the problem with caves: there's only one route in, which means it can be easily covered.'

'So it is simple,' a voice volunteered. 'We go in knowing we will be detected. We allow ourselves to get drawn into the spider's web. If nothing else, it will very likely reveal to us what they are doing there.'

Jaeger eyed the speaker: Narov. 'Great. One problem. How do we get out again?'

Narov gave a dismissive toss of the head. 'We fight. We go in heavily armed. When we have found what we are looking for, we shoot our way out.'

'Or die trying.' Jaeger shook his head. 'No, there's got to be a better way . . .'

For a moment he glanced at Narov, and the corners of his mouth twitched into a mischievous half-smile.

'You know what, I may just have thought of one. And you know something else? You're going to love it.'

31

'This is a fully fledged game reserve, right?' Jaeger queried. 'I mean, it comes complete with safari drives, game lodges, the works?'

Peter Miles nodded. 'It does. The Katavi Lodge. It's a five-star facility.'

'Right, let's say you were a visitor to the lodge, but let's say you weren't exactly thinking straight. En route to the lodge you decide to climb Burning Angels Peak, just 'cause it's there. The high point of the crater rim lies outside the borders of the sanctuary – the shoot-to-kill zone – right?'

'It does,' Miles confirmed.

'So you're driving to the lodge and you spy this awesome peak. You've got time to spare and you figure, what the hell? It's a steep scramble, but when you reach the summit you see a sheer rock face dropping to the crater below. You see the mouth of a cave: dark, mysterious, compelling. You won't know its forbidden territory. Why would you? You decide to abseil down to explore. That's our route into the caves, and at least there's a good cover story.'

'So what's not to like?' Narov demanded.

'You're not thinking straight, remember. That's the key. What kind of people don't think straight? Not a bunch of hardened operators like us.' Jaeger shook his head. 'Newly-weds, that's who. A rich, wealthy newly-wed couple – the kind of people who honeymoon at five-star game ranches.'

Jaeger swung his gaze from Narov to James and back again.

'That's you two. Mr and Mrs Bert Groves, whose wallets are stuffed with cash and whose brains are addled with love.'

Narov stared at the hulking bearded form of Joe James. 'Me and him? Why us?'

'You, 'cause none of us is sharing a safari lodge with another guy,' Jaeger answered. 'And James, 'cause once he's shaved his beard and cut his hair, he'll be perfect.'

James shook his head and smiled. 'And what'll you be doing, while the lovely Irina and I head off into the African sunset?'

'I'll be right behind you,' Jaeger answered, 'with the guns and the backup.'

James scratched his massive beard. 'One problem, aside from shaving this off . . . Can I be trusted to keep my hands off Irina? I mean, much as I—'

'Zip it, Osama bin Liner,' Narov cut in. 'I can look after myself.'

James shrugged good-naturedly. 'But seriously, there is a problem. Kamishi, Alonzo and me – we're under the cosh, re-member. We've got cutaneous leishmaniasis; we're banned from any strenuous activity. And by anyone's reckoning, this is going to be tough.'

James wasn't bullshitting about the sickness. At the end of their Amazon expedition, he, Alonzo and Kamishi had been trapped in the jungle for several weeks. During their epic exfil-tration they'd been eaten alive by sand flies – tiny tropical mites the size of a pinhead.

The flies had laid their larvae under the men's skin, to feed off the living flesh. The bites had turned into open, weeping sores. The only treatment was a series of injections of Pentostam, a highly toxic drug. Each shot felt as if acid was burning through your veins. Pentostam was so noxious it could weaken your heart and respiratory systems – hence the ban on any strenuous physical activity.

'There's still Raff,' Jaeger ventured.

James shook his head. 'With all due respect, Raff just won't cut it. Sorry, mate, but it's the tattoos and the hair. No one would buy it. And that,' he eyed Jaeger, 'leaves only you.'

Jaeger glanced at Narov. She didn't appear the slightest bit perturbed at what was being proposed here. He wasn't entirely surprised. She seemed to possess few of the normal human sensitivities to how people should and shouldn't interact, especially between the sexes.

'What if Kammler's people recognise us? We've got reason to believe they have photos of me, at the very least,' Jaeger objected. It was the main reason he hadn't suggested that he team up with Narov in the first place.

'Two options,' a voice cut in. It was Peter Miles. 'And let me just say – I like this plan. You'll be disguised. The extreme option is to have plastic surgery. The less extreme option is to change your appearance as much as we can without going under the knife. Either way, we have people who can do this.'

'Plastic surgery?' Jaeger queried, incredulous.

'It is not so unusual. Ms Narov has already had it done twice. Each time we suspected that those she hunted knew of her appearance. In fact, the Secret Hunters have a long history of going under the knife.'

Jaeger threw up his hands. 'Okay, look, can we just do this without a nip 'n' tuck and nose job?'

'We can, in which case you will be a blonde,' Miles announced. 'And for good measure, your wife will be a ravishing brunette.'

'Or how about a fiery redhead?' James suggested. 'That's far more suited to her temperament.'

'Get a life, Osama,' Narov hissed.

'No, no. A blonde and a brunette.' Peter Miles smiled. 'Trust me, that will be perfect.'

With that agreed, the briefing broke up. All were tired. Being locked away deep underground made Jaeger feel strangely restless and irritable. He longed for a breath of wind and a touch of sunshine.

But there was one more thing he needed to do first. He

loitered as the room thinned out, before approaching Miles, who was busy packing away his computer gear.

'Any chance of a private word?'

'Of course.' The elderly Miles glanced around the bunker. 'We're pretty much alone, I think.'

'So, I'm curious,' Jaeger ventured. 'Why the stress you keep placing on human testing? The relevance you seem to think it has to me personally?'

'Ah, that . . . I'm not very good at hiding things, not when they trouble me . . .' Miles powered up his laptop again. 'Let me show you something.'

He clicked on a file and pulled up an image. It showed a shaven-headed man, in a black and white striped pyjama suit, slumped against a plain tiled wall. His eyes were screwed shut, his brow heavily furrowed and his mouth open in a silent scream.

Miles glanced at Jaeger. 'The Natzweiler gas chamber. As with most things, the Nazis documented their poison gas experiments in great detail. There are four thousand such images. Some are far more disturbing, because they feature tests on women and children.'

Jaeger had a sickening sense of what Miles was driving at here. 'Give it to me straight. I need to know.'

The elderly Miles blanched. 'I do not relish having to say this. And remember, these are only my suspicions . . . But Hank Kammler has seized your wife and child. He holds them. He – or his people – sent you proof that they are still alive; or at least they were alive not so long ago.'

A few weeks back, Jaeger had been sent an email, with an attachment. When he'd opened it, the image had shown a kneeling Ruth and Luke holding up the front page of a newspaper: proof that they were alive as of its date. It was all part of the attempt to torment and break Jaeger. 'He seized your family, and eventually he will need to test his *Gottvirus* on live humans, if he is to prove beyond all doubt . . .'

The elderly man's words faded into nothing. His eyes were

full of a dark pain. He left the rest unsaid. As for Jaeger, he didn't need telling.

Miles stared at Jaeger, searchingly. 'Again, I'm sorry we felt the need to test you. For the R2I.'

Jaeger didn't respond. It was the last thing on his mind right now.

32

Jaeger kicked off with his boots, forcing his body outwards into space and letting gravity do the rest. The rope hissed through the belay plate as he plummeted downwards in an abseil, the floor of the crater coming closer with every second.

Some fifty feet below him, Narov was hanging on her climbing gear: a D-shaped carabiner clicked into a chock – a wedge-like piece of metal jammed into a convenient crack in the rock face, with a strong steel loop attached. She was well anchored as she waited for Jaeger to reach her, after which she'd begin the next leg of the descent.

The eight hundred metres of near-vertical rock that formed the interior face of Burning Angels crater made for some fourteen separate abseils, on a sixty metre climbing rope – which was about the maximum size that a man could carry.

It was proving to be quite an undertaking

Some seventy-two hours earlier Jaeger had sat in stunned silence. Peter Miles' briefing had left little to the imagination. It wasn't just about Ruth and Luke anymore. Quite possibly, the survival of the entire human species was at stake.

As honeymooners might, he and Narov had flown club class direct to the main international airport here, before hiring a 4x4 and heading west into the sun-baked African bush. After an eighteen-hour drive, they'd reached Burning Angels Peak, pulled over, locked their hire vehicle and begun their epic climb.

Jaeger's boots made contact again, and he kicked hard, booting himself away from the cliff face. But as he did so, large chunks of rock broke off and plummeted downwards ... towards where Narov was hanging on her climbing gear.

'Rock fall!' Jaeger yelled. 'Watch out below!'

Narov didn't so much as glance upwards. She didn't have the time. Instead, Jaeger saw her grasp with her bare fingers at the rock face, as she scrabbled to flatten her torso to its surface, pressing her face into its sun-warmed hardness. Against the massive expanse of the crater she looked small and fragile somehow, and Jaeger held his breath as the mini-avalanche crashed down.

At the last instant, the boulders smashed into a narrow lip of rock just above where she was positioned, ricocheting outwards and missing her by bare inches.

That had been close. If just one rock had hit, it would have cracked her skull open, and Jaeger wouldn't be able to rush her to a hospital any time soon out here.

He let the last of the rope whistle through his fingers, and pulled to a halt beside her.

She eyed him. 'There are enough things here that want to kill us. I don't need you as well.' She seemed fine. Not even shaken.

Jaeger clicked himself on to the climbing gear, detached from the rope and handed it over. 'Your turn. Oh, and be careful with the rocks. Some of them are a little loose.'

As he knew only too well, Narov wasn't great with his teasing sense of humour. Generally she tried to ignore him, which just made it all the funnier.

She scowled. '*Schwachkopf.*'

As he'd learned in the Amazon, she was fond of that German curse word – *idiot*. He presumed it was something she'd picked up during her time with the Secret Hunters.

As Narov readied herself, Jaeger gazed westwards over the crater's steaming interior. He could see where a massive archway sliced right through the crater wall. The opening allowed the lake due west of there to flood in during the height of the rains, so boosting the level of the floodwaters in the crater.

And that was what made this place so very dangerous.

Lake Tanganyika, the world's longest freshwater lake, stretched north for several hundred kilometres from here. The lake's isolation and its vast age – it was some twenty million years old – had enabled a unique ecosystem to evolve. Its waters harboured giant crocodiles, huge crabs and massive hippos. The lush forests that crowded the lake were home to herds of wild elephant. And with the coming of the rains, much of that life was washed outwards from the lake and into Burning Angels crater.

Between Jaeger and that imposing archway lay one of the caldera's main waterholes. He could barely see it, due to the lush forest cover. But he sure could hear it. The blow and suck and bellowing of the hippos reached him clearly on the hot and humid air.

A one-hundred-strong 'bloat' was gathered there, mushing the waterhole into the mother of all mudbaths. And as the merciless African sun beat down and the waterhole began to shrink, so the massive animals were forced closer and closer, hippo tempers fraying.

No doubt about it, that kind of terrain was to be given as wide a berth as possible. The watercourses linking the mud holes were also to be avoided. They harboured crocodiles, and after Jaeger and Narov's encounter with one of those murderously powerful reptiles in the Amazon, they didn't fancy another.

They'd stick to dry land wherever possible.

But of course, even there was danger.

33

Twenty minutes after triggering the rock fall, Jaeger's tough Salewa boots thumped into the rich black volcanic soil of the crater bottom, the rope bouncing him up and down a few times before it finally found its equilibrium.

Strictly speaking they'd have been better using a static line – a rope possessing zero elasticity – for the epic series of abseils. But you don't want to climb on a static line, just in case you take a tumble. The elasticity of a climbing rope is what serves to break your fall, in a similar way to how a bungee-jumper decelerates at jump's end.

But a fall is still a fall, and it hurts.

Jaeger unhooked himself, pulled the rope free from the final abseil point above and let it drop with a hiss at his feet. Then, starting from the middle, he coiled it and slung it over his shoulder. He took a brief moment to search out the way ahead. The terrain before him was quite simply out of this world, and so different from the climb in here.

When he and Narov had scaled the mountain's outer slopes, the ground had proved remarkably friable and treacherous underfoot. It had been washed by the seasonal rains into a latticework of deep, plunging gulleys.

The climb to the high point had been a harsh, burning hot, disorienting slog. In many places they had laboured in the shadow of a ravine, blocked from all view and with no easy means to navigate. It had been next to impossible to get any purchase on the dry, gravelly surface, and with each step they'd slipped a good distance back again.

But Jaeger had been driven on relentlessly by one thought: that of Ruth and Luke imprisoned within the caves below and threatened with the terrible fate that Peter Miles had intimated. That conversation was but days old, and that image – that terrible apparition – burned in Jaeger's mind.

If there was a germ warfare laboratory secreted somewhere beneath this mountain – with Jaeger's family very likely caged and ready for the final weapons testing – it would require an assault by Jaeger's entire team to neutralise it. The present mission was an attempt to prove its existence, one way or the other.

For now they'd left the rest of the team – Raff, James, Kamishi, Alonzo and Dale – at the Falkenhagen bunker, busy with their preparations. They were scoping out options for the coming assault, plus gathering together the weaponry and kit that would be required.

Jaeger felt driven by a burning need to find his family and to stop Kammler, but at the same time he knew how vital it was to prepare properly for what was coming. If they didn't, they'd fall at the first battle, and before they had any chance of winning the wider war.

While serving in the military, one of his favourite maxims had been the five Ps: proper planning prevents piss-poor performance. Or put another way: fail to prepare, prepare to fail. The team at Falkenhagen were busy making sure that when they found Kammler's germ lab, they would be totally prepared, and they wouldn't fail.

For Jaeger, it had been a dual relief to reach the high point of the crater's rim, the evening before. *One step closer. One step nearer to the dark truth.* To left and right the jagged ridge had stretched away from him, a switchback of what had once been red-hot volcanic fire and magma, but was now a harsh grey razor's edge, with a rocky, sun-blasted, windswept profile.

They'd made camp upon it – or rather on a rock ledge set a few dozen feet below the rim. That hard, cold, unwelcoming shelf had been accessible only by abseiling down to it, which meant it would render them immune to any attack by wild animals. And there were predators in abundance here in Hank Kammler's lair. Apart from the obvious – lions, leopards and hyenas – there were the massive Cape buffalo, plus the hippos, which killed more people every year than any kind of carnivore.

Powerful, territorial, surprisingly fast for their bulk, and intensely protective of their young, the hippo was the single most dangerous animal in Africa. And Katavi's dwindling water sources had brought them crowding together in their packed, irritable and stressed-out masses.

If you put too many rats in a cage, they'd end up eating each other. If you put too many hippos in a waterhole, you'd end up with the mother of all heavyweight fights.

And if you were a hapless human caught in the middle, you'd end up a squidge of bloody puree under a charging hippo's feet.

Jaeger had awoken on the crater rim to a breathtaking sight: the entire floor of the caldera was a sea of fluffy white cloud. Illuminated a burning pink by the early-morning sun, it had looked almost firm enough that they could step out from their rocky ledge and walk across from one side of the crater to the other.

In truth it was an expanse of low-lying mist, thrown up by the lush forest that carpeted much of the caldera's interior. And now that he was down amongst it, the view – plus the smells and sounds – took Jaeger's breath away.

The rope coiled, Jaeger and Narov began to move. But their arrival here had set off alarm bells already. A flock of flamingoes rose from the nearby lake, taking to the air like a giant pink flying carpet, their high-pitched cackling squawks and cries echoing around the crater walls. The sight was awe-inspiring: there had to be thousands of the distinctive birds, drawn here by the rich minerals deposited in the volcanic waters of the lake.

Here and there Jaeger could see where a geyser – a hot spring – gushed a fountain of steaming water high into the air. He took a moment to check the way ahead, then signalled Narov to follow.

They flitted through the alien landscape, just the odd hand gesture pointing out the route to take. They understood instinctively each other's quiet. There was a breathtaking other-worldliness to this place; a sense of a world lost in time; a sense almost that humans should never set foot here.

Hence their desire to slip through in utter silence, unnoticed by anything that would make of them its prey.

34

Jaeger's boots broke through a crust of dried, sun-baked mud. He paused at the pool before him. It was shallow – too shallow for any crocs – and crystal clear. It looked as if it would be good to drink, and marching under the burning sun had left his throat as dry as sandpaper. But a quick dip of the fingers and a flick of the tongue confirmed what he had suspected. *This water would kill you.*

Welling up from deep below ground and heated to near boiling point by the magma, it was still hot to the touch. More to the point, it was so salty it made him want to gag.

The crater floor was peppered here and there with these steamy, volcanic springs, bubbling toxic gases. Where the sun had baked the saline waters dry, a thin layer of salt had crystallised around the edges, giving the bizarre impression that frost had somehow dusted the ground this close to the equator.

He glanced at Narov. 'Saline,' he whispered. 'Not good. But there should be water aplenty in the caves.' It was blistering hot. They needed to keep drinking.

She nodded. 'Let's get moving.'

As Jaeger stepped into the hot, briny pool, the crisp white crust crunched under his mud-covered boots. Before them lay a grove of baobab trees – Jaeger's favourites. Their massive squat trunks were silvery grey and smooth, reminding him of the flanks of a powerful bull elephant.

He headed towards them, passing one that would require the full complement of his team just to link their arms around its swollen circumference. From that massive base the trunk rose statuesque and bulbous to a stubby crown of branches, each like a gnarled finger reaching out to grasp at the air.

Jaeger had first had a close encounter with a baobab a few years back, and in the most memorable of ways. En route to the safari that he'd taken with Ruth and Luke, they'd paid a visit to South Africa's Sunland Big Baobab, in Limpopo province, famous for its 150-foot girth and its vast age.

Baobab trees start to hollow out naturally once they are a few hundred years old. So large was the Sunland Baobab's interior that it had a bar built inside it. Jaeger, Ruth and Luke had sat in the cavernous heart of the tree, drinking chilled coconut milk through straws and feeling like a family of Hobbits.

Jaeger had ended up chasing Luke around the knobbly, gnarly interior, rasping out Gollum's favourite phrase: *My precious. My precious.* Ruth had even lent Luke her wedding ring to add a little authenticity to the scene. It had been magical and hilarious – and in retrospect, utterly heartbreaking.

And now here was a grove of baobab trees standing sentinel before the dark and gaping maw of the entrance to Kammler's lair; his kingdom beneath the mountain.

Jaeger believed in portents. The baobabs were here for a reason. They spoke to him: *you're on the right path.*

He knelt before a dozen fallen fruit pods – each a delicate yellow in colour and looking like a dinosaur egg lying in the dirt.

'The baobab is known here as the upside-down tree,' he whispered to Narov. 'It's like it's been uprooted by a giant's fist and thrust into the earth the wrong way around.' He knew as much from the time he'd spent soldiering in Africa, which was when he'd picked up some of the local language too. 'The fruit is rich in antioxidants, vitamin C, potassium and calcium: it's the most nourishing on earth. Nothing else comes close.'

He scooped several of the pods into his rucksack, urging Narov to do likewise. They'd brought ration packs with them, but he'd learned in the military never to pass up the opportunity to gather a little fresh food, as opposed to the dried stuff they carried. Dry rations were great for longevity and weight. They weren't great for keeping the bowels regular.

A sharp cracking sound echoed through the grove of baobab trees. Jaeger scanned all around. Narov was equally alert, eyes searching the undergrowth, nose scenting the wind.

The noise came again. Its source seemed to be a nearby grove of African stinkwood trees – so named because of the foul odour given off when a trunk or branch was cut. Jaeger recognised the sound for what it was: a herd of elephants were on the move, snacking as they went – ripping off bark and tearing down the juiciest, leafiest branches.

He had suspected they would encounter elephants here. The caves had been hugely enlarged by the actions of the herds over the years. No one knew for sure if it was the cool shade or the salt that had first drawn them in. Whichever, they had adopted the habit of spending days at a time underground, intermittently dozing on their feet and gouging at the cave walls, using their massive tusks as makeshift wrecking bars. With their trunks they'd whisk the broken rock into their mouths and grind it between their teeth, so releasing the salt bound up in the ancient sediment.

Jaeger figured the elephant herd was heading for the cave entrance right now, which meant that he and Narov had to make it in there before them.

They locked eyes. 'Let's go.'

Boots flashing across the hot earth, they crossed a final patch of grassland that grew within the shade of the crater wall, and darted towards the darkest patch of shadow. The rock face loomed before them, the cave mouth a massive, jagged-edged slash cut into it, some seventy feet or more across. Moments later – with the elephant herd hot on their heels – they had darted inside.

Jaeger took a moment to glance around. The best place to position any motion sensors was in the choke point of the cave entrance, but they'd be next to useless without cameras.

There were numerous types of motion sensors, but the simplest were about the size and shape of a shotgun cartridge. British military sets came with eight sensors, plus one transmit/receive handset, which looked something like a small radio. The sensors would be buried just below ground level, and would detect any seismic activity within a twenty-metre radius, sending a message to the receiver.

The cave entrance being seventy feet across, one pack of eight sensors would cover the entire expanse. But with the amount of wildlife that passed in and out of here, anyone guarding this place would require a video camera plus feed, in order to check whether the movement was caused by a hostile intruder, as opposed to a herd of salt-hungry tuskers.

Buried, the motion sensors would be almost impossible to detect. It was the hidden cameras that Jaeger was alert for, plus any aerials or cabling. He could see nothing obvious, but that didn't mean a thing. During his time in the military, he'd come across CCTV cameras disguised as rocks and dog turds, to name just a few permutations.

He and Narov pressed ahead, the cave opening out before them to form an enormous cathedral-like edifice. They were in the twilight zone now – the last vestiges of grey before the darkness stretched unbroken into the bowels of the mountain. They fished out their Petzl head torches. There was no point in using night-vision goggles where they were going. The technology relied upon boosting ambient light – that thrown off by moon and stars – to enable a person to see in the dark.

Where they were headed, there would be no light at all.

Only darkness.

They could have used thermal imaging kit (TI), but it was heavy and bulky and they needed to travel light and fast. And if caught, they didn't want to be carrying anything that would distinguish them from a couple of over-zealous and adventurous tourists.

Jaeger pulled his Petzl over his head and reached up with his gloved hand, twisting the glass of the lens. A blueish light stabbed out from the torch's twin xenon bulbs, playing like a laser show across the cavernous interior, and catching on a layer of what resembled old, dry manure lying thick across the ground. He reached down to inspect it.

The entire floor of the cave was thick with elephant droppings, peppered with chewed-up rock fragments. It was testament to the sheer brute strength of the animals. They had the power to rip apart the cave's very walls and grind them to dust.

The herd was thundering in behind them now.

There would be no easy escape for Jaeger and Narov.

35

Jaeger reached around to the small of his back and patted his waistband, checking that the angular bulge was still there. They'd debated long and hard whether to go in armed, and if so, with what.

On the one hand, carrying weapons didn't exactly marry up with being a honeymooning couple. On the other, abseiling into a place such as this without some form of protection would be potential suicide.

The longer they'd argued, the more it had become clear that to carry no weapons at all would just seem strange. This was wild Africa after all, red in tooth and claw. No one ventured into this kind of terrain without the means to protect themselves.

In the end they'd each opted to bring a P228, plus a couple of magazines. No silencers, of course, for those were the preserve of professional killers and assassins.

Reassured that his pistol hadn't come loose during the long march in, Jaeger glanced at Narov. She too had been checking her weapon. Though they were supposed to be acting as newly-weds, old habits died hard. The drills had been hammered into them remorselessly over the years, and they couldn't just stop functioning overnight as the elite warriors that they were.

Jaeger was seven years out of the military. He'd left in part to set up an eco-expeditioning company called Enduro Adventures, a business he'd pretty much abandoned when Luke and Ruth were stolen from him. That had led in turn to the present mission: to get his family and his life back, and very possibly to prevent an incalculable evil.

The light dimmed further and a series of deep, throaty snorts echoed around the enclosed space. The elephants were surging into the cave behind them. It was the prompt that Jaeger and Narov needed to move.

Signalling Narov to do likewise, Jaeger reached down, grabbed a handful of dung and rubbed it up the legs of his plain combat-style trousers, doing the same to his T-shirt and the exposed skin of his arms, neck and legs, before lifting up his T-shirt to do his belly and back. As a final gesture, he rubbed the last of the elephant dung through his recently dyed blonde hair.

The dung had a faint smell of stale urine and fermented leaves, but that was about all he could detect. Yet to an elephant – whose universe was defined first and foremost by its sense of smell – it might make Jaeger appear to be just another harmless pachyderm; a fellow tusker.

That was his hope, anyway.

Jaeger had first learned this trick on the slopes of Mount Kili-manjaro, Africa's highest peak. He'd been on a training exercise with one of the Regiment's legendary survivalists, who'd ex-plained how it was possible to move through a herd of Cape buffalo if you first rolled yourself head to toe in fresh buffalo dung. He'd proved it to them most powerfully by making each man in the troop – Jaeger included – do exactly that.

Like Cape buffalos, elephants had poor eyesight at anything other than close range. The light from Jaeger and Narov's head torches was unlikely to bother them. They detected food, predators, sanctuary and danger via their sense of smell, which was second-to-none in the animal world. Their nostrils were positioned on the end of their trunk, and so sensitive was the elephant's smell that it could detect a water source up to nine-teen kilometres away.

They also had an acute sense of hearing, which could detect sounds well outside of the normal human range. In short, if

Jaeger and Narov could take on the smell of an elephant and keep largely silent, the herd shouldn't even know they were here.

They pushed onwards across a flat shelf thick with dry dung, boots kicking up puffs of detritus as they went. Here and there the heaps of old faeces were streaked with splashes of dark green, as if someone had been through flicking daubs of paint around the cave.

Jaeger guessed it had to be guano.

He flicked his head up, his twin beams sweeping the roof high above. Sure enough, clusters of skeletal black figures could be seen hanging upside down from the ceiling. Bats. Fruit bats, to be precise. Thousands and thousands of them. Green slime – their digested fruit droppings; guano – was smeared down the walls.

Nice, Jaeger told himself. They were pushing into a cave plastered from floor to ceiling in faeces.

In the light of Jaeger's head torch, a tiny pair of orange eyes flickered open. A bat that had been sleeping was suddenly awake. The flare of the Petzl woke more of them now, and a ripple of angry disturbance pulsed across the animals hanging from the roof of the cave.

Unlike most bats, fruit bats – often called megabats – don't use the echo-location navigation system, in which high-pitched squeaks and squeals are bounced off the walls. Instead, they possess large, bulbous eyes, which enable them to find their way in the twilight of cave systems. Hence they are drawn to the light.

The first megabat broke from its perch – where its claws had been hooked into a cranny in the cave roof, bony wings wrapped around itself like a cloak – and took flight. It plunged earthwards, no doubt mistaking Jaeger's torch for a beam of sunlight flooding through the cave entrance.

And then a cloud of the things were upon him.

36

B*am! Bam! Bam! Bam! Bam!*
Jaeger felt the first of the megabats cannon into his head, as the dark horde tried to fly down the beam of light. The ceiling was over one hundred feet high, and from that kind of distance the bats had appeared minuscule. Up close, though, they were monsters.

They had a wingspan of up to two metres, and must weigh in at a good two kilos. That kind of weight going at great speed sure hurt, and with their bulging eyes shining an angry red and their gleaming rows of teeth set in long, narrow, bony skulls, they looked positively demonic.

Jaeger was knocked to the floor, as more of the ghostly forms swooped from the heights. He reached up and killed the light with his cupped hands, which also served to shield his head from the blows.

Just as soon as he had doused the light, the bats were gone, drawn instead to the sunlight seeping in through the cave entrance. As they swept out in a massive black-winged storm cloud, the big bull elephant leading the herd trumpeted and flapped his ears angrily. He clearly appreciated the megabats about as much as Jaeger had done.

'*Megachiroptera*,' Narov whispered. 'Also called the flying fox. You can see why.'

'Flying wolf, more like.' Jaeger shook his head in disgust. 'Definitely *not* my favourite animal.'

Narov gave a silent laugh. 'They rely on their keen sense

of sight and smell to locate food. Normally it is fruit. Today they obviously thought it was you.' She sniffed ostentatiously. 'Though I am surprised. You smell like shit, Blondie.'

'Ha, ha,' Jaeger muttered. 'And you smell truly delectable, of course.'

Blondie. The nickname had been inevitable. With his eyebrows and even his eyelashes dyed peroxide blonde, he was amazed how much his appearance had altered. As disguises went, it was surprisingly effective.

They picked themselves up from the dirt, brushed themselves down and pressed on in silence. Above them, the last ghostly whisperings of the bats died away. The only other noise came from behind now – the steady, ground-shaking beat of a hundred or so elephants pushing ever deeper into the cave.

To one side of the cavern floor ran a dark, sluggish waterway, which vented out of the cave entrance. They climbed over a series of ledges that took them higher than the water by a good few metres. Finally they crested a rise, and a stunning sight unfolded before them.

The river widened out into a massive expanse of water, forming a vast lake beneath Burning Angels mountain. Jaeger's torch beam couldn't even reach the far shore. But even more fantastical were the intricate forms that lunged out of the water in bizarre, seemingly frozen animation.

Jaeger stared for several seconds in astonishment, before he realised what exactly it was that they had stumbled upon. It was a petrified jungle – here, the jagged-toothed skeletal forms of giant palm trees thrusting out of the lake at crazed angles; there, a serried rank of hardwood trunks puncturing the water like the pillars of a long-lost Roman temple.

At some stage this must have been a lush prehistoric forest. A volcanic eruption must have rained down ash upon the greenery, burying it, Over time, the volcano had risen higher and the jungle had turned to stone. It had been transformed into the most incredible minerals: into opal – a beautiful reddish mineral streaked with fluorescent blues and greens; malachite – a gemstone rendered in stunning, swirling coppery greens; plus bolts of smooth, glittering, jet-black chert.

Jaeger had seen much of the world with the military, visiting some of the most remote terrain the planet had to offer, yet still it had the power to amaze and confound him – although rarely like it did right now. Here, in this place where he had expected to encounter only darkness and evil, they'd stumbled upon mind-blowing beauty and splendour.

He turned to Narov. 'Don't ever let me hear you complain about where I took you for your honeymoon.'

She couldn't help but smile.

The lake had to be a good three hundred yards across – more than three football fields set end to end. As to its length, that was anyone's guess. A ledge ran around the southern flank, and that was clearly the route they had to take.

As they set off, a thought struck Jaeger. If somewhere up ahead lay Kammler's dark secret – his factory of death – there was little sign of it from this side. In fact, there was no sign of any human presence anywhere.

No boot prints.

No pathways used by humans.

Not a hint that any vehicles had ever passed this way.

But the cave system was clearly massive. There were sure to be other entrances; other water-worn passageways leading to other galleries.

They pressed on.

The shelf forced them closer to the cave's wall. It glittered beguilingly. The rock was pierced with a myriad of frosty quartz crystals that glowed blue-white in the torchlight, their tips as sharp as razor blades. Spiders had strung their webs between them, the entire wall seemingly coated with a thin skein of silk.

The webs were thick with dead bodies. Fat black moths; giant butterflies of stunning colours; enormous orange-and-yellow-striped African hornets, each the length of your little finger;

all enmeshed and mummified in the silk. Everywhere Jaeger looked, he could see spiders feasting upon what they had caught.

Water meant life, Jaeger reminded himself. The lake would draw beasts of all kinds. Here, the hunters – the spiders – were waiting. And the spider bided its time to trap its prey, as did many other predators.

As they pushed further into the cave, the thought wasn't lost on Jaeger.

37

Jaeger doubled his guard. He'd not been expecting this amount of wildlife so deep in Burning Angels cave.

In amongst the glittering crystals and the shimmering webs there was something else too, jutting out of the cave wall at odd angles. It was the petrified bones of whatever animals had inhabited the prehistoric – now fossilised – jungle: giant armoured crocodiles; massive beasts that were the ancient forebears of the elephant; plus the heavyweight age-old ancestor to the hippo.

The ledge narrowed.

It forced Jaeger and Narov skin-close to the rock.

A sharp fissure opened up between the ledge and the wall. Jaeger glanced into it. *There was something in there.*

He peered closer. The tangled, tortured mass of yellowish brown resembled the flesh and bones of something that had once been living – the skin mummified to a consistency like leather.

Jaeger felt a presence at his shoulder. 'Baby elephant,' Narov whispered, as she peered into the crevasse. 'They feel their way in the dark using the tips of their trunks, and they must fall in there by accident.'

'Yeah, but you see those marks.' Jaeger focused his twin beams on a bone that looked badly gnawed. 'Something did that. Something big and powerful. Some carnivore.'

Narov nodded. Somewhere in this cave there were flesh-eaters.

For an instant, she flashed her light across the lake to their rear. 'Look,' she whispered. 'They come.'

Jaeger glanced over his shoulder. The column of elephants was surging into the lake. As the water deepened, the smaller amongst them – the adolescents – plunged in over their heads. They lifted their trunks until just the tips were showing, the nostrils on the ends sucking in air greedily, as if through a snorkel.

Narov turned to check the path that she and Jaeger had taken. Smallish grey forms could be seen hurrying forward. The youngest of the herd: the babies. They were too small to wade across, and so they had to take the long way around, sticking to dry land.

'We need to hurry,' she whispered, a real edge of urgency to her tone now.

They set off at a jog.

They hadn't gone far when Jaeger heard it.

A low, ghostly sound broke the silence: it was like a cross between a dog's growl, a bull's bellow and a monkey's whooping cackle.

It was echoed by an answering cry.

It sent a tingle up Jaeger's spine.

If he hadn't heard that type of cry before, he'd have been convinced that the cave was inhabited by a demonic horde. As it was, he recognised it for what it was: *hyenas*.

Up ahead on the path, there were hyenas – an animal that Jaeger had come to know well.

Something like a cross between a leopard and a wolf, the largest can weigh more than a fully grown human male. Their jaws are so powerful, they can crush the bones of their prey and eat them. Normally they only take on the weak, the sick and the old. But if cornered, they are as dangerous as a pack of lions.

Maybe more so.

Jaeger didn't doubt there was a pack of hyenas on the path, waiting to ambush the youngest of the herd.

As if to confirm his fears, from behind them a bull elephant gave an answering challenge to the hyena's ghastly call, unleashing a screaming trumpet from his massive trunk. It tore through the cave system like a thunderclap, his giant ears flapping and his head swinging towards the direction of the threat.

The lead bull veered off course, bringing two others with him. As the main body of the herd surged onwards through the lake, the three bulls tore through the water towards the rock shelf – the source of the hyena howls.

Jaeger didn't underestimate the danger. The elephants were facing down a pack of hyenas, and he and Narov were sandwiched in the middle. Every second was vital. There was no time to search for an alternative route around the hyenas, and no time to waver, much as he might baulk at what they were about to do.

Jaeger reached behind and whipped out his P228, then glanced at Narov. She already had her weapon in hand.

'Head shots!' he hissed, as they started to sprint forward. '*Head shots*. A wounded hyena is a killer . . .'

The light of their head torches bounced and spun as they ran, casting weird, ghostly shadows across the walls. From behind them the bull elephants trumpeted again and surged ever closer.

Jaeger was the first to catch sight of their adversaries. A massive spotted hyena wheeled towards the sound of their footfalls and the glare of the torches, its eyes glowing evilly. It had the typical squat hindquarters, massive shoulders, short neck and bullet-shaped head, plus the distinctive shaggy mane running down its backbone. The beast's jaws were open in a snarl, showing off short, thick canines and rows of huge, bone-crushing premolars.

It was like a wolf on steroids.

The female of the spotted hyena was larger than the male and she dominated the pack. She swung her head low, and to either side of her Jaeger could see other sets of glowing eyes. He counted seven animals in all, as behind him the enraged bull elephants tore through the last of the lake water.

Jaeger's pace didn't falter. Two-handed, and aiming on the run, he pulled the trigger.

Pzzzt! Pzzzt! Pzzzt!

Three 9mm rounds tore into the queen hyena's skull. She fell hard, her torso slamming into the rock shelf – dead before she even came to rest. Her cohorts snarled and sprang to attack.

Jaeger sensed Narov on his shoulder, firing as she ran.

The distance between them and the rabid pack had closed to a matter of yards.

38

Even as Jaeger vaulted into the air to avoid the bloodied corpses, his P228 spat rounds.

His boots slammed down on the far side and he sprinted onwards, as behind him the bull elephants closed in – the water boiling under their massive feet; their eyes blazing, ears flapping, trunks sensing the threat.

As far as the bulls were concerned, there was blood and death and combat on the path before them, on the very route their little ones needed to take. For elephants, the strongest urge was seemingly to protect their own. The entire one-hundred-strong herd was one big, extended family, and right now the bulls' offspring were in mortal danger.

Jaeger could understand the animals' desperation and rage, but that didn't mean he wanted to be anywhere around when it was unleashed upon the enemy.

As he instinctively checked over his shoulder, searching for Narov, he realised with a shock that she wasn't there any more. He came to a juddering halt. He spun around, spotting her bent over the form of a hyena, trying to drag it off the path.

'GET MOVING!' Jaeger screamed. 'MOVE IT! NOW!'

Narov's only response was to redouble her efforts with the dead weight of the corpse. Jaeger hesitated for just an instant, and then he was back beside her, hands gripping the animal's once-powerful shoulders as together they heaved it into the crevasse at the side of the path.

Barely had they done so when the lead elephant was upon them. Jaeger was hit with a wall of sound that seemed to turn his innards to jelly as the elephant trumpeted its earth-shattering rage. Seconds later, tusks stabbed inwards, trapping the pair of them on the narrowest part of the rock shelf.

Jaeger dragged Narov back into the crook, where the cave roof met the inner edge of the shelf. Jammed against the thick webs and the needle-sharp crystals, they shaded their torches with their hands, lying motionless in the dirt.

Any movement would attract the bull elephant's wrath. But if they stayed still and silent in the darkness, they might just survive the carnage that was being unleashed.

The massive bull speared the first of the hyenas, lifting it up on its tusks and flinging it bodily into the waters of the lake.

The power of the animal was simply fearsome.

One by one the hyena bodies were picked up and hurled into the lake. When the shelf was clear of corpses, the lead elephant seemed to calm a little. Jaeger watched, both fascinated and fearful, as the massive animal used the soft, flat end of its trunk to check what had happened.

He could see the huge nostrils dilating as they sucked in the scent. Every smell would tell a story. Hyena blood. To the elephant, that was good. But it was also intermingled with a scent that would be alien to the animal: cordite fumes. A smog of smoke from the pistol fire hung thick in the cool air of the cave.

The elephant appeared perplexed: *what smell was this?*

The trunk reached deeper. Jaeger could see its moist pink end groping towards him. That trunk – as thick as a tree, and capable of lifting 250 kilos – could snake around a thigh or torso and rip them out of there in a flash, dashing them to pieces against the rock wall.

For an instant Jaeger considered going on the offensive. The elephant's head was no more than ten feet away: an easy shot.

He could see its eyes clearly now, the long, fine eyelashes catching in the light thrown off by his torch.

Weirdly, he felt as if the animal could see right through him, even as its trunk reached out to make first contact with his skin. There was something just so human – so humane – about its gaze.

Jaeger abandoned all thoughts of opening fire. Even if he could bring himself to do so, which he doubted, he knew a 9mm subsonic round would never pierce a bull elephant's skull.

He abandoned himself to the elephant's caress.

As the trunk made contact with the skin of his arm, he froze. It was so gentle, it felt as if a faint breeze was rippling his arm hairs. He heard the snuffling as the elephant sucked in his scent.

What could it smell, Jaeger wondered? He hoped to hell that the elephant dung had done the trick. But was there also an underlying human scent that the animal would still detect? Surely, there had to be?

Gradually the familiar smell of its own species seemed to calm the big bull. A few more caresses and sniffs, and the trunk moved on. Jaeger was using the bulk of his body to shield Narov, so the elephant was only able to take a few perfunctory sniffs at her.

Seemingly satisfied, the animal turned to its next task: herding its offspring through the bloodied mess that was all that remained of the hyenas. But before it moved away, Jaeger caught a glimpse in its eyes; those ancient, deep, all-seeing eyes.

It was as if the elephant knew. He knew what he had encountered here. But he had decided to let them live. Jaeger was convinced of it.

The elephant moved away to where the young ones were clustered on the rock shelf in fear and uncertainty. It used its trunk to settle and comfort them, before nudging those at the front to get moving again.

Jaeger and Narov grabbed the chance to clamber to their feet and scuttle onwards, ahead of the baby elephants, and towards safety.

Or so they thought.

39

They ran on, moving at a fast jog along the path.

The rock shelf broadened out into a flat expanse, where the lake came to a natural end. It was here that the rest of the herd had gathered. From the juddering thud of their tusks as they made gouging contact with the rock walls, this was also clearly the site of their salt mine.

This was what they had come for.

Jaeger crouched down in the cover of the cave wall. He needed a moment to catch his breath, and to try to get his pulse under control. He pulled out a water bottle and drank deep.

He waved it in the direction of the path they'd just taken. 'What's with moving the corpse? The hyena? It didn't matter where it fell – dead's still dead.'

'Those baby elephants – they would not cross a path blocked by a dead hyena. I was trying to clear a way.'

'Yeah, but twenty tons of daddy elephant was incoming to do the job properly.'

Narov shrugged. 'I know that now, but . . . The elephant is my favourite animal. I could never leave the young ones trapped.' She eyed Jaeger. 'And in any case, daddy elephant did not so much as harm a hair on your head, did he?'

Jaeger rolled his eyes in exasperation. What was there to say?

Narov had a magical, almost childlike way with animals. Jaeger had realised as much during their expedition into the Amazon. At times she acted almost as if she had a closer relationship with animals than she did with her fellow humans;

as if she understood them far better than her own species.

It didn't seem to matter what kind of animals, either. Venomous spiders, spine-crushing snakes, carnivorous fish – sometimes all she seemed to care about were the non-humans on this earth. God's creatures all of them, great or small. And when she had to kill an animal to protect her fellow operators – as now with the hyenas – she was haunted by regrets.

Jaeger drained the bottle and thrust it back into his pack. As he tightened the shoulder straps and prepared to move again, the light of his torch caught momentarily on something lying far below them.

Nature rarely follows straight, angular lines of design or construction, such as humans tend to favour. In nature, they are anathema. It was that – that blocky anomaly; that noticeable, unnatural difference – that had caught Jaeger's eye.

A river drained into the lake from deeper inside the cave. Just before the point where it did so, there was a bottleneck. A natural constriction.

And on the near side of that narrow point stood a building.

It looked more like a Second World War shelter – like part of the Falkenhagen bunker – than it did a generator housing or a pumping station. But set that close to the water, Jaeger was certain that was what it had to be.

They crept down to the water's edge. With his ear pressed close to the concrete, Jaeger could hear a faint, rhythmic whir coming from the interior and knew for certain what lay inside.

This was a hydropower unit, sited where the water was funnelled swift and powerful through the choke point. Part of the river ran into the building via a duct, and inside would lie a rotor blade – the modern form of the ancient water wheel. The thrust of the current would spin the blade, which would in turn drive an electricity generator. The building's massive construction was to safeguard the mechanics from being crushed by a curious herd of elephants.

All of Jaeger's scepticism had evaporated in an instant. There was something beneath this mountain all right, something hidden way deep; something man-made that required electricity.

He jabbed a finger further into the darkness. 'We trace the cable. It'll lead us to whatever needs the power. And this far beneath the mountain—'

'Any laboratory has need of electricity,' Narov cut in. 'It's here! We are close.'

Jaeger's eyes blazed. 'Come on – let's go!'

They moved forward at a fast pace, tracing the cable deeper in. Encased in a steel sarcophagus to safeguard it from any harm, it snaked far into the bowels of the mountain. Step by step, they were closing in on their target.

The cable terminated at a wall.

The massive structure cut across the entire breadth of the cave. It was several metres high – taller than the biggest elephant. Jaeger didn't doubt that was why it had been placed here: to stop the herds from penetrating any further.

Where the wall met the river, there were sluices in the structure that allowed the water to gush through. He figured there would be further turbines set within those, the downstream unit being a backup power source.

They paused in the cold shadow of the wall. Jaeger was gripped by a grim determination. The mountain was about to yield its secrets, whatever they might be.

Soon now.

He eyed the structure. It was a vertical sheet of smooth reinforced concrete.

It was the border; but the border to what?

What might lie beyond it?

Who might lie beyond it, even? An image of Ruth and Luke – chained and caged – flashed through his mind.

Always forward. Keep moving. It had been a mantra with Jaeger when he had served with the Royal Marines. *In a fight, close the distance.* He'd kept it at the forefront of his mind in the hunt to find his family, just as he did now.

He scanned with his eyes for handholds. There were few, if any. It was all but unclimbable. Unless . . .

He moved across to the side; to where the man-made wall met the natural cave wall. Sure enough, here was a line of weakness. Where the smooth structure butted up against the sharp crystals and bony outcrops, it might just be scalable. He could see where whoever had built the wall had smashed off some of the outcrops during construction.

They'd done so randomly, as those outcrops had got in their way, leaving just enough to offer handholds and footholds.

'This wasn't built to stop people,' Jaeger whispered, as he mapped out the route of the climb in his head. 'It's here to stop salt-hungry elephants from going any further. To protect whatever lies on the far side.'

'Whatever is there that requires electricity,' Narov hissed, her eyes gleaming. 'We are close now. So close.'

Jaeger shrugged off his rucksack and dropped it at his feet. 'I'll go first. Tie on the packs once I'm up, and I'll haul them over. You bring up the rear.'

'Got it. After all, you are – how do you say? – the rock jock.'

Ever since Jaeger was a kid, rock-climbing had been his thing. At school, in response to a bet from a fellow pupil, he'd scaled the bell tower, free-climbing – so using no ropes at all. In the SAS, he'd served in Mountain Troop – the one that specialised in all aspects of mountain warfare. And during their recent Amazon expedition, he'd pulled off several perilous ascents and descents.

In short, if there was something to be climbed, he was the one to attempt it.

It took several tries, but by tying a rock on to the end of the climbing rope, Jaeger was able to hurl it up and snag one of the highest of the bony outcrops. With it looped over that, he had an anchor point of sorts; he could begin the climb with a reasonable degree of safety.

He stripped down to the bare minimum, stuffing all extraneous gear – even his pistol – into his pack. Reaching up with his left hand, he closed his fingers around a knobby outcrop. Was it the fossilised jawbone of an ancient giant hyena? Right now, Jaeger didn't particularly care.

His feet made contact with similar nodules, as he used the prehistoric remains embedded in the cave wall to haul himself up the first few metres. He grabbed the rope and dragged himself up to the next solid handhold.

The rope held fast, and he was making good progress.

All he cared about now was reaching the apex of that wall, and discovering what it had been built here to safeguard – and to hide.

40

Jaeger groped for the lip of the upper surface. His fingers wriggled their way on to it, and with burning shoulder muscles he hauled his body upwards, using first his stomach and then his knees to worm his way on to the high point.

He lay there for several seconds, his breath coming in sharp, heaving gasps. The wall was broad and flat on top, testament to the massive effort that had gone into its construction. As he had suspected, it hadn't been placed here to stop humans. There wasn't so much as a coil of razor wire atop it. No one had been expected to arrive here uninvited and with the intent of scaling it – that much was clear.

Whoever had built this barrier – and Jaeger didn't doubt any more that Kammler was somehow responsible – they had never imagined that this place would be discovered. They had clearly believed it to be undetectable, and thus secure.

Jaeger risked a peek over the far side. The twin beams of his head torch reflected back at him from a completely still, black, mirror-like surface. There was a second lake concealed behind the wall, one set within a vast circular cave gallery.

The entire space appeared to be utterly deserted, but it wasn't that which drew a gasp of astonishment from Jaeger.

Set way out in the centre of the water was a simply fantastical sight. Floating on the lake's mirror surface was an apparition that was shockingly unexpected, yet strangely familiar all at the same time.

Jaeger tried to keep control of his emotions and his excitement; his pulse was off the scale right now.

He unhooked the rope from where it had snagged itself precariously and secured it properly around a small pinnacle, before lowering one end to Narov. She attached the first pack and he hauled it up, repeating the process with the second. Then Narov scaled the barrier, as Jaeger acted as her belay point, his legs straddling the wall.

Once she was up, Jaeger flashed his light across the lake. 'Take a look,' he hissed. 'Feast your eyes upon that.'

Narov stared. Jaeger had rarely seen her lost for words. She was now.

'At first I thought I had to be dreaming,' he told her. 'Tell me I'm not. Tell me it's for real.'

Narov couldn't drag her gaze away. 'I see it. But how in the name of God did they get it in here?'

Jaeger shrugged. 'I haven't the faintest idea.'

They lowered their packs to the far side, before abseiling down to join them on the ground. They squatted in the utter stillness, contemplating the next, seemingly impossible challenge. Short of swimming – and Lord only knew what was in the water – how were they going to make it to the centre of that lake? And having done so, how were they to get aboard what lay tethered there?

Jaeger figured maybe they should have been expecting this. In a sense, they'd been forewarned in the Falkenhagen briefing. But still, to find it here, and so utterly unblemished and intact – it took his very breath away.

In the centre of the lake beneath the mountain was anchored the giant form of a Blohm and Voss BV222 seaplane.

Even from this distance it was simply stupendous – a six-engine behemoth tethered by its cruelly beaked nose to a buoy. The incredible size of the thing was betrayed by the antique-looking motorboat that was lashed to its side, dwarfed by the graceful wing stretching high above it.

But perhaps even more than the warplane's size and presence, what confounded Jaeger most was how utterly perfect she appeared to be. There was no layer of bat guano coating the BV222's upper surface, which was painted in what had to be its original camouflage green. Likewise, its blue-white undersurface – contoured like the V-shaped hull of a speedboat – was free of any algae or weed.

From the upper surface of the warplane sprouted a forest of gun turrets: the BV222 was designed to operate without the need for any escort. It was a massive flying gun-platform, which was supposed to be able to shoot down any Allied fighters.

The Perspex of the gun turrets appeared to be almost as clear and clean as the day she had left the factory. Along her side ran a row of portholes, which terminated at the fore end in the iconic insignia of the Luftwaffe – a black cross superimposed over a larger white one.

It looked as if it had been painted only yesterday.

Somehow, this BV222 had lain here for seven decades, being carefully tended to and looked after. But the biggest mystery – one that Jaeger couldn't for the life of him fathom – was how on earth the aircraft had got in here.

With a 150-foot wingspan, she was too wide to have made it through the cave entrance.

This had to be Kammler's doing. Somehow, he'd got her in here.

But why had he done so?

For what purpose?

For an instant Jaeger wondered whether Kammler had sited his hidden germ warfare laboratory inside this aircraft secreted deep beneath the mountain. But just as soon as he'd entertained the idea he discounted it. Were it not for their head torches, the BV222 would be lying here enshrouded in utter darkness.

Jaeger didn't doubt that she was deserted.

As he rested, racking his brains, he became aware of how quiet it was. The massive concrete structure of the wall blocked off nearly all sound from further down the cave system: the gouging of the elephants; the rhythmic crunching of rock fragments; the odd contented stamp or bellow.

Here it was utter stillness. Devoid of all life. Ghostly. Deserted. Here was a place where all life apparently came to an end.

41

Jaeger gestured at the seaplane. 'There's nothing for it. We're going to have to swim.'

Narov nodded her silent assent. They began to strip down to the bare minimum. It was a one-hundred-and-fifty yard dash, and the last thing they needed in the cold water was to be weighed down by rucksacks, pouches and ammo. They'd leave everything but the essentials – the clothes they stood up in, plus footwear – by the lakeside.

Jaeger hesitated only when it came to discarding his pistol. He hated the thought of proceeding unarmed. Most modern weaponry worked just fine after a good dousing in water, but the key now was to move fast on the long, freezing swim that lay ahead.

He laid his P228 next to Narov's under a small rock, beside their pile of gear.

Jaeger wasn't surprised to see that Narov had kept one weapon on her person, though. He'd learned in the Amazon that she was never to be parted from her Fairbairn-Sykes fighting knife. It had a talismanic significance for her, supposedly being a gift from Jaeger's grandfather.

He glanced at her. 'You ready?'

Her eyes glittered. 'Race you.'

Jaeger made a mental note of the warplane's location, fixing it in his mind, before extinguishing his head torch. Narov did likewise. By feel alone they stuffed the Petzls into waterproof Ziploc pouches. All was total darkness now; utter, unrelenting black.

Jaeger brought his hand in front of his face. He couldn't see anything. He moved it closer, until his palm touched his nose, yet still he'd not discerned the slightest thing. Not the faintest glimmer of light made it in here, this far underground.

'Stick close,' he hissed. 'Oh, and one more thing . . .'

He didn't finish the sentence. Instead he plunged into the icy lake, hoping to have thrown Narov and gained himself a head start. He sensed her hit the water just yards behind him, thrashing madly to catch up.

Using long, powerful strokes to surge ahead, Jaeger's head only left the water to grab quick gasps of air. A former Royal Marine, he felt very much at home in or on the water. The draw of that aircraft was irresistible, yet still the utter darkness was horribly disorientating.

He'd almost given up hope of having navigated true when his hand made contact with something hard. It felt like cold, unyielding steel. He figured it had to be one of the warplane's floats. He dragged himself out of the water, and sure enough was able to haul himself on to a flat surface.

He reached for his head torch, pulled it out and flicked it on, flashing it over the surface of the lake. Narov was bare seconds behind him, and he used the light to guide her in.

'Loser,' he whispered as he pulled her out, needling her gently.

She scowled. 'You cheated.'

He shrugged. 'All's fair in love and war.'

They crouched, taking a few seconds to catch their breath. Jaeger shone his torch around, the light gleaming off the massive sweep of the wing that stretched above them. He remembered from the Falkenhagen briefing that the BV222 actually had two decks – the upper one for passengers and cargo, the lower harbouring ranks of machine-gun positions, from which the warplane could be defended.

This close to the fuselage, he could well believe it. Here, he could finally appreciate the sheer size of the thing, coupled with her compelling grace and her incredible presence. He needed to get inside.

He stood, helping Narov to her feet. He took a step or two ahead, but no sooner had he done so than a scream rent the silence. A rhythmic, blaring wail blasted out across the lake, echoing deafeningly off the unyielding rock walls.

Jaeger froze. He knew instantly what had happened. The BV222 had to be fitted with infrared sensors. As soon as they'd started moving, they'd exposed themselves to the sensor's invisible beams, so triggering the alarm.

'Kill your light,' he hissed.

Moments later, they were plunged back into deep blackness, but it didn't last long.

A powerful beam of illumination stabbed outwards from the southern shore of the lake, chasing away the deepest shadows. It swept across the water, coming to rest upon the warplane, half blinding Jaeger and Narov.

Fighting the urge to take cover and prepare for battle, Jaeger shaded his eyes from the glare.

'Remember,' he hissed, 'we're a married bloody couple. Tourists. Whoever it is, we're not here to fight.'

Narov didn't answer. Her eyes were fixed on the apparition all around them, as if she were hypnotised. The powerful searchlight had illuminated much of the cavern, showing off the glittering form of the BV222 in all her mind-bending glory.

It was almost as if she were a prize exhibit in a museum.

Incredibly, she looked good enough to fly.

42

A cry rang out across the water. 'Stay right where you are! Do not move!'

Jaeger stiffened. The accent was European-sounding. Not a native English speaker, certainly. German, maybe? The word 'where' had been pronounced with a slight 'v', suggestive of a Germanic tongue.

Was it Kammler? It couldn't be. The people at the Falkenhagen bunker were keeping very close tabs on Hank Kammler, ably assisted by their contacts at the Central Intelligence Agency. And anyway, the voice had sounded far too young.

Plus there was something wrong about the tone. It lacked the arrogance that one would expect of Kammler.

'Stay right where you are,' the voice commanded again, a clear hint of menace lying behind the words. 'We come to you now.'

There was the snarl of a powerful engine, and the form of a RIB drew out from its place of hiding. It cut through the lake's surface, shortly arriving at Jaeger and Narov's feet.

The figure in the prow had a shock of untidy sandy hair above a straggly beard. He had to be a good six foot two inches tall, and he was white, as opposed to the rest of the men in the boat, who were local Africans. He was dressed in plain green combat-style fatigues, and it hadn't escaped Jaeger's notice that he had an assault rifle cradled in his arms.

The rest of those in the boat were dressed and armed likewise, and they had Narov and Jaeger covered with their weapons.

The tall man fixed them with a stare. 'What are you doing here? Some mistake that you are here, I think?'

Jaeger decided to play dumb. He thrust out a hand in greeting. The figure in the boat didn't make a move to take it.

'And you are?' he demanded icily. 'And please – explain why you are here.'

'Bert Groves, and my wife, Andrea. We're English. Tourists. Well, more adventurers, I guess. Couldn't resist the lure of the crater – had to take a peek. Cave drew us in.' He gestured at the warplane. 'Then this thing drew us further. Kind of incredible.'

The figure in the boat frowned, suspicion further creasing his brow. 'Your presence here is remarkably ... adventurous for tourists, to put it mildly. And it is also dangerous, on many levels.' He gestured at his men. 'I had reports from my guards that you were poachers.'

'Poachers? No way.' Jaeger glanced at Narov. 'We're newly-weds. I guess we were swept away by our African adventure and maybe not thinking straight. Call it honeymoon spirit.' He shrugged apologetically. 'I'm sorry if we caused any trouble.'

The figure in the boat readjusted the hold on his rifle. 'Mr and Mrs Groves – the name is familiar, I think. You are booked into the Katavi Lodge, for an arrival date of tomorrow morning?'

Jaeger smiled. 'You got it. That's us. Tomorrow morning at eleven. For five days.' He glanced at Narov, trying his best to act like the world's most besotted husband. 'Newly married and determined to live life to the max!'

The eyes of the man in the boat remained cold. 'Well of course, if you are not poachers then you are most welcome.' There was little corresponding welcome in his tone. 'I am Falk Konig – the head conservationist at the Katavi Game Reserve. But this is not the recommended route via which to begin a honeymooner safari, or to make your way to our lodge.'

Jaeger forced a laugh. 'Yeah, so I figured. But like I said, couldn't resist the draw of Burning Angels Peak. And once you're on that ridge, well – you just can't stop. It's like a real-life Lost World out there. Then we saw the elephants heading into the caves. I mean, that's one awesome spectacle.' He shrugged. 'We just had to follow.'

Konig nodded stiffly. 'Yes, the caldera shelters a very species-rich ecosystem. A truly unique habitat. It is the breeding reserve for our elephants and rhino. And that is why we make it off-limits to *all visitors*.' He paused. 'I have to warn you, we have a free-fire policy within the breeding reserve. Intruders can be shot on sight.'

'We understand,' Jaeger glanced at Narov. 'And we're sorry for any upset caused.'

Konig eyed him, suspicion still lingering in his gaze. 'Mr and Mrs Groves, this was not the wisest thing to have done. Next time, please come via the normal route, or you may not enjoy such a peaceful reception.'

Narov reached out to shake Konig's hand. 'My husband – it is all his fault. He is headstrong and always thinks he knows best. I tried to dissuade him . . .' She smiled, apparently adoringly. 'But it's what I love about him too.'

Konig seemed to relax a little, but Jaeger found himself choking back a suitably cutting response. Narov was playing her part to perfection. Maybe too well – he almost got the impression that she was enjoying this.

'Indeed.' Konig offered Narov hand the barest of handshakes. 'But you, Mrs Groves – you do not sound so English?'

'It is Andrea,' Narov replied. 'And these days, as you know, there are many English who do not sound very English. For that matter, Mr Konig, you do not sound so very Tanzanian.'

'Indeed, I am German.' Konig glanced at the massive warplane tethered in the water. 'I am a German wildlife conservationist living in Africa, working with a local Tanzanian staff, and part of our responsibility is also to safeguard this aircraft.'

'It's Second World War, right?' Jaeger asked, feigning igno-rance. 'I mean . . . unbelievable. How in the name of God did it end up here, so far beneath the mountain? Surely it's too wide to have made it through the cave entrance.'

'It is,' Konig confirmed. There was a wariness to his gaze still. 'They removed the wings and hauled the aircraft in here during the height of the rains, in 1947, I believe. Then they hired local Africans to bring the wings in afterwards, in sections.'

'Mind-blowing. But why here in Africa? I mean, how did it land here, and why?'

For the briefest of instants a dark shadow flitted across Konig's features. 'That I do not know. That part of the story is long before my time.'

Jaeger could tell that he was lying.

43

K onig gave a curt nod towards the warplane. 'You must be curious, no?'

'To see inside? Of course!' Jaeger enthused.

Konig shook his head. 'Unfortunately, it is strictly off limits. All access is forbidden, as is any access to this entire area. But I think now you understand that?'

'Got it,' Jaeger confirmed. 'Still, it's disappointing. It's not allowed by whom?'

'The man who owns this place. Katavi is a private game sanctuary, run by an American of German descent. That is part of our attraction to foreigners. Unlike the government-run national parks, Katavi is operated with a certain Teutonic efficiency.'

'It is a game reserve that works?' Narov queried. 'Is that what you mean?'

'Pretty much. There is a war being waged against Africa's wildlife. Sadly the poachers are winning. Hence the shoot to-kill policy introduced here, as a desperate measure to try to help us win that war.' Konig eyed them both. 'A policy that very nearly got the two of you killed today.'

Jaeger chose to ignore the last comment. 'You've got our vote,' he remarked, genuinely. 'Butchering an elephant for its tusks, or a rhino for its horn – it's a tragic waste.'

Konig inclined his head. 'I agree. We lose one elephant or rhino on average every day. Wasteful death.' He paused. 'But for now, Mr and Mrs Groves, enough questions, I think.'

He ordered them into the RIB. It wasn't exactly at gunpoint, but it was clear that they had no option but to comply. The boat pulled away from the warplane, the bow wave setting the seaplane rocking. For her size, the BV222 had an undeniable grace and beauty, and Jaeger was determined to find an opportunity to return here and uncover her secrets.

The RIB took them to where an access tunnel threaded its way out of the cave system. Konig flicked a switch set into the wall, and the rock-cut passageway blazed into life, courtesy of electric lighting recessed into the roof.

'Wait here,' he ordered. 'We will go to fetch your things.'

'Thanks. You know where they are?' Jaeger queried.

'Of course. My men have been observing you for some time.'

'They have? Wow. How d'you do that?'

'Well, we have sensors positioned in the caves. But you can imagine, with animals always in and out, they are forever being triggered. And anyway, no one ever trespasses this deep inside the mountain.' He eyed Narov and Jaeger pointedly. 'Or at least, not normally . . . Today, something surprised my guards. An entirely unexpected sound. A series of gunshots—'

'We shot hyena,' Narov cut in, defensively. 'A pack of them. We did it to safeguard the elephants. They had young ones.'

Konig held up a hand to silence her. 'I am quite aware that you killed the hyena. And certainly they are a menace. They come here to scavenge juveniles. They cause stampedes, young ones get trampled, and we do not have many of those to spare. The hyena – we ourselves have to cull them, to keep their numbers down.'

'So your guards heard gunshots?' Jaeger prompted.

'They did. They called me in some alarm. They feared poachers had made their way into the cave. Hence I arrived and found . . . *you*.' A pause. 'A newly-wed couple who scale mountains, penetrate caves and eliminate a pack of spotted hyena. It is most unusual, Mrs Groves, is it not?'

Narov didn't so much as flinch. 'Would you abseil into this place without being armed? It would be madness to do so.'

Konig's face remained expressionless. 'Possibly so. But still, regrettably, I will have to take your weapons. For two reasons. One, you are trespassing in a closed zone. No one but myself and my guards are permitted to carry arms in here. '

He eyed Narov and Jaeger. 'And two, because the man who owns this place has ordered anyone found here to be arrested. I think perhaps this second ruling did not extend to guests of the lodge. But I will reserve judgement, and keep your weapons, at least until I have spoken with the owner.'

Jaeger shrugged. 'No problem. We'll have no need of them where we're going.'

Konig forced a smile. 'Of course. In Katavi Lodge you will not require any weapons.'

Jaeger glanced after two of Konig's guards, as they headed off to retrieve the gear that he and Narov had stashed by the lakeside.

'The pistols are under a small rock, next to our supplies!' he shouted after them. He turned back to Konig. 'I guess it doesn't look too good, carrying weapons into a restricted zone like this?'

'You are right, Mr Groves,' Konig replied. 'It doesn't look good at all.'

44

Jaeger went to give Narov a refill, but there was little point, for she'd hardly touched her drink. He was doing so for appearances only.

Narov frowned. 'Alcohol – I do not like the taste.'

Jaeger sighed. 'Tonight you've got to loosen up a little. You need to look the part.'

He'd chosen a bottle of chilled Saumur – a French dry sparkling wine, and a little less ostentatious an option than champagne. He'd wanted to order something to celebrate their newly-wed status, but something that wouldn't turn too many heads. He figured the Saumur – with its royal blue label embossed discreetly in white and gold lettering – was about right.

They were thirty-six hours into their stay at the fabulous Katavi Lodge. It consisted of a cluster of whitewashed safari bungalows, each sculpted on the outside with gentle curves designed to soften the hard lines of the walls, and situated within a bowl-like slope in the foothills of the Mbizi mountains. Each came complete with traditional-style high ceilings, fitted with roof fans that kept the rooms relatively cool.

Similar fans turned lazily above tonight's diners, throwing a light breeze over the setting – the lodge's Veranda Restaurant. Positioned with great care to overlook a waterhole, it offered a perfect vantage point. And tonight the scene below sure was busy, the noisy snorting of the hippos and the blowing of the elephants punctuating the diners' conversations.

With every hour they'd spent here, Jaeger and Narov had

become ever more aware of the challenges of getting back on to that warplane. At Katavi Lodge, everything was done for you – cooking, washing, cleaning, bed-making, driving – plus there was the daily itinerary of safari tours. The people here sure knew how to run a game reserve, but all that left precious little scope for any freelance activity – like an unsanctioned return to the caves.

At the back of Jaeger's mind, a dark worry was gnawing away at him: were Ruth and Luke also hidden somewhere beneath that mountain? Were they imprisoned in some lab, like rats awaiting the touch of the ultimate killer virus?

As much as Jaeger knew that he and Narov had to play a convincing act, he was burning with frustration. They needed to get moving; to get results. But Konig was still suspicious of them: they could risk doing nothing to further fuel those suspicions.

He took a sip of the Saumur. It was chilled to perfection in the ice bucket set to one side; he couldn't deny that it was good.

'So, you find all this at all weird?' he asked, lowering his voice to ensure they couldn't be overheard.

'Weird like how?'

'Mr and Mrs Groves? The honeymooners thing?'

Narov glanced at him blankly. 'Why would I? We are playing a part. How is that weird?'

Either Narov was in denial, or all of this somehow came naturally to her. It was bizarre. Jaeger had spent months trying to fathom out this woman; to get to truly know her. But he didn't feel a great deal closer to doing so.

With her Falkenhagen bunker makeover – her new raven-headed look – there was something of the Irish Celtic beauty about Narov. In fact it struck Jaeger that there was something reminiscent of his wife, Ruth, in her look.

He found the idea distinctly unsettling.

Why had that come into his head?

It had to be the alcohol.

A voice cut into his thoughts. 'Mr and Mrs Groves. You are settling in well? You are enjoying the dinner?'

It was Konig. The reserve's head conservationist did a nightly round of the diners, checking that all was as it should be. He still didn't sound overly welcoming, but at least he hadn't had the two of them arrested for their trespassing beneath the mountain.

'We can't fault it,' Jaeger replied. 'Any of it.'

Konig gestured at the view. 'Stunning, isn't it?'

'It's to die for.' Jaeger lifted the bottle of Saumur. 'Fancy joining us for a celebratory drink?'

'Thank you, no. A newly-wed couple? You I think have no need of company.'

'Please, we'd like it,' said Narov. 'You must know so much about the reserve. We're fascinated – bewitched – aren't we, Spotty?'

She'd addressed that last remark to a cat sprawled beneath her chair. The lodge had several resident moggies. Typically, Narov had adopted the one that was the least attractive; the one that the other diners tended to shoo away from their tables.

'Spotty' was a white mongrel with black splodges. She was as thin as a rake, and at some time she'd lost one of her rear legs. Half of Narov's baked Nile perch – a locally caught fish – had been fed to the cat during the course of the evening, and she'd grown ever more contented.

'Ah, I see you and Paca have become friends,' Falk remarked, his tone softening a little.

'Paca?' Narov queried.

'Swahili for "cat".' He shrugged. 'Not very imaginative, but the staff found her in one of the local villages, half dead. She'd been run over by a vehicle. I adopted her, and as no one knew her real name, we took to calling her Paca.'

'Paca.' Narov savoured the word for an instant. She held out what remained of her fish. 'Here, Paca, don't chew too noisily – some people are still eating.'

The cat reached out a paw, tapped down the chunk of flesh and pounced.

Konig allowed himself a brief smile. 'You, I think, Mrs Groves, are a hopeless lover of animals?'

'Animals,' Narov echoed. 'So much simpler and more honest than humans. They either want to eat you, they want you to pet them or feed them, or to give them loyalty and love – which they give back to you one hundred times over. And they never decide on a whim to leave you for another.'

Konig allowed himself a chuckle. 'I think perhaps you need to be worried, Mr Groves. And I think perhaps I will join you. But just for the one drink: I have an early start tomorrow.'

He signalled to the waiter for a third glass. It was Narov's love for the Katavi Lodge's most unattractive cat that seemed to be winning him over.

Jaeger poured some Saumur. 'Great staff, by the way. And you should congratulate the chef on the food.' A pause. 'But tell me – how does the reserve function? I mean, is it successful?'

'On one level, yes,' Konig answered. 'We run a very profitable business here at the lodge. But I am first and foremost a conservationist. For me, all that matters is that we protect the animals. And in that . . . in that, if I am honest, we are failing.'

'Failing like how?' Narov queried.

'Well, this is not really a honeymoon type of conversation. It would be distressing, particularly for you, Mrs Groves.'

Narov nodded at Jaeger. 'I am married to a guy who takes me into Burning Angels crater just for the hell of it. I think I can handle it.'

Konig shrugged. 'Very well then. But be warned: it is a dark and bloody war being fought out there.'

45

'Very few guests choose to get here by driving, as you did,' Konig began. 'Most are doing Africa on a tight schedule. They fly into Kilimanjaro International Airport, from where they are whisked down here by light aircraft.

'They arrive, keen to get their big game animals ticked off. The Big Seven: lion, cheetah, rhino, elephant, giraffe, Cape buffalo and hippo. That done, most fly out to Amani Beach Resort. It is it is a truly magical resort set right on the Indian Ocean. Amani means "peace" in Swahili, and trust me – it's the perfect place to get away from it all in utter privacy.'

Konig's face darkened. 'But I spend my days very differently. I spend them trying to ensure that enough of the Big Seven survive to satisfy our visitors. I am a pilot, and I fly anti-poaching patrols. Well, "patrol" is perhaps too grand a word for it. It's not as if we can do anything, for the poachers are very heavily armed.'

He pulled out a battered map. 'I spend my days flying transects, which are recorded on video and married up to a computerised mapping system. That way we get a real-time video map of poaching incidents, pinpointed to their exact location. It's a state-of-the-art system, and trust me, it is only due to the backing of my boss, Mr Kammler, that we can afford such things. We get precious little support from the government.'

Kammler. He'd said it. Not that Jaeger had ever doubted who called the shots around here, but it was nice to have it confirmed absolutely.

Konig lowered his voice. 'Last year we had three thousand two hundred elephants. Sounds pretty healthy, no? That is until you learn that during that year we lost some seven hundred. Around two elephants killed for every day. The poachers shoot them with assault rifles, slice off their tusks with chainsaws and leave the carcasses to rot in the sun.'

Narov looked horrified. 'But if it goes on like that, in five years you'll have none left at all.'

Konig shook his head despondently. 'It is worse. We are four months into this year and I have not flown a single day without encountering the butchery . . . In those four months already we have lost approaching eight hundred elephants. *In just four months*. It is little short of a catastrophe.'

Narov looked white with shock. 'But that is *sickening*. Having seen the herd in that cave . . . I mean all of them, and so many more, being slaughtered . . . It's hard to believe. But why the recent upsurge? Without knowing that, it is difficult to counter it.'

'The great thing about the mapping system is it allows us to deduce certain things, like the focus of the poaching activity. We have narrowed it down to one village, plus a certain individual. A Lebanese dealer; a buyer of ivory. It is his arrival in the area that has triggered the upsurge.'

'So report your findings to the police,' Jaeger suggested. 'Or the wildlife authorities. Whoever it is who deals with such issues.'

Konig gave a bitter laugh. 'Mr Groves, this is Africa. The amounts of money being made – everyone is paid off at all levels. The chances of someone taking action against this Lebanese dealer are just about zero.'

'But what's a Lebanese doing here?' Jaeger queried.

Konig shrugged. 'There are dodgy Lebanese business rackets running all over Africa. I guess this guy just decided to make himself the Pablo Escobar of the ivory trade.'

'And what about the rhino?' It was the Jaeger family favourite, and he felt a deep attachment to the magnificent animals.

'With rhino it is even worse. The breeding sanctuary where we have the shoot-to-kill policy – that is mostly for the rhino. With a few thousand elephants, we still have viable breeding herds. With the rhino, we have had to fly in fully grown males, to bolster the numbers. To keep them viable.'

Konig reached for his glass and drained it. The subject of their conversation clearly troubled him. Without asking, Jaeger poured him a refill.

'If the poachers are so heavily armed, you must be a prime target?' he queried.

Konig smiled grimly. 'I consider that a compliment. I fly very low and very fast. Just above the treetops. By the time they see me and have readied their weapons, I have flashed past. Once or twice there have been bullet holes in my aircraft.' He shrugged. 'It's a small price.'

'So you over-fly, locate the poachers, and then what?' Jaeger queried.

'If we spot signs of activity, we radio the ground teams and they try to intercept the gangs, using our vehicles. The problem is response times, personnel, level of training and sheer scale, not to mention the mismatch in weaponry. In short, by the time we get anywhere near close the tusks or horns, plus the poachers, are long gone.'

'You must be scared,' Narov probed. 'For yourself and the animals. Scared but enraged all at the same time.'

There was genuine concern in her voice, plus a certain admiration burning in her eyes. Jaeger told himself that he shouldn't be surprised. Narov and this German wildlife warrior had an obvious bond – their shared love of animals. It drew them close, and it was a closeness from which he felt oddly excluded.

'Sometimes, yes,' Konig answered. 'But I am more often angry than scared. That anger – at the scale of the slaughter – it drives me on.'

'In your position, I would be enraged,' Narov told Konig. She fixed him with a very direct look. 'Falk, I would like to see this at first hand. Can we fly with you tomorrow? Join a patrol?'

It took a good second or more for Konig to answer. 'Well, I don't think so. I have never taken guests on a flight. You see, I fly very low and fast – like a roller coaster, only worse. I do not think you would enjoy it. Plus there is the risk of gunfire.'

'Regardless, will you fly us?' Narov persisted.

'It is really not a good idea. I cannot just take anyone . . . And for insurance reasons, it's just not —'

'We're not just anyone,' Narov cut in, 'as you may have realised in that cave. Plus I think we can help. I honestly believe we can help you put a stop to the slaughter. Bend the rules, Falk. Just this once. For the sake of your animals.'

'Narov's right,' Jaeger added. 'We really could help you deal with the threat.'

'Help like how?' Konig asked. He was clearly intrigued. 'How could you ever help combat such slaughter?'

Jaeger looked hard at Narov. A plan of sorts was coalescing in his mind, one that he figured might just work.

46

Jaeger eyed the big German. He was in great shape, and would very likely have made a fine elite soldier, had his life followed a different path. He'd certainly shown little apparent fear upon their first encounter.

'Falk, we're going to let you in on a secret. We're both ex-services. Special forces. A few months back we left the military and got married, and I guess we're both searching for something: a cause to get involved with that's bigger than us.'

'We think we may have found it,' Narov added. 'Today, here with you at Katavi. If we can help put a stop to the poaching, that would mean more to us than a whole month of safaris.'

Konig glanced from Narov to Jaeger. There was still a hint of uncertainty as to whether he should trust them.

'What do you have to lose?' Narov prompted. 'I promise you – we can help. Just get us in the air so we can see the lie of the land.' She glanced at Jaeger. 'Trust me, my husband and I have dealt with far worse than poachers before.'

That pretty much put an end to the debate. Konig had developed a soft spot for the beguiling Narov, that much was clear. No doubt he was keen to bend the rules and to show off his prowess in the air. But the chance of furthering his mission – of saving his wildlife – that had been the clincher.

He got up to leave. 'Okay, but you come as independents. Not as guests of Katavi. Clear?'

'Of course.'

He shook hands with them both. 'It is most unorthodox, so please keep it quiet. We meet at seven a.m. sharp at the airstrip. There will be breakfast once we lift off, that's if you still have the stomach for it.'

It was then that Jaeger fired a final question at him, as if in afterthought.

'Falk, I'm curious – have you ever set foot inside that aircraft in the cave? Have you seen inside it?'

Caught off his guard, Konig couldn't disguise the evasiveness in his answer. 'The warplane? Seen inside it? Why would I have? It is of little interest to me, to be honest.'

With that he wished them goodnight and was gone.

'He's lying,' Jaeger told Narov, once he was out of carshot. 'About never having been on that plane.'

'He is,' Narov confirmed. 'When someone says "to be honest", you can know for sure they're lying.'

Jaeger smiled. Classic Narov. 'Question is, why? On all other fronts he seems genuine. So why lie about that?'

'I think he is scared. Scared of Kammler. And if our experience is anything to go by, he has every reason to be.'

'So we join his game patrol,' Jaeger mused. 'How does that help us get back beneath the mountain; get on to that warplane?'

'If we can't get on to it, the next best thing is to speak to someone who has – and that's Konig. Konig knows everything that goes on here. He knows there is darkness behind the glossy facade. He knows all the secrets. But he's scared to talk. We need to draw him on side.'

'Hearts and minds?' Jaeger queried.

'First his heart, then his mind. We need to bring him to a place where he feels safe enough to talk. In fact, where he feels *obliged* to. And by helping to save his wildlife, we can do that.'

Together they wandered back to their safari bungalow, passing under a giant spreading mango tree. A troop of monkeys screeched at them from the branches, before hurling down some gnawed mango stones.

Cheeky sods, Jaeger thought.

Upon arrival here, he and Narov had been handed a brochure regarding proper etiquette to be maintained around monkeys. If confronted by one, you had to avoid eye contact. They would see it as a challenge, and it would send them into a rage. You had to back away quietly. And if a monkey grabbed some food or a trinket off you, you were supposed to give it up voluntarily and report the theft to one of the game guards.

Jaeger didn't exactly agree with the advice. In his experience, capitulation invariably led to greater aggression. They reached their bungalow and slid back the heavy wooden screen that served as a shutter to the large glass doors. Jaeger was immediately on his guard. He could have sworn they'd left the screen open.

As soon as they stepped inside, it was clear that someone had been in their room. The massive bed had had the mosquito netting lowered all around it. The air was chill; someone had switched on the air conditioning. And there were handfuls of red petals scattered across the pristine white pillows.

Jaeger remembered now. This was all part of the service. Whilst they had been dining, one of the maids had been in to lend that added honeymoon touch. It had been like this the first night too.

He flicked off the air con. Neither of them liked sleeping with it.

'You take the bed,' Narov called to him, as she went to use the bathroom. 'I'm on the sofa.'

The previous night, Jaeger had slept on the couch. He knew better than to argue. He stripped down to his boxers and threw on a dressing gown. Once Narov was done, he went to brush his teeth.

When he came out again, he found her wrapped up in the thin sheet on the bed. The contours of her body could clearly be seen through the bedclothes. She had her eyes closed, and he presumed the alcohol had sent her straight to sleep.

'I thought you said *you'd* take the sofa,' he muttered, as he prepared to settle down on it . . . again.

47

The only sign that Jaeger could detect that Narov had a hangover was the sunglasses. This early in the morning, the sun was still to rise over the African plains. Or maybe she was wearing them to shield her eyes from the dust kicked up by the ancient-looking helicopter.

Konig had decided to take the Katavi Reserve's Russian-made Mi-17 HIP helicopter, as opposed to the twin-engine Otter light aircraft. He was doing so because he was worried about his passengers getting airsick, and the chopper made for a more stable air platform. Plus he had a little surprise in store for his guests, one that would only be possible via a chopper.

Whatever the surprise might be, it must entail some degree of risk, for he'd returned to Jaeger and Narov their SIG Sauer P228s.

'This is Africa,' Konig had explained as he'd handed over the pistols. 'Anything can happen. But I'm bending the rules, so try and keep your weapons hidden. And I will need them back at the end of today's proceedings.'

The HIP was a bulbous, ugly grey beast of a thing, but Jaeger wasn't overly worried. He'd flown numerous missions before in this type of aircraft, and he knew it to be of typically simple, rugged Russian design.

It was bulletproof-reliable, and well deserved the nickname given it by NATO forces – 'the bus of the skies'. Although in theory the British and US militaries didn't operate any such former Soviet-era kit, in practice of course they did. A HIP was ideal for flying unmarked, deniable operations, hence Jaeger's easy familiarity with the machine.

Konig had the helo's five blades spooled up to speed, spinning into a blur. It was vital to get airborne as soon as possible. The HIP would achieve maximum purchase in the cool of early morning. As the heat rose through the day, the air would thin, making it more and more challenging to fly.

From the cockpit Konig flashed a thumbs up. They were good to go. Hot blasts of burning avgas fumes washed over Jaeger, as he and Narov made a dash for the open side door and vaulted aboard.

The tang of the exhaust was intoxicating, bringing back memories of countless former missions. Jaeger smiled to himself. The dust thrown up by the rotor wash had that familiar smell of Africa: hot, sun-baked earth; age beyond measure; a history stretching back deep into the prehistoric past.

Africa was the crucible of evolution – the cradle within which humankind had evolved from an original, ape-like predecessor. And as the HIP clawed into the skies, so Jaeger could see the awe-inspiring and timeless terrain rolling out before him on all sides.

To their left – port – side, the humped foothills of the Mbizi mountains rose like a sagging layer cake, sludge grey in the pre-dawn light. A good distance north-west lay the twin lips of Burning Angels Peak, the eastern, slightly higher point marking where Jaeger and Narov had made their climb and descent.

And somewhere out of sight deep beneath that mountain lurked the hulking form of the BV222 seaplane. From the air, Jaeger could well imagine how it had remained hidden in the trackless wilderness of the Mbizi mountains for seven long decades.

He turned to the right – starboard – side. Patches of mountain forest rolled eastwards, petering out into a brown, hazy savannah-like landscape dotted with clumps of flat-topped acacia trees. Dry watercourses wound like so many serpents all the way to the distant horizon.

Konig dipped the helo's nose and it leapt ahead with remarkable swiftness for such a snub-nosed and bulging pig of a machine. Within moments they were free of the open expanse of the airstrip and speeding over dense thickets of woodland, practically clipping the treetops as they went. The door was latched open, offering Jaeger and Narov the best view possible.

Prior to take-off, Konig had explained today's objective: to fly a series of transects over the Lake Rukwa seasonal flood plain, where big game animals congregated around the few major waterholes. Lake Rukwa was prime poaching territory. Konig had warned them that he would have to keep the aircraft down lower than a snake's belly, and to be prepared for evasive action should they come under fire.

Jaeger reached behind him for the bulge of his P228. He flicked it out of his waistband, using the thumb of his right hand to depress the magazine release mechanism. He was left-handed, but he'd taught himself to shoot with his right, as so many weapons were designed for a right-handed shooter.

He slipped off the near-empty mag – the one with which he'd taken on the pack of hyenas – and stuffed it into the side pocket of his combat trousers. That big, deep compartment was perfect for stashing used ammo. He reached into the pocket of his fleece jacket and pulled out a fresh magazine, slotting it on to the weapon. It was something he'd done a thousand times before, both in training and on operations, and he did it now almost without thinking.

That done, he plugged himself into the helo's intercom, via a set of headphones that linked him direct to the cockpit. He could hear Konig and his co-pilot, a local guy called Urio, calling out the landmarks and flight details.

'Dog-leg in dirt track,' Konig reported. 'Port side of aircraft, four hundred metres.'

Co-pilot: 'Check. Fifty klicks out from Rukwa.'

Pause. Then Konig again. 'Airspeed: ninety-five knots. Direction of travel: 085 degrees.'

Co-pilot. 'Check. Fifteen minutes out from run cameras.'

At their present speed – over a hundred miles per hour – they'd be reach the the Rukwa flood plain shortly, at which moment they'd set the video cameras rolling.

Co-pilot: 'ETA waterhole Zulu Alpha Mike Bravo Echo Zulu India fifteen minutes. Repeat, waterhole Zambezi in fifteen. Look for dog's-head kopje, then clearing one hundred metres east of there . . .'

Konig: 'Roger that.'

Through the open door, Jaeger could see the odd acacia flashing by. He felt close enough almost to reach out and touch the treetops, as Konig weaved the aircraft between them, hugging the contours.

Konig flew well. If he took the HIP any lower, its rotors would be shaving the branches.

They sped onwards, the noise killing all chance of any chat. The racket from the HIP's worn turbines and rotor gear was deafening. There were three other figures riding in the rear along with Jaeger and Narov. Two were game guards, armed with AK-47 assault rifles; the third was the aircraft's loadmaster – the guy who managed any cargo or passengers.

The loadie kept moving from one doorway to the other, glancing upwards. Jaeger knew what he was doing: he was checking for any smoke or oil coming from the turbines, and that the rotors weren't about to sheer off or splinter. He settled back to enjoy the ride. He'd flown in countless HIPs.

They might look and sound like a sack of shit, but he'd never known one to go down.

48

Jaeger reached for a 'havabag', as they'd nicknamed them in the military – a brown paper bag stuffed full of food. There was a pile of them sitting in a cool box lashed to the HIP's floor.

When serving in the British military, the best you could hope for from a havabag was a stale ham and cheese sandwich, a warm can of Panda cola, a bag of prawn cocktail crisps and a Kit Kat. The contents never seemed to differ, courtesy of the RAF caterers.

Jaeger peered inside: boiled eggs wrapped in tin foil; still warm to the touch. Pancakes, freshly fried that morning, and laced with maple syrup. Grilled sausages and bacon slapped between slices of buttered toast. A couple of crispy croissants, plus a freezer bag full of freshly sliced fruit: pineapple, watermelon and mango.

In addition, there was a flask of fresh coffee, hot water for making tea, plus chilled sodas. He should have guessed, given the care the Katavi Lodge caterers took of their guests and staff.

He tucked in. Beside him – hangover or no – Narov was likewise getting busy.

Breakfast was done and dusted by the time they hit the first signs of trouble. It was approaching mid-morning, and Konig had already flown a series of survey transects across the Lake Rukwa region, finding nothing.

All of a sudden he was forced to throw the HIP into a series of fierce manoeuvres, the noise from the screaming turbines rebounding off the ground deafeningly as the helo dropped lower and almost kissed the very dirt.

The loadie peered from the doorway and jabbed a thumb towards their rear.

'Poachers!' he yelled.

Jaeger thrust his head into the raging slipstream. He was just in time to see a group of stick-like figures being swallowed by the thick dust. He glimpsed the flash of a raised weapon, but even if the gunman did manage to unleash any rounds, they would be too late to find their target.

This was the reason for the ultra-low-level ride: by the time the bad guys had noticed the HIP, it would be long gone.

'Cameras running?' Konig came up over the intercom.

'Running,' his co-pilot confirmed.

'For the benefit of our passengers,' Konig announced, 'that was a poaching gang. Maybe a dozen strong. Armed with AK47s and what looked like RPGs. More than enough to blast us out of the sky. Oh, and I hope you still have your breakfasts in your stomachs!'

Jaeger was surprised at how tooled up the poachers were. AK47 assault rifles could do the HIP some serious damage. As for a direct hit from an RPG – a rocket-propelled-grenade – that would blast them out of the skies.

'We're just plotting their line of march, and it seems they're returning from a . . . kill.' Even via the intercom, the tension in Konig's voice was palpable. 'Looked like they were carrying tusks. But you can see our predicament. We're outnumbered and outgunned, and when they're armed to the teeth like that, we have little chance of arresting them, or seizing the ivory.

'We'll be over the most likely area – a waterhole – in a matter of seconds now,' he added. 'So brace yourselves.'

Moments later, the helo decelerated massively as Konig threw it into a screaming turn, circling over what had to be the water-hole. Jaeger peered out of the starboard-side porthole. He found that he was looking down almost directly at the ground. Several dozen feet from the muddy gleam of the water, he spotted two shapeless grey forms.

The elephants possessed little of their poise or magical grace any more. Compared to the magisterial animals that he and Narov had encountered deep within Burning Angels cave, these had been rendered into unmoving bundles of lifeless meat.

'As you can see, they captured and tethered a baby elephant,' Konig announced, his voice tight with emotion. 'They used that to lure the parents in. Both the bull and the mother have been shot and butchered. Tusks gone.

'I know many of the animals here by name,' he continued. 'The big bull looks like Kubwa-Kubwa; that's Swahili for "Big-Big". Most elephants don't live past seventy years of age. Kubwa-Kubwa was eighty-one years old. He was the elder of the herd, and one of the oldest in the reserve.

'The baby is alive, but it'll be badly traumatised. If we can get to it and calm it down, it may live. If we're lucky, the other matriarchs should take it under their wing.'

Konig sounded remarkably calm. But as Jaeger well knew, dealing with such pressure and trauma day after day, took its toll.

'Okay, now for your surprise,' Konig announced grimly. 'You said you wanted to see this . . . I'm taking you down. A few minutes on the ground to witness the horror close up. The guards will escort you.'

Almost instantly Jaeger felt the HIP start to lose what little altitude it had. As it flared out, the rear end dropping towards a narrow clearing, the loadie hung out of the doorway, checking that the rotor blades and tail were clear of the acacia trees.

There was a jolt as the wheels made contact with the hot African earth, and the loadie gave the thumbs up.

'We're good!' he yelled. 'De-bus!'

Jaeger and Narov leapt from the doorway. Bent double and heads bowed they scuttled off to one side until they were clear of the rotors, which were whipping up a storm of dirt and blasted vegetation. They went down on one knee, pistol in hand, just in case there were any poachers remaining in the area. The two game guards rushed over to join them. One gave a thumbs up to the cockpit, Konig flashed it back, and an instant later the HIP rose vertically and was gone.

The seconds ticked by.

The juddering beat of the rotors faded.

Shortly the aircraft was no longer audible at all.

Hurriedly the game guards explained that Konig was returning to Katavi to fetch a harness. If they could get the baby elephant darted and put to sleep, they could sling it beneath the HIP and fly it back to the reserve. There, they'd hand-rear the animal for as long as it took to get it over the trauma, at which stage it could be reunited with its herd.

Jaeger could see the sense in this, but he didn't exactly relish their present situation: surrounded by the carcasses of recently butchered elephants, and armed with only a pair of pistols between them. The game guards seemed calm, but he doubted how skilled they'd be if it all went south.

He rose to his feet and glanced at Narov.

As they made their way toward the scene of unspeakable carnage, he could see the rage burning in her eyes.

49

As carefully as they could, they approached the trembling, traumatised form of the baby elephant. It was lying on its side now, seemingly too exhausted to even stand. The ground betrayed the signs of its recent struggles: the rope tethering it to the tree had cut deep into its leg, as it had fought to get free.

Narov knelt over the poor thing. She lowered her head, whispering soft words of reassurance into its ear. Its small – human-sized – eyes rolled in fear, but eventually her voice seemed to calm it. She stayed close to the animal for what seemed like an age.

Finally she turned. There were tears in her eyes. 'We're going after them. Those who did this.'

Jaeger shook his head. 'Come on . . . The two of us armed with pistols. That's not brave: it's foolish.'

Narov got to her feet. She fixed Jaeger with a tortured look. 'Then I'll go alone.'

'But what about . . .' Jaeger gestured at the baby elephant. 'It needs protection. Safeguarding.'

Narov jabbed a finger in the direction of the guards. 'What about them? They are better armed than we are.' She glanced west, in the direction the poachers had taken. 'Unless someone goes after them, this will continue until the last animal is killed.' Her expression was one of cold and determined fury. 'We need to hit them hard, mercilessly, and with the same kind of savagery as they used here.'

'Irina, I hear you. But let's at least work out how best to do this. Konig's twenty minutes out. They had spare AKs stashed in the HIP. At the very least let's get ourselves properly armed. Plus the chopper's stuffed full of supplies: water, food. Without that, we're finished before we've even begun.'

Narov stared. She didn't speak, but he could tell that she was wavering.

Jaeger checked his watch. 'It's 1300 hours. We can be on our way by 1330. The poachers will have a two-hour start on us. If we move fast, we can do this; we can catch them.'

She had to accept that his was the voice of reason.

Jaeger decided to go check out the corpses. He didn't know quite what he expected to find, but he went anyway. He tried to act dispassionately: to inspect the kill scene like a soldier. But still he found his emotions running away with him.

This had been no accurate, professional hit. Jaeger figured the elephants had been charging to protect their young, and the poachers must have panicked. They'd peppered the once-mighty beasts indiscriminately, using assault rifles and machine guns to take them down.

One thing was for sure: the animals would have had no quick and painless death. They'd have sensed danger; possibly even known they were being lured to their doom. But they came anyway, to safeguard their family, charging to the defence of their offspring.

With Luke missing three long years, Jaeger couldn't help but relate. He wrestled with unexpected emotions and blinked back the tears.

Jaeger turned to leave, but something made him stop. He figured he'd seen movement. He checked again, dreading what he might find. Sure enough – unbelievably – one of the mighty animals was still breathing.

The realisation was like a punch to the guts. The poachers had gunned the bull elephant down, hacked off its tusks and left it in a pool of its own blood. Riddled with bullets, it was dying a slow and agonising death under the burning African sun.

Jaeger felt rage burning through him. The once-mighty animal was well beyond any hope of saving.

Though he was sickened, he knew what he had to do.

He turned aside and made his way to one of the guards, from whom he borrowed an AK47. Then, with hands shaking with anger and emotion, he levelled the weapon at the magnificent animal's head. For just an instant he thought the bull opened his eyes.

With tears blurring his vision, Jaeger fired, and the stricken animal breathed its last.

In a daze, Jaeger went back to rejoin Narov. She was still comforting the baby elephant, though he could tell by her pained look that she knew what he had been forced to do. For both of them this was personal now.

He crouched beside her. 'You're right. We do have to go after them. Just as soon as we've grabbed some supplies off the HIP, let's get moving.'

Minutes later, the noise of rotor blades cut through the hot air. Konig was ahead of schedule. He brought the HIP down into the clearing, the rotors throwing up a choking cloud of dust and debris. The bulbous wheels hit the dirt, and Konig began to power down the turbines. Jaeger was about to rush forward to help unload when his heart skipped a beat.

He'd spotted a flash of movement way off in the bush; the tell-tale glint of sunlight on metal. He saw a figure rise from the undergrowth, hefting a rocket-launcher on his shoulder. He was a good three hundred yards away, so there was sod-all that Jaeger could do with a pistol.

'RPG! RPG!' he screamed.

An instant later he caught the unmistakable sound of the armour-piercing projectile firing. Normally RPGs were notoriously inaccurate, unless fired at close quarters. This one tore out of the bush, hammering towards the HIP like a bowling pin on its side, trailing a fiery dragon's breath in its wake.

For an instant Jaeger figured it would miss, but at the last moment it ploughed into the rear of the helo, just forward of the tail rotor. There was the blinding flash of an explosion, which ripped the entire tail section off the aircraft, the impact throwing the HIP through ninety degrees.

Jaeger barely hesitated. He was on his feet and racing forward, as he yelled orders at Narov and the game guards to form a defensive cordon, putting steel between them and their attackers. Already he could hear fierce bursts of gunfire, and he didn't doubt the poachers were closing for the kill.

Even as flames sparked from the HIP's shattered rear Jaeger vaulted into the torn and buckled hold. Thick, acrid smoke billowed all around him as he searched for survivors. Konig had flown in with four extra guards, and Jaeger could tell instantly that three of them were peppered with shrapnel, and very dead.

He grabbed the fourth, who was injured but still alive, hoisted his bloody form and hauled him out of the stricken aircraft, dumping him in the bush, before turning back for Konig and his co-pilot.

Fire leapt through the chopper now, the hungry flames taking hold. Jaeger needed to move fast, or Konig and Urio would be burned alive. But if he tried to brave those flames unprotected, he'd never make it.

He threw off his pack, reached inside and pulled out a large spray can, with COLDFIRE stamped across the matt-black exterior. Turning the nozzle on himself, he sprayed himself from head to toe before dashing for the HIP, can gripped in hand. Coldfire was a miracle agent. He'd seen soldiers spray their hands with it, then play a blowtorch across their bare skin and feel nothing.

Taking a massive gulp of air, he dived through the smoke towards the heart of the flames. Incredibly, he felt no sensation of burning; no heat at all. He lifted the can and let rip, the foam cutting through the toxic vapours and dousing the flames · within seconds.

Fighting his way forward into the cockpit, he unbuckled the

unconscious form of Konig and hauled him from the HIP. Konig looked as if he'd taken a blow to the head, but otherwise he seemed relatively unharmed. Jaeger was soaked with sweat by now, and choking from the smoke, yet he turned a further time and ripped open the other door to the HIP's cockpit.

With a final burst of energy, he grabbed the co-pilot and began to drag him towards safety.

50

Jaeger and Narov had been moving at speed for a good three hours now. Sticking to the cover of a wadi – a dry water-course – they'd managed to overtake the poaching gang, and without any sign that they had been spotted.

They pressed ahead to a thick grove of acacia trees, from which they could get eyes on the poachers as they passed. They needed to assess numbers, weaponry, strengths and weaknesses, in order to determine the best way to hit them.

Back at the helicopter, the poachers had been driven off by the weight of defensive fire, and the injured had been stabilised. They'd called for a medevac chopper, which Katavi Lodge was getting sorted. They planned to lift the baby elephant out at the same time as picking up the wounded.

But Jaeger and Narov had left long before any of that could happen, hard on the trail of the poachers.

From the cover of the acacia grove they watched the gang approach. There were ten gunmen. The RPG operator who'd hit the HIP, plus his loader, would be bringing up the rear, making twelve in all. To Jaeger's practised eye, they looked tooled up to the nines. Long bandoliers of ammo were hanging off their torsos, and magazines were stuffed into bulging pockets, plus rakes of grenades for the launchers.

Twelve poachers, with a veritable war in a box. It wasn't the sort of odds he relished.

As they watched the gang pass, they saw the ivory – four massive bloodied tusks – being passed between them. Each man took his turn, staggering along with a tusk slung over his shoulder, before passing it on to another.

Jaeger didn't doubt the energy expended in doing so. He and Narov had moved light, but still they were drenched in sweat. His thin cotton shirt was glued to his back. They had grabbed some bottled water out of the HIP, but even so they were already running short. And these guys – the poachers – were carrying many times more weight.

Jaeger guessed that each tusk was a good forty kilos, so as heavy as a small adult. He figured they'd be breaking march and setting camp any time soon. They'd have to. Dusk was only a short time away, and they would need to drink, eat and rest.

And that meant the plan forming in his mind might just be doable.

He settled back into the cover of the wadi, signalling Narov to do likewise. 'Seen enough?' he whispered.

'Enough to want to kill them all,' she hissed.

'My sentiments exactly. Trouble is, if we take them on in open battle, it'll be suicide.'

'Got a better idea?' she rasped.

'Maybe.' Jaeger delved into his backpack and pulled out his compact Thuraya satphone. 'From what Konig told us, elephant ivory is solid, like a massive tooth. But like all teeth, at the root end there's a hollow cone: the pulp cavity. And that's filled with soft tissue, cells and veins.'

'I'm listening,' Narov growled. Jaeger could tell she still wanted to go in and hit them right here and now.

'Sooner or later the gang will have to call a halt. They camp up for the night, and we go in. But we don't hit them. Not yet.' He held up the Thuraya. 'We stuff this deep into the pulp cavity. We get Falkenhagen to track the signal. That leads us to their base. In the meantime, we order up some proper hardware. Then we go in and hit them at a time and place of our choosing.'

'How do we get close enough?' Narov demanded. 'To plant the satphone?'

'I don't know. But we do what we do best. We observe; we study. We find a way.'

Narov's eyes glinted. 'And what if someone calls the phone?'

'We set it to vibrate mode. Silent.'

'And if it vibrates its way loose and falls out?'

Jaeger sighed. 'Now you're just being difficult.'

'Being difficult keeps me alive.' Narov rummaged in her pack and pulled out a tiny device no bigger than a pound coin. 'How about this? GPS tracker device. Solar-powered Retrievor. Accurate up to one and a half metres. I figured we might need one to keep tabs on Kammler's people.'

Jaeger held out a hand for it. Stuffing this deep into the tusk's pulp cavity was certainly feasible, if only they could get close enough.

Narov held off from passing it over. 'One condition: I get to place it.'

Jaeger eyed her for a second. She was slight, nimble and smart, that much he knew, and he didn't doubt that she might move more quietly than he could.

He smiled. 'Let's do this.'

They pressed on for another three gruelling hours. Finally the gang called a halt. The giant, blood-red African sun was sinking swiftly towards the horizon. Jaeger and Narov crept closer, belly-crawling along a narrow ravine that ended at a patch of dark and stinking mud, marking the fringes of a waterhole.

The poachers were camped on the far side, which made perfect sense. After the long day's march, they'd have need of water. The waterhole, though, looked to be a festering mud pit. The heat had dissipated slightly, but it remained stultifying, and every crawling, buzzing, stinging thing seemed to be drawn here. Flies as big as mice, rats as big as cats and vicious stinging mosquitoes – the place was swarming.

But nothing bothered Jaeger as much as the dehydration. They'd drained the last of their water a good hour back, and he had little or no fluid left in his body to sweat out. He could feel the onset of a splitting headache. Even lying utterly still, keeping watch on the poachers, the thirst was unbearable.

They both needed to rehydrate, and soon.

Darkness descended across the landscape. A light wind got up, whipping away the last of the sweat from Jaeger's skin. He lay in the dirt, still as a rock and staring into the wall of the night, Narov beside him.

Above them a faint shimmer of starlight flickered through the acacia canopy, with just the faintest hint of the moon breaking through. To left and right a firefly skittered in the darkness, its fluorescent blue-green glow floating magically above the water.

The absence of light was to be welcomed. On a mission such as this, the darkness was their greatest friend.

And the more he watched, the more Jaeger realised that the water – repulsive though it might be – offered the ideal route in.

51

Neither Jaeger nor Narov had a clue how deep the water was, but it would take them right into the heart of the enemy's camp. On the far side of the waterhole, the light of the poachers' cooking fire gleamed on its stagnant surface.

'Ready to go to work?' Jaeger whispered, gently nudging Narov's boot with his own.

She nodded. 'Let's get moving.'

It was gone midnight and the camp had been still for a good three hours. During their time spent observing the place, they'd not seen a single sign of any crocs.

It was time.

Jaeger turned and slid himself in, feeling with his boots for something solid. They came to rest in the thick, gloopy detritus that formed the bottom of the waterhole. He was in up to his waist, but at least the bank shielded him from view.

To either side, unseen, nameless beasts slithered and slopped about. Unsurprisingly, there wasn't the faintest hint of any flow to the water. It was stagnant, fetid and nauseating. It stank of animal faeces, disease and death.

In short, it was perfect – for the poachers would never think to watch for an attack from here.

During his time in the SAS, Jaeger had been taught to embrace what most normal souls feared; to inhabit the night; to welcome darkness. It was the cloak to hide his and his brother warriors' movements from hostile eyes – just as he hoped it would prove now.

He had been trained to seek out the kind of environments – sun-blasted desert, remote, hostile bush and fetid swamps – that normal human beings tended to shun. No other sane people would be there, which meant that a small group of elite operators could sneak through unnoticed.

No poachers would be joining Jaeger and Narov in this foul and stinking waterhole, which was why – despite the numerous downsides – it was perfect.

Jaeger got himself down on to his knees, his eyes and nose just above the water, his hand gripping his pistol. Like this he could maintain the lowest profile possible, while crawling and shuffling silently ahead. He made sure to keep the P228 out of the water. While most pistols still worked when wet, it was always better to keep them dry – just in case the dirty water fouled up the weapon.

He glanced at Narov. 'You happy?'

She nodded, her eyes sparkling dangerously in the moonlight.

The tips of the fingers of Jaeger's left hand gripped the squelchy, gooey mush as his feet shoved him into forward motion. He flailed about amongst a mass of rotting, putrid vegetation, his hand sinking up to the wrist with each thrust.

He prayed there weren't any snakes in here, then drove the thought from his mind.

He pressed ahead for three minutes, counting each forward thrust by hand and feet, and translating that into a rough estimate of distance travelled. He and Narov were moving blind here, and he needed a sense of where the poachers' camp lay. When he figured they'd covered about seventy-five yards, he signalled a halt.

He approached the left bank and raised his head, inching it above the cover. He felt Narov tight beside him, her head practically on his shoulder. Together they emerged from the swamp, their hands gripping their pistols. Each covered one half of the terrain before them as they whispered details back and forth, building up a picture of the enemy encampment as rapidly as possible.

'Campfire,' Jaeger whispered. 'Two guys sat beside it. Sentry.'

'Direction of watch?'

'South-east. Away from the waterhole.'

'Lights?'

'None that I can see.'

'Weapons?'

'AKs. Plus I see guys to left and right of the fire, sleeping. I count . . . eight.'

'That's ten accounted for. Two unseen.'

Narov swivelled her eyes this way and that, scanning her section of the terrain.

'I see the tusks. One guy standing sentry over them.'

'Weapon?'

'Assault rifle slung across his shoulder.'

'That leaves one unaccounted for. One missing.'

Both were aware of the passage of time, but it made sense to find that missing poacher. They kept watch for a few minutes longer, but still they couldn't locate the last man.

'Any sign of extra security measures? Tripwires? Booby traps? Motion sensors?'

Narov shook her head. 'Nothing visible. Let's move ahead thirty. Then we'll be right beside the tusks.'

Jaeger slid back into the murk and pushed on. As he did so, he could hear the sounds of mystery beasts thrashing about in the thick darkness. His eyes were about level with the water, and he could sense vile movement to all sides. Worst of all, he could feel things slithering their way in.

Beneath his shirt, around his neck – on his inner thighs, even – he could detect the faintly stinging sensation, as a leech inserted its jaws under his skin and began sucking greedily, filling its gut with his blood.

It was sickening; revolting.

But there was nothing he could do about it right now.

For some reason – most likely the electrifying adrenalin buzz he was feeling – Jaeger was also dying for a pee. But he had to fight the urge. The golden rule of crossing such watery terrain was: never take a leak. If you did, you risked opening up your urethra and allowing a swampload of germs, bacteria and parasites to swim up your urine stream.

There was even a tiny *fish* – the candiru, or 'toothpick fish' – that liked to insert itself into your tube and extend its spines, so you couldn't pull it out again. The very thought made Jaeger shudder. No way could he allow himself to take a leak. He'd hold it in until the mission was done.

Finally they stopped and did a second scan of the terrain. To their immediate left the four giant tusks gleamed eerily in the moonlight, maybe thirty yards away. The lone sentry had his back to them, facing out into the bush – where any obvious threat would come from.

Narov held up the tracker device. 'I'm going in,' she whispered.

For a moment Jaeger was tempted to argue. But this was not the time. And very possibly she could do this better than him. 'I've got your back. You're covered.'

Narov paused for an instant, then scooped up a handful of shitty gunk from the bank and smeared it all over her face and hair.

She turned to Jaeger. 'How do I look?'

'Ravishing.'

With that she slithered up the bank like a ghostly serpent and was gone.

52

Jaeger counted out the seconds. He figured seven minutes had passed, and still no sign of Narov. He was expecting her to reappear at any moment. He had his eyes glued to the sentries by the fire, but there was no sign yet of any trouble.

Still, the tension was unbearable.

Suddenly he detected a weird, strangled gurgling noise coming from the direction of the ivory pile. Momentarily he swivelled his eyes across to check. The lone watchman had disappeared from view.

He saw the sentries by the fire stiffen. His heart was beating like a machine gun, as he pinned them in the sights of his SIG.

'Hussein?' one of them cried. 'Hussein!'

They'd clearly heard the noise too. There was no answer from the lone sentry, and Jaeger could make a good guess as to why.

One of the figures at the fireside got to his feet. His words – in Swahili – drifted across to Jaeger. 'I'll go take a look. Probably gone for a piss.' He set off through the bush, moving in the direction of the ivory pile; in the direction of Narov.

Jaeger was about to raise himself over the lip and dash to her aid, when he spotted something. A figure was belly-crawling through the bush towards him. It was Narov all right, but there was something odd about the way she was moving.

As she got closer, he realised what it was: she was dragging a tusk behind her. Laden down like that, she was never going to make it. Jaeger broke cover, dashed across in a crouch, grabbed the heavy tusk and staggered back the way he'd come.

He lowered himself into the water, sliding the tusk in beside him. Narov joined him. He could barely believe they'd not been seen.

Without a word, the two of them began to move silently away. No words needed to be spoken. Had Narov not accomplished her mission, she'd have told him. But what the hell had she brought one of the tusks for?

Suddenly, gunshots split the night. *PCHTHEW! PCHTHEW! PCHTHEW!*

Jaeger and Narov froze. That was three rounds from an AK, and they'd been fired from the direction of the tusk pile. No doubt Narov's handiwork had been discovered.

'Warning shots,' Jaeger mouthed. 'Sounding the alarm.'

There was a series of irate yells, as figures woke all across the camp. Jaeger and Narov sank lower into the water, faces pressed tight into the mud. All they could do was keep utterly still and try to work out what was happening by hearing alone.

Voices cried out and boots pounded across the terrain. Weapons could be heard being made ready. The poachers yelled and screamed confusedly. Jaeger sensed a figure appear on the bank just a few metres away from where they were hiding.

Momentarily, the gunman's eyes scanned the water, and Jaeger felt his gaze sweep across them. He braced himself for a cry of alarm; for gunfire; for the bite of bullets slicing into flesh and bone.

Then a voice – a commanding voice – yelled out: 'No one's in that shit pit, you idiot! Get searching – out there!'

The figure turned and dashed towards the open bush. Jaeger sensed the focus of the search melting away, as the poachers spread out to comb the surrounding terrain. It was sticking to this fetid, disease-ridden stretch of water that had saved them.

They moved off at a slow crawl, until finally they reached the point from which they'd started. Having checked that it was clear of poachers, they pulled themselves on to dry land, retrieving their backpacks from where they'd stashed them.

For a brief moment Narov paused. She pulled out her knife and proceeded to rinse its blade in the water.

'One of them had to die. I took that,' she gestured at the tusk, 'as cover. To make it look like theft.'

Jaeger nodded. 'Smart thinking.'

They could hear the odd yell, and an occasional burst of gunfire, echoing out of the darkness. The search seemed to have moved east and south, away from the waterhole. The poachers were clearly spooked, and chasing after ghosts and shadows.

Jaeger and Narov left the lone tusk hidden in the shallows and set off through the bush. They had a long trek ahead of them, and the dehydration was really starting to bite now. But there was one priority even more pressing than water.

When he figured they'd gone far enough to be safe from detection, Jaeger called a halt. 'I need a pee. Plus we should check for leeches.'

Narov nodded.

It was not the place to stand on ceremony. Jaeger turned away from her and dropped his trousers. Sure enough, his groin was a dark mass of writhing bodies.

He had always hated bloody leeches. Literally. Even more than bats, they were his least favourite animal. After a good hour feasting on his blood, each of the fat black bodies was engorged to several times its normal length. He prised them off one by one and flicked them away, each leaving a stream of blood oozing down his leg.

Groin done, he pulled off his shirt and did a repeat performance with neck and torso. The leeches injected an anticoagulant that kept the blood running for a while: by the time he was done, his body was a bloodied mess.

Narov turned away from him and dropped her own pants.

'Need a hand?' Jaeger asked jokingly.

She snorted. 'In your dreams. I'm surrounded by leeches, you included.'

He shrugged. 'Fine. Bleed away.'

Once the de-leeching was done, they each took a moment to clean their gun. It was crucial to do so, for mud and moisture would have got into the working parts. Then they set out due east, moving at a fast walk.

They had no water or food remaining, but there should be plenty in the ruins of the helicopter.

That was if they ever made it back there.

53

Jaeger and Narov passed the hip flask back and forth between them. It had been a bonus finding that amongst the wreckage of the HIP. Though Narov rarely drank, they were both exhausted, and in need of the whisky for the psychological boost.

They'd made it back by close to midnight, to discover the place utterly deserted. Even the baby elephant was gone, which was good news. At least hopefully they'd saved one animal. They'd emptied the HIP of water, sodas and food, sating both their thirst and their hunger.

That done, Jaeger had made some calls on his Thuraya. The first was to Katavi, and he had been elated to speak to Konig. The reserve's chief conservationist was made of strong stuff, that much was clear. He'd regained consciousness and was back on the case.

Jaeger had explained the basics of what he and Narov were up to. He'd asked for a flight to come in and pick them up, and Konig had promised to be airborne by first light. Jaeger had also warned him to expect a delivery of cargo on the next flight in, and told him not to open the crates when they arrived.

His second call had been to Raff, at Falkenhagen, giving him a shopping list of hardware and weaponry. Raff had promised to get it shipped out to Katavi within twenty-four hours, courtesy of a British diplomatic bag. Finally Jaeger had briefed Raff on the tracking device that he needed them to keep eyes on. The moment it went static Jaeger and Narov needed to know, for that would mean the poachers had reached home base.

Calls done, they'd sat back against an acacia tree and broken out the hip flask. For a good hour they'd sat together sharing the drink and making plans. It was well past midnight by the time Jaeger realised the flask was nearly empty.

He shook it, the last of the whisky sloshing about inside. 'Last sippers, my Russian comrade? So, what do we talk about now?'

'Why the need to talk? Listen to the bush. It is like a symphony. Plus there is the magic of the sky.'

She leant back and Jaeger followed suit. The rhythmic *preep-preep-preep* of the night-time insects beat out a hypnotic rhythm, the stunning expanse of the heavens stretching wide and silken above them.

'Still, it's a rare opportunity,' Jaeger ventured. 'Just the two of us; no one else for miles around.'

'So what do you want to talk about?' Narov murmured.

'You know what? I think we should talk about you.' Jaeger had a thousand questions he'd never got to ask of Narov, and now was as good a time as any.

Narov shrugged. 'It is not so interesting. What is there to say?'

'You can start by telling me how you knew my grandfather. I mean, if he was like a grandfather to you, what does that make us – some kind of long-lost siblings or something?'

Narov laughed. 'Hardly. It is a long story. I will try to keep it short.' Her face grew serious. 'In the summer of 1944, Sonia Olschanevsky, a young Russian woman, was taken prisoner in France. She had been fighting with the partisans and serving as their radio link to London.

'The Germans took her to a concentration camp, one that you already know of: Natzweiler. It was the camp for the *Nacht und Nebel* prisoners – those that Hitler decreed would disappear into the night and the fog. If the Germans had realised that Sonia Olschanevsky was an SOE agent, they would have tortured and executed her, as they did all captured agents. Fortunately, they did not.

'They set her to work at the camp. Slave labour. A senior-ranking SS officer was visiting. Sonia was a beautiful woman. He chose her as his bedfellow.' Narov paused. 'Over time, she found a means to escape. She managed to wrestle some wooden slats off a pigpen and built herself an escape ladder.

'Using that ladder, she and two fellow escapees clambered over the electrified wire. Sonia made it to the American lines. There she met a pair of British officers embedded with US forces – fellow SOE agents. She told them about Natzweiler, and when the Allied forces broke through, she led them to the camp.

'Natzweiler was the first concentration camp found by the Allies. No one had ever imagined such horrors could exist. The effect of liberating it was incalculable for those two British officers.' Narov's face darkened. 'But by then Sonia was four months pregnant. She was carrying the child of the SS officer who had raped her.'

Narov paused, her eyes searching the skies above. 'Sonia was my grandmother. Your grandfather – Grandpa Ted – was one of those two officers. He was so affected by what he had witnessed, and by Sonia's fortitude, that he offered to be the godfather to the unborn child. That child was my mother. And that's how I came to know your grandfather.

'I am the grandchild of Nazi rape,' Narov announced, quietly. 'So you will understand why for me this is personal. Your grandfather saw something in me from an early age. He honed me – he shaped me – to take up his mantle.' She turned to Jaeger. 'He schooled me to be the foremost operative of the Secret Hunters.'

They sat in silence for what seemed like an age. Jaeger had so many questions, he didn't know where to start. How well had she known Grandpa Ted? Had she ever visited him at the Jaeger family home? Had she trained with him? And why had this been kept a secret from the rest of the family, Jaeger included?

Jaeger had been close to his grandfather. He'd admired him, and he'd been inspired by his example to join the military. He felt hurt, somehow, that he'd never once breathed the slightest word.

Eventually the cold got the better of them. Narov moved in closer to Jaeger. 'Pure survival, that's all,' she murmured.

Jaeger nodded. 'We're grown-ups. What's the worst that can happen?'

He was drifting off to sleep when he sensed her head drop on to his shoulder, and her arms snake around his torso as she snuggled in tight.

'I'm still cold,' she murmured sleepily.

He could smell the whisky on her breath. But he could also smell the warm, sweaty, spicy tang of her body so close to his, and he felt his head spinning.

'It's Africa. It's not that cold,' he muttered, as he slipped an arm around her. 'Better now?'

'A little.' Narov held on to him. 'But remember, I am made of ice.'

Jaeger suppressed a laugh. It was so tempting just to go with it; to go with the easy, intimate, intoxicating flow.

A part of him felt tense and jumpy: he had Ruth and Luke to somehow find and rescue. But another part of him – the slightly inebriated part – remembered for a moment what it was like to feel the caress of a woman. And deep within himself he longed to return it.

After all, this wasn't just any woman he was holding right now. Narov had a startling beauty. And under the moonlight, she looked utterly arresting.

'You know, Mr Bert Groves, if you play an act for long enough, sometimes you start to believe it's for real,' she murmured. 'Especially when you have spent so long living close to the thing you really want, but you know you cannot have it.'

'We can't do this,' Jaeger forced himself to say. 'Ruth and Luke are out there, somewhere beneath that mountain.

230

They're alive, of that I'm certain. It can't be long now.'

Narov snorted. 'So, better to die of the cold? *Schwachkopf.*'

But despite her signature curse, she didn't relinquish her grip, and neither did he.

54

The last twenty-four hours had been an absolute whirlwind. The kit they'd ordered from Raff had arrived as requested, and was now stuffed deep in the rucksacks they carried.

The one thing they'd forgotten to ask for was two black silk balaclavas to hide their features. They'd had to improvise. In keeping with their honeymooning cover, Narov had brought with her some sheer black stockings. Pulled over their heads and with eyeholes slashed in them, they were the next best thing.

Once Raff had warned them that the tracker had gone stationary, Jaeger and Narov knew they had their target. As a bonus, the building the tusks had been taken to turned out to be known to Konig. It was where the Lebanese dealer was thought to have his base, complete with a hand-picked contingent of bodyguards.

Konig had explained how the dealer was the first link in a global smuggling chain. The poachers would sell the tusks to him, and once the deal was done the goods would be smuggled onwards, on a journey that invariably ended in Asia – the prime market for such illegal wares.

Jaeger and Narov had moved out from Katavi using their own transport – a white Land Rover Defender that they'd hired in-country under false names. It had the hire company name – Wild Africa Safaris – emblazoned across its doors, as opposed to the Katavi Lodge's Toyotas, which carried the reserve's distinctive logo.

They had needed someone trusted to remain with their ve-hicle when they went in on foot. There was only one person it made sense to use: Konig. Once acquainted with their plans – and assured that the coming action could never be traced back to Katavi – he was fully on side.

As dusk had fallen, they'd left him with the Land Rover, well hidden in a wadi, and melted into the flat, ghostly light, navi-gating on GPS and compass across dry savannah and scrub. They were equipped with SELEX Personal Role Radios, plus headsets. With a good three miles' range, the SELEX sets would enable them to keep in touch with each other and with Konig.

They'd had no opportunity to test-fire the main weapons they carried, but their sights were factory-zeroed to 250 yards, which was good enough for tonight.

Jaeger and Narov came to a halt three hundred yards short of the building pinpointed by the tracker. They spent twenty min-utes lying prone on a ridge of higher ground, silently observing the place. Beneath Jaeger's belly, the soil still held the warmth from the day.

The sun was well down, but the windows of the building before them were lit up like the proverbial Christmas tree. So much for security. The poachers and the smugglers clearly didn't believe there was any real and present danger; any threat. They figured they were above the law. Tonight they were going to learn otherwise.

For this mission, Jaeger and Narov were one hundred per cent rogue; a law unto themselves.

Jaeger scanned the building, counting six visible guards armed with assault rifles. They were sitting out front, clustered around a card table, their weapons either leant against the wall or thrown casually across their backs on slings.

Their faces were illuminated in the warm glow of a storm lantern.

More than enough light to kill by.

On one corner of the building's flat roof Jaeger spotted what he figured was a light machine gun, covered with blankets to hide it from curious onlookers. Well, if everything went to plan, the enemy would all be stone-cold dead before they ever got near that weapon.

He picked up his lightweight thermal imaging scope and gave the building the once over, making a mental note of where there were people. They showed up as bright yellow blobs – the heat thrown off by their bodies making each appear like a burning man on the scope's dark screen.

Music drifted across to him.

There was a ghetto blaster set to one side of the card table. It was playing some kind of distorted, wailing Arab-pop beat, reminding him that most of those here would be the Lebanese dealer's men. And by rights they should be half-decent operators.

'I make it twelve,' Jaeger whispered into his headset. It was set to open mic, so there was no need to push any awkward buttons.

'Twelve humans,' Narov confirmed. 'Plus six goats, some chickens and two dogs.'

Good point. He'd need to take care – those animals might be domesticated, but they would still sense an unfamiliar human presence and might raise the alarm.

'You good to deal with the six out front?' he asked.

'I'm good.'

'Right, once I'm in position, hit them on my word. Radio me a warning when you're good to follow me in.'

'Got it.'

Jaeger delved into his backpack and removed a slender black attaché case. He flicked it open to reveal the constituent parts of a compact VSS Vintorez 'Thread Cutter' sniper rifle. Beside him, Narov had already started to assemble her own identical weapon.

They'd chosen the Russian-made VSS because it was

ultra-lightweight, allowing them to move fast and silently. Its accurate range was five hundred metres, so less than half that of many sniper rifles, but it weighed in at only 2.6 kilograms. It also fired a twenty-round magazine, whereas most sniper rifles were bolt action, each round having to be chambered separately.

With the Thread Cutter you could hit repeated targets in quick succession.

Equally as important, it was designed specifically as a silenced weapon; it could not be fired without its wrap-around suppressor. Like the P228, it fired heavy, subsonic 9mm rounds. It was pointless using a silenced sniper rifle if each time it unleashed a bullet it made a deafening crack as the round went through the sound barrier.

The 9mm slugs were tipped with tungsten points to enable them to pierce light armour, or walls for that matter. Due to their low muzzle velocity, they lost energy more slowly, hence the remarkable range and power of the weapon for its weight and size.

Jaeger left Narov and circled around to the east, moving in a fast but low crouch. He made sure to stay downwind of the building, so the animals wouldn't detect his scent on the breeze and get spooked. He kept a good distance from any possible security lighting, which would be triggered by movement, and stuck to the low ground and cover.

Jaeger came to a halt sixty yards short. He studied the target through his thermal imaging scope, making a mental note of where those inside were now situated. That done, he settled himself into position lying prone on the dirt, the tubular stock of the VSS nestling in the crook of his shoulder, its thick silenced barrel supported on one elbow.

Not many weapons could rival the VSS as a silent night killer. Yet a sniper rifle was only ever as good as its operator. There were few better than Jaeger, especially when he was on a covert mission and hunting in the dark.

And tonight he was about to get busy.

55

A light westerly breeze blew off the Mbizi mountains.
The weapon's sight enabled Jaeger to compensate for bullet drop and wind speed. He estimated the breeze to be around five knots, so adjusted his aim to fire one mark to the left of the target.

Up on the ridgeline, Narov would have notched her sight two marks left and one chevron higher, to allow for the fact that the weapon was being used at approaching the limit of its range.

Jaeger slowed his breathing and talked himself into the calm and absolute focus that a sniper needed. He was under no illusions as to the challenges now before them. He and Narov had to hit multiple targets in quick succession. A wounded man could blow the element of surprise.

Plus there was one man – the Lebanese Mr Big – that Jaeger wanted to take very much alive.

The VSS made no visible muzzle flash, so the rounds would come tearing out of the darkness with little chance for the enemy to return fire. But one cry of alarm and the assault would be blown.

'Okay, I'm scanning the building,' Jaeger whispered. 'I count seven seated outside now; six in the interior. That's thirteen. Thirteen targets.'

'Got it. I will take the seven.'

Narov's reply had about it the ice-cold calm of a total professional. If there was one shooter in the world that Jaeger rated more highly than himself, it was possibly Narov. In the Amazon, her chosen weapon had been the sniper rifle, and she'd left Jaeger in little doubt as to why.

'Targets outside seated around table, head and shoulders mostly visible,' Jaeger whispered. 'You'll need to go for head shots. You good with that?'

'Dead is still dead.'

'If you hadn't noticed, those outside are smoking,' Jaeger added.

The glowing butts showed up like fiery pinpricks each time one of the figures inhaled. It illuminated their faces nicely, making for easier targets.

'Someone should tell them – smoking kills,' Narov breathed.

Jaeger spent a last few seconds rehearsing the moves he'd make to hit those inside the building. From his direction he figured three of the six could be taken out via shots through the walls.

He studied those three figures: he guessed they were watching TV. He could make out their forms resting on some kind of seating arranged around the glowing rectangle of what had to be a flat-screen TV.

He wondered what was playing: football; a war movie?

Either way, for them the show was almost over.

He decided to go for head shots. Body shots were easier – there was a bigger target to aim for – but they were less immediately lethal. Jaeger had the principles of sniping ingrained in his brain. The crucial thing was that each shot had to be released and followed through with no disturbance to the aim.

He used to tell Luke the same thing as a joke, when having a wee.

Jaeger smiled grimly. He breathed in deeply and let out a long, level breath. 'Engaging now.'

There was a faint *fuzzt!* Without pausing, he swung the weapon a fraction right, fired again, swung back left and squeezed off a third shot.

The entire move had taken barely two seconds.

He had seen each of the figures twitch and jerk as the rounds struck, before slumping into a formless heap. For a second or so he didn't move his eye from the scope. He just kept watching, silently, like a cat sizing up its prey.

There had been a barely audible *tzzsing* as the last bullet had cut through the wall. The sparks from the tungsten-tipped round had lit up the centre of Jaeger's sight a burning white. He figured there had to be some metal – maybe piping or electrics – running through the walls.

The seconds ticked by with no movement from those he'd hit, or any sign that the noise had been heard. The Arab beat pumping out from the boombox had very likely deadened any sound.

Narov's voice broke the silence. 'Seven down. Moving from ridge to front of building.'

'Got it. Moving now.'

In one smooth action Jaeger rose to his feet, his weapon in the shoulder, and began to race across the dark terrain. He had done this countless times before – moving swift and silent on a seek-and-destroy mission. In many ways it was where he felt most at home.

Alone.

In the darkness.

Hunting down his prey.

He rounded the front of the building and vaulted over Narov's handiwork, kicking aside a chair that barred his route to the entranceway. The boombox still blared out its beat, but none of the seven gunmen were in any shape to do any listening.

As Jaeger went to crash through into the interior, the door swung inwards and a figure was framed in the light that spilled outside. Someone had seemingly heard something suspicious and had come to investigate. The guy was swarthy-looking, powerful and thickset. He had an AK47 held in front of him, but in a relaxed kind of a grip.

Jaeger fired on the run. *Fuzzt! Fuzzt! Fuzzt!* In rapid succession three 9mm rounds left the Thread Cutter's barrel, nailing the figure in the chest.

He leapt over the fallen form, hissing an update at Narov. 'I'm in!'

Two voices were making simultaneous counts in Jaeger's head now. One had reached six: he was six bullets down from a twenty-round magazine. It was crucial to keep a count, or else the mag might run dry and he would get the fateful 'dead man's click' – when you pulled the trigger and nothing happened.

The other voice was making the body count: *eleven down*.

He stepped into the dimly lit corridor. Off-white walls, smeared here and there with dirt and unidentifiable scuffmarks. In his mind's eye Jaeger could see heavy elephant tusks being dragged down this hallway, dried blood and gore smeared along the walls. Hundreds and hundreds of them, like a conveyor belt of mindless death and murder.

The ghosts of so much bloody slaughter seemed to haunt the very shadows.

Jaeger slowed, moving on the balls of his feet with the grace of a ballet dancer but none of their benign intent. Through an open door to his right he heard a fridge door close. The clink of bottles.

A voice called out in what had to be Lebanese Arabic. The only word that Jaeger recognised was the name: Georges.

Konig had given them the name of the Lebanese ivory dealer. It was Georges Hanna. Jaeger figured one of his men was fetching the boss a chilled beer.

A figure stepped through the doorway, beer bottles clutched in his hands. There was barely time for him to register Jaeger's presence, or for the surprise and terror to flash through his eyes, before the VSS spat again.

Two rounds tore into his left shoulder just above the heart, spinning him around and slamming him into the wall. The bottles fell, the noise of their breaking echoing down the hallway.

A voice called out from a room up ahead. The words sounded

mocking. They were followed by laughter. There was still no sign of any evident alarm. The caller had to figure that the guy was drunk and had dropped the bottles accidentally.

A red smear slithered down the wall, tracing the dead man's trajectory to the floor. He had collapsed slowly, folding in on himself with a hollow, wet *whump*.

Twelve, the voice in Jaeger's head breathed. By rights, that should leave only one now – the Lebanese Mr Big. Konig had shown them a photo of the guy and it was seared into Jaeger's mind.

'Moving in to take Beirut,' he whispered.

They'd kept the language for the assault simple-stupid. Their only codeword was for their target, and for that they'd chosen the name of the Lebanese capital city.

'Thirty seconds out,' Narov replied, her breath coming in heaving gasps as she sprinted for the entranceway.

For an instant Jaeger was tempted to wait for her. Two brains – two gun barrels – were always better than one. But every second was precious now. Their objective was to wipe out this gang and terminate their operation.

The key thing now was to cut the head off the snake.

56

Jaeger paused for a second, slipping the part-used mag off the sniper rifle and clicking a fresh one into place – just in case.

As he moved forward, he heard the muffled sound of a TV blaring out from his right front. He caught the odd word of commentary in English. Football. A Premier League match. Had to be. In that room would be the three he had shot through the wall. He made a mental note to get Narov to check that they were all dead.

He crept towards the half-open doorway ahead of him, stopping a pace back from it. Muted voices came from inside. A conversation. What sounded like haggling, in English. More than just the Lebanese Mr Big in there, that was for sure. He raised his right leg and booted the door fully open.

In the adrenalin-fuelled, hyped intensity of combat, time seemed to slow to a prehistoric pace, and a second could last a lifetime.

Jaeger's eyes swept the room, taking in the key aspects in a microsecond.

Four figures, two seated at a table.

One, on his far right, was the Lebanese dealer. His wrist dripped a gold Rolex. His bulging belly oozed a lifetime's overindulgence. He was dressed in a khaki designer safari suit, though Jaeger doubted it had ever seen much of the real bush.

Opposite him was a black guy in a cheap-looking collared

shirt, grey slacks and black business shoes. Jaeger figured he had to be the brains behind the poaching operation.

But standing against the window facing Jaeger was the main threat: two seriously tooled-up, mean-looking individuals. Seasoned poachers – elephant and rhino killers – no doubt.

One had a belt of machine-gun ammo slung around his torso, Rambo style. In his hands he cradled the distinctive form of a PKM – the Russian equivalent of the British general-purpose machine gun. Perfect for cutting down elephants out on the wide-open plains, but not a great choice of weaponry for close-quarters combat.

The second figure held an RPG7 – the archetypal Russian-made rocket launcher. Great for blowing up vehicles, or blasting a helicopter out of the sky. Not good for stopping Will Jaeger in the close confines of a cramped room.

Part of the reason for the lack of space in here was the ivory piled in one corner. Dozens of massive tusks, each ending in a jagged, bloodied rosette where the poachers had hacked them off the animals they had slaughtered.

Fuzzt! Fuzzt!

Jaeger nailed the tooled-up poachers with head shots, right between the eyes. As they fell, he riddled them with six further rounds, three to each torso – the shots driven as much by rage as by any desire to ensure they were dead.

He caught a flash of movement as the big Lebanese went for a gun. *Fuzzt!*

A scream rent the room as Jaeger pumped a bullet into the fat man's gun hand, blowing a jagged hole through his palm. Then he pirouetted and nailed the African in his sights, putting a bullet through his hand too, at close to point-blank range.

That hand had been scrabbling about on the table, trying to gather up and hide a pile of US dollar notes, which were now getting soaked with his blood.

'Have Beirut. Repeat: have Beirut,' Jaeger reported to Narov. 'All hostiles down, but check room second on right with TV. Three hostiles – check dead.'

'Got it. Moving into corridor now.'

'Once you're done, secure building's entryway. In case we missed any or they called for reinforcements.'

Jaeger stared down his gun barrel at two faces wide-eyed with shock and fear. Keeping his trigger finger at the ready and holding the Thread Cutter one-handed, he reached behind him with the other and grabbed his pistol, bringing it forward. He let the Thread Cutter drop on to his front, suspended on its sling, then brought the P228 into the aim. He needed one hand free for what was coming.

He reached into his pocket and pulled out a tiny black rectangular device. It was a Spy Chest Pro Minicam – a tiny, ultra-compact, idiot-proof video recording device. He placed it on the table, making a show of switching it on. Like most Lebanese businessmen, the dealer was sure to speak reasonable English.

Jaeger smiled, but his features remained indecipherable behind the stocking mask. 'Show time, gentlemen. You answer all my questions, you might just get to live. And keep your hands on the table, where I can see them bleed.'

The fat Lebanese shook his head disbelievingly. His eyes were awash with pain, plus the glazed look of distress. But still Jaeger could tell that his spirit of resistance – his arrogant belief in the unassailability of his own position – wasn't completely broken.

'What in the name of God?' He gasped out the question through teeth clenched in pain. His accent was thick, his English broken, but it was still quite intelligible. 'Who in hell are you?'

'Who am I?' Jaeger snarled. 'I'm your worst nightmare. I'm your judge, jury and probably your executioner too. You see, Mr Georges Hanna, I decide if you live or if you die.'

In part Jaeger was playing an act here – one designed to strike utter fear into his adversaries. Yet at the same time he was consumed by a burning fury at what these people had done; at the carnage they had wrought.

'You know my name?' The Lebanese dealer's eyes bulged. 'But are you insane? My men. My guards. You think they will let you leave this place alive?'

'Corpses don't tend to put up much resistance. So start talking, unless you want to join them.'

The dealer's face contorted into a snarl. 'You know something – screw you.'

Jaeger didn't exactly relish what he was about to do now, but he needed to force this bastard to talk, and quickly. He had to break his spirit of resistance, and there was only one way to do so.

He twitched the P228's barrel down and to the right a fraction, and shot the dealer in the kneecap. Blood and shattered bone spattered across the safari suit as the dealer tumbled off his chair.

Jaeger strode around, leant down and smashed the butt of the P228 into the big man's nose. There was a sharp crack of breaking bone, and a stream of blood spurted down the front of his white shirt.

Jaeger dragged him to his feet by his hair, and thrust him back into his chair. Then he drew his Gerber knife and slammed it point down into the guy's remaining good hand, nailing it to the table.

He swivelled his gaze across to the local poacher chief, his eyes blazing murder from behind the distorted veil of the mask.

'You watching?' he hissed. ''Cause you mess around, you'll get some of the same.'

The poacher was frozen with terror. Jaeger could see where he had pissed himself. He figured he had these guys exactly where he wanted them now.

He raised the gun until the dark maw of the barrel was levelled at the dealer's forehead. 'You want to live – start talking.'

Jaeger fired off a series of questions, delving further and further into the details of the ivory-smuggling business. Answers spilled forth: routes out of the country; destinations and buyers overseas; names of the corrupt officials facilitating the smuggling at every level – airports, customs, the police, a handful of government ministers, even. And finally, the all-important bank account details.

When he had milked the Lebanese man for all he could, he reached forward, switched off the SpyChest camera and pocketed it.

Then he turned around and shot Mr Georges Hanna twice between the eyes.

The big Lebanese keeled over, but his hand was still nailed to the table. His weight pulled it with him, overturning it, his body ending up crumpled beneath it and slumped against the heap of plundered ivory.

Jaeger turned. The local poacher leader was suffering from a full-on adrenal freeze now. All energy had drained from his system, and his mind had little control over his body any more. The fear had shut his brain down completely.

Jaeger bent until his face was spitting-distance close. 'You've seen the fate of your buddy there. Like I said – I'm your worst nightmare. And you know what I'm going to do with you? I'm going to let you live. A privilege you never afforded any rhino or elephant.'

He smashed the butt of the pistol across the man's face, twice. An expert at Krav Maga – a self-defence system developed by the Israeli military – Jaeger knew only too well how a blow delivered by your own hands could end up hurting you almost as much as your opponent.

Think teeth embedded in knuckles, or broken toes resulting from kicking a hard, unyielding part of your adversary, like his skull. It was always better to use a weapon, one that shielded your body from the blow. Hence his use now of the pistol butt.

'Listen carefully,' he announced, his voice laced with a sinister quiet. 'I am going to let you live so that you can go give your pals a warning. You tell them from me.' He jerked a thumb in the direction of the Lebanese man's corpse. 'That is what will happen to you – *all of you* – if one more elephant dies.'

Jaeger ordered the man to his feet and marched him down the corridor, to where Narov was standing guard at the entranceway.

He shoved the sorry figure at her. 'This is the guy who has orchestrated the slaughter of several hundred of God's most beautiful creatures.'

Narov turned her cold eyes on him. 'He is the elephant killer? This man?'

Jaeger nodded. 'He is. And we're taking him with us, at least for part of the way.'

Narov drew her knife. 'One breath out of place – the slightest excuse – and I will carve your guts out.'

Jaeger stepped back inside and made for the building's kitchen. There was a stove of sorts: a burner ring attached to a gas bottle. He reached down and turned the gas to the 'on' position. It hissed reassuringly. Then he stepped outside, grabbed the lighted storm lantern and placed it midway along the building's hallway.

As he hurried from the building into the darkness, a thought struck him. He was well aware that their recent actions had been way outside the strict rule of law. He wondered why it didn't bother him. But after witnessing the elephant slaughter, the boundaries between right and wrong had become irrevocably blurred.

He tried to figure out if this was a good thing, or whether it was a reflection of how his moral compass was being led astray. Morality had become a blur in so many ways. Or maybe it was all crystal clear. In a sense he'd never seen with such clarity. If he listened to his heart, buried deep under the pain that was his constant companion, he had few doubts that what he'd done was right.

If you joined forces with the devil and targeted the defenceless – as the poaching gangs had – then you had to expect retribution.

57

J aeger reached forward and powered down the SpyChest camera. He, Narov and Konig were seated in the privacy of Konig's bungalow. They'd just watched Georges Hanna's confession, from bloody beginning to bloody end.

'So there is it,' Jaeger remarked, handing the camera to Konig. 'You've got it all. What you do with it is your decision. But either way, that's one African poaching cartel closed down for good.'

Konig shook his head in astonishment. 'You weren't kidding – you nailed the entire network. That's a game-changer in terms of conservation. Plus it'll help the local communities involved in the wildlife here to thrive.'

Jaeger smiled. 'You opened the door; we just oiled the hinges.'

'Falk, you played a key part,' Narov added. 'And to perfection.'

In a way Konig *had* played a key role. He'd guarded Jaeger and Narov's back, keeping watch over their getaway vehicle. And as they'd driven away from the scene, the gas-filled building had erupted into a ball of flame, incinerating all evidence in its wake.

Konig scooped up the SpyChest gratefully. 'This – it will change everything.' He eyed them for a second. 'But I feel as if there must be some way I can repay you. This – it is not your war. Your battle.'

Now was the time. 'You know, there is one thing,' Jaeger ventured. 'The BV222. The warplane beneath the mountain. We'd like to see inside it.'

248

Konig's face dropped. He shook his head. 'Ah, this . . . this is not possible.' A pause. 'You know, I have just taken a call from the boss. Herr Kammler. From time to time he checks in. I had to report to him your . . . transgression. Straying into his domain beneath the mountain. He wasn't best pleased.'

'Did he ask if you'd arrested us?' Jaeger queried.

'He did. I told him it was impossible. How do I arrest two foreign nationals for doing something that isn't a crime? And especially when they are paying guests of the lodge. It was plainly ridiculous.'

'How did he react?'

Konig shrugged. 'As always. Very angry. Ranted and raved for a while.'

'And then?'

'And then I told him you had hatched a plan to take out the poaching gang; that you were fellow wildlife lovers. True conservationists. At which stage he seemed to relax a little. But he reiterated: the BV222 is off limits to all but himself and . . . one or two others.'

Jaeger fixed Konig with an inquisitorial look. 'Which others, Falk? Who are they?'

Konig averted his eyes. 'Ah . . . just some people. It doesn't matter who.'

'*You* have access to that warplane, don't you, Falk?' Narov queried. 'Of course you do.'

Konig shrugged. 'Okay, yes, I do. Or at least I have had. In the past.'

'So you can fix a brief visit for us?' she pressed. 'Quid pro quo and all that.'

By way of an answer, Falk reached forward and pulled something from his desk. It was an old shoebox. He hesitated for a second, before handing it to Narov.

'Here. Take it. Video tapes. All filmed inside the BV222. Several dozen of them. I expect there is not an inch of that aircraft that has not been covered.' Konig raised one shoulder apologetically. 'You gave me a film to die for. This is the best I can offer in return.' He paused, then glanced at Narov with a tortured look. 'But please – one thing. Do not watch them until you are gone.'

Narov held his gaze. Jaeger could see that there was real compassion in her eyes. 'Fine, Falk. But why?'

'They are . . . somehow personal, as well as being of the seaplane.' He shrugged. 'Don't watch until you leave. That is all I ask.'

Jaeger and Narov nodded their consent. Jaeger didn't doubt Konig's honesty, and he was dying to see what was on those tapes. They'd stop somewhere on the drive out and spin through a few of them.

Either way, they knew now what lay beneath the mountain. They could always return, parachuting in there in force if need be, and fight their way on to that warplane.

But first, sleep. He craved rest. As his body came down from the massive rush – the buzz of the assault – he felt waves of deadening fatigue wash over him.

Tonight, doubtless, he'd sleep like the dead.

58

It was Narov who woke first. In an instant she'd grabbed her
P228 from beneath the cushions. She could hear a desperate
hammering on the door.

It was 3.30 a.m. – not the best of times to have been dragged
out of such a deep and leaden sleep. She stepped across the
room and wrenched the door open, thrusting her gun into the
face of . . . Falk Konig.

Narov brewed coffee as a visibly distressed Konig went about
explaining why he was there. Apparently, when he'd reported
their trespassing into the caves, Kammler had asked to see
some of the video surveillance footage. Konig had thought
nothing of it; he'd emailed over some clips. He'd just received
a call.

'The old man seemed very agitated; overwrought. He wants
you detained for twenty-four hours, minimum. He said that
after what you achieved with the poachers, you were the kind
of people he could use. He said he wants to recruit you. He told
me to use all means necessary to make sure you do not leave. If
necessary, to disable your vehicle.'

Jaeger didn't doubt that Kammler had somehow recognised
him. The blonde makeover seemingly wasn't as foolproof as its
Falkenhagen creators had intended it to be.

'I just don't know what to do. I had to tell you.' Konig hunched
over his knees, as if in severe pain. Jaeger figured it was the tension and nerves twisting up his guts. He lifted his head slightly
and gazed at the two of them. 'I do not think he wants you kept

here for any good reason. I fear he is lying. There was something in his voice . . . Something . . . predatory almost.'

'So, Falk, what do you suggest?' Narov asked.

'You must leave. At times Mr Kammler has been known to have a . . . long reach. Leave. But take one of the Katavi Lodge Toyotas. I will send two of my men in a different direction, driving your Land Rover. That way, we will have a decoy vehicle.'

'Surely those guys will be bait?' Jaeger queried. 'Bait in a trap.'

Falk shrugged. 'Perhaps. But you see, not all of our workers here are what they seem. Almost all of us have been offered bribes by the poaching gangs, and not all have stayed strong. For some the temptation proves too much. The men I will send have sold many of our secrets. They have much innocent blood on their hands. So if something happens, it is . . .'

'Divine retribution?' Narov suggested, finishing the sentence for him.

He smiled weakly. 'Something like that, yes.'

'There is a lot you're not telling us, isn't there, Falk?' Narov probed. 'This Kammler; his warplane beneath the mountain; your fear of him.' She paused. 'You know, it always makes it easier to share a burden. And maybe we can help.'

'Some things can never be altered,' Falk muttered, 'or helped.'

'Okay, but why not start with your fears?' Narov pressed.

Konig glanced around nervously. 'All right. But not here. I will be waiting by your vehicle.' He got up to leave. 'And do not ask for help when you leave. No one to carry your bags. Who we can trust – I do not know. The story I will tell is that you stole away secretly, in the night. Please – make it convincing.'

Fifteen minutes later, Jaeger and Narov were packed. They'd travelled light, and they'd already given Falk all the kit and weaponry they'd used to execute the assault. He was going to drive it out to Lake Tanganyika shortly, where he would dump it, never to be discovered.

They made their way to the lodge's vehicle park. Konig was waiting, a figure at his side. It was Urio, the co-pilot.

'Urio you know,' Konig announced. 'I trust him absolutely. He will drive you south, towards Makongolosi – no one ever leaves that way. Once he's got you on to a flight, he'll return with the vehicle.'

Urio helped them to load their kit into the Toyota's rear, then grabbed Jaeger's arm. 'I owe you. My life. I will get you out of here. Nothing will happen with me at the wheel.'

Jaeger thanked him, and then Konig led him and Narov into the shadows, talking as he did so. His voice was barely above a whisper. They had to lean in close to hear.

'So, there is a side to the business you know nothing about: Katavi Reserve Primates Limited. KRP for short. KRP is a monkey-export business, and it is Mr Kammler's baby. As you've seen, the monkeys are like pests around here and it is almost a blessing whenever they do a round-up.'

'And?' Narov prompted.

'Firstly, the level of secrecy surrounding KRP's business is un-precedented. The round-ups happen here, but the exports go out from some other place – one that I have never seen. I do not even know its name. The local staff are flown there blindfolded. All they see is a dirt airstrip, where they unload the crates of an-imals. I have always wondered: why the need for such secrecy?'

'Have you never asked?' Jaeger probed.

'I have. Kammler just says the trade is highly competitive and he doesn't want his rivals to know where he keeps his monkeys immediately prior to transport. If they did, he claims they could give the animals some kind of sickness. And exporting a batch of sick primates would not be good for business.'

'Where do the exports go?' Jaeger asked.

'America. Europe. Asia. South America . . . All the world's major cities. Anywhere with medical laboratories involved in testing drugs on primates.'

Konig was silent for a second. Even by the faint light, Jaeger could tell how troubled he looked. 'For years I chose to believe him – that it was a legit business. But that was until the case of

. . . the boy. The monkeys are flown to the export house by a chartered aircraft. A Buffalo. Maybe you know it?'

Jaeger nodded. 'Used for getting cargo into and out of difficult places. The US military flies them. Carries about twenty thousand pounds of freight.'

'Exactly. Or in primate terms around a hundred crated monkeys. The Buffalo shuttles the primates from here to the export house. It flies out loaded, and returns empty. But six months back it flew in here with something unexpected. It had a human stowaway.'

Konig's words were coming faster now, almost as if he was desperate to unburden himself now that he had started to talk. 'The stowaway was a kid. A Kenyan boy about twelve years old. A kid out of the Nairobi slums. You know of those slums?'

'A little,' said Jaeger. 'They're big. Several million people, so I heard.'

'One million at least.' Konig paused, darkly. 'I was away from here at the time. On leave. The kid sneaked off the aircraft and hid. By the time my staff found him, he was more dead than alive. But they build them tough in those slums. If you live to the age of twelve, you are a true survivor.

'He didn't know his exact age. Kids tend not to in the slums. There is rarely any reason to celebrate birthdays.' Konig shuddered, almost as if he was sickened by what he was about to say. 'The boy told my staff an unbelievable story. He said he was part of a group of orphans who'd been kidnapped. Nothing so unusual there. Slum children being sold like that – it happens all the time.

'But this kid's story – it was unreal.' Konig ran his hand through his wild blonde hair. 'He claimed they were kidnapped and flown to some mystery location. Several dozen of them. At first things weren't so bad. They were fed and looked after. But then came a day when they were given some kind of injections.

'They were placed in this huge sealed room. People only ever entered in what the kid described as spacesuits. They fed them through these slots in the walls. Half the kids had had the injections, half not. The half who had no injections started to get ill.

'At first they started sneezing and their noses ran.' Konig gave a dry retch. 'But then their eyes turned glazed and red and they took on the look of a zombie; of the living dead.

'But you know the worst thing?' Konig shuddered again. 'Those kids – they died weeping blood.'

59

The big German conservationist fished in his pocket. He thrust something at Narov. 'A memory stick. Photos of the kid. While he stayed with us, my staff took photos.' He glanced from Narov to Jaeger. 'I have no power to do anything. This is way bigger than me.'

'Go on. Keep talking,' Narov reassured him.

'There's not much more to say. All the kids who weren't injected died. All those who were injected – the survivors – were herded outside, into the surrounding jungle. A large hole had been dug. They were gunned down and shovelled into that hole. The kid wasn't hit, but he fell amongst the bodies.'

Konig's voice dropped to a whisper. 'Imagine it – he was buried alive. Somehow he dug his way out again. It was night. He found his way to the airstrip and climbed aboard the Buffalo. The Buffalo flew him here . . . and the rest you know.'

Narov placed a hand on Konig's arm. 'Falk, there has to be more. *Think*. It is very important. Any details, whatever you can remember.'

'There was maybe one thing. The kid said that on the flight in, they headed over the sea. So he figured this all took place on some kind of an island. That was why he knew he had to board the aircraft to have any chance of getting out of there.'

'An island where?' Jaeger probed. 'Think, Falk. Any details – anything.'

'The kid said the flight out from Nairobi took around two hours.'

'A Buffalo's got a cruising speed of three hundred m.p.h.,' Jaeger remarked. 'That means it's got to be within a six-hundred-mile radius of Nairobi, so somewhere on the Indian Ocean.' He paused. 'You have a name? The kid's name?'

'Simon Chucks Bello. Simon is his English first name, Chucks his African. It's Swahili. It means "great deeds of God".'

'Okay, so what happened to this kid? Where is he now?'

Konig shrugged. 'He went back to the slums. He said it was the only place he would feel safe. It was where he had family. By that he meant his slum family.'

'Okay, so how many Simon Chucks Bellos are there in the Nairobi slum?' Jaeger mused. It was as much a question to himself as to Konig. 'Twelve-year-old boy with that name – could we find him?'

Falk shrugged. 'There are probably hundreds. And the people of the slums – they look after their own. It was the Kenyan police who rounded up those kids. Sold them for a few thousand dollars. The rule in the slum is: trust no one, and certainly not those in authority.'

Jaeger glanced at Narov, then back at Konig. 'So, before the two of us do our Cinderella act, is there anything else we need to know?'

Konig shook his head morosely. 'No. I think that is it. It is enough, yes?'

The three of them made their way back towards the vehicle. When they reached it, Narov stepped across and embraced the big German stiffly. It struck Jaeger that he had rarely seen her offer anyone simple physical closeness. A spontaneous hug.

This was a first.

'Thank you, Falk – for everything,' she told him. 'And especially for all that you do here. In my eyes you are . . . a hero.' For an instant their heads collided, as she gave him an awkward farewell kiss.

Jaeger climbed into the Toyota. Urio was behind the wheel with the engine running. Moments later, Narov joined them.

They were about to pull away when she put out a hand to stop them. She gazed at Konig through the open side window.

'You're worried, aren't you, Falk? There's more? Something more?'

Konig hesitated. He was clearly torn. Then something inside him seemed to snap. 'There is something . . . strange. It has been torturing me. This last year. Kammler told me that he had stopped worrying about the wildlife. He said: "Falk, keep alive a thousand elephants. A thousand will be enough."'

He paused. Narov and Jaeger let the silence hang in the air. *Give him time.* The Toyota's diesel engine thumped out a steady beat, as the conservationist mustered his courage to continue.

'When he comes here, he likes to drink. I think he feels safe and secure in the isolation of this place. He is near his warplane in his sanctuary.' Konig shrugged. 'The last time he was here, he said: "There's nothing more to worry about, Falk, my boy. I hold the final solution to all our problems in my hands. The end, and a new beginning."'

'You know, in many ways Mr Kammler is a good man,' Konig continued, a little defensively. 'His love of wildlife is – or was – genuine. He speaks about his worries for the earth. Of extinction. He talks about the crisis of overpopulation. That we are like a plague. That humankind's growth needs to be curtailed. And in a way, of course, he makes a fair point.

'But he also enrages me. He speaks about the people here – the Africans; my staff; *my friends* – as savages. He laments the fact that black people inherited paradise and then decided to slaughter all the animals. But you know who buys the ivory? The rhino horn? You know who drives the slaughter? It is *foreigners*. All of it – smuggled overseas.'

Konig scowled. 'You know, he speaks about the people here as the *Untermenschen*. Until I heard it from him, I did not think anyone still used that word. I thought it had died with the Reich. But when he is drunk, that is what he says. You know of course the meaning of this word?'

'*Untermenschen*. Sub-humans,' Jaeger confirmed.

'Exactly. So I admire him for setting up this place. Here, in Africa. Where things can be so difficult. I admire him for what he says on conservation – that we are ruining the earth with blind ignorance and greed. But I also loathe him for his horrific – his *Nazi* – views.'

'You need to get out of here,' Jaeger remarked quietly. 'You need to find a place where you can do what you do, but working with good people. This place – *Kammler* – it'll consume you. Chew you up and spit you out again.'

Konig nodded. 'You are probably right. But I love it here. Is there any place like this in the world?'

'There isn't,' Jaeger confirmed. 'But still you need to go.'

'Falk, there is an evil here in paradise,' Narov added. 'And that evil emanates from Kammler.'

Konig shrugged. 'Perhaps. But this is where I have invested my life and my heart.'

Narov eyed him for a long second. 'Falk, why does Kammler feel he can trust you with so much?'

Konig shrugged. 'I am a fellow German and a fellow lover of wildlife. I run this place – his sanctuary. I fight the battles . . . I fight his battles.' His voice faltered. It was clear that he was reaching the absolute heart of the matter now. 'But most of all . . . most of all it is because we are family. I am his flesh and blood.'

The tall, lean German glanced up. Hollow-eyed. Tortured. 'Hank Kammler – he is my father.'

60

High above the African plains the General Dynamics MQ9 Reaper drone – the successor to the Predator – was preparing to gather its deadly harvest. From the bulbous head of the UAV – unmanned aerial vehicle – an invisible beam fired earthwards, as the drone began to 'paint' the target with the hot point of its laser.

Some 25,000 feet below, the distinctive form of a white Land Rover – 'Wild Africa Safaris' emblazoned on its doors – ploughed onwards, those inside utterly oblivious to the threat.

Woken in the early hours, they had been sent on an urgent errand. They were to drive to the nearest airport, at Kigoma, some three hundred kilometres north of Katavi, to collect some spares for the replacement HIP helicopter.

Or at least that was what Konig had told them.

The sun had not long risen, and they were just an hour or so out from the airport. They were intent on getting the errand done and dusted as soon as possible, for they planned an unscheduled stop on their return. They had prize information to pass to the local poaching gang, information that would earn them good money.

As the Reaper's laser beam secured 'lock-on' with the Land Rover, so the calipers holding a GBU-12 Paveway laser-guided bomb released their grip. The sleek gunmetal-grey projectile dropped away from the UAV's wing and plummeted earthwards, its homing system locking on to the hot point of the laser reflecting off the Land Rover's upper surface.

The fins on the rear section folded out to better perform their 'bang-bang' guidance function. Adjusting minutely to every move made by the vehicle, they steered the smart bomb in a snaking flight path, constantly correcting its trajectory.

According to Raytheon, the Paveway smart bomb's manu-facturers, the GBU-12 yielded a circular error probable of 3.6 feet. In other words, on average the Paveway struck within less than four feet of the hot point of the laser. As the Land Rover Defender barrelling through the African bush was five feet wide by thirteen long, there should be ample room for error.

Bare seconds after its release, the Paveway cut through the dust cloud thrown up by the vehicle.

By chance, this bomb wasn't quite as smart as the majority of its brother munitions. It ploughed into the African earth three feet wide of the Land Rover, and just off its front nearside wing.

It didn't particularly alter the outcome of the kill mission.

The Paveway detonated in a massive punching explosion, the blast wave driving a storm of jagged shrapnel into the Land Rover and flipping it over and over, as if a giant hand had grabbed it and was pounding it into oblivion.

The vehicle rolled several times, before coming to rest on its side. Already, hungry flames were licking around the twisted re-mains, engulfing those unfortunate enough to have been riding inside.

Some eight thousand miles away in his Washington DC office, Hank Kammler was hunched over a glowing computer screen, watching a live feed of the Reaper strike.

'Goodbye, Mr William Jaeger,' he whispered. 'And good riddance.'

He reached for his keyboard and punched a few buttons, pulling up his encrypted email system. He sent a quick mes-sage, with the video from the Hellfire hit as a low-resolution attachment, then clicked his mouse and fired up IntelCom, a secure and encrypted US military version of Skype. In essence, via IntelCom, Kammler could place untraceable calls to anyone anywhere in the world.

There was the buzzing of IntelCom's distinctive ringtone before a voice answered.

'Steve Jones.'

'The Reaper strike has gone ahead,' Kammler announced. 'I've just emailed you a video clip, with GPS coordinates embedded in the footage. Take a Katavi Lodge vehicle and go check it out. Find whatever remains and ensure it's the right bodies.'

Steve Jones scowled. 'I thought you said you wanted to torture him for as long as possible. This robs you – *us* – of revenge.'

Kammler's expression hardened. 'It does. But he was getting close. Jaeger and his pretty little sidekick had found their way to Katavi. That's more than close enough. So I repeat: I need to know that their remains are within the wreckage of that vehicle. If they've somehow escaped, you're to track them down and finish them.'

'I'm on it,' Jones confirmed.

Kammler killed the link and leaned back in his chair. On one level it was a pity to have put an end to the torture of William Jaeger, but sometimes even he tired of the game. And it was fitting, somehow, that Jaeger had died in Katavi – Hank Kammler's favourite place in all the world.

And for what was coming – his sanctuary.

Steve Jones stared at his mobile, a frown scrunching up his massive, brute features. The twin Otter light aircraft droned onwards across the African savannah, buffeted by pockets of hot, riotous air.

Jones cursed. 'Jaeger dead ... What's the point of bloody being here? Sent to scrape up some roasted body parts ...'

He became aware that someone was watching him. He glanced towards the cockpit. The pilot – some hippy-dippy-looking Kraut called Falk Konig – was staring at him intently. He had clearly been listening in on the phone call.

The veins in Jones's neck began to throb, and under his shirt his muscles bunched aggressively.

'What?' he growled. 'What are you staring at? Just do your job and fly the bloody aircraft.'

61

Jaeger shook his head in amazement. He still couldn't get over it. 'Did you ever see that coming?'

Narov settled back into her seat and closed her eyes. 'See what? There have been any number of surprises over the past few days. And I am tired. We have a long flight ahead of us and I would like to sleep.'

'Falk. Being Kammler's son?'

Narov sighed. 'We should have seen it coming. We clearly did not listen properly to the Falkenhagen briefing. When SS General Hans Kammler was recruited by the Americans, he was forced to change his name to, amongst other things, Horace Konig. His son changed his name back to Kammler to reclaim the family's glorious heritage. General Kammler's grandson clearly didn't feel it was quite so glorious, and decided to revert to Konig; Falk Konig.'

She cast a withering glance at Jaeger. 'As soon as he introduced himself we should have known. So, sleep. It might sharpen you up a little.'

Jaeger grimaced. Back to the old Irina Narov. In a sense he regretted it. He'd rather liked the Katavi version.

They'd chartered a flight in a light aircraft, routed direct from Makongolosi's tiny provincial airport direct to Nairobi. On touchdown, they planned to track down Simon Chucks Bello, which would mean heading into the chaotic and lawless world of the Nairobi slums.

Narov tossed and turned under her airline blanket. The small plane was being buffeted by the turbulence, and sleep just wouldn't come. She flicked on her reading light and pressed the call button. The hostess appeared. They were the only passengers, this being a private charter.

'Do you have coffee?'

The hostess smiled. 'Of course. How do you take it?'

'Hot. Black. Strong. No sugar.' Narov glanced at Jaeger, who was trying to sleep. 'Bring two cups.'

'Of course, madam. Right away.'

Narov nudged Jaeger. 'You, I think, are not asleep.'

Jaeger grumbled. 'Not now I'm not. I thought you said you wanted to rest.'

Narov frowned. 'I have too much going on in my head. I have ordered some—'

'Coffee.' Jaeger completed the sentence for her. 'I heard.'

She jabbed him harder. 'So wake up.'

Jaeger gave up trying to rest. 'Okay. Okay.'

'Tell me: Kammler, what is he up to? Let's put the pieces of the puzzle together and see what we have got.'

Jaeger tried to shake the sleep from his head. 'Well, first up we go find the kid and verify his story. Two, we head back to Falkenhagen and get access to their resources and expertise. Everything and everyone we need to take this further is there.'

The coffee arrived. They sat quietly, savouring the brew.

It was Narov who broke the silence. 'So how exactly do we go about finding the boy?'

'You saw Dale's message. He knows people in the slums. He'll meet us there and together we'll find the kid.' Jaeger paused. 'That's if he's still alive, if he's willing to talk, and if he is for real. A lot of ifs.'

'So what is Dale's connection to the slums?'

'A few years back he volunteered to teach slum children camera operating. He teamed up with a guy called Julius Mburu, who grew up in the slums. He was a small-time gangster, but then he saw the light. These days, he runs the Mburu

Foundation, teaching orphans video and photography skills. Dale's got him searching for the kid, using his ghetto network.'

'He is confident we will get to him?'

'Hopeful. Not confident.'

'It's a start.' Narov paused. 'What did you make of Falk's videos?'

'His home movies?' Jaeger shook his head. 'That his daddy is a sick bastard. Imagine holding your son's tenth birthday party in a BV222 buried beneath a mountain. Bunch of old men teaching Falk and his friends Hitler salutes. Kids done up in shorts and lederhosen. All those Nazi flags around the walls. No wonder Falk turned against him.'

'The BV222 – it is Kammler's shrine,' Narov remarked quietly. 'His shrine to the Thousand-Year Reich. Both the one that never was and the one he hopes to usher into existence.'

'Sure looks that way.'

'And what about finding Kammler's island? If the kid is for real, how do we track its location?'

Jaeger took a gulp of coffee. 'Tough one. Within a six-hundred-mile radius of Nairobi there are hundreds of possibilities. Maybe thousands. But my guy Jules Holland is on to it. They'll get him to Falkenhagen and he'll start digging. Trust me, if anyone can track that island, the Ratcatcher can.'

'And if the kid's story is true?' Narov pressed. 'Where does that leave us?'

Jaeger stared into the distance – into the future. Much as he was trying to downplay it, he couldn't keep the worry and tension from his voice.

'If the kid is right, Kammler's got the *Gottvirus* refined and tested. All the kids who weren't inoculated died. That means it's back up to a near one hundred per cent lethality. It *is* the God Virus once more. And as all the inoculated kids survived, it looks as if he's sorted his antidote. All he needs now is a weapon delivery system.'

'That's if he intends to use it.'

'From what Falk told us, the signs are that he will.'

'So how close d'you think he is?'

'Falk said the kid escaped six months ago. So Kammler's had at least that long to work on delivery. He'd need to ensure the virus is infective via airborne means, so that it'll spread as far and fast as possible. If he's cracked that, his vision is nearing completion.'

Narov's face darkened. 'We'd better find that island. And I mean like yesterday.'

62

They'd ordered an in-flight meal and it proved surprisingly good. Pre-packed, frozen and microwaved – but for all that eminently edible. Narov had gone for the seafood selection – a platter of smoked salmon, prawns and scallops, served with an avocado salsa.

Jaeger watched curiously as she proceeded to push the food around her plate, rearranging it with seemingly exacting precision. It wasn't the first time he'd seen her do this segregation act. She didn't seem able to start eating until each type of food had been moved into a place where it couldn't touch – contaminate? – the others.

He nodded at her plate. 'Looks good. But what's with quarantining the smoked salmon from the salsa? You worried they're going to fight?'

'Foods of differing colours should never touch,' Narov replied. 'The worst is red on green. Like salmon on avocado.'

'Okay . . . but why?'

Narov glanced at him. The shared mission – the sheer emotional intensity of the past few days – seemed to have softened her hard edges a little.

'The experts say I am autistic. High-functioning, but autistic nonetheless. Some people term it Asperger's. I am "on the spectrum", they say – my brain is wired differently. Hence red food and green cannot touch.' She glanced at Jaeger's plate. 'But I don't much care for labels, and frankly, the way you shove your food around like a cement mixer makes me want to be sick.

Rare lamb speared on a fork with green beans: I mean, *how can you do that?'*

Jaeger laughed. He loved the way she'd turned it right back on him.

'Luke had a friend – his best buddy, Daniel – who was autistic. The Ratcatcher's son, in fact. Great kid.' He paused guiltily. 'I said "had a friend". I meant "has". Luke *has* a friend. As in present and still very much with us.'

Narov shrugged. 'Using the wrong tense doesn't affect your son's fate. It won't determine whether he lives or dies.'

Were Jaeger not so used to Narov by now, he could have punched her. The comment was typical: lacking in empathy; a bull-in-a-china-shop kind of remark.

'Thanks for the insight,' he shot back, 'not to mention the sympathy.'

Narov shrugged. 'You see, this is what I do not understand. I thought I was telling you something you needed to know. It is logical and I thought it would be helpful. But from your viewpoint – what? I have just been rude?'

'Something like that, yeah.'

'Many autistic people are very good at one thing. Exceptionally gifted. They call it savant. Autistic savant. Often it is maths, or physics, or prodigious feats of memory, or perhaps artistic creativity. But we are often not very good at many other things. Reading how other – so-called normal – people tend to think isn't our strong point.'

'So what's your gift? Beyond tact and diplomacy?'

Narov smiled. 'Hardly. I know I am hard work. I understand that. It is why I can seem so defensive. But remember, to me *you* are very hard work. For example, I do not understand why you were angered by my advice about your son. To me it was the obvious thing to say. It was logical and I was trying to help.'

'Okay, I get it. But still – what's your gift?'

'I excel at one thing. I am truly obsessed by it. It is hunting. Our present mission. At its most basic you could say *killing*. But

I do not see it that way. I see it as ridding the earth of unspeakable evil.'

'Mind if I ask a further question?' Jaeger prompted. 'It's kind of . . . personal.'

'For me, this entire conversation has been very personal. I do not normally speak to people about my . . . gift. You see, that is how I think of it. That I am indeed gifted. Exceptionally so. I have never met another person – a hunter – as gifted as I am.' She paused and eyed Jaeger. 'Until I met you.'

He raised his coffee. 'I'll drink to that. That's us – a brotherhood of hunters.'

'Sisterhood,' Narov corrected him. 'So, the question?'

'Why do you speak so oddly? I mean, your voice has a kind of odd, flat, robotic ring to it. Almost like it's devoid of feeling.'

'Have you ever heard of echolalia? No? Most people haven't. Imagine when you are a child, you hear words spoken but *all* you hear is the words. You do not hear the stresses, the rhythm, the poetry or the emotion of the language – because *you can't*. You do not understand any of the emotional inflexions, because that is not how your brain is wired. That is how I am. It was via echolalia – mimicking but not understanding – that I learned to talk.

'Growing up, no one understood me. My parents used to sit me in front of the TV. I heard the Queen's English spoken, plus American English, and my mother also used to play Russian movies for me. I didn't differentiate between the accents. I didn't understand not to mimic – to echo – those on screen. Hence my accent is a mishmash of many ways of speaking, and typical of none.'

Jaeger speared another succulent chunk of lamb, resisting the temptation to do the unthinkable and add some green beans. 'So what about the Spetsnaz? You said you served with the Russian special forces?'

'My grandmother, Sonia Olschanevsky, moved to Britain after the war. That was where I was raised, but our family never forgot that Russia was the mother country. When the Soviet Union collapsed my mother took us back there . I got most of my schooling there and went on to join the Russian military. What else was I to do? But I never felt at home, not even in the Spetsnaz. Too many stupid, mindless rules. I only ever truly felt at home in one place: the ranks of the Secret Hunters.'

'I'll drink to that,' Jaeger announced. 'The Secret Hunters – may our work one day be complete.'

It wasn't long before the food lulled both of them to sleep. Jaeger awoke at some stage to find Narov snuggled close. She had her arm linked through his, her head on his shoulder. He could smell her hair. He could feel the soft touch of her breath upon his skin.

He realised that he didn't particularly want to move her. He was growing used to this closeness between them. He felt that stab of guilt again.

They'd gone to Katavi posing as a honeymooning couple; they were leaving looking like one.

63

The battered-looking Boeing 747 taxied into the cargo terminal at London's Heathrow airport. It was remarkable only in that it lacked the usual row of porthole like windows running down the sides.

That was because air freight isn't normally alive, so what need would it have for windows?

But today's cargo was something of an exception. It was very much alive, and made up of a bunch of very angry and stressed-out animals.

They'd been cooped up bereft of any daylight for the whole of the nine-hour flight, and they were not happy. Enraged cries and whoops rang out all down the 747's echoing hold. Small but powerful hands rattled cage doors. Big, intelligent primate eyes – brown pupils ringed with yellow – flickered this way and that, searching for a means to escape.

There was none.

Jim Seaflower, the chief quarantine officer at Heathrow Terminal 4, was making sure of that. He was issuing orders to get this shipment of primates moved across to the big, sprawling quarantine centre that was tucked away to one side of the rain-swept runway. The business of primate quarantine was taken very seriously these days, and for reasons that Seaflower understood well.

In 1989, a shipment of monkeys out of Africa had landed at Washington DC's Dulles airport on a similar flight. Upon arrival, the cages of animals were trucked from the airport to a laboratory – a 'monkey house' as those in the trade called it – in Reston, one of the city's upmarket suburbs.

Back then, quarantine laws were somewhat less stringent. The monkeys started dying in their droves. Laboratory workers fell sick. It turned out that the entire shipment was infected with Ebola.

In the end, the US military's chemical and biological defence specialists had to move in and 'nuke' the entire place, euthanising every single animal. Hundreds and hundreds of diseased monkeys were put to death. The Reston monkey house was rendered into a dead zone. Nothing in there – not the smallest microorganism – was allowed to live. Then it was sealed off and abandoned pretty much for ever.

The only reason the virus hadn't killed thousands – maybe millions – of people was because it wasn't transmitted via aerial means. Had it been more flu-like, 'Reston Ebola', as it became known, would have ripped through the human population like a viral whirlwind.

As luck would have it, the Reston Ebola outbreak was contained. But in the aftershock, far tougher and more stringent quarantine laws were introduced – ones that Jim Seaflower had to ensure were observed at Heathrow airport today.

Personally, he felt that a six-week quarantine period was somewhat draconian, but the risks very likely justified the new laws. And either way, it gave him and his staff decent, reliable, well-paid employment, so who was he to complain?

As he observed the crates of animals being unloaded from the aircraft – each with the words 'Katavi Reserve Primates Limited' stamped across the side – he figured that this was an unusually healthy batch. Normally a few animals died in transit; the stress of the journey saw to that. But none of these little guys had succumbed.

They looked full of beans.

He'd expect nothing less of Katavi Reserve Primates. He'd

overseen dozens of KRP shipments, and he knew the company to be a class act.

He leaned down to look into one of the cages. It was always best to get a sense of a shipment's general health, so you could better manage the quarantine process. If there were any sick primates, they'd need to be isolated, so the others didn't fall ill. The silver-haired, black-faced vervet monkey inside retreated to a far corner. Primates don't tend to enjoy close-up eye contact with humans. They view it as threatening behaviour.

This little guy was a fine specimen, though.

Seaflower turned to another cage. This time, as he peered inside, the occupant charged at the bars, pounding them angrily with his fists and baring his canines. Seaflower smiled. This little guy was certainly full of fight.

He was about to turn away when the animal sneezed, right into his face.

He paused, and gave it the visual once-over, but it seemed to be perfectly healthy otherwise. Probably just a reaction to the cold, damp, moisture-laden London air, he reasoned.

By the time the seven hundred primates had been transferred to their quarantine pens, Jim's working day was done. If fact he'd stayed an extra two hours to oversee the last of the shipment.

He left the airport and drove home, stopping for a beer at his local. It was the usual crowd, as always enjoying a chat with their drinks and their snacks.

Totally unsuspecting.

Jim bought a round of drinks. He wiped the beer foam off his beard with the back of his hand, and shared some packets of crisps and salted peanuts with his mates.

From the pub he drove home to his family. He greeted his wife at the door with a beery hug, and was just in time to kiss his three young children goodnight.

In homes across the London area, Jim's Heathrow staff were doing likewise.

The following day, their kids went to school. Their wives

and girlfriends travelled here and there: shopping, working, visiting friends and relatives. Breathing. Everywhere and always – breathing.

Jim's buddies from the pub went to their places of work, taking tubes, trains and buses to the four corners of this massive, bustling metropolis. Breathing. Everywhere and always – breathing.

All over London – a city of some eight and a half million souls – an evil was spreading.

64

Steve Jones moved surprisingly fast for such a massive beast of a man. Using fists and feet, he delivered a series of machine-gun-swift blows, smashing into his adversary with a fearsome force and leaving little time for recovery, or to fight back.

Sweat poured off his semi-naked torso as he weaved, ducked and whirled, striking again and again, merciless despite the searing heat. Each blow was more violent than the last; each delivered with a ferocity that would shatter bone and shred internal organs.

And with each strike from fist or foot, Jones imagined himself cracking Jaeger's limbs; or better still, beating his oh-so-well-bred face to a bloodied pulp.

He'd chosen a patch of shade in which to train, but even so the midday stupor made such intense physical activity doubly exhausting. He thrilled to the challenge. Pushing himself to the limit – that was what gave him a sense of self; of his own stature. It always had done.

Few were the men who could deliver – or take – such extreme and sustained physical punishment. And as he'd learned in the military – before Jaeger had got him thrown out for good – *train hard, fight easy*.

Finally he called a halt, grabbing the heavy RDX punchbag that he'd strung from a convenient tree and bringing it to a standstill. He hung on to it for a second, catching his breath, before he swung away and headed for his safari bungalow.

Once there, he kicked off his boots and laid his sweaty bulk on the bed. No doubt about it, at Katavi Lodge they knew how to do luxury. Shame about the company: Falk the hippy-dippy shit, and his band of tree-hugging jungle-bunny locals. He flexed his aching muscles. Who the hell was he going to drink with this evening?

He reached across to the side table, grabbed a packet of pills and swallowed several. He hadn't stopped taking the performance-enhancing drugs. Why would he? They gave him an edge. Made him unstoppable. Unbeatable. The military had been wrong. Dead wrong. If the SAS had listened, they could all be taking them now. Via the drugs, they could have made themselves into superheroes.

Just as he had. Or so he believed.

He propped himself on the pillows, punched the keys of his laptop and called up IntelCom, dialling in Hank Kammler's details.

Kammler was quick to answer. 'Tell me.'

'Found it,' Jones announced. 'Never knew a Land Rover could do such a fine impression of a crushed sardine can. Completely burned out. Ruined.'

'Excellent.'

'That's the good news.' Jones ran a massive hand across his close-cropped hair. 'Bad news is, only two bodies inside, and both were deep-fried locals. If Jaeger and his woman were in that vehicle, they escaped. And no one could escape from that.'

'You're certain?'

'Sure as eggs is eggs.'

'That's a yes, is it?' Kammler snapped. Sometimes he found this Englishman's phraseology – not to mention his uncouth manner – insufferable.

'Affirmative. Roger that. It is.'

Kammler would have found the thinly veiled sarcasm infuriating, were it not for the fact that this man was about as good as it got in terms of enforcers. And right now, he had need of him.

'You're on the ground. What do you think happened?'

'Simple. Jaeger and his woman didn't leave in that vehicle. If they had, their body parts would now be scattered across the African bush. And they're not.'

'Have you checked – is one of the Lodge's vehicles missing?'

'One Toyota is gone. Konig says they found it parked up at some provincial airport. One of his guys is bringing it back tomorrow.'

'So Jaeger stole a vehicle and escaped.'

Well done, Einstein, Jones mouthed. He hoped Kammler hadn't caught the gist. He had to be careful. Right now the old man was his sole employer, and he was getting paid big bucks to be here. He didn't want to blow it just yet.

He had his eyes on a little piece of paradise. A lakeside house in Hungary, a country where he figured they had the good sense to hate foreigners – non-whites – almost as much as he did. He was banking on Kammler's little gig earning him enough to achieve that dream.

More to the point, with Jaeger having survived the Reaper strike, there was still every chance that Jones might get to kill him. Plus the woman. He'd love nothing more than to mess her up, right in front of Jaeger's very eyes.

'Okay, so Jaeger lives,' Kammler announced. 'We need to turn this to our advantage. Let's up the psychological warfare. Let's hit him with some images of his family. Let's wind him up and lure him in. And when we've wound him in far enough, we'll finish him.'

'Sounds good,' Jones growled. 'But one thing: leave that last part to me.'

'You keep delivering, Mr Jones, and I may just do that.' Kammler paused. 'Tell me, how would you like to pay a visit to his family? They're being held on an island not so far away from where you are now. We can fly you out there direct. How d'you think your buddy Jaeger would react to a nice picture of you with his wife and child? "Hello from an old friend." That kind of thing.'

Jones smiled evilly. 'Love it. It'll finish him.'

'One thing. I run a monkey export business from that island. I have a high-security laboratory there, for researching some fairly nasty primate diseases. Some places are strictly off limits – the labs for developing cures for those pathogens.'

Jones shrugged. 'I wouldn't give a damn if you were deep-freezing African babies' body parts. Just get me out there.'

'I keep the location of this venture a strict secret,' Kammler added, 'to deter my would-be business rivals. I'd like you to do the same.'

'Got it,' Jones confirmed. 'Just fly me to wherever his family are, and let's get this show on the road.'

65

Over the years, Nairobi had earned the nickname 'Nairobbery', and with good reason. It was a hectic and lawless kind of a place; a place where anything could happen.

Jaeger, Narov and Dale edged into the downtown chaos, honking bumper-to-bumper through streets crammed with cars and battered *matatus* – garishly painted minibus-taxis – plus people heaving cumbersome handcarts. Somehow, in spite of the desperate crush, the riotous mass of humans and machines continued to function.

Just.

Jaeger had spent a good deal of time in this city, for it was a transit point for British military training grounds in desert, mountain and jungle warfare. Yet he'd never once set foot in the teeming Nairobi slums, and for good reason. Any foreigners – *mzungus* – dumb enough to stray into the forbidden city tended to disappear. Down there in the ghetto, a person with a white skin wouldn't stand much of a chance.

The tarmac gave way to a rutted track, the vehicle kicking up a trail of dust. The surroundings had changed utterly now. The concrete and glass office blocks of downtown were no more. Instead, they were driving through a mass of rickety wooden hovels and stalls.

Figures squatted at the dusty roadside selling their wares: a heap of tomatoes, blood red in the fierce sunlight; piles of puce onions; mountains of dried fish, scales shimmering golden brown; an avalanche of worn, dusty shoes – battered and down-at-heel, but all still for sale.

A view opened before Jaeger: a vast shallow valley filled with the choking haze of cooking fires and smouldering heaps of refuse. Wood and plastic shacks rose one on top of the other, scattered in hopeless confusion, narrow alleyways slithering amidst the chaos. Here and there he spotted a bright patchwork of colour – washing hung to dry amidst the rank, toxic smoke. He was instantly fascinated, and somehow also unsettled.

How did people *live* here?

How did they survive amongst such lawless deprivation?

Their vehicle overtook a man running along pulling a handcart, gripping wooden shafts worn smooth by the passage of the years. He was barefoot, and dressed in ragged shorts and T-shirt. Jaeger glanced at his face, which was glistening with sweat. As their eyes met, he sensed the gulf between them.

The carter was one of the teeming hordes of the slum-dwellers, who fed the insatiable hunger of this city. This wasn't Jaeger's world, and he knew it. It was utterly alien territory, and yet somehow it drew him to it like a moth towards a candle flame.

Jaeger's all-time favourite terrain was the jungle. He thrilled to its ancient, wild, primordial otherness. And this place was the ultimate urban jungle. If you could survive here, with its gangs, drugs, shacks and *changa'a* – illegal drinking – dens, you could survive anywhere.

As he gazed out over the sprawling wasteland, sensing the raw ebb and pulse of the place, Jaeger heard the ghetto's signal challenge. In any new and hostile environment, you had to learn from those who knew how to fight and survive there, and he would need to do the same. This was a place of unspoken rules; unwritten hierarchies. The ghetto had its own laws, to protect its own, which was why outsiders steered clear.

Back at their hotel, Dale had briefed them extensively. The more affluent Kenyans were never to be seen in the ghetto. It was a place of shame, to be kept strictly hidden; a place of hopelessness, brutality and despair. Hence how Simon Chucks Bello and his fellow orphans could disappear without trace – sold for a few thousand dollars.

The vehicle drew to a halt at a roadside bar.

'This is it,' Dale announced. 'We're here.'

The ghetto-dwellers stared. They stared at the vehicle, for there were few smart new Land Rover Discoveries in this part of town; in fact, few vehicles at all. They stared at Dale – this moneyed *mzungu* who dared to stray into their territory – and the others who dismounted from the Discovery.

Jaeger felt so alien here; so set apart; more different perhaps than he had ever felt before. And strangely – worryingly – vulnerable. This was one jungle in which he had never been trained to operate, and one terrain in which no camouflage was ever going to be possible.

As he, Narov and Dale moved towards the roadside bar – stepping over a putrid open drain-cum-sewer made of cracked and flaking concrete – he felt as if he had a target pinned to his back.

He passed a woman squatting on a wooden stool at a rickety roadside stall. She had a charcoal-fired stove at her feet, and was deep-frying small fish in a crescent of seething oil. She gazed out at the riot of life, waiting for a customer.

A distinctive figure waited on the sidewalk: squat, broad-chested and with massive shoulders. Jaeger could tell that he was immensely powerful and battle-hardened; a born street fighter. His face was flat and scarred, yet his expression was strangely open; an island of calm amidst the chaos.

He wore a T-shirt with the slogan: *I FOUGHT THE LAW*.

Jaeger recognised the line from his teenage years. Back then, he'd been a big fan of the Clash. Momentarily, the lyrics flashed through his head: *Breaking rocks in the hot sun, I fought the law and the law won* . . .

He had few doubts who this was.

It was Julius Mburu, their passport into the slum.

66

Jaeger's fingers curled around the cool bottle, tight with tension and unease. He ran his eye around the bar, with its battered plastic furniture and greasy, smoke-stained walls. A rough concrete balcony opened on to the noisy, fume-filled street below.

Figures clustered around the tables, gazing at the TV with something approaching rapture. The voice of the commentator boomed out from the tiny screen set above the bar, where racks of bottles sat behind thick metal mesh. It was showing some game from the UK Premier League. Football was massive in Africa – even more so in the slums, where it was close to a religion.

But Jaeger's mind was all on Simon Chucks Bello.

'So, I have found him,' Mburu announced, his voice deep and gravelly. 'It wasn't easy. This kid had gone deep. Real deep.' He eyed Dale. 'And he's scared. After what he's been through, he's not inclined to warm to *mzungus*.'

Dale nodded. 'That's understandable. But tell me, do you believe him?'

'I believe him.' Mburu's gaze flicked from Dale to Jaeger and Narov and back again. 'Despite what you may think, kids here know the difference between right and wrong. They don't lie – not about shit like that, anyway.' His eyes flashed defiantly. 'There's a brotherhood here in the ghetto. It's like nothing you will ever find outside.'

Mburu had clearly had a tough life. Jaeger had sensed it in

the hard, calloused hand that had gripped his in welcome. It showed in the lines of his face and the smoky yellowing around his dark eyes.

Jaeger gestured around the bar. 'So? Can we meet him?'

Mburu gave a faint nod. 'He's here. But there is one condition. What the kid says goes. If he doesn't want to play ball – if he won't come with you guys – he stays.'

'Got it. Agreed.'

Mburu turned and called into the shadows. 'Alex! Frank! Bring him.'

Three figures emerged: two older kids – big, muscled teenage boys – steering a smaller one between them.

'I run a charity – the Mburu Foundation – doing education and development in the slums,' Mburu explained. 'Alex and Frank are two of my guys. And this,' he gestured at the smaller figure, 'is one of the Mburu Foundation's smartest kids. Simon Chucks Bello, as you may have figured.'

Simon Chucks Bello was one striking-looking dude. His dusty, wiry hair stood out at crazed angles, as if he'd just been electrocuted. He was wearing a red T-shirt displaying a print of the Eiffel Tower, with the word *PARIS* emblazoned beneath it. It was several sizes too big and hung off his sparse, bony frame.

A big gap between his two front teeth gave him an even cheekier, more streetwise look than he would have had otherwise. Below his ragged shorts his knees were scuffed and scarred, and his bare feet sported cracked and broken toenails. But somehow it all seemed to add to his indefinable charm.

Yet right now, Simon Bello wasn't exactly smiling.

Jaeger tried to break the ice. He glanced at the TV. 'You a Man U fan? They're taking a beating today.'

The kid eyed him. 'You want to talk football 'cause you think football's the key. I like Man U. You like Man U. So suddenly we're friends. It makes us seem the same.' He paused. 'Mister, why not just tell me what you came for.'

Jaeger held up his hands in mock surrender. The kid sure had attitude. He liked that. 'We were told a story. First off, we just want to know if that story's true.'

Simon Bello rolled his eyes. 'I told this story a thousand times over. Again?'

With Mburu's help, they persuaded the kid to give them a potted version of his tale. It turned out to be exactly as Falk Konig had related it – with one notable exception. The kid talked a lot about 'the boss', as he called him – the *mzungu* who had called the shots on the island, overseeing all the horrors that had unfolded there.

From the description, Jaeger figured it had to be Hank Kammler.

'So Kammler was there,' Narov muttered.

Jaeger nodded. 'Seems like. I guess we shouldn't be surprised that Falk glossed over that detail. It's not exactly what you'd want in a father.'

Jaeger outlined to the kid the deal he was proposing. They wanted to take him away from the slum, just for long enough to ensure that he was safe. They feared that those who had kidnapped him might come again, especially if they learned that he had survived.

The kid's response was to ask for a soda. Jaeger ordered them all some drinks. He could tell by the way the boy fingered his cold bottle of Fanta what a rare treat it was.

'I want your help,' Simon announced, once he'd drained his bottle.

'That's why we're here,' Jaeger told him. 'Once we're out of this place—'

'No, I want your help now,' the boy cut in. He eyed Jaeger. 'You do for me, I do for you. I need your help now.'

'What d'you have in mind?'

'I got a brother. He's sick. I need you to help him. You're a *mzungu*. You can afford it. Like I said: you do for me, I do for you.'

Jaeger glanced at Mburu questioningly. By way of answer, Mburu got to his feet. 'Come. Follow me. I'll show you.'

He led them across the street to a roadside stall. A young boy, maybe nine years old, was seated alone, half-heartedly spooning up lentil stew. He was stick-thin, the hand that held the spoon shaking horribly. A black Mburu Foundation T-shirt hung from his skeletal frame.

From the way Simon Bello talked to the boy and comforted him, Jaeger figured this had to be his brother.

'He's got malaria,' Jaeger remarked. 'Has to be. I'd know that shaking anywhere.'

Mburu related the boy's story. His name was Peter. He'd been sick for several weeks. They'd tried to get him to a doctor, but he couldn't afford the fees. His mother was dead and his father was addicted to *changaa* – the illegal, lethal knockout brew they fermented in the slums.

In short, Peter had no one to look out for him, and Jaeger could tell that he was in desperate need of help. It didn't escape his notice that the boy was about the same age as Luke had been when he had disappeared.

He glanced at Simon Bello. 'Okay. Let's do it. Let's get him to a doctor. Where's the nearest clinic?'

For the first time, the kid cracked a smile. 'I'll show you.'

As they went to leave, Julius Mburu bade them farewell. 'You're safe with Alex and Frank. But come say goodbye before you go.'

Jaeger thanked him, then he, Narov and Dale followed Simon Bello, Peter and the Mburu boys into the maze of narrow, twisting alleyways. As they pushed deeper into the slum the stench of raw sewage assailed them, plus the noise – so many human souls crammed in so close together. It was hugely claustrophobic, and Jaeger felt his senses reeling.

Here and there their progress was barred by a heavy gate made of beaten corrugated iron, nailed to whatever waste wood the ghetto-dwellers could scavenge. They were covered in graffiti.

Simon Bello held one open so that they could pass. Jaeger asked what they were for.

'The gateways?' Simon's face darkened. 'To stop the cops when they do round-ups. Like when they grabbed me.'

67

By Western standards, the Miracle Medical Centre was a dirty, run-down dump of a place. But to the people here, it was clearly about as good as it got. As they queued to see the doctor, Jaeger, Narov and Dale got some very strange looks. A crowd of kids had gathered, peering in and pointing.

Alex went to fetch some roast corncobs. He broke them into fist-sized lengths, offering the first to Jaeger. Once they'd stripped off the juicy maize grains, the kids took turns using the cores to juggle, laughing the whole time. Simon Chucks Bello turned out to be the biggest joker of all. He finished his juggling act with a mad shuffling dance that had everyone in stitches. In fact they were making so much racket that the doctor had to lean out of his window and tell them to keep it down.

No one seemed overly concerned about Peter. It was then that it struck Jaeger that getting sick like this – practically on the brink of death – was normal for these guys. It happened all the time. So you had no money for medical fees? Who did around here? And what were the chances of some white guy pitching up to whisk you off to hospital? Pretty near zero.

Having run some basic tests, the doctor explained that most likely Peter had malaria *and* typhoid. They would have to keep him in for a week, just to ensure that he pulled through. Jaeger knew what the doctor was also driving at. It would be costly.

'How much?' he asked.

'Nine hundred and fifty Kenyan shillings,' the doctor replied.

Jaeger did a quick bit of mental arithmetic. That was less than fifteen American dollars. He handed the doctor a thousand-shilling note, and thanked him for all he had done.

As they left, a young nurse came running after them. Jaeger wondered what was wrong. Maybe they'd decided to add on some extras, as he'd seemed so easy with the fees.

She held out her hand. In it was a fifty-shilling note. She'd come to give him his change.

Jaeger stared at the note in amazement. Mburu had been right. That kind of honesty, in the midst of all of this – it was humbling. He handed the money to Simon Bello.

'Here. Treat yourself and the guys to another soda.' He ruffled the kid's hair. 'So, are we good? Are you okay to hang with us for a while? Or do we need to go seek permission from your father?'

Simon frowned. 'My father?'

'Your and Peter's dad.'

He gave Jaeger a look. 'Duh. Peter – he's not my *brother* brother. He's my ghetto brother. Me – I don't have anyone. I'm an orphan. I thought you knew that. Julius Mburu is the nearest I got to family.'

Jaeger laughed. 'All right. You got me.' The kid was smart, as well as having attitude. 'But are you good to come with us now we've got your *ghetto* brother sorted?'

'Yeah. I guess. As long as Julius is okay with it.'

They made their way back towards the vehicle, Jaeger falling into step with Narov and Dale. 'The kid's testimony – in terms of nailing Kammler, it's key. But where can we take him? Somewhere utterly away from it all where we can hide him?'

Dale shrugged. 'He's got no passport, no papers – not even a birth certificate. He doesn't know how old he is or when he was born. So he's not exactly travelling anywhere far any time soon.'

Jaeger cast his mind back to something Falk Konig had said in passing. He glanced at Narov. 'Remember that place Konig mentioned? Amani. Remote, isolated beach retreat. Totally private.' He turned to Dale. 'Amani Beach Resort, set on the Indian

Ocean way south of Nairobi. You think you can check it out? If it looks right, can you take him there, at least until we get his papers sorted?'

'It's got to be better than here, that's for sure.'

They turned up an alleyway, heading for the dirt road. All of a sudden, Jaeger heard the wail of a siren. He sensed the figures to either side of him stiffen, their eyes going wide with fear. Seconds later, the sharp crack of a pistol shot rang out. One shot, close, and echoing along the twisting alleyway. Feet thundered in all directions – some running away from the trouble, but others – mainly youths – running towards it.

'Cops,' Simon Bello hissed.

He gestured for Jaeger and the others to join him, as he stole ahead and crouched at the far corner.

'You doubt anything I told you; you doubt the cops could do what they did to me: watch.' He jabbed a finger in the direction of the gathering crowd.

Jaeger spotted a Kenyan policeman, pistol in hand. Lying before him was a teenage kid. He'd been shot in the leg and was pleading for his life.

Simon explained what was going down, his voice a tense, tight whisper. He recognised the young guy on the ground. He'd tried to make it as a ghetto gangster, but he'd proved too soft to hack it. He was a layabout, but no big-time villain. As for the cop, he was notorious. The ghetto-dwellers knew him by his nickname: Scalp. It was Scalp who'd led the round-up in which Simon and the other orphans had been captured.

As the seconds ticked by, the ghetto crowd swelled in size, but everyone was fearful of Scalp. He brandished his pistol, screaming at the wounded boy to move. The kid staggered to his feet, swaying on his bloodied leg, his face a mask of pain and terror. Scalp shoved him along the nearby alleyway, towards the top of the hill where the cop cars were waiting, complete with more men with guns.

A spasm of wild rage swept through the crowd. Scalp could

sense the threat pulsing all around him. As the cops well knew, the slum could spark into a paroxysm of violence if pushed to the edge.

Scalp started beating the wounded boy with his pistol and yelling at him to move faster. The ghetto crowd surged closer, and all of a sudden Scalp just seemed to lose it. He raised his pistol and shot the young guy in his good leg. Howling in agony, the boy collapsed to the ground.

Some of the crowd rushed forward now, but Scalp brandished his pistol in their faces.

The wounded boy had both his hands up, begging for his life. Jaeger could hear his pitiful pleas for mercy, but Scalp seemed lost in a crazed bloodlust, drunk with the power of the gun. He opened fire again, shooting the boy in the body. Then he bent forward and placed the muzzle of his pistol against his head.

'He's dead,' Simon Bello announced, through gritted teeth. 'Any second now, he's dead.'

For an instant the ghetto seemed to hold its breath, and then a shot rang out through the press of bodies, echoing around the fury-filled alleyways.

The crowd lost all control now. Figures surged forward, howling with fury. Scalp raised his weapon and began firing in the air, driving them back. At the same time, he yelled into his radio for backup.

Police reinforcements pounded down the alleyway towards the confrontation. Jaeger could sense that the ghetto was about to explode. The last thing they needed right now was to get caught up in all that. Sometimes, as he'd learned, discretion *was* the better part of valour.

They needed to save Simon Bello. That was the priority.

He grabbed the kid and, yelling at the others to follow, took to his heels.

68

The big, powerful Audi barrelled along the Autobahn at breakneck speed. Raff had met them at the airport, and he was clearly in a hurry. In fact, they all were, and as Raff was as fine a driver as any, Jaeger wasn't particularly worried.

'So you found the kid?' Raff asked, without taking his eyes from the dark road.

'We did.'

'Is he for real?'

'The story he told us – no one could have made it up, and certainly not an orphaned kid from the slums.'

'So what did you learn? What did he say?'

'What Konig told us is pretty much the full story. The kid added a few minor details. Nothing significant. So, are we any closer to finding that island? Kammler's island?'

Raff smiled. 'Yeah, we might be.'

'Like how?' Jaeger pushed.

'Wait for the briefing. As soon as we get to Falkenhagen. Wait for that. So where is the kid now? Is he safe?'

'Dale's got him in his hotel. Adjoining rooms. The Serena. Remember it?'

Raff nodded. He and Jaeger had stayed there once or twice, when rotating through Nairobi with the British military. For a hotel in the centre of the city, it was a rare island of peace and tranquillity.

'They can't stay there,' Raff remarked, stating the obvious. 'They'll get noticed.'

'Yeah, so we figured. Dale's taking him to a remote retreat. Amani Beach, several hours south of Nairobi. That's the best we could come up with for now.'

Twenty minutes later, they pulled into the dark and deserted grounds of the Falkenhagen bunker. Oddly, considering the gruesome testing that Jaeger had been subjected to here, it felt somehow good to be back.

He woke Narov. She'd dozed through the journey curled up on the Audi's rear seat. They'd hardly slept at all in the last twenty-four hours. Having extricated themselves and the kid from the knife-edge chaos of the slums, they'd been on a whirlwind journey ever since.

Raff checked his watch. 'Briefing is at 0100 hours. You got twenty minutes. Show you to your rooms.'

Once in his bedroom Jaeger splashed some water on his face. No time for a shower. He'd left his few personal effects in Falkenhagen: his passport, phone and wallet. Since he'd travelled to Katavi under a pseudonym, he'd had to make sure he was one hundred per cent sterile in terms of being Will Jaeger.

But Peter Miles had furnished the room with a MacBook Air laptop, and he was keen to check email. Via ProtonMail – an ultra-secure email service – he knew he could check his messages with little risk of Kammler and his people being able to monitor it.

Before discovering ProtonMail, all their previous communication systems had been hacked. They'd used a draft email account from which messages were never actually sent; all you ever did was log on to the account using a shared password, and read the drafts.

With no messages being sent, it should have been secure.

It wasn't.

Kammler's people had hacked it. They'd used that account to torture Jaeger – first with photos of Leticia Santos in captivity; then with photos of his family.

Jaeger paused. He couldn't resist the urge – the dark

temptation – to check it now. He hoped that Kammler's people would somehow mess up; that they'd email something – some image – from which he could extract a clue as to their whereabouts. Something via which to track them – and his family.

There was one message sitting in the draft folder. As always, it was blank. It simply had a link to a file in Dropbox – an online data storage system. No doubt it would be part of Kammler's ongoing mind warfare.

Jaeger breathed deeply. A darkness descended upon him like a black cloud.

With shaking hands he clicked on the link, and an image began to download. Line by line it filled the screen.

The image showed a dark-haired, emaciated woman kneeling beside the figure of a boy, both dressed in nothing but their underclothes. She had one arm thrown around the child protectively.

The boy was Jaeger's son, Luke. His shoulders were thin and hunched, as if he had the weight of the world piled upon them, and in spite of his mother's protective stance. He was holding a strip of torn bedsheet before him, like a banner.

On it was written: *DADDY – HELP US.*

The image faded out. A blank white screen replaced it, with a message typed in black across it:

> Come find your family.
> *Wir sind die Zukunft.*

Wir sind die Zukunft: we are the future. It was Hank Kammler's calling card.

Jaeger clenched his hands into fists to try to stop them shaking, then slammed them repeatedly into the wall.

He doubted if he could go on. He couldn't do this any more.

Every man had his breaking point.

69

At Kenya's Jomo Kenyatta Airport, a Boeing 747 cargo aircraft was in the process of being loaded. A forklift raised crate after crate marked with the KRP logo and slotted them into the hold.

When fully loaded, this flight would be routed to the east coast of the USA, to Washington's Dulles airport. America imported some 17,000 primates every year, for the purposes of medical testing. Over the years, KRP had grabbed a good chunk of that market.

Another KRP flight was scheduled to fly to Beijing, a third to Sydney, a fourth to Rio de Janeiro . . . Within a matter of forty-eight hours, all those flights should have landed and the evil would be complete.

And in that, Hank Kammler had just received an unexpected boost, although he wasn't to know it.

After the British, Kammler hated the Russians almost as much. It was on the Eastern Front, mired in snowy wastes, that Hitler's mighty *Wehrmacht* – his war machine – had finally ground to a halt. The Russian Red Army had played a pivotal role in its subsequent defeat.

Accordingly, Moscow was Kammler's second key target, after London. A 747 cargo aircraft had recently touched down at the city's Vnukovo airport. Even now, Sergei Kalenko, Vnukovo's quarantine officer, was busy overseeing the transfer of the caged primates to the nearby pens.

But this was Vladimir Putin's Russia, where everything was

somewhat negotiable. Kalenko had directed that a few dozen cages – containing thirty-six vervet monkeys – should be stacked to one side.

Centrium – Russia's largest pharmaceutical testing company – had run out of animals for an ongoing drugs trial. Each day's delay was costing the company some $50,000. Money – bribes – talked in Russia, and accordingly Kalenko wasn't about to object to a few dozen of his charges evading quarantine. He figured the risk was negligible. After all, KRP had never once sent an unhealthy shipment, and he didn't expect them to have done so now.

Quickly the cages were loaded on to the rear of a flatbed truck and sheeted over with a dull green canvas. That done, Kalenko pocketed a large wad of cash and the vehicle sped away into the frost-kissed Moscow night.

He watched the truck's red tail lights disappear before reaching into the voluminous pocket of his overcoat. Like many airport workers, Kalenko took the occasional nip of vodka to ward off the mind-numbing cold. He treated himself to an extra large gulp now, to celebrate his lucky windfall.

The heater in the Centrium truck cab was on the blink. All day, the man at the wheel had been likewise fighting off the icy chill, and mostly via the bottle. As he headed towards Centrium's vast facility, he swung the vehicle into the first of a series of bleak suburbs that lay on the south-eastern fringes of the city.

The truck hit a patch of black ice. The driver's reactions – numbed by the alcohol – were a fraction too slow. It took only an instant, but suddenly the vehicle had skidded off the highway and tumbled down a snowy bank, the canvas ripping open and throwing its load across the ground.

Primates screamed and cackled in fear and rage. The door of the cab had been thrown open at a crazed angle by the impact. The bloodied and dazed form of the driver stumbled out, collapsing in the snow.

The door to the first of the cages was pushed ajar by a terrified hand. Small but powerful fingers tested the strange coat of glistening cold – this alien whiteness. The confused animal sensed freedom – or a freedom of sorts – but could it really walk on this frozen surface?

Up above, vehicles drew to a halt. Faces peered over the incline. Seeing what had happened, some decided to film it on their mobile phones, but one or two actually made the effort to help. As they skidded down the icy bank, the monkeys heard them coming.

It was now or never.

The first broke free from its cage, scattering a cloud of powdery snow in its wake as it made a dash for the nearest shadows. Other cages had likewise burst open, and those animals followed the first monkey's lead.

By the time the dazed driver had managed to do a body count, he was twelve primates down. A dozen vervet monkeys had escaped into the snowbound streets of this Moscow suburb – cold, hungry and frightened. There was no way the driver could raise the alarm. He'd broken strict quarantine laws. He, Kalenko and Centrium would be in the shit if the cops were alerted.

The monkeys would have to fend for themselves.

The truck happened to have deposited the primates on a road running along the Moskva river. Forming themselves into a makeshift troop, they gathered on the riverbank, huddling together for warmth.

An old woman was hurrying along the riverside. She spied the monkeys and, fearing she was seeing things, started to run. As she skidded on the icy surface and tumbled, the fresh bread stuffed in her shopping bag was strewn across the path. The famished monkeys were upon it in a flash. The woman – dazed and confused – tried to beat them off with her gloved hands.

A vervet snarled. The woman didn't heed the warning. It struck with its canines, ripping through her gloves and raking a bloodied track across the upper surface of her hand. The woman screamed, monkey saliva mixed with the thick red blood dripping from her wound.

At a cry from the troop's self-proclaimed leader, the vervets grabbed what bread they could and set off into the busy night – running, climbing and hunting for more food.

A few hundred yards along the river, an after-school club was coming to an end. Moscow kids were learning Sambo, a Soviet-era martial art originally perfected by the KGB but now increasingly popular with the mainstream.

The monkeys were drawn to the noise and the warmth. After a moment's hesitation, the leader took the troop through an open window. A blow heater propelled currents of hot air into the hall, where the youths were busy with their final bouts of the evening.

One of the monkeys sneezed. Tiny droplets were propelled into the atmosphere, and were wafted with the heat into the hall. Sweaty, panting fighters breathed hard, gasping for air.

Across a city of some eleven million unsuspecting souls, the evil was spreading.

70

Peter Miles stood up to speak. Bearing in mind the intense pressure they were all under, he appeared remarkably calm. Right now, Jaeger wasn't feeling that way at all. The challenge was to drive from his mind that terrible image of his wife and child – *DADDY – HELP US* – so that he could focus on what was coming.

At least this time he *had* gleaned something potentially useful from the image; something that might help him track down his family and their captors.

'Welcome, everyone,' Miles began. 'And especially a returning William Jaeger and Irina Narov. There are several new faces in the room. Rest assured, all are trusted members of our network. I will introduce them as we go, and feel free to fire in any questions.'

He spent a few minutes summarising Jaeger and Narov's discoveries, both at the Katavi Reserve and in the Nairobi slums, before reaching the crux of the matter.

'Falk Konig revealed that his father, Hank Kammler, runs a highly secretive primate export business – Katavi Reserve Primates – from an island off the coast of East Africa. The primates are air-freighted around the world for medical research purposes. The level of secrecy surrounding this island operation is unprecedented.

'So, how likely is it that this monkey export facility doubles as Kammler's bio-warfare lab? Highly likely, as it happens. During the war, Kurt Blome – the godfather of the *Gottvirus* – set up his germ warfare testing facility off Germany's Baltic coast, on the island of Riems. Reason being, you can test a pathogen on an island with a reasonable likelihood that it won't escape. In short, an island is the perfect isolated incubator.'

'But we still don't know what Kammler intends to do with the virus,' a voice cut in. It was Hiro Kamishi, as ever the voice of measured reason.

'We don't,' Miles confirmed. 'But with the *Gottvirus* in Kammler's hands, we have the architect of a conspiracy to bring back Hitler's Reich possessing the world's most fearful weapon. That alone is an utterly terrifying scenario, regardless of what exact use he intends to make of it.'

'Do we have any better idea what the *Gottvirus* is?' a voice cut in. It was Joe James. 'Where it came from? How to stop it?'

Miles shook his head. 'Unfortunately not. From all our research, there is no record anywhere of it ever having existed. Officially, the two SS officers who discovered it – Lieutenants Herman Wirth and Otto Rahn – are both recorded as deceased due to "death by misadventure". According to official records, the pair went hiking in the German Alps, got lost and froze to death in the snow. Yet by Blome's own account, those two men were the discoverers of the *Gottvirus*, and finding it killed them. In short, the Nazis had the *Gottvirus* purged from all official records.'

'So, the million-dollar question,' Jaeger ventured. 'Where is Kammler's island? I understand we may have a fix on it?'

'You don't need a great deal of land for this kind of work,' Miles replied, by way of an answer. 'Working on the basis of a landmass the size of Riems, there are approximately a thousand possible candidates off the coast of East Africa – which did make finding it something of a challenge. That is, until . . .'

He cast around his audience until his gaze came to rest upon one distinctive individual. 'At this stage I'll hand over to Jules Holland. He is his own best introduction.'

A dishevelled figure shuffled forwards. Overweight, scruffily dressed and with his greying hair tied back in a straggly pony-tail, he looked somewhat out of place in the former nuclear command bunker of the Soviet Union.

He turned to face the audience and smiled his snaggle-toothed smile. 'Jules Holland, but to all who know me well, the Ratcatcher. The Rat for short. Computer hacker, working for the good guys. Mostly. Quite an effective one too, if I might say so. And usually rather expensive.'

'It's via Will Jaeger's good offices that I'm here.' He gave a slight bow. 'And I must say, I'm very glad to be of service.'

The Rat glanced at Peter Miles. 'This gentleman gave me the gen. Not a lot to go on: find me an island of anything more than postage-stamp size where this Nazi lunatic may have sited his germ warfare laboratory.' He paused. 'I've had easier briefs. Took a bit of lateral thinking. Whether or not it's a germ war-fare lab, the one thing we *do* know is that it's a monkey export facility. And that is what cracked it. The monkeys were the key.'

Holland brushed back his lank hair, wisps of which were fall-ing free. 'The monkeys are captured in and around the Katavi Reserve, and flown from there to the island. Now, every flight leaves a trace. Numerous flights leave numerous traces. So I . . . erm . . . paid an unauthorised visit to the Tanzanian Air Traffic Control computer. It proved most accommodating.

'I found three dozen KRP flights of interest over the past few years, all to the same location.' He paused. 'Around one hundred miles off the coast of Tanzania lies Mafia Island. Yes, "Mafia" as in the Sicilian bad guys. Mafia Island is a popular high-end tour-ist resort. It is part of an island chain; an archipelago. On the far southern end of that chain lies tiny, isolated Little Mafia Island.

'Until two decades or so, Little Mafia was uninhabited. The only visitors were the local fishermen, who stopped there to repair their wooden boats. It is heavily forested – jungle, ob-viously – but it has no natural water source, so no one could afford to stay for long.

'Twenty years ago, it was purchased by a private foreign buyer.

Pretty shortly, even the fishermen stopped visiting. Those who had occupied the island weren't exactly friendly. More to the point, a population of monkeys moved in alongside the humans, and they proved less than welcoming. Many were horribly, terribly diseased. Glazed eyes. Walking-dead killer zombie look. Plus lots and lots of bleeding.'

Holland eyed his audience darkly. 'The locals coined a new name for the place, one that I fear is aptly suited. They call it Plague Island.'

71

'Little Mafia – Plague Island – is Kammler's primate export facility,' Holland explained. 'The air traffic control records alone prove that. What else it may be, and what we do about it . . . well, I guess that's up to you, the action men – and women – in the room, to decide.'

His eyes sought out Jaeger. 'And before you ask, my friend: yes I did leave my usual signature: "Hacked by the Rat". No matter how much more mature one is supposed to get with the passing years, I just can't seem to resist.'

Jaeger smiled. The same old Ratcatcher. A maverick genius whose life had been defined by anarchic rule-breaking.

Holland made his way back to his seat, Peter Miles taking his place. 'Jules makes it sound easy. It was far from that. Thanks to you, we have a fix on the location. Now, consider the nightmare scenario. Somehow Kammler ships his virus off this island and releases it worldwide. He and his cronies are inoculated. They sit out the coming global meltdown somewhere safe. Somewhere underground, no doubt: in fact, probably in a facility similar to this one.

'Meanwhile, the *Gottvirus* gets to work. The nearest equivalent pathogen that we know of is Ebola. The lethal dose of Ebola Zaire is five hundred infectious virus particles. That number could hatch out of one single human cell. In other words, one infected person whose blood has been transformed into a viral soup can infect *billions* of fellow humans.

'A tiny amount of Ebola, if airborne, could nuke an entire

place. Airborne Ebola would be like plutonium. In fact, it would be far more dangerous, because unlike plutonium, it is *alive*. It replicates. It breeds, multiplying exponentially.

'That's the nightmare scenario with Ebola, a virus that we have been able to study for close on three decades. This – it's a total unknown. A hot-zone killer of unimaginable ferocity. It has a total fatality rate. Human beings have zero immunity.'

Miles paused. He could no longer keep the worry from his eyes. 'If the *Gottvirus* gets into the human population, it will wreak utter devastation. The world as we know it will cease to exist. If Kammler manages to unleash it, he can sit it out as the virus works its dark evil, and then emerge – inoculated – to a brave new world. So please forgive the melodrama, ladies and gents, but for the sake of humankind, Kammler and his virus have to be stopped.'

He gestured toward a grey-haired, grizzled-looking man seated amongst his listeners. 'Right – I'm going to hand over now to Daniel Brooks, the director of the CIA. And by way of introduction, I'd just like to mention that our top cover has just got a whole lot more serious.'

'Gentlemen. Ladies,' Brooks began gruffly. 'I'll keep this short. You've done great work. Amazing work. But it still isn't enough to nail Hank Kammler, the deputy director of my agency. For that we need absolute proof, and at the moment that island facility could just conceivably be a bona fide disease control centre for a monkey export business.

Brooks glowered. 'Much as I hate it, I have to tread carefully. Kammler has powerful friends, right up to the level of the American President. I cannot go after him without absolute proof. Get me that proof and you will have every support – every goddam asset – the US military and intelligence community can bring to bear. And in the meantime, there are a few dark assets we can push your way, unofficially I might add.'

Brooks took his seat, and Miles thanked him. 'One final thing. When Jaeger and Narov left the Katavi Reserve, they did so in a Katavi Lodge Toyota 4x4. Their Land Rover was driven out at the same time by two of the lodge staff. Several hours after its departure, it was taken out by a Reaper drone. Hank Kammler ordered the kill mission, no doubt believing Jaeger and Narov were at the wheel. In short, he knows we're after him. The hunt is on – you for him, and him for us.

'Let me remind you: if you use any personal communications devices, he will find you. He has the services of the CIA's most technologically accomplished people at his disposal. If you use insecure email, you're as good as done for. If you return to your home addresses, he will track you there. It's kill or be killed. Use only the comms systems as provided: secure encrypted means. Always.'

Miles eyed each of them in turn. 'Make no mistake, if you speak on open means; if you email on open networks – you're dead.'

72

Five thousand miles across the Atlantic Ocean, the architect of the evil was putting the finishing touches to a momentous message. Kammler's Werewolves – the true sons of the Reich; those who had remained steadfast for over seven decades – were poised to reap their rewards.

Stupendous rewards.

The time was almost upon them.

Hank Kammler ran his eye over the closing paragraphs, polishing them one final time.

Gather your families. Make your way to your places of sanctuary. It has begun. It is unleashed. In six weeks it will start to bite. You have that time, before those who are not with us will start to reap the whirlwind. We who are chosen – we precious few – stand on the brink of a new age. A new dawn.

It will be a new millennium in which the sons of the Reich – the Aryans – grasp our rightful inheritance once and for all.

From here we will rebuild, in the name of the Führer.

We will have destroyed to create anew.

The glory of the Reich will be ours.

Wir sind die Zukunft.

HK

Kammler read it, and it was good.

His finger punched the 'send' button.

He leant back in his leather chair, his eyes drifting to a framed photo on his desk. The middle-aged man in the pinstriped suit bore a striking resemblance to Kammler: they had the same thin, hawkish nose; the same ice-blue eyes brimful of arrogance; the same gaze betraying an easy assumption that power and privilege were theirs as a birthright, and due them long into old age.

It wasn't hard to imagine them as father and son.

'At last,' the seated figure whispered, almost as if speaking to the photo. '*Wir sind die Zukunft.*'

His gaze dwelt upon the framed image a moment longer, but his eyes were looking inwards; menacing pools of thick darkness that sucked in all that was good. All life – all innocence – was drawn into them, suffocating mercilessly.

London, Kammler reflected. London – the seat of the British government; the site of the late Winston Churchill's War Rooms, from where he had orchestrated resistance to Hitler's glorious Reich when all defiance had seemed futile.

The cursed British had held on for just long enough to draw the Americans into the war. Without them, of course, the Third Reich would have triumphed and ruled as the Führer had intended – for a thousand years.

London. It was only right that the darkness had begun there.

Kammler tapped his keyboard and pulled up his IntelCom link. He dialled, and a voice answered.

'So tell me, how are my animals?' Kammler asked. 'Katavi? Our elephants are thriving, despite the greed of the locals?'

'The elephant populations are stronger by the day,' Falk Konig's voice replied. 'Less attrition – especially since our friends Bert and Andrea—'

'Forget them!' Kammler cut in. 'So they snuffed out the Lebanese dealer and his gang. Their motives weren't entirely altruistic, let me assure you.'

'I had been wondering . . .' Falk's voice tailed off. 'But either way, they did a good thing.'

Kammler snorted. 'Nothing compared to what I intend. I mean to kill them all. Every last poacher, every last trader, and every last buyer – all of them.'

'So why not hire Bert and Andrea?' Konig persisted. 'They're good people. Professionals. And especially in Andrea's case, a genuine lover of wildlife. They're ex-military and in need of work. If you want to defeat the poachers, you could use them to run an anti-poaching drive.'

'It won't be necessary,' Kammler snapped. 'You liked them, did you?' His voice was laced with sarcasm now. 'Made some fine new friends?'

'In a way, yes,' Konig replied defiantly. 'Yes, I did.'

Kammler's voice softened, but it was all the more sinister for it. 'Is there something you haven't told me, my boy? I know our opinions can tend to differ, but our key interests remain aligned. Conservation. Wildlife protection. The herds. That is what matters. There's nothing that might threaten Katavi, is there?'

Kammler sensed his son's hesitation. He knew he was afraid of him, or rather of the kind of people – the enforcers – that he at times sent out to Katavi; like the present incumbent, the fearsome shaven-headed Jones.

'You know, if you're holding something back, you really shouldn't,' Kammler wheedled. 'It will be the wildlife that suffers. Your elephants. Your rhino. Our beloved animals. You know that, don't you?'

'It's just . . . I did mention the kid to them.'

'What kid?'

'The slum kid. Turned up here a few months back. It was nothing . . .' Again Konig's voice tailed off into silence.

'If it was nothing, no reason not to share it with me, is there?' Kammler wheedled, a real edge of menace to his tone now.

'It was just a story about some boy who stowed away on one of the flights . . . It didn't make any sense to anyone.'

'A *slum* kid, you say?' Kammler was silent for a long second. 'We need to get to the bottom of this . . . Well, I will be out there with you soon. Within the next forty-eight hours. You can tell me everything then. I have just a few things to deal with here first. In the meantime, a nurse will be flying in. She needs to give you an injection. A follow-up booster for a childhood illness. You were too young to remember much, but trust me, it's worth doing as a precaution.'

'Father, I'm thirty-four,' Konig protested. 'I don't need looking after.'

'She is already on her way,' Kammler replied, with finality. 'I will be flying in shortly thereafter. Returning to my sanctuary. And when I get there, I'll look forward to you telling me all about this boy – this slum kid. We have much to catch up on . . .'

Kammler said goodbye and finished the call.

Falk wasn't exactly the son he would have wished for, but at the same time he wasn't wholly bad. They shared a key passion: conservation. And in Kammler's brave new world, wildlife, the environment – the health of the planet – would once again be ascendant. The dangers facing the world – global warming, overpopulation, extinctions, habitat destruction – would be dealt with in an instant.

Kammler had used computer simulations to predict the death count from the coming pandemic. The world population would experience an almost total eclipse. It would be reduced to a few hundred thousand souls.

The human race was a veritable plague upon the earth.

It would be wiped out by the mother of all plagues.

It was all just so perfect.

Some isolated peoples would doubtless survive. Those on remote, rarely visited islands. Tribes in the deep jungle. And of course, that was as it should be. After all, the Fourth Reich would have need of some natives – *Untermenschen* – to serve as their slaves.

Hopefully, once the pandemic had run its course, Falk would see the light. In any case, he was all that Kammler had. His wife had died during childbirth, and Falk was their first and only child.

Come the rise of the Fourth Reich, Kammler was determined to make him an heir worthy of the cause.

He dialled up another IntelCom ID.

A voice answered. 'Jones.'

'You have a new task,' Kammler announced. 'A story about some kid from the slums did the rounds of Katavi Lodge. I have a particular interest in this. There are two members of staff who will do anything for a few beers. Try Andrew Asoko first; if he knows nothing, speak to Frank Kikeye. Let me know what you find.'

'Got it.'

'One more thing. A nurse will fly in today with an inoculation for Falk Konig, my head conservationist. Make sure he allows her to administer it. I don't care if you have to forcibly restrain him, but he gets his injection. Understood?'

'Got it. An injection. Some story about a kid.' He paused. 'But tell me, when do I get to do something really pleasurable, like hitting Jaeger?'

'The two tasks you've just been given are of key importance,' Kammler snapped. 'Get them done first.'

He killed the call.

He didn't like Jones. But he was an efficient exterminator, which was all that mattered. And by the time he would be ready to claim his first – very handsome – pay cheque, he would be as good as dead, along with the rest of humanity . . . bar the chosen.

But this story about a slum kid was worrisome. A few months back Kammler had received reports that a grave on the island had been disturbed. They'd presumed it was the work of wild animals. But was it just possible that someone had survived, and escaped?

Either way, Jones was sure to get to the bottom of it. Kammler put his worries to one side, and refocused.

The resurrection of the Reich – it was almost upon them.

73

As Jaeger was well aware, if you wanted to get a small force of elite operators on to a distant target ultra-fast and ultra-low-profile, a civilian jet airliner was the way to do it.

A force could be flown across nations and continents on a bog-standard airliner, following a flight path and altitude open to commercial carriers, and posing as a bona fide flight of one of those airlines. Once over the target, they could leap from the aircraft in a high-altitude parachute jump, remaining immune to detection by radar, the airliner continuing on to its destination as if nothing untoward had ever happened.

Taking advantage of CIA director Daniel Brooks' offer of tacit support, Jaeger and his team had been made last-minute additions to the passenger list of BA Flight 987, routed from Berlin's Schonefeld airport to Perth, Australia. Upon arrival at its destination, BA 987 would be six passengers short. They would have exited en route – at 0400 hours local time and somewhere off the coast of East Africa.

An airliner's doors cannot be opened in flight, because of the massive pressure differential between the interior and exterior of the aircraft. The exits are 'plug doors'; they're closed from the inside and kept shut partly by the higher pressure in the cabin. Even if someone did manage to unlock a door during flight, the pressure differential would make it impossible to pull it inwards and open it.

Not so the specially adapted hatch and 'jump cage' of this Boeing airliner.

In a top secret deal with UK Special Forces, one or two supposedly standard BA airliners had been modified to facilitate such
covert high-altitude parachute jumps. In an isolated section of
the fuselage a reinforced steel cabin had been constructed, complete with a man-sized jump hatch. Flight 987 was one of these
specially adapted aircraft, and it was via this means that Jaeger
and his team would be leaping into the thin and screaming blue.

With the team scattered in pairs around the aircraft, Jaeger
and Narov had lucked out. They were flying club class – the
only seats available at a few hours' notice, which was all the
time Brooks had had to muscle them on to the flight. It was
indicative of the quiet cooperation from high-level corporations
that the CIA director enjoyed. When someone of his influence
asked, people tended to accommodate.

The pilot of BA 987 – a former air force fighter jock – would
be opening the jump hatch over a specific set of GPS coordinates. He would make sure to override any warning systems. It
wasn't a dangerous manoeuvre, and the door would only be ajar
for a matter of seconds.

Jaeger and his team would change into their high-altitude
survival and parachutist gear in the aircraft's crew quarters, well
away from the other passengers' view. In the Boeing 747-400's
jump cabin – which could be depressurised independently from
the rest of the aircraft – a row of six bulging rucksacks had been
laid to one side, along with a heap of high-altitude parachutist
kit and weaponry.

After they'd tumbled free of the aircraft, the jump hatch
would swing shut, BA 987 continuing on her way as if no unscheduled unloading of passengers had ever taken place.

The reasons for making such a rapid and ultra-secret insertion
were simple. Time was of the essence, and if Little Mafia Island
was all that it was suspected to be, Kammler's surveillance and
security was bound to be second to none. He'd doubtless have
co-opted some CIA hardware – satellites; UAVs; spy planes
– to keep a permanent watch rotation over the island, not to

mention whatever security systems he had in place on the ground.

Any assault would be up close in the jungle, where visibility was never more than a few dozen yards at best. Stashed in the 747's jump cabin were half a dozen Hechler & Koch MP7s, an ultra-short-barrelled sub-machine gun. With a total length of just twenty-five inches, it was perfect for close-quarter battle and jungle warfare.

Each weapon was fitted with a suppressor, to silence its distinctive bark. Equipped with a forty-round magazine, the MP7 packed a real punch, especially as it fired bespoke armour-piercing bullets. The DM11 Ultimate Combat round boasted an alloy-plated steel core, making it ideal for penetrating any buildings or bunkers that Kammler might have sited on the island.

Jaeger's team numbered six, and they expected to be heavily outnumbered. Nothing new there, he noted.

Lewis Alonzo and Joe James had organised the jump kit, plus parachutes. Leaping from an airliner at some 40,000 feet required seriously specialist high-altitude gear. Hiro Kamishi – who was something of a CBRN defence specialist – had sorted the protective suits they'd need.

Any attack on such a place was a truly daunting proposition. The jungle was one of the most hostile of environments in which to operate, but this was no ordinary jungle. It was bound to be teeming with Kammler's guard force, plus his laboratory workers.

Plus it could well be overrun with sick and infected primates, in which case it would have to be treated as one huge Level 4 biohazard zone. A Level 4 biohazard is the most dangerous of all, denoting contamination with a pathogen of unprecedented lethality.

All the evidence suggested that Little Mafia Island – Plague Island – was awash with such a threat. Jaeger and his team would not only be battling the jungle and Kammler's security forces; they would also be facing whatever killer diseases lingered there.

One bite from an infected and rabid monkey; one stumble against a sharp tree branch that ripped gloves, mask or boots; one nick from either bullet or shrapnel that tore open their protective suits: any one of those would leave them vulnerable to infection by a pathogen for which there was no cure.

To counter such a threat, they'd be going in dressed in Bio Level 4 'spacesuits' – something similar to what astronauts wore. Clean filtered air would be pumped in continuously, keeping a positive pressure inside the suit at all times.

If the suit were pierced, the outrush of air should prevent the killer pathogen from entering – at least for long enough for the operator to tape up the breach. Each team member would keep a roll of tough gaffer tape – a vital tool for Hot Zone Level 4 operators – handy at all times.

Jaeger settled further into his luxurious seat and tried to force such fears to the back of his mind. He needed to relax, focus and recharge his batteries.

He was drifting off to sleep when Narov's voice jolted him fully awake.

'I hope you find them,' she remarked quietly. 'Both of them. Alive.'

'Thanks,' Jaeger murmured. 'But this mission – it's bigger than my family.' He glanced at Narov. 'It's about all of us.'

'I know that. But for you, your family . . . finding them . . . Love – it is the most powerful of human emotions.' She glanced at Jaeger, an intensity burning in her eyes. 'I should know.'

Jaeger too had felt this growing closeness between them. It was as if they had grown inseparable over the past few weeks, as if one couldn't operate – couldn't function – without the other. He knew only too well that rescuing Ruth and Luke would change all of that.

Narov smiled wistfully. 'Anyway, I have already said too much. As is my way.' She shrugged. 'It is impossible, of course. So let us forget. Let us forget *us*, and go to war.'

74

A Boeing 747-400 cruises at around 40,000 feet of altitude. To jump from such a height – some 11,000 feet higher than Mount Everest – and survive requires some seriously high-tech equipment, not to mention training.

Those at the cutting edge of special forces have developed a whole new paradigm for such jumps, designated HAPLSS; the High Altitude Parachutist Life Support System.

At 40,000 feet, the atmosphere is so thin you have to breathe off an air bottle, or you suffocate to death rapidly. But unless the right combination of gases is used, the jumper can suffer altitude decompression sickness, more commonly known as 'the bends' – what scuba divers suffer when ascending from depth.

During a normal high-altitude jump, from around 30,000 feet, terminal velocity – the maximum speed of your free fall – is some 320 k.p.h. But the thinner the air, the faster you plummet. Jumping from 40,000 feet, terminal velocity would be around 440 k.p.h.

If Jaeger and his team tried to pull their chutes at that kind of speed, either they'd suffer serious injury as a result of the impact, or they'd experience a canopy explosion. The chute would deploy out of its pack and all they'd likely hear would be a series of cracks as the cells tore open, leaving a patchwork of shredded silk flapping uselessly above them.

In short, if they pulled their chutes at anything above 35,000 feet, and at terminal velocity, they'd be unlikely to make it down alive. Hence the standard operating procedure with HAPLSS was to free-fall a good 20,000 feet, until the thicker air slowed their fall.

Jaeger had insisted on having eyes-in-the-sky over the target; an air asset standing permanent watch over Plague Island. Accordingly, Peter Miles had made contact with Hybrid Air Vehicles, the operators of the Airlander 50 – the world's largest aircraft.

A modern-day airship, the Airlander was helium-filled – as opposed to hydrogen – so totally inert. Unlike the Zeppelins of First World War renown, she wouldn't be exploding into a ball of flame any time soon. Four hundred feet long and two hundred wide, she was designed for performing persistent wide area surveillance – keeping long-term watch over specific targets – and was equipped with state-of-the-art radar and infrared scanners.

With a 105-knot cruise speed and a 2,320 nautical mile range, she was capable of making the flight to the coast of East Africa. As an added bonus, her crew and Jaeger and his team had worked together closely on their previous mission to the Amazon.

Once over the coast of East Africa, the Airlander would remain in continuous orbit for the duration of the mission. She didn't need to be directly over Little Mafia Island to keep watch; she could perform her duties from as much as seventy kilometres away.

She also had great cover in case she came to Kammler's attention. Beneath the waters of this part of the Indian Ocean there lay some of the world's richest gas reserves. The Chinese – in the form of China National Offshore Oil Corporation – were surveying several concessions in the area. Officially, the Airlander was there at the behest of CNOOC, carrying out an aerial survey function.

The Airlander had arrived over Little Mafia Island some thirty-six hours previously. Since then she'd beamed back scores of surveillance photos. The jungle appeared almost unbroken

– apart from the one dirt airstrip, which was only long enough to accommodate a Buffalo or similar aircraft.

Wherever Kammler had sited his monkey houses, labs and accommodation facilities, they appeared to be craftily hidden – either positioned under thick jungle canopy, or underground. That promised to make the team's mission doubly challenging, and that in turn made the Airlander's extra capabilities all the more welcome.

The Airlander 50 dispatched to East Africa was actually a top-secret developmental version of the aircraft. Aft of the flight pod slung below the massive bulbous hull was a cargo bay, one normally reserved for whatever heavy loads the airship might be carrying. But this Airlander was a little different. She was an airborne aircraft carrier and gun platform, with a seriously lethal capability. Two British Taranis drones – an ultra-high-tech stealth warplane – were parked within the cargo bay, which doubled as a well-equipped flight deck.

With a wingspan of ten metres, and just a fraction longer in length, the Taranis – named after the Celtic god of thunder – was a third the size of the American Reaper drone. And with a speed of Mach 1 – some 767 m.p.h. – it was twice as swift in the air. With two internal missile bays, the Taranis packed a serious punch, plus the sleek stealth technology made the drone all but invisible to any enemy.

The inspiration behind converting the Airlander to such a carrier function was a pre-Second World War airship, the USS *Macon*, the world's first – and until now only – flying aircraft carrier. Using technology that was now many decades old, the *Macon* had a series of trapezes slung beneath her cigar-shaped hull. Sparrowhawk biplanes had been able to fly under the airship and hook themselves up to these trapezes, after which the airship had been able to winch them in.

Inspired by the *Macon*, the Airlander 50 also carried an AW-159 Wildcat helicopter – a fast and highly manoeuvrable British chopper capable of carrying eight troops. The rationale behind bringing the Wildcat was that she would be able to pull Jaeger and his team out of Little Mafia Island once their mission was complete.

And at that stage Jaeger fervently hoped they would be eight in total – Ruth and Luke having joined them.

He was certain that his wife and son were being held on the island. In fact he had proof that that was the case, although he'd not mentioned it to any of the others. It was something he wasn't prepared to share. There was too much at stake, and he didn't want to risk anyone deterring him from his primary mission.

The photograph that Kammler had emailed him had shown Ruth and Luke kneeling in a cage. Across one side of that cage had been stamped a faded name: Katavi Reserve Primates.

Jaeger – the Hunter – was closing in.

75

Leaping out of the dark slash of the 747's jump hatch was like plummeting into a coffin – but there was no other way.

Jaeger threw himself forward into the churning, empty blackness, and instantly he hit the 747's hurricane-force slipstream. The pilot had reduced the 747's airspeed, but still he felt the punishing blast spinning him around, as the massive jet engines roared and snorted like a dragon just above him.

Moments later he was through the worst and rocketing to earth like a human-shaped missile.

Directly below he could just make out the ghostly silhouette of Lewis Alonzo, the man who'd jumped immediately ahead of him, as a darker spot against the dark night sky. Jaeger stabilised his position, then accelerated into a head-first dive in an effort to catch Alonzo.

His body moulded into a delta shape – arms tight by his sides, legs dead straight behind him – he was like a giant arrowhead plummeting towards the ocean. He remained like that until he got to within fifty feet of Alonzo, at which point he eased his limbs back into a star shape. The drag served to slow him down and stabilise his position.

That done, he turned his head into the snarling slipstream, searching the heavens above for Narov, number five in the stick. She was two hundred feet behind, but catching up fast. One further human-sized arrowhead was strung out behind her, which would be the last man, Hiro Kamishi.

Far above Kamishi he could just make out the ghostly form

of BA Flight 987 powering onwards into the darkness, its lights flashing reassuringly. For an instant his mind drifted to the passengers: sleeping; eating; watching movies – blissfully unaware of the small part they had played in the unfolding drama.

A drama that would determine the course of all their lives.

Jumping from 40,000 feet, Jaeger and his team would spend just sixty seconds free-falling. He did a rapid visual check of his altimeter. He needed to keep one eye on their altitude, or they could crash through their parachute release height, with potentially devastating consequences.

At the same time, the assault plan was running through his mind at warp-factor speed. They'd set their jump point some ten kilometres east of the target, out over the open ocean. That way they could drift under their chutes undetected, but were well within range of Plague Island.

Raff was the stick leader, and it was his job to choose the exact spot to land. He'd seek out an area devoid of trees or other obstructions, plus obvious enemy positions. Keeping the stick together was the key priority right now. It would be all but impossible to find someone again if they got lost during the free fall.

Far below him, Jaeger saw the flash of the first canopy unfurling in the darkness.

He stole a quick glance at his altimeter. He needed to deploy his chute. He reached for the rip cord handle located on his chest and pulled. An instant later the spring-loaded pilot chute billowed upwards, dragging with it the main canopy.

Jaeger braced for the violent deceleration as the main chute caught the air, and the deafening roar that would follow. He was looking forward to what would come after – the calm and relative silence of the descent, which would give him time to run through the assault plan once more in his mind.

But nothing happened. Where there should have been the ghostly form of his chute blossoming above him in the darkness, instead there was mostly empty space and something that looked like a bundle of tangled washing raging in the slipstream.

It spun and twisted angrily. Jaeger knew instantly what must have happened. One of the chute's rigging lines must have got caught up with the main canopy, preventing it from opening.

There was just a chance he might be able to pump the brakes or risers and free the rigging lines. He'd then have a fully or partially inflated chute above him, and maybe he could avoid the need to 'cut away' and deploy his reserve.

But time was not on his side.

Seconds later he plummeted past Alonzo. He'd lost well over a thousand feet by now. Every second brought him closer to a shattering impact with the ocean, which at this speed would feel like solid concrete. Water might seem soft and yielding when stepping into the bath. Slamming into it at several hundred feet per second would prove lethal.

The adrenalin was burning through Jaeger's system now, like a forest fire doused in gasoline.

After a few frantic attempts to free his lines, Jaeger realised they were too badly tangled. He had no option but to cut away. He grabbed the reserve handle, attached to his chest rigging.

Time to give it everything you've got, he screamed at himself. *Time to bloody rip that handle free.*

76

Whatever the hell had happened during Jaeger's exit, or in the free fall, only one course of action lay open to him now. He reached around and tore away the emergency release straps from his shoulders, jettisoning his main chute. It was ripped into the darkness above him and was gone.

That done he grabbed the reserve handle and yanked at it with all his strength, so triggering his emergency chute. Moments later there was a crack like a ship's canvas filling with wind, and a wide expanse of silk blossomed above him.

Jaeger was left hanging in the silence and stillness, and saying his prayers of thanks. He yanked his head upwards to check the reserve canopy. All seemed good.

He'd gained three thousand feet on the others, which meant he had to massively slow his descent. He reached up for the handheld steering toggles, giving them a sharp tug, forcing air the full length of the chute and making small adjustments to reduce his speed.

Glancing beyond his feet, he searched for Raff, the stick leader. He flicked down his night-vision goggles, which were attached to his jump helmet, and switched them to infrared mode, scanning the night. He was looking for the faint strobing of an IR firefly, a flashing infrared light unit.

There was no sign of it anywhere. Jaeger must have gone from being number four to number one in the stick. He had a similar IR unit attached to the rear of his helmet, so hopefully the others would be able to home in on that.

He pressed the light button on his GPS unit. It displayed a dotted line stretching from his present position to the exact point where they intended to put down. He could afford to leave the GPS powered up: at this altitude – some 20,000 feet – no one could see it from the ground. He figured he was travelling at around thirty knots, and drifting westwards with the prevailing wind. Another eight minutes and they should be over Plague Island.

Below his Goretex HAPLSS suit, Jaeger was wearing full cold-weather gear, including a pair of warm silk gloves beneath his thick Goretex overmitts. But still his hands were cramping up with the cold as he adjusted his line of flight to try to help the others catch him.

In a matter of minutes, five IR fireflies appeared in the night sky above him: the stick was complete. He let Raff overtake, taking up pole position once more, and they drifted onwards, six figures alone on the dark roof of the world.

When Jaeger had studied the Airlander's surveillance photos, there had seemed to be only one viable landing zone – the island's dirt airstrip. It was likely to be heavily guarded, but it was the one significant patch of terrain devoid of any tree cover.

He hadn't liked it. None of them had. Landing there would be like flying down the very throats of the enemy. But it had seemed like it was the airstrip or bust.

Then Kamishi had outlined their actions-on, which were vital upon landing. And it wasn't pretty.

They would need to find a location where they could change from one set of survival kit – HAPLSS high-altitude jump gear – to another, their Bio Level 4 space suits. And all while potentially having dropped right into the hornets' nest.

The thick HAPLSS suits provided life-saving warmth and oxygen, but they would offer little protection in a Level 4 hot zone. The team needed a safe environment in which to don their air-purifying respirators and space suits.

The kit included FM54 masks – the same as they'd worn when rescuing Leticia Santos – linked by a crushproof S-profile hose to a series of battery-operated filters, making up a space-age-looking pack on the operator's back. That filter unit would pump clean air into their bulky space suits – olive-green Trell-chem EVO 1Bs, made of a Nomex fabric with a chemically resistant Viton rubber topcoat, providing one hundred per cent protection.

Whilst transforming themselves from high-altitude para-chutists to Hot Zone 4 operators, the team would be highly vulnerable, which ruled out the airstrip as a landing point. That had left only one other possibility: a narrow stretch of pristine white sand that lay to the western side of the island.

From the surveillance photos, 'Copacabana Beach', as they'd dubbed it appeared just about doable. At low tide there was maybe fifty feet of sand between where the jungle ended and the sea began. All being well, they would switch gear there, then move into the jungle and hit Kammler's facility, striking with total surprise from out of the dark and empty night.

That, at least, was the plan.

But one person would have to remain at the beach. Their role was to establish a 'wet decon line' – consisting of a makeshift decontamination tent complete with scrub-down kits. Once the team re-emerged from the jungle, mission complete, they would need to douse their suits in buckets of seawater laced with EnviroChem – a potent chemical that killed viruses.

With the suits sanitised, they'd change out of them and scrub down a second time, this time decontaminating their bare skin. They'd then step over the clean/dirty line into the non-contaminated universe, leaving their CBRN kit behind.

On one side of that line would lie a Level 4 Hot Zone.

The other side – the open, wave-washed beach – would hopefully be safe and contamination-free. At least that was the theory. And Kamishi – their CBRN specialist – was the obvious candidate to oversee the wet decon line.

Jaeger glanced westwards, in the direction of Plague Island, but still he couldn't make out a thing. His chute was buffeted by a gust of wind, and rain droplets pinged into his exposed skin, each like a tiny sharp blade.

Ominously, all he could see was a cold and impenetrable darkness.

77

As he followed the route that Raff was steering, Jaeger's mind was full of images of Ruth and Luke. The next few hours would reveal everything. For better or for worse.

The question that had been dogging him for the last three years was about to be answered. Either he was going to pull off the seemingly impossible and rescue Ruth and Luke. Or he would discover the grisly truth – that one or both of them were dead.

And if the latter were the case, he knew to whom he would turn.

Their recent missions, and Narov's confessions – her dark and traumatic family history; her link to Jaeger's late grandfather; her autism; their growing attachment – had drawn him perilously close to her .

And if he flew too close to Narov's sun, Jaeger knew for sure that he would get burnt.

Jaeger and his fellow jumpers were still at altitude, and they were completely untraceable by any known defence system. Radar bounces off solid, angular objects – an aircraft's metal wings, or a helicopter's rotor blades – but simply bends around human forms and carries on uninterrupted. They were pretty much silent as they flew, so there was little risk of them being heard. They were dressed all in black, suspended beneath black chutes, and practically invisible from the ground.

They approached a high bank of cloud, which was piling up way out to sea. They'd already flown through one level of wet cloud, but nothing as thick or substantial as this. They had no option but to pass right through.

They slipped into the dense grey fug, the cloud becoming blindingly thick. As he drifted through the opaque mass, Jaeger could feel more and more icy water droplets condensing on his exposed skin and running down his face, forming tiny rivulets. By the time he emerged on the far side, he was freezing cold.

He picked up Raff right away, on a level with him and to his front. But when he turned to search behind, there was no sign of Narov, or any of the others.

Unlike in free-falling, when comms are impossible due to all the buffeting of the slipstream, you can radio each other when drifting under chutes. Jaeger pressed send and spoke into his mouthpiece.

'Narov – Jaeger. Where are you?'

He repeated the call several times, but still there was no answer. He and Raff had lost the rest of the stick, and by now they were very likely out of radio range.

Raff's voice came up over the air. 'Let's crack on. We'll hit the IP and reorg on the ground.' IP meant the impact point – in this case Copacabana Beach.

Raff was right. There was sod all they could do about losing contact with the rest of the stick, and too much radio traffic might lead to detection.

Several minutes later, Jaeger noticed Raff accelerate as he started to spiral vertically downwards, making for the island below and the small strip of beach. He made landfall with an almighty thump.

At a thousand feet, Jaeger hit the metal release levers to free his rucksack. It dropped away until it was suspended some twenty feet below him.

He heard the bulky pack thud into the ground.

He flared his chute, to slow his rate of descent, and seconds later his boots slammed into the stretch of sand, which glowed a surreal blue-white in the moonlight. He ran forward several paces as the expanse of silk drifted down, tangling in a bundle beside the sea.

Immediately he unslung his MP7 from his right shoulder and slotted a bullet into the breech. He was a few dozen yards from Raff, and he was good.

'Ready,' he hissed into his radio.

The two of them converged on the muster point. Moments later, Hiro Kamishi appeared out of the night sky and landed nearby.

But there was zero sign of the rest of Jaeger's team.

78

Hank Kammler ordered a bottle of Le Parvis de la Chapelle, the 1976 vintage. Nothing too flashy, but a quality French red nonetheless. He'd resisted cracking open a bottle of the finest champagne. There was much to celebrate, but he never liked to start the party early.

Just in case.

He powered up his laptop, and as it came to life, he let his eyes wander over the scene below. The waterhole was wonderfully busy. The humped, rounded, oily forms of hippos lazed contentedly in the mud. A herd of graceful roan antelopes – or were they sable? Kammler was never quite certain how to tell the difference – nosed towards the murky water, fearful of crocodiles.

All seemed good in paradise, which buoyed his already ebullient mood. He clicked the laptop's keys, pulling up the same draft email account that Jaeger had accessed just a few days earlier. Kammler kept a regular watch on it. He could tell which messages Jaeger had looked at, and when.

A frown creased his brow.

The most recent messages dreamed up by himself and Steve Jones had yet to be opened. Kammler clicked on one, savouring the dark intent, yet at the same time unsettled that his nemesis hadn't yet seen it.

The image opened, showing the distinctive shaven-headed form of Jones crouching behind Jaeger's wife and son, his massive bare arms around their shoulders, his face beaming an utterly sinister smile.

Words typed themselves below the photo: *Hello from an old friend*.

A pity, Kammler told himself, that Jaeger hadn't yet got to enjoy that one. It was a masterstroke. That in turn made him wonder where Jaeger and his crew might be right now.

He checked his watch. He was expecting company. Bang on cue, the hulking form of Steve Jones lowered himself into the seat opposite, largely blocking Kammler's view.

It was typical of the man. He had the sensitivity – the subtlety – of a dinosaur. Kammler glanced at the wine. He'd asked for only the one glass.

'Good evening. I presume you'd like a Tusker?' Tusker was a brand of Kenyan lager popular with tourists and expats alike.

Jones eyes narrowed. 'Never touch the stuff. It's African, which means it's piss-weak. I'll have a Pilsner.'

Kammler ordered the beer. 'So, what news?'

Jones poured his beer. 'Your man – Falk Konig – got to take his medicine. He was a little reluctant, but he wasn't about to argue.'

'And? Any progress on this boy?'

'Apparently a kid did arrive here, around six months back, as a stowaway on a transport aircraft. He came complete with some wild story. Sounds like a heap of bullshit to me.'

Kammler's eyes – reptilian, cold and predatory – fixed themselves on Jones. 'It may sound like bullshit to you, but I need to hear it. All of it.'

Jones proceeded to relate a similar story as Konig had told Jaeger and Narov several days back. By the end of it, Kammler knew pretty much everything, including the boy's name. And of course, he didn't doubt that the tale was one hundred per cent accurate.

He felt the cold claws of uncertainty – of an impossible eleventh-hour dread – tearing at him. If the same story had made its way to Jaeger's ears, what had he learned? What had he deduced? And where had that taken him?

Was there anything in the boy's story that might have revealed Kammler's wider plan? He didn't think so. How could it? Already the seven flights had landed at their chosen destinations. Their cargoes had been unloaded, and as far as Kammler knew, the primates were parked in quarantine right now.

And that meant the genie was out of the bottle.

No one was about to put it back in again.

No one could save the world's population from what, even now, was spreading.

Unseen.

Undetected.

Unsuspected even.

In a few weeks' time it would start to rear its ugly head. The first symptoms would be flu-like. Hardly alarming. But then would come the first of the bleeding.

Well before that time, the world's population would be infected. The virus would have spread to the four corners of the earth, and it would be unstoppable.

And then it hit him.

The realisation was so forceful it made Kammler choke on his wine. His eyes bulged and his pulse spiked as he contemplated the utterly unthinkable. He grabbed a napkin and dabbed at his chin absent-mindedly. It was a long shot. Next to impossible. But nonetheless, there was still just the sliver of a chance.

'You all right?' a voice queried. It was Jones. 'Look like you just seen a ghost.'

Kammler waved the question away. 'Wait,' he hissed. 'I need silence. To think.'

His teeth locked and ground against each other. His mind was a maelstrom of seething thoughts, as he tried to work out how best to combat this new and utterly unforeseen danger.

Finally he turned his gaze on Jones. 'Forget every order I've given you. Instead, concentrate on this one task exclusively. I need you to find that boy. I don't care what it costs, where you have to go, which of your . . . comrades you may need to recruit – *but find him*. Find this damn kid and shut him down permanently.'

'I hear you,' Jones confirmed. It was a long way from going after Jaeger, but at least it was a manhunt of sorts. Something to get his teeth into.

'I'll need something to go on. A starting point. A lead.'

'All will be provided. These slum dwellers – they use cell phones. Mobiles. Mobile internet. I'll have the best people we've got listen out for him. Search. Hack. Monitor. They'll find him. And when they do, you will go in and terminate with extreme prejudice. Are we understood?'

Jones flashed a cruel smile. 'Perfectly.'

'Right, go make your preparations. You'll need to travel – most likely to Nairobi. You'll need help. Find people. Offer them whatever it takes, but get this done.'

Jones departed, his unfinished glass of beer gripped in his hand. Kammler turned to his laptop. His fingers flashed across the keyboard, placing a call via IntelCom. It was routed to a nondescript grey office in a complex of low-lying grey buildings, hidden within a swathe of grey forest in remote rural Virginia, on the eastern coast of the USA.

That office was stuffed full of the world's most advanced signals intercept and tracking technology. On the wall next to the entryway was a small brass plaque. It read: *CIA – Division of Asymmetric Threat Analysis (DATA)*.

A voice answered. 'Harry Peterson.'

'It's me,' Kammler announced. 'I'm sending you a file on one specific individual. Yes, from my vacation in East Africa. You are to use all possible means – internet, email, cell phones, travel bookings, passport details, *anything* – to find him. Last known location believed to be the Mathare shanty town, in the Kenyan capital, Nairobi.'

'Understood, sir.'

'This has the absolute highest priority, Peterson. You and your people are to drop everything – absolutely everything – to concentrate on this one tasking. Are we understood?'

'Yes, sir.'

'Let me know as soon as you learn anything. No matter what time of day or night, contact me immediately.'

'Understood, sir.'

Kammler killed the call. His pulse rate was starting to return to something like normal. *Let's not overdo this,* he told himself. Like any threat, it could be managed. Eliminated.

The future was still one hundred per cent his for the taking.

79

There was a crackle in Jaeger's earpiece. Message incoming.
'We lost you in the cloud.' It was Narov. 'We're three, but we took a while to find each other. We put down on the airstrip.'

'Understood,' Jaeger responded. 'Stay out of sight. We'll move across to your location.'

'One thing. There's no one here.'

'Say again?'

'The airstrip. It's utterly deserted.'

'Okay, lie low. Leave your fireflies on strobe.'

'Believe me, there's not a soul here,' Narov repeated. 'It's like the whole place . . . It's deserted.'

'We're on our way.'

Jaeger and Raff prepared to move out, leaving Kamishi to guard the wet decon line.

Jaeger laid out the components for his Plague Island space walk on the sands. The thick, chemically resistant material of the Trellchem suit gleamed sinisterly in the moonlight. Beside it he placed the rubber overboots, plus thick rubber gloves. On a nearby rock he laid his roll of all-important gaffer tape.

He glanced at Raff. 'Me first.'

Raff stepped around to assist. Jaeger clambered into the suit feet-first. He pulled it up to his armpits, then shrugged it over his arms and shoulders. With Raff's assistance, he zipped himself inside, then pulled the bulbous hood over so that it encased his head completely.

He gestured at the gaffer tape, then held out his hands. Raff taped the wrists of his suit to the rubber of the gloves, doing the same with the boots around Jaeger's ankles.

The tape would be their first line of defence.

Jaeger twisted a switch, changing his respirator kit on to active powered-air mode. There was a faint whir as the electric motors began to blow in clean, filtered air, billowing out his suit until the toughened rubber skin went rigid. Already it felt hot, unwieldy and constricting, plus it proved noisy whenever he tried to move.

Kamishi helped Raff suit up, and it wasn't long before they were ready to step into the jungle.

For a moment Raff hesitated. He glanced at Jaeger from behind his visor. Inside, his face was enclosed within his FM54 mask, as was Jaeger's. That way, they had a double line of defence.

Jaeger saw Raff's lips move. The words reverberated in his earpiece, sounding muffled and distant.

'She's right. Narov. There's no one here. I can sense it. This island – it's deserted.'

'You don't know that,' Jaeger countered. He had to raise his voice to make himself heard above the throb of the air flow.

'There's no one here,' Raff repeated. 'When we came in to land, did you see a single light? A glimmer? Movement? Anything?'

'We still have to clear the place. First the airstrip. Then Kammler's labs. Every step of the way.'

'Yeah, I know. But trust me – there's no one here.'

Jaeger eyed him through the barrier of their visors. 'If you're right, what does that signify? What does it mean?'

Raff shook his head. 'Dunno, but it can't be good news.'

Jaeger sensed the same, but there was something else eating at his mind – something that made him feel physically sick.

If this island was deserted, where had Kammler taken Ruth and Luke?

They moved out, lumbering towards the dark wall of forest

like astronauts, but without the benefit of comparative weight-lessness to ease their way. As they stepped awkwardly into the waiting jungle, each had his stubby MP7 sub-machine gun slung across his front.

As soon as they were beneath the canopy, the darkness was upon them. The tree cover cut out all ambient light. Jaeger flicked the switch on the torch attached to his MP7, a beam of illumination piercing the gloom as he swept the way ahead.

Before him was an almost impenetrable wall of brooding veg-etation, the jungle thick with creepers, plus giant fan-like palm leaves and vines as thick as a man's thigh. Thank God they only had a few hundred yards of this to fight their way through to make the airstrip.

Jaeger had taken a few ungainly paces under the dark canopy when he sensed movement above him. A bunched, alien form darted at him from out of the shadowed tree limbs, springing with an impossibly acrobatic and lithe sure-footedness. Jaeger raised his bulky gloved right hand to block the movement, and punched with his left, going for the creature's throat in a typical Krav Maga thrust.

In hand-to-hand combat you had to hit instantly and hard, landing repeated blows on your adversary's areas of greatest vulnerability – the foremost of which was the neck. But what-ever this beast might be, it proved too agile; or maybe Jaeger's movements were just too constricted by the suit. He felt as if he were mired in a thick sludge.

His assailant dodged the first blows, and an instant later he felt something powerful snake its way around his suited neck. Whatever had gripped him began to squeeze.

The strength of the thing – for its size – was unbelievable. Jaeger felt adrenalin surge around his system as his suit puck-ered and buckled, four powerful limbs closing around his head. He fought with his hands to tear them free, but then – suddenly and shockingly – a face appeared before him, red-eyed, rabid and snarling, and the creature struck with its canines, the long yellow fangs slashing at his visor.

For whatever reason, primates find humans encased in space suits even more terrifying and provocative than they do in the flesh. And as Jaeger had been warned in the Falkenhagen briefings, a primate – even one as small as this – could make for a fearsome adversary.

Doubly so when its brain was fried with a mind-altering viral infection.

Jaeger groped for its eyes, one of the most vulnerable points of the body. His gloved fingers made contact, and he drove his thumbs in, gouging deep – a classic Krav Maga move, and one that didn't require particular agility or speed.

His fingers slid and slewed on a slick, greasy wetness: he could feel it even through the gloves. The animal was leaking liquid – blood – from its eye sockets.

He forced his thumbs deeper, hooking out one living eyeball. Finally the monkey relented, dropping off him in screaming, agonised rage. It let go last with its tail, the limb that had snaked around Jaeger's neck in a stranglehold.

It made a desperate leap for cover, wounded and hopelessly sick though it was. Jaeger raised his MP7 and fired: one shot that took it down.

The monkey fell dead on the forest floor.

He bent to inspect it, sweeping his torch beam across its motionless form. Beneath its sparse hair, the primate's skin was covered in swollen red blotches. And where the bullet had torn apart its torso, Jaeger could see a river of blood pooling.

But this wasn't anything like normal blood.

It was black, putrid and stringy.

A deadly viral soup.

The air roared in Jaeger's ears like an express train steaming down a long, dark tunnel. What must it be like to live with that virus? he wondered.

Dying, but with no idea what was killing you.

Your brain a fried mush of fever and rage.

Your organs dissolving inside your skin.

Jaeger shuddered. This place was evil.

'You okay, kid?' Raff queried, via the radio.

Jaeger nodded darkly, then signalled the way ahead. They pressed onwards.

The monkeys and the humans on this cursed island were close cousins, their shared lineage stretching back countless millennia. Now they would have to fight to the death. Yet a much older life force – a primeval one – was stalking both of them.

It was tiny and invisible, but far more powerful than them all.

80

Donal Brice peered through the bars into the nearest cage. He scratched his beard nervously. A big, lumbering lump of a guy, he'd only recently got the job at Washington Dulles airport's quarantine house, and he still wasn't entirely certain how the whole darned system worked.

As the new guy, he'd landed more than his share of night shifts. He figured that was fair enough, and in truth he was glad of the work. It hadn't been easy finding this job. Painfully unsure of himself, Brice tended to cover up his insecurities with bursts of booming, deafening laughter.

It didn't tend to go down too well at job interviews – especially as he tended to laugh at all the wrong things. In short, he was glad to have a job at the monkey house, and he was determined to do well.

But Brice figured that what he saw before him now was not good news. One of the monkeys looked real sick. Crook.

It was nearing the end of his shift, and he'd entered the monkey house to administer their early-morning feed. His last duty before clocking off and heading home.

The recently arrived animals were making a horrendous racket, banging on the wire mesh, leaping around their cages and screaming: *we're hungry*.

But not this little guy.

Brice sank to his haunches and studied the vervet monkey closely. It was crouched at the rear of the cage, its arms wrapped around itself, an odd, glazed expression on its otherwise cute features. The poor little critter's nose was running. No doubt about it, this guy wasn't well.

Brice racked his brains to remember the procedure for when they had a sick animal. That individual was to be removed from the main facility and placed in isolation, to prevent the illness from spreading.

Brice was a hopeless lover of animals. He still lived with his parents, and they had all kinds of pets at home. He felt strangely ambivalent about the nature of his work here. He liked being close to the monkeys, that was for sure, but he didn't much like the fact that they were here for medical testing.

He sloped off to the storeroom and grabbed the kit required for moving a sick animal. It consisted of a long pole with a syringe attached to one end. He charged the syringe, returned to the cage, poked the stick inside and, as gently as he could, stuck the monkey with the needle.

It was too sick even to react much. He pushed the lever at his end, and the shot of drugs was injected into the animal. A minute or so later, Brice was able to unlatch the cage – which had the exporter's name, Katavi Reserve Primates, stamped across it – and reach inside to retrieve the unconscious animal.

He carried it to the isolation unit. He'd pulled on a pair of surgical gloves in order to move the primate, but he wasn't using any extra protection, and certainly not the suits and masks piled in one corner of the storeroom. No sickness had yet been reported in the monkey house, so there was no reason to do so.

He laid the comatose animal in an isolation cage and was about to close the door when he remembered something one of the friendlier workers had told him. If an animal was sick, you could usually smell it on its breath.

He wondered if he should give it a try. Maybe he could earn some brownie points with his boss that way. Remembering how his colleague had said to do it, he leant into the cage and used his hand to waft the monkey's breath across his nostrils, inhaling deeply a couple of times. But there was nothing distinctive that he could detect, above the faint smell of stale urine and food in the cage.

Shrugging, he shut and bolted the door, and glanced at his watch. He was a few minutes overdue his shift changeover. And in truth, Brice was in a hurry. Today was Saturday – the big day at the Awesome Con comic convention in downtown. He'd forked out some serious money for tickets to the 'Geekend', and to get access to the Power Rangers 4-Pack VIP event.

He had to hurry.

An hour later, he'd made it to the Walter E. Washington Convention Centre, having done a quick stopover at home to change out of his work clothes and grab his costume. His parents had objected that he had to be tired after his night shift, but he'd promised them he'd get some proper rest that evening.

He parked up and headed inside, the roar of the massive air-conditioning units adding a reassuring baseline hum to the chatter and laughter that filled the cavernous convention centre's interior. Already it was buzzing.

He made a beeline for the breakfast hall. He was starving. Once fed and watered, he headed into a changing booth, emerging minutes later as a . . . *superhero*.

Kids flocked to the Hulk. They pressed close, wanting to have their photo taken with their all-powerful comic idol – especially as the Hulk seemed to be far more smiley and fun in the flesh than he ever appeared in the movies.

Donal Brice – aka the Hulk – would spend the weekend doing what he loved most: laughing his booming, heroic laugh in a place where everyone seemed to like it, and no one ever held it against him. He'd spend the day laughing and breathing, and breathing and laughing, as the vast air-conditioning system recycled his exhalations . . .

Mixing them with those of ten thousand other unsuspecting human souls.

81

'We maybe got something,' Harry Peterson, the director of the CIA's Division of Asymmetric Threat Analysis – DATA – announced via the IntelCom link.

'Tell me,' Kammler commanded.

His voice sounded oddly echoing. He was sitting in a room carved out of one of the many caves situated close to the BV222 – his beloved warplane. The surroundings were spartan, but remarkably well equipped for somewhere positioned within immense rock walls deep beneath Burning Angels mountain.

It was both an impregnable fortress and a technologically sophisticated nerve centre. The perfect kind of place to sit out what was coming.

'Okay, so a guy named Chucks Bello sent an email,' Peterson explained. 'DATA picked it up using keywords based on namecheck combinations. There's more than one Chucks Bello active on the internet, but this one grabbed our attention. There are several districts in the Nairobi slums. One – Mathare – lit up with this Chucks Bello's comms.'

'Which means?' Kammler demanded impatiently.

'We're ninety-nine per cent certain this is your guy. Chucks Bello sent an email to one Julius Mburu, who runs something called the Mburu Foundation. It's a social-action kind of charity that works in the Mathare slum. With kids. A lot of them are orphans. I'll forward you the email. We're sure this is your guy.'

'So d'you have a fix? A location?'

'We do. The email was generated from a commercial address:

guest@amanibeachretreat.com. There is an Amani Beach Re-treat approximately four hundred miles south of Nairobi. It's a high-end, exclusive resort set on the Indian Ocean.'

'Great. Forward me the comms chain. And keep digging. I want to be absolutely one hundred per cent certain this is our guy.'

'Understood, sir.'

Kammler cut the IntelCom link. He punched the words 'Amani Beach Resort' into the Google search engine, then clicked on the website. It showed images of a pristine white crescent of sand, washed with stunning turquoise waters. A glimmering, crystal-clear swimming pool situated on the very fringes of the beach, complete with a discreet bar service and shaded sunloungers. Locals in traditional-looking batique dress serving fine food to the elegant foreign guests.

No slum kid ever went to a place like this.

If the kid was at Amani Beach, someone must have taken him there. It could only be Jaeger and his group, and they could only have done so for one reason: to hide him. And if they were shielding him, maybe they *had* realised the impossible hope that a penniless kid from the African slums might offer humankind.

Kammler checked his email. He clicked on the message from Peterson, running his eye down Simon Chucks Bello's email.

This Dale guy gave me *maganji*. Spending money – like real *maganji*. Like, Jules man, I'm gonna pay you back. All I owe you. And you know what I'll do next, man? I'm gonna hire a jumbo jet with a casino and a swimming pool and dancing girls from all over – London, Paris, Brazil and Russia and China and Planet Mars and even America; yeah – Miss USA by the busload – and you'll all be invited 'cause you're my *brothers* and we'll zoom above the city dropping empty beer bottles 'n' stuff so that everyone will know what a cool party we're having, and behind that jumbo we'll drag a banner announcing: MOTO'S JUMBO BIRTHDAY PARTY – BY INVITATION ONLY!

Mburu had replied:

> Yeah, well you don't even know your own age, Moto, so how will you know when it's your birthday? Plus where's all the dough gonna come from? You need a lot of *maganji* to hire a jumbo. Just take it easy and lie low and do as the *mzungu* tells you. Plenty of time for partying when all this is over.

Clearly 'Moto' was the kid's nickname. And clearly he was being treated well by his *mzungu* benefactors, *mzungu* being a word that Kammler knew well. In fact, the kid was being treated so nicely that he was even planning a birthday party.

Oh no, Moto, I don't think so. Today it's my time to party.

Kammler punched in Steve Jones's ID on his IntelCom link with furious fingers. After a few short rings Jones answered.

'Listen, I have a location,' Kammler hissed. 'I need you to get there with your team and eliminate the threat. You'll have Reaper overhead if you need backup. But it's one slum kid and whoever is guarding him. It should be – forgive the pun – child's play.'

'Got it. Send me the details. We're on our way.'

Kammler typed a short email providing a link to the resort, then sent it to Jones. Next, he googled the word 'Amani'. It turned out to be Swahili for 'peace'. He smiled his thin smile.

Not for much longer.

That peace – it was about to be ripped asunder.

82

Jaeger shoulder-barged the last of the doors with all of the force of his cumulative rage. It was coursing through his veins like burning acid.

He stopped for an instant, the cumbersome space suit snagging on the door frame, and then he was through, his torch beam sweeping the darkened interior, his weapon doing likewise. The light reflected off shelves of gleaming scientific equipment, most of which Jaeger couldn't begin to recognise.

The lab was deserted.

Not a soul anywhere.

Just as they'd discovered with the rest of the complex.

No guard force. No boffins. All he and his team had used their guns on were the disease-ravaged monkeys.

Finding this place so deserted was utterly eerie; chilling. And Jaeger felt cruelly cheated. Against all odds they'd found Kammler's lair. But Kammler – and his people – had flown the nest before justice and retribution could be visited upon them.

But mostly Jaeger felt tortured by the emptiness – the lack of life – where it hit him most personally: there was no sign of Ruth and Luke anywhere.

He stepped forward, and the last man in closed the door behind him. It was a precaution to prevent contamination spreading from one room to another.

As the door clicked shut, Jaeger heard a sharp, deafening hiss. It had come from just above the door frame, and it had sounded like a truck letting off its air brakes. Like a compressed-air explosion.

At the same instant he felt a wave of tiny pinpricks pierce his skin. His head and neck seemed fine, protected as they were by the thick rubber of the FM54 mask, and the tough filter unit seemed to have shielded his back.

But his legs and arms were on fire.

He glanced down at his suit. The tiny puncture holes were clearly visible. He'd been hit by some kind of booby-trapped device, which had pierced the fabric of the Trellchem. He had to presume the rest of the team were likewise hit.

'Tape up!' he screamed. 'Tape up vents! Every man help the other!'

In a flurry of near-panic, he turned to Raff and began ripping off lengths of gaffer tape to seal up the tiny holes torn in the big Maori's suit. Once he was finished, Raff did the same for him.

Jaeger had kept monitoring his suit pressure the entire time. It had remained positive – the filter pack automatically blowing in clean air, which would have kept flowing out through the tears in the fabric. That outward pressure should have kept any contamination at bay.

'Sitrep,' Jaeger demanded.

One by one his team reported in. All their suits were compromised, but they had been resealed effectively. Positive air pressure seemed to have been maintained by all, thanks to their powered-air units.

But still Jaeger could feel a tingling sensation where whatever it was that had been blasted through his suit had cut into his skin. He didn't doubt that it was time to get out of there. They had to head back to the wet decon line at the beach and do a damage inspection.

He was just about to issue the order when the utterly unexpected happened.

There was a faint hum, and the electric power came to life in the complex, bathing the lab in blinding halogen light. At one end of the room a giant flat-screen terminal flickered into life, and a figure appeared on what had to be some kind of live link.

It was unmistakable.

Hank Kammler.

'Gentlemen, leaving so soon?' His voice echoed around the laboratory, as he spread his arms in an expansive gesture. 'Welcome . . . welcome to my world. Before you do anything rash, let me explain. That was a compressed air bomb. It fired tiny glass pellets. No explosives. You will feel a slight tingling on your skin. That is where the pellets cut into you. The human skin is a great barrier to infection: one of the best. But not when it is punctured.

'The lack of any explosives means the agent – the dry virus – remained unharmed and viable. As the glass entered your skin – driven in there by four-hundred-bar pressure – it carried the inert agent with it. In short, you have all been infected, and I don't think I need to tell you with what type of pathogen.'

Kammler laughed. 'Congratulations. You are some of my first victims. Now, I'd like you to fully appreciate your delicious predicament. You might decide it best to remain trapped on this island. You see, if you go out into the world, you will be mass murderers. You are infected. Already, you are plague bombs. So you might argue that you have no option but to stay and die, and to that end you will find the premises well stocked with food.

'Of course, the *Gottvirus* has already been released,' Kammler continued. 'Or should I say *unleashed*. Even now it is making its way into the four corners of the world. So alternatively, you can help me. The more carriers the merrier, as it were. You can opt to go out into the world and help spread the virus. The choice is yours. But just for a moment, make yourselves comfortable while I tell you a story.'

Wherever Kammler was speaking from, he was seemed to be enjoying himself immensely. 'Once upon a time, two SS scientists found a frozen corpse. She was perfectly preserved, even down to her long golden hair. My father, SS General Hans Kammler, gave her a name, that of an ancient Nordic god: Var, the Beloved. Var was the five-thousand-year-old ancestor of the Aryan people. Sadly, she had fallen ill before she died. She had been infected by a mystery pathogen.

'At the Deutsche Ahnenerbe, in Berlin, they unfroze her and began to clean her up, in an effort to make her presentable to the Führer. But the corpse started to collapse from the inside out. Her organs – liver, kidneys, lungs – seemed to have rotted and died, even as the outer being still lived. Her brain had been transformed into a mush; a soup. In short, she had been something close to a zombie as she'd stumbled into the icy crevasse and perished.

'The men tasked to make her perfect – a perfect Aryan ancestor – didn't know what to do. Then one, an archaeologist and pseudo-scientist called Herman Wirth, tripped while carrying out his work. He reached out to save himself, but in doing so he cut both himself and his Deutsche Ahnenerbe colleague – a myth-hunter called Otto Rahn – with a small glass inspection slide. No one thought too much about it, until both men sickened and died.'

Kammler raised his eyes to his long-distance audience, and a terrible darkness seemed to have filled them. 'They died voiding thick, black, putrid blood from every orifice, and with terrible, zombified expressions on their features. No one needed to carry out a post-mortem to know what had happened. A five-thousand-year-old killer disease had survived, deep-frozen in the Arctic ice, and now it had come back to life. Var had claimed her first victims.

'The Führer named this pathogen the *Gottvirus*, because nothing like it had ever been seen. It was clearly the mother of all viruses. That was in 1943. The Führer's people spent the next two years perfecting the *Gottvirus*, fully intending to use it to repel the Allied hordes. In that, sadly, they failed. Time was against us . . . But not any more. Now, today, as I speak to you, time is very much on our side.'

Kammler smiled. 'So, gentlemen – and one lady, I believe – now you know exactly how you are going to die. And you know what choice you have before you. Stay on that island and die quietly, or help spread my gift – my virus – to the world. You see, you British never understood: you cannot defeat the Reich. The Aryan. It has taken seven decades, but we are back. And we have survived to conquer. *Jedem das Seine*, my friends. Everyone gets what they deserve.'

As he reached out to cut the live link, Kammler paused.

'Ah! I almost forgot . . . One last thing. William Jaeger – presumably you were expecting to find your wife and child on my island, were you not? Well, you can relax: they are indeed there. They have been enjoying my hospitality for quite some time. And it's high time you were reunited with them.

'Like you, of course, they are also infected. Unharmed, but infected all the same. We injected them several weeks ago. This is so you will be able to watch them die. I mean, I didn't want you to die as one happy family. No, they must go first, so you can witness it at first hand. You'll find them in a bamboo cage, tethered in the jungle. And feeling more than a little sick already, I believe.'

Kammler shrugged. 'That's it. *Auf Wiedersehen*, my friends. It only leaves me to say a final *Wir sind die Zukunft*.'

His teeth gleamed in a perfect smile. 'We – my kind – we really are the future.'

83

A form struck out at Jaeger, driving a sharpened bamboo stake repeatedly towards his face. The figure whirled around, wielding the crude weapon like an ancient gladiator would a spear. It yelled curses. Cruel insults. The kind of words Jaeger had never imagined her capable of, not in his wildest dreams.

'GET AWAY! KEEP AWAY! I'LL SLICE YOU UP, YOU . . . YOU EVIL BASTARD! TOUCH MY SON AND I'LL RIP YOUR BLACK HEART OUT!'

Jaeger shuddered. He could barely recognise the woman he loved; the one he'd spent the last three years searching for relentlessly.

Her hair was long and matted into thick clumps, like dreadlocks. Her features were haggard and drawn, her clothes hanging in dirty rags around her shoulders.

My God, how long had they kept her like this? Caged like an animal in the jungle.

He sank to his haunches before the crude bamboo structure, repeating the same phrase over and over, trying to reassure her.

'It's me. Will. Your husband. I've come for you, like I promised I would. I'm here.'

But each utterance was met only with another swing of the stave towards his tortured features.

To the rear of the cage Jaeger spied Luke's emaciated form lying prone – presumably unconscious – as Ruth did all in her power to defend him from what she perceived to be her enemies.

The image broke his heart.

In spite of everything, he felt he loved her more now than he had ever thought possible, and especially for this spirited, desperate, frantic defence of their son. But had she lost her mind? Had the terrible incarceration and the virus broken her?

Jaeger couldn't be sure. All he wanted to do was take her in his arms and let her know that they were safe now. Or at least until the *Gottvirus* started to bite and to fry their very minds.

'It's me, Ruthy. It's Will,' he repeated. 'I've been searching. I found you. I've come for you and for Luke. To take you home. You're safe now . . .'

'You bastard – you're lying!' Ruth shook her head violently, striking out again with the stake. 'You're that cruel bastard Jones . . . You've come here for my child . . .' She swung the stake again, threateningly. 'YOU TRY TAKING LUKE, I'LL . . .'

Jaeger reached out towards her, but as he did so he was reminded of how he must look, encased in the space suit and visor and the thick rubber gloves.

Of course. She'd have no idea who he was.

No way of recognising him at all.

Dressed like this, he could be any one of those who had tortured her. And the mask's voice projection system meant that he was speaking like some kind of alien cyborg, so she wouldn't even know his tones.

He reached up and pulled back his hood. Air gushed out of the suit, but Jaeger didn't give a damn. He was infected. He had nothing left to lose. With feverish fingers he unstrapped the respirator and pulled that up and over his head.

He gazed at her. Beseechingly. 'Ruth, it's me. It really is me.'

She stared. Her grip on the bamboo stake seemed to falter. She shook her head disbelievingly, even as recognition flared in her eyes. Then she seemed to collapse in on herself, throwing her body at the cage door with the last of her energy, and letting out a piercing, strangled cry that cut Jaeger to the heart.

She reached for him, desperately, disbelievingly. Jaeger's

hands met hers. Fingers meshed through the bars. Heads came together, skin-close; hungry for a loving touch, for intimacy.

A figure moved beside Jaeger. It was Raff. As discreetly as he could, he undid the bolts that kept the cage fastened from the outside, then stepped back to give them their privacy.

Jaeger leaned inside and brought her out to him. He held her close, hugging her as tightly as he could, while trying not to cause any more pain to her bruised and battered form. As he did so, he could feel how hot she was, the fever of the infection coursing through her veins.

He held her as she shuddered and sobbed. She cried for what seemed like an age. As for Jaeger, he let the tears fall freely too.

As gently as he could, Raff retrieved Luke from the rear of the cage. Jaeger held his son's emaciated form in one arm, with his other keeping Ruth from collapsing. The three of them sank slowly to their knees, Jaeger clutching tight to both of them.

Luke remained unresponsive and Jaeger laid him down, while Raff broke out their medical kit. As the big Maori bent over the boy's unconscious form, Jaeger figured he could see tears in his eyes. Together they worked on treating Luke, as Ruth sobbed and talked.

'There was this man, Jones . . . He was evil. Pure evil. What he said he was going to do to us . . . What he did to us . . . I thought you were him.' She glanced around fearfully. 'He's not still here? Tell me he's not here.'

'There's no one else here but us.' Jaeger pulled her closer. 'And no one's going to hurt you. Trust me. No one's going to hurt you ever again.'

84

The Wildcat helicopter clawed through the dawn skies, climbing fast.

Jaeger squatted on its cold steel floor at the head of a pair of stretchers, clutching the hands of his wife and son. They were both desperately ill. He wasn't even certain if Ruth could recognise him still.

He could see a filmy, distant expression in her eyes now – the stage directly before it turned into the glazed stare of the walking dead; the kind of look he'd seen in the eyes of the monkeys, before he'd put them out of their misery.

He felt gripped by a terrible fatigue and dark sense of hopelessness; waves of exhaustion, mixed with a crushing sense of utter failure, washed over him.

Kammler had been one step ahead of them every inch of the way. He'd sucked them into his trap and spat them out again, like dead, dried husks. And to Jaeger he'd just delivered the ultimate in revenge, ensuring that his last days would be horrific beyond imagining.

Jaeger felt paralysed by grief. He was awash with it. Three long years searching for Ruth and Luke, and finally he had found them – *but like this.*

For the first time in his life, a terrible thought flashed through his mind: *suicide.* If he were forced to witness Ruth and Luke perish in such an unspeakable and nightmarish way, better to die with them, and at his own hand.

Jaeger resolved that was what he would do. If his wife and son were taken from him for a second time – and this time for ever – he would choose an early death. He'd put a bullet in his brain.

At least then he would rob Kammler of his ultimate victory.

It hadn't taken him and his team long to make the decision to abandon Plague Island. They could have done nothing there: nothing for Ruth and Luke, or for each other, not to mention the wider human population.

Not that they were kidding themselves. There was no cure. Not for this; not for a five-thousand-year-old virus brought back from the dead. Everyone on that aircraft was as good as finished, along with the vast majority of planet earth's human population.

Some forty-five minutes earlier the Wildcat had put down on the beach. Before boarding, each team member had gone through the wet decon tent, sluicing down and discarding their suits, before dousing themselves with EnviroChem and scrubbing out the shards of glass.

Not that any of that could alter the fact of their own contamination.

As Kammler had told them, they were all now virus bombs. For the uninfected, their every breath spelled a potential death sentence.

That was why they'd chosen to keep their FM54 masks on. The respirators not only filtered the air they breathed in; with a DIY modification courtesy of Hiro Kamishi, they could also filter the air breathed out, so preventing them spreading the virus.

Kamishi's bodge was rough and ready, and it came with its own risks, but it was the best they had. They'd each taped a particulate filter – similar to a basic surgical mask – over the respirator's exhaust port. It created greater resistance, with the unfortunate result that the lungs were less able to exhale and void the virus.

Instead, the *Gottvirus* would pool in the confines of the respirator, so around eyes, mouth and nose. With that would come a greater risk of increased virus loading – in other words, accelerated infection – which could precipitate a rapid onrush of the symptoms. In short, in striving to not infect others, they risked doubly poisoning themselves.

But that didn't particularly seem to matter, with all of humanity seemingly doomed.

Jaeger felt a comforting hand on his shoulder. It was Narov's. He glanced up at her, a look of pained emptiness in his eyes, before flicking his gaze back to Ruth and to Luke.

'We found them . . . But after everything, it's all so bloody hopeless.'

Narov crouched beside him, her eyes – her striking, clear, ice-blue eyes – level with his now.

'Maybe not.' Her voice was tight with intensity. 'How has Kammler got his virus out to the world? Think about it. He said that the virus has already been *unleashed*. "Even now it is making its way into the four corners of the world." That means he has weaponised it. How did he *achieve* that?'

'What does it matter? It's out there. It's in people's blood.' Jaeger swept his eyes across the forms of his wife and child. 'It's in *their* blood. Breeding. Taking them over. What does it matter how it's spreading?'

Narov shook her head, her grip tightening on his shoulder. 'Think about it. Plague Island was deserted, and not just of people. Every single monkey cage was empty. He'd emptied the place of primates. That's how he sent the virus global – he exported it via those KRP shipments. Trust me. I'm sure of it. And those few animals that already showed signs of sickness – he let them loose in the jungle.

'The Ratcatcher can trace those monkey export flights,' Narov continued. 'The monkeys may still be in quarantine. That won't stop the virus completely, but if we can nuke the monkey houses, it may at least slow its spread.'

'But what does it matter?' Jaeger repeated. 'Unless those aircraft are still in the air, and we can somehow stop them, the virus is already out there. Sure, it might buy us a little time. A few days. But without a cure, the outcome will still be the same.'

Narov's expression darkened, her features seeming to collapse in on themselves. She had been grasping at that hope, yet in truth it was a chimera.

'I hate losing,' she muttered. She went as if to drag her hair into a ponytail – as if pulling herself together for action – before remembering she was still wearing the respirator. 'We have to try. We *have* to. It is what we do, Jaeger.'

They did, but the question was how. Jaeger felt utterly defeated. With Ruth and Luke lying there beside him, being slowly consumed by the virus, he felt as if there was nothing left worth fighting for.

When the kidnappers had first ripped them away from him, he had failed to protect them. He'd clung to the hope of finding and rescuing them; of redemption. Yet now he had done so, he felt doubly impotent; utterly powerless.

'Kammler – *we cannot let him win.*' Narov's fingers dug deeper into Jaeger's flesh, where her hand still gripped his shoulder. 'Where there is life, there is hope. Even a few days might make a difference.'

Jaeger glanced at Narov, blankly.

She gestured at Ruth and Luke, lying on the stretchers. 'Where there is life there is still hope. You need to lead us. To take action. You, Jaeger. *You*. For me. For Ruth. For Luke. For every person who loves and laughs and breathes – take action, Jaeger. We go down fighting.'

Jaeger didn't say a word. The world seemed to stop revolving, time itself standing still. Then, slowly, he squeezed Narov's hand and raised himself to his feet. On legs that felt like jelly, he stumbled towards the cockpit. He spoke to the pilot, his words sounding cold and alien through the FM54's voice-projection unit.

'Raise me Miles on the Airlander.'

The pilot did as asked and handed over the radio handset.

'It's Jaeger. We're inbound.' His voice was steel. 'We're bringing in two stretcher cases – both infected. Kammler's shipped his primates off the island. It's via the monkeys that he's spreading the virus. Get the Rat on to it. Trace the flights, find the monkey houses and nuke them.'

'Understood,' Miles replied. 'I'm on it. Leave it with me.'

Jaeger turned to the Wildcat pilot. 'We've got urgent casualties to deliver to the Airlander – so why not show me how fast this thing can go.'

The pilot pushed his throttles forward. As the Wildcat soared towards the heights, Jaeger felt a stirring in his spirits. *Go down fighting.*

They would fight this battle, and maybe they would lose, but as his scoutmaster used to say to him when he was a kid, quoting Baden-Powell, the scouting founder: 'Never say die until you're dead.'

They had a matter of weeks in which to save his family, and all of humankind.

85

Figures dashed hither and thither across the Airlander's flood-lit hold. Voices echoed, shouted orders reverberating off the smooth lines of the Taranis drones. Above it all, the harsh whine of the Wildcat's rotors was quieting as the pilot prepared for turbine shutdown.

A medical team had taken over, and even now they were manoeuvring Ruth towards an Isovac 2004CN-PUR8C – a portable patient isolation unit. It consisted of a transparent plastic cylinder, with five hooped ribs inserted inside, the whole thing sitting on a wheeled stretcher.

Its purpose was to isolate patients who were infected with a Level 4 pathogen, while still allowing them to be cared for – and right now, Ruth and Luke were in urgent need of all the treatment they could get.

Tough rubber surgical gloves were built into the sides of the unit, so the medics could insert their hands and deal with the patient without any risk of contamination. It also came complete with an airlock, to allow medicines to be administered. Plus there was an 'umbilical connection' that enabled IV drips and oxygen to be fed to the patient.

Luke was already zipped tight into his unit, and hooked up to its umbilical, and Ruth was being lifted out of the Wildcat's hold in preparation for her own entombment.

For Jaeger, this was the worst moment yet of what had been his darkest day. He felt as if he were losing his wife and child all over again, having only just found them.

He couldn't get the terrible association out of his head – that for him, the PIUs were Ruth and Luke's body bags. It was as if they had already been declared dead; or at least, beyond saving.

As he exited the chopper with the team carrying his wife's semi-conscious form, he felt as if he were being sucked into a dark and swirling void.

He watched as Ruth was slid feet-first into the unit – like a bullet being slotted into a shotgun's breech. Sooner or later, he would have to let go of her hand. Her unresponsive hand.

He held on until the last moment, his fingers twined around hers. And then, just as he was about to relinquish his grip, he sensed something. Had he imagined it, or was there a spasm of life – of consciousness – in his wife's outstretched fingers?

Suddenly her eyes flickered open. Jaeger gazed into them, an impossible spark of hope kindling in his heart. The near-zombie look was gone, and for an instant, his wife was back. He could read as much in her wild, sea-green eyes, which were once again flecked with their signature specks of gold.

Jaeger saw her gaze dart hither-and-thither, taking everything in. Understanding everything. Her lips moved. Jaeger moved nearer, so he could hear.

'Come closer, my darling,' she whispered.

He bent further, until his head was kissing-distance close to hers.

'Find Kammler. Find his chosen,' she murmured. There was a blaze of fire in her eyes. 'Find those like himself that he inoculated . . .'

With that, the brief moment of lucidity seemed to be gone. Jaeger felt her fingers relax their grip, as her eyes fluttered shut again. He glanced at the medics and nodded, allowing them to slide her the rest of the way into the unit.

He stepped back as they zipped the coffin closed. At least for a moment there – a wonderful, precious moment – she had known him.

Jaeger's mind was racing. *Find Kammler and those he inoculated.*

Fucking genius, Ruth. He felt his heart start to race. Maybe – just maybe – here was the elusive spark of hope.

With a last look at his loved ones, Jaeger allowed them to be wheeled off towards the Airlander's sickbay. Then he called together his team, and hurried towards the front of the airship.

They gathered on the flight deck. Jaeger dispensed with the niceties. Now was not the time. 'Listen up. And listen good. Just for a few seconds there my wife was conscious. Remember, she's been in Kammler's lair for a very long time. She's seen it all.'

He eyed the team, his gaze coming to rest upon the elderly Miles. 'This is what she said: "Find Kammler. Find those like himself that he inoculated." She's got to mean that we could isolate a cure from them. But is that even possible? Is it doable, scientifically speaking?'

'Could we extract and synthesise a cure? In theory we could,' Miles answered. 'Whatever antidote Kammler has injected into his system, we would be able to copy and inject into our own. It would be a challenge to manufacture enough drugs in time, but with several weeks, it's doable. Probably. The challenge is finding him, or one of his acolytes. That we have to do pretty much immediately— -'

'Right, let's get moving,' Narov cut in. 'Kammler will have anticipated this. He will be prepared for us. We will need to scour the ends of the earth to find him.'

'I'll get Daniel Brooks up to speed immediately,' Miles announced. 'We'll have the CIA and every other intelligence agency begin the search. We'll—'

'Whoa, whoa, whoa.' Jaeger held up his hands for silence. 'Just a second.' He shook his head, trying to clear it. He'd just been struck by an ultimate moment of clarity, and he had to capture it; to crystallise it fully.

He glanced around at his team, his gaze burning with an impossible excitement. 'We already have it. The cure. Or the source of the cure.'

Brows furrowed. What the hell was Jaeger talking about?

'The kid. The slum kid. Simon Chucks Bello. He survived. He survived because Kammler's people inoculated him. *He's immune*. He has that immunity in his blood. We have the kid, or rather Dale does. Through him we can isolate the source of the immunity. Culture it. Mass-produce it. *The kid is the answer.*'

As he saw the realisation – the blinding flash of understanding – firing off in the eyes of his team, Jaeger felt a new-found burst of energy burning through his system.

He locked eyes with Miles. 'We need to get the Wildcat airborne again. Contact Dale. Get him to move the kid somewhere we can fly in and pick them up. Get them away from any crowded beaches, on to a stretch of easily accessible sand.'

'Understood. You'll be bringing them back here directly, I take it?'

'We will. But tell them to stay under cover, in case Kammler's watching. He's been one step ahead of us all the way. We can't allow him to be this time.'

'I'll launch both Taranis. Get them orbiting over Dale's location. That way you'll have cover.'

'Do that. Radio us their pickup coordinates once you have them. Just give us a distance due north or south along the beach from Amani itself, and we'll know where to put down. Tell Dale not to show himself until he can see the whites of our eyes.'

'Understood. Leave it to me.'

Jaeger led his team in a rush for the Airlander's hold. He grabbed the Wildcat's pilot. 'We need you to turn your ship around. Make for an area called Ras Kutani. Should be pretty much due west of here. We're going to do a pickup from a resort called Amani Beach.'

'Give me five,' the pilot replied, 'and we're good to go.'

86

The three Nissan Patrol 4x4s tore southwards, their massive tyres juddering like machine guns as they ripped across the ridged surface of the rough, unmade dirt road. Behind them they threw up a huge plume of dust, which would be visible from miles around – that was if anyone was watching.

In the passenger seat of the lead vehicle sat the hulking form of Steve Jones, his shaven head gleaming in the early-morning light. He felt his cell phone vibrate. They were barely thirty kilometres out from the airport, and thankfully they still had a good mobile signal.

'Jones.'

'You're how long to Amani?' a voice demanded. Kammler.

'Twenty minutes, at the most.'

'Too long,' he snapped. 'It can't wait.'

'What can't wait?'

'I've got a Reaper drone overhead, and it's picked up a Wildcat chopper inbound. Fast. Maybe five minutes out. It might be nothing, but I can't risk it.'

'What're you suggesting?'

'I'm going to hit the resort. Amani. And I'll earmark a first Hellfire for the Wildcat.'

Steve Jones paused for an instant. Even he was shocked by what he'd just heard. 'But we're almost there. Fifteen minutes if we really push it. Just hit the helo.'

'Can't risk it.'

'But you can't just take out a beach resort. It'll be full of tourists.'

'I'm not seeking your advice,' Kammler snarled. 'I'm warning you what's about to happen.'

'You'll bring seven tons of shit down on our heads.'

'Then get in and out fast. Kill the kid and anyone who gets in your way. This is Africa, remember. And in Africa the cavalry takes a long time to arrive, if ever. Do it right and you'll get your biggest ever payday. Do it wrong, and I'll deal with it by Reaper alone.'

The call went dead. Jones glanced around, somewhat apprehensively. He was starting to get the sense that he was working for some kind of power-crazed lunatic. Deputy director of the CIA or not, Kammler was a law unto himself.

But the money was good. Too good to complain.

He'd never earned so much for doing so little. Plus Kammler had offered him a double-pay bonus on proof of death; proof that the kid had been terminated.

Jones was determined to earn it all.

Anyway, Kammler was probably right. Who was going to rush to investigate, this far out in the African bush? By the time anyone bothered, he and his crew would be long gone.

He turned to his driver. 'That was the boss. Get a move on. We need to be there like bastard yesterday.'

The driver floored the accelerator. The needle crept up to 60 m.p.h. The big Nissan felt as if it were about to tear itself apart on the uneven surface of the dirt road.

Jones didn't give a damn. It wasn't his problem.

They were hire vehicles.

87

Kicking up a wind-whipped plume of ocean spray, the Wildcat put down on the damp sand. The tide was receding, and the beach was at its firmest where it was soaked with water.

The pilot kept the rotors turning as Jaeger, Narov, Raff, James, Kamishi and Alonzo piled off. They'd landed amongst the most stunning of landscapes. Dale had led the kid south, until they'd rounded a rocky headland taking them out of sight of Amani resort itself. Here, the low cliffs dropped abruptly into the sea, the red rock being cut into a series of dramatic wave-sculpted forms.

They fanned out into defensive positions, taking cover behind the rocky outcrops. Jaeger dashed forward. A figure came running out to meet him. It was Dale, and beside him was the distinctive form of the kid.

Simon Chucks Bello: the most wanted person in the world right now.

After a few days at Amani, the kid's hair looked even wilder, stiffened by exposure to salt, sand and sun. He was wearing faded shorts that were two sizes too big for him, plus a pair of shades that Jaeger figured he'd borrowed off Dale.

Simon Chucks Bello was one cool dude. And he didn't have a clue how important he was to all of humankind right now.

Jaeger was about to scoop him up and run him the fifty metres to the waiting chopper, when a chill froze him to the bone. With zero warning, something tore apart the mist of sea spray swirling above the Wildcat's rotors, the scream of its descent ripping into Jaeger's consciousness.

The missile ploughed into the roof of the Wildcat, ripping open the thin skin like a tin-opener. It detonated in a blinding flash, a storm of red-hot shrapnel slicing through the helo's hold and piercing the twin fuel tanks. They ignited, punching a dragon's breath of fiery death through the disintegrating fuselage.

Jaeger stared, transfixed, as the plume of destruction tore upwards and outwards, the noise of its eruption pounding into his ears and echoing back and forth across the seashore.

It was all over in less than a second.

He'd called in enough Hellfire strikes to recognise the high-pitched, tortured wolf-howl of the missile. He and his team – and Simon Chucks Bello – were the target of one right now, which meant there had to be a Reaper overhead.

'HELLFIRE!' he screamed. 'Get back! Get under the trees!'

He dived into some thick vegetation, dragging the kid and Dale with him. Unsurprisingly, Simon Chucks Bello was wide-eyed and frozen with fear, his pupils dilated to an impossible size.

'Keep hold of the kid!' Jaeger yelled at Dale. 'Calm him. And whatever you do, *do not lose him.*'

He rolled on to his back and delved into his combats, pulling out his compact Thuraya satphone and punching speed-dial for the Airlander. Miles answered almost immediately.

'The helo's been hit! There must be a Reaper above us.'

'We're on it. We have the Taranis involved in a nasty little dogfight with a Reaper right now.'

'Win it, or we're toast.'

'Understood. Plus get this. We've detected three 4x4s making for the resort. They're moving fast, maybe five minutes out from the front gate. I don't believe they're coming with any good intentions.'

Shit. Kammler must have deployed a ground force, as well as drones. It made sense for him to have done so. He was too careful to leave the kid to an unverified Reaper strike from ten thousand feet.

'Once we kill his drones, we can get the Taranis to deal with the road convoy,' Miles continued. 'But they'll likely be in amongst you by then.'

'Right, there's a bunch of boats along the beach, at the jetty,' Jaeger told him. 'I'm gonna grab one and bring the kid out that way. Can you get the Airlander down for a pickup at sea?'

'One moment, I'm passing you across to the pilot.'

Jaeger spoke a few words to the Airlander's pilot. Pickup plan sorted, he prepared to move.

'On me!' he yelled into his radio. 'All, on me!'

One by one his team gathered. Having taken good cover, all had survived the Hellfire strike.

'Okay, let's move it – and fast.'

With that, Jaeger started sprinting down the beach, his team right on his heels. They knew better than to ask for any kind of an explanation.

'Keep the kid in the centre of us!' Jaeger yelled over his shoulder. 'Shield him from fire. The kid is all that matters!'

88

A short burst of machine-gun fire echoed out of the resort, a few hundred yards along the beach. Amani had guards, and maybe they'd tried to put up some form of resistance. But somehow Jaeger doubted it.

The shots were most likely Kammler's force shooting their way in.

Jaeger shoved Dale and the kid aboard the RIB. It was a big, sleek ocean-going craft, and he prayed the thing was fuelled and good to go.

'Spark up the engine,' he yelled at Dale.

He ran his eye along the smart-looking wooden pier. There were maybe a dozen boats that could conceivably give chase. Too many to disable, and especially with Kammler's ground force closing in.

He was about to order his team to break from their defensive positions when the first figures came dashing on to the open sand. Jaeger counted six, with more arriving by the second.

They scanned the beach with their weapons, but Raff, Alonzo, James and Kamishi were quicker. Their MP7s barked, and two of the distant figures crumpled. The first savage return of fire came cutting in. The beach spat vicious gouts of sand, the long eruption ending in the water at Jaeger's feet.

Narov dashed across to him, dodging fire as she went.

'Move it!' she yelled. 'Go, go, go! We'll hold them off. GO!'

For an instant, Jaeger wavered. This went against all his

instincts and training. You never left a guy behind. These were his team. His crew. He couldn't just abandon them.

'GET MOVING!' Narov screamed. 'SAVE THE KID!'

Without a word, Jaeger forced himself to turn away from his team. At his signal, Dale gave a quick burst of power and the craft tore away from the pier, a storm of bullets chasing after it.

Jaeger searched for Narov. She was sprinting down the length of the pier, unleashing rounds from her MP7 into the engines of the tethered craft. She was trying to ensure that Kammler's gunmen had no vessel in which to mount a pursuit, but in doing so she was exposing herself to a murderous amount of fire.

As the RIB rounded the end of the pier, she made a final dash and a leap. For the briefest of moments she sailed through the air, her arms reaching for the speeding craft, and then she hit the water.

Jaeger reached over, grabbed her by the scruff of her shirt and, with powerful arms, hauled her sodden form aboard. She lay in the bottom of the RIB, fighting for breath and choking out seawater.

The RIB approached the first reef. Already it was well out of range of any accurate fire. Jaeger helped Dale lift the heavy outboard engine and tilt it forward, so it was free of the water. The hull bumped over the shallows, where there was a narrow gap in the coral, and then they glided out into the open sea beyond.

Dale went to full throttle, and the boat powered away from the dark, smoke-enshrouded beach, leaving the burning wreckage of the Wildcat, plus the dead aircrew, behind her. Yet Jaeger remained painfully aware that most of his crew was trapped on that beach, embroiled in the fight of their lives.

Narov glanced at him. 'I always hated beach holidays,' she yelled over the noise of the engine. 'The kid's alive. Focus on that. Not your team.'

Jaeger nodded. Narov seemed able to read his mind, always. He wasn't sure he liked that.

He searched out Simon Chucks Bello. The boy was crouched

in the lowest point of the RIB, eyes wide with fear. He seemed a lot less cool now. More like the orphan kid he really was. In fact, he looked distinctly ashen-faced. Jaeger didn't doubt this was the first time this kid from the ghetto had ever been in a boat, let alone experienced a full-on firefight.

All things considered, he was bearing up remarkably well. Jaeger was reminded of Falk Konig's words: *they build them tough in those slums.*

They sure did.

Jaeger wondered where Konig was now, and where his allegiances ultimately lay. They say blood is thicker than water, but he still figured that Falk was on the side of the angels. Even so, he couldn't exactly bank humanity's future on it.

He turned to Narov, jabbing a finger in the kid's direction. 'Keep him company. Calm him down. I'll sort the RV.'

He pulled out his Thuraya, punching speed-dial. A flood of relief washed over him as he heard the calm tones of Peter Miles.

'I'm on a RIB with the kid,' Jaeger yelled. 'We're moving due east at thirty knots. D'you see us?'

'I have you visual via the Taranis. And you'll be happy to hear the Reaper drones are no more.'

'Nice one! Give me a grid to head for, for the pickup.'

Miles gave him a set of GPS coordinates some thirty kilometres out from the coast, well into international waters. With the Airlander needing to descend from ten thousand feet to sea level, it was also the closest practicable interception point.

'Half my team is on the beach fighting a rearguard action. Can you get the drones over them to mallet Kammler's guys?'

'There's only one Taranis remaining, plus it's all out of missiles. Gone in the dogfight. But it can fly low-level runs at Mach 1, burning up the sand.'

'Do it. Keep eyes on the team. We're safe. The kid's safe. Give them all the support you can.'

'Understood.'

Miles would get his drone operator to bring the Taranis low

across the beach, flying repeated shows-of-force. That should drive the gunmen's heads down. And under the shock of those low-level passes, Jaeger's team would have to seize their chance to escape.

He allowed himself a moment to relax now. He rested against the RIB's side, fighting off the waves of exhaustion. His mind drifted to thoughts of Ruth and Luke. He thanked God they were still alive, and that Simon Bello was too.

It was close to miraculous that they had the kid safely in that boat.

More to the point, he was the key to Jaeger's family's survival.

89

As they sped across the ocean, Jaeger thought about the aircrew of the Wildcat. Not a nice way to go, but at least it had been instantaneous. Theirs had been a sacrifice to save humankind; they were heroes and he would not forget. His job now was to make their sacrifice worthwhile. And to ensure that Raff, Alonzo, Kamishi and James got off that beach alive.

Jaeger reminded himself that they were good operators. Some of the best. If anyone could get out of there, they could. But that stretch of open sand offered precious little cover, and they were outnumbered three to one. He wished he were back there, fighting shoulder-to-shoulder with his team.

His mind flipped to thoughts of the orchestrator of so much death and suffering, the architect of the evil; to Kammler. Surely they had enough evidence now to nail him ten times over. Surely his boss, Daniel Brooks, would start hunting for him properly. Surely, that hunt must have already begun.

But as Narov had warned, Kammler would have anticipated it, and he would be hidden where he figured no one would ever find him.

The ringing of the Thuraya brought Jaeger's mind crashing back to the present. He answered.

'It's Miles. And I'm afraid you've got company. There's a fast motor yacht bearing down on you. It's Kammler's people; they somehow made it out of Amani.'

Jaeger cursed. 'Can we outrun them?'

'It's a Sunseeker Predator 57. It can top forty knots. They'll catch you, and soon.'

'Can the Taranis deal with it?'

'It's all out of missiles,' Miles reminded him.

A sudden thought struck Jaeger. 'Listen: remember the kamikazes. Japanese pilots who deliberately flew their aircraft into Allied ships, in World War Two. Can your drone operator do something similar? Take out the Sunseeker with a missile-less drone strike? Slam the one remaining Taranis into it at Mach 1?'

Miles told him to wait while he checked. Seconds later he was back on the line. 'He can. It's unorthodox. Not exactly what they train for. But he figures it's doable.'

Jaeger's eyes blazed. 'Perfect. But that means we're leaving our guys on the beach with nothing: with zero top cover.'

'It does. But we're all out of options. Plus the kid is the priority. He has to be.'

'I know,' Jaeger replied reluctantly.

'Right, we'll re-task the Taranis. But the Sunseeker's catching you fast, so prepare to put down fire. We'll bring the drone around as quickly as possible.'

'Got it,' Jaeger confirmed.

'And just so we're absolutely certain the boy will be safe, once you're on board, we'll shortly have a pair of F-16s flying escort. Brooks has scrambled them from the nearest US airbase. He says he's ready to go overt on the whole Kammler thing.'

'About bloody time.'

Jaeger killed the call and readied his MP7, signalling Narov to do likewise. 'We've got company. Fast pursuit boat. Should be visible any time now.'

The RIB powered on, but just as Jaeger had feared, they spotted the distinctive white bow wave and plume of spray heading fast towards them. He and Narov took up position, kneeling at the RIB's gunwale, MP7s braced against its topside. It was at times like this that Jaeger wished he had a longer weapon, one blessed with a more generous range.

The Sunseeker's sharply raked prow cleft the sea like a knife, the wash from its engines throwing up a massive swirl of white water in its wake. Those on board were armed with AK-47s, which in theory had an effective range of 350 metres, as opposed to half that for the MP7s.

But firing accurately from a boat moving at speed was difficult, even for the best of operators. Plus Jaeger had to hope that Kammler's men had sourced their weapons locally, in which case they were unlikely to be properly zeroed.

The Sunseeker gained on them rapidly. Jaeger could make out several figures. Two were perched in the boat's forward compartment, to the fore of the sharply raked cockpit, their weapons braced on the Sunseeker's rail. In the seats set high and aft were a further three gunmen.

Those in the bow opened fire, unleashing a torrent of rounds towards the speeding RIB. Dale began to throw the craft into a series of tight random turns, in an effort to confuse the shooters, but they were running out of time and options.

Jaeger and Narov held their aim but still didn't open fire. The Sunseeker thundered closer. Rounds skipped and juddered off the surface of the ocean to either side of the speeding RIB.

Jaeger took a momentary glance behind him. Simon Bello was curled up in the footwell, shaking, his eyes rolling with fear.

Jaeger squeezed off a short burst that peppered the Sunseeker's hull. But it seemed to have no effect on the speeding craft. He forced himself to calm his nerves and concentrated on his breathing, blocking out all other thoughts. He glanced at Narov, and together they unleashed a second burst.

Jaeger saw a round strike one of the figures in the Sunseeker's bow compartment. The guy slumped forward over his weapon. As Jaeger watched, the other gunman lifted him up effortlessly and proceeded to throw him overboard.

It was an utterly ruthless move, and a chilling thing to have done.

The gunman had dumped the body in the sea using the

strength in his massive arms and shoulders. For a moment Jaeger's mind flipped back to a moment in his past: the gunman's form and bulk and his movements seemed somehow chillingly familiar.

And then it hit him. The night of the attack. The night of his wife and child's abduction. The massive, hulking form and the hateful tones behind the gas mask. *That man and this were one and the same.*

The figure in the bow of the Sunseeker was Steve Jones, the guy who'd very nearly managed to kill Jaeger during SAS selection.

The guy Jaeger suddenly knew with an instinctive realisation was the kidnapper of his wife and child.

90

Jaeger reached down to the kid – the precious kid – lying flat in the bottom of the RIB, where he was shielded from the worst of the fire. Simon Chucks Bello couldn't see a thing down there, and Jaeger didn't doubt how much he was suffering, both physically and mentally. He'd heard him puke once already.

'Hang on in there, hero!' he yelled at the boy, flashing him a bracing smile. 'I'm not letting you die, I promise!'

Still the Sunseeker bore down fast. It was no more than 150 metres to their stern, and it was only the rough ocean swell that was keeping the RIB shielded from its fire.

But that wouldn't last.

Any closer, and the rounds unleashed by Jones and his co-horts were bound to find their mark. Worse still, Jaeger was running dangerously low on ammo.

He and Narov had each emptied six mags, so some 240 rounds in all. It sounded like a lot, but not when trying to repulse an assault by a score of gunmen on a speeding pursuit boat, using two short-range weapons.

It was only a matter of time before the RIB took a cata-strophic hit.

Jaeger was tempted to grab the Thuraya and call Miles, screaming for the Taranis strike. But he knew he couldn't afford to drop his guard, or relax his aim. As soon as the Sunseeker hove into view again, they needed to hit it doubly hard and accurately.

Moments later, the sleek motorboat reappeared, its powerful

form slicing across their wake. Jaeger and Narov traded savage fire with fire. They saw the unmistakable figure of Jones raise himself and unleash a long burst on automatic. The rounds cut a chasm through the sea, one that reached out directly for the RIB. No doubt about it, Jones was a crack shot, and this burst was going to find them.

And then, at the very last moment, Dale powered the craft over the crest of a swell and the RIB dropped out of view, the fire ripping apart the air above their heads.

The howl of the Sunseeker's massive engines was audible now. Jaeger tensed over his weapon, scanning the horizon for where the boat would make its next move.

It was then that he heard it. A stupendous noise – an earth-shattering, thunderous roar – filled the air, as if a deep-ocean earthquake was ripping apart the sea floor. It reverberated through the skies, drowning out all other sounds.

Moments later, a dart-like form tore out of the heavens, its single Rolls-Royce Adour turbofan jet engine powering it along at a punishing 800 m.p.h. It streaked above them in a shallow dive, twisting this way and that as the drone operator corrected the Taranis's flight path to keep it on course with its target.

Jaeger heard deafening gunfire erupt from the direction of the Sunseeker, as those in the pursuit boat tried to blast the drone out of the skies. He pinned Jones in the sights of his MP7, squeezing off short aimed bursts, as his arch-enemy unleashed savage fire in return.

Beside him Narov was likewise eking out the last of her bullets.

But it was then that Jaeger sensed it.

His ears caught the soft, sickening hollow crunch of a high-velocity round striking human flesh. Narov barely cried out. She had no time to. The impact of the shot threw her backwards, and moments later she'd tumbled from the craft into the sea.

As her bloodied form slipped beneath the swell, the dart-like form of the speeding Taranis struck the horizon. There was a blinding flash of light, and a split second later a deafening explosion rolled across the ocean, chunks of blasted debris raining down on all sides.

Flames boiled and seethed around the stricken form of the Sunseeker, as the RIB powered onwards across the ocean. The motorboat had been struck in the stern, and flames and smoke were pouring off the vessel.

Desperately Jaeger scanned the waters immediately to their rear, searching for Narov, but there was no sign of her. The RIB was flying along at top speed, and in no time they would lose her.

'Spin the boat around!' he screamed at Dale. 'Narov's overboard and hit!'

Dale had been facing forward the entire time, steering a tortuous course through the ever-shifting swell. He hadn't seen what had happened. He slowed the RIB in preparation to make the turn, just as a call came in on the Thuraya.

Jaeger punched answer. It was Miles. 'The Sunseeker's down, but not out. We've got several figures alive, and they still have their weapons.' He paused, as if monitoring something from his vantage point, then added: 'And whatever you've slowed for, get moving and make for the RV. *You have to save the boy.*'

Jaeger slammed his fist into the bulwark of the RIB. If they turned back towards the smouldering wreck of the Sunseeker, in order to search for Narov, the risk of the boy getting hit was too high. He knew that.

He knew the right thing to do was to press on – for his family's sake; for the sake of humanity. But he cursed himself for the decision that he was being forced to make here.

'Get under way again,' he snarled at Dale. 'Move! Make for the RV.'

As if to reinforce the good sense of that decision, a burst of fire hammered out of the distance. Some of Kammler's men – Jones himself possibly included – were clearly determined to go down fighting.

Jaeger moved around the craft, busying himself trying to comfort Simon Bello, while scanning the skies ahead for the squat, bulbous form of the Airlander. He didn't know what else he could do.

'Listen, kid, stay calm, okay. Not long now, and we'll have you out of all this shit.'

But Simon's reply was lost to Jaeger, for inside he was burning up with rage and frustration.

Minutes later, the airship came looming into view, the ghostly white presence descending from the sky like an impossible apparition. The pilot took her massive bulk into a perfect hover, inching her towards the surface of the sea. The giant five-bladed propulsors – one set to each corner of the airship's hull – whipped up a storm of spray as the Airlander's skids made contact with the waves.

The pilot inched lower, until the open cargo ramp dipped its end beneath the ocean swell. The Airlander's turbines screamed as the pilot held her rock-steady, the downdraught whipping a storm of seawater around the faces of the two men on the RIB.

Jaeger took control of the boat now. What he was about to attempt was a manoeuvre he'd only ever seen done by one of his former commando coxswains, back when he was a young marine recruit. It had taken that guy years of training to get it just right, yet Jaeger had just one shot to execute it perfectly.

He turned the RIB until its prow was facing directly into the hold. The loadmaster gave a thumbs up from the Airlander's open ramp, and in response Jaeger gunned the powerful outboard. He was thrown back against the helm seat as the engine roared and the RIB surged ahead.

Any moment now they would slam into the Airlander's open ramp at full speed, so Jaeger hoped to hell he had got this dead right.

91

Moments before the point of impact, Jaeger raised the outboard engine to the point where the prop was hardly in the water, and then cut the power. The giant airship loomed above them, there was a sharp jolt as the RIB hit the ramp, leapt upwards and slammed down with a sickening thud, slewing its way into the hold.

The boat careered forward on to the flight deck, skidded sideways and came to a juddering halt.

They were in.

Jaeger flashed a thumbs up to the loadmaster. The propulsors screamed above them as they went to full power, the massive airship preparing to lift her impossible bulk from the sea, along with her extra cargo.

The airship rose a fraction, the swell sucking greedily at her skids.

Jaeger turned and ruffled Simon Chucks Bello's hair.

They might have saved him, but had they saved humanity?

Or Ruth and Luke?

Kammler must have anticipated that they'd go for the kid, for why else would he have risked sending out his hunter force; his dogs of war? He must have got wise to the fact that Simon Bello was the answer; the cure.

And in his heart of hearts Jaeger was convinced that the boy would prove to be their collective saviour. But right now, he felt little sense of joy or achievement. That final, horrific image of Narov being blasted off the RIB was seared into his mind.

Abandoning her to her fate – it was torturing him.

He peered out of the cargo ramp. The surface of the ocean was being whipped into a frenzied spray. The propulsors screamed at maximum revs, but the airship seemed momentarily stuck fast. He glanced to one side, darkly, and his eyes came to rest upon the distinctive form of one of the Airlander's life rafts.

In a flash, a plan crystallised in his mind.

Jaeger hesitated for barely an instant. Then, with a yell at Dale to safeguard the kid, he leapt from the RIB, ripped down the life raft and sprinted along the Airlander's ramp, until he was perched on the very edge of the abyss.

He grabbed the radio headset that the loadmaster would use, and called up Miles. 'Get this thing airborne, but stay under fifty feet. Take us due west, and slow.'

Miles confirmed the message, and Jaeger felt the four massive propulsors rev to an even greater pitch. For long seconds the Airlander seemed to hang there, the propulsors cutting through the air to either side of the craft, the swell crashing powerfully against her hull.

Then the giant airship seemed to tremble once along the whole of her bulk, and with a final effort she shook herself free of the sea's embrace. Suddenly they were airborne.

The giant beast of an aircraft turned and began to ease a path west across the waves. Jaeger scanned the ocean surface, using his GPS and the burning hulk of the Sunseeker as his reference points.

Finally he saw it – a tiny figure amongst the waves.

The airship was about a hundred metres away from her.

Jaeger didn't hesitate for an instant. He figured the drop was over fifty feet. It was high but survivable, if he entered the water properly. The crucial thing was to let go of the life raft. Otherwise, its buoyancy would bring him up short, as if he'd driven into a brick wall.

Jaeger let the raft fall, and seconds later he jumped, plunging towards the ocean. Just prior to impact, he assumed the classic position – legs tight together, toes pointed, arms linked over his chest and chin tucked well in.

The collision knocked the wind out of him, but as he sank beneath the waves, he thanked God that nothing was broken. Seconds later he surfaced, hearing the distinctive hiss of the life raft self-inflating. It had an inbuilt system that automatically triggered on impact with water.

He glanced upwards. The Airlander was powering skywards and away from danger with its precious cargo.

The term 'life raft' did Jaeger's inflatable something of an injustice. As it pumped full of air, it resolved itself to be a miniature version of the RIB, complete with a tough zip-over cover, plus a pair of oars.

Jaeger clambered aboard and orientated himself. A former bootneck – a Royal Marine commando – he felt almost as at home on water as he did on land. He fixed the position where he'd last seen Narov and began to row.

It was several minutes before he spotted something. It was a human figure all right, but Narov wasn't alone. Jaeger's eye was drawn to the distinctive V shape of a dorsal fin slicing through the surface of the water, circling her bloodied form. They were well beyond the protective barrier of the reefs here, which kept the beaches shielded from such predators.

This was a shark for sure, and Narov was in trouble.

Jaeger scanned the waters, spotting another and yet another razor-tipped fin. He redoubled his efforts, his aching shoulders screaming out in pain as he forced himself to row ever faster, in a desperate effort to reach her.

At last he pulled in close and stowed his oars, then reached into the sea and dragged her over the side and to safety. They collapsed as one, a heaving, sodden mess in the bottom of the life raft. Narov had been treading water for an age now, and bleeding profusely, and Jaeger didn't have a clue how she could still be conscious.

As she lay there, gasping for air and her eyes tight shut, Jaeger busied himself tending to her wounds. Like all good life rafts, this one came complete with the basic survival essentials, including medical kit. She'd taken a bullet in the shoulder, but as far as Jaeger could tell it had passed right through the flesh, missing any bone.

Luck of the devil, he thought. He stemmed the bleeding, then bound up the wound. The key thing now was to get water into her, to rehydrate and make up for the blood loss. He thrust a bottle at her.

'Drink. No matter how bad you feel, you got to drink.'

She took it and gulped some down. Her eyes found his and she mouthed a few inaudible words. Jaeger leaned close. She repeated them, her voice barely above a croaking whisper.

'You took your time . . . What kept you?'

Jaeger shook his head, then smiled. Narov – she was unbelievable.

She tried to stifle a laugh. It petered out into a watery cough. Her face twisted in agony. Jaeger had to get her to some proper medical help, and quickly, that was for sure.

He was about to take up the oars and start rowing again when he heard it. Voices, coming from the west, their position obscured by the thick pall of smoke drifting across from the burning wreckage of the Sunseeker.

Jaeger had little doubt who it might be – or what he had to do.

92

Jaeger cast around for a weapon. There was nothing in the life raft, and Narov's MP7 had to be somewhere at the bottom of the sea.

Then he spied it. Strapped in her chest sheath, as always: Narov's distinctive commando knife, the one that had been a gift to her from his grandfather. With its razor-sharp seven-inch blade it was perfect for what Jaeger had in mind.

He reached across and unfastened the sheath, strapping it around himself. In response to her enquiring look, he leaned close.

'Stay here. Keep still. Something I've got to deal with.'

With that he raised himself on to the side of the craft and dropped backwards into the sea.

Once in the water, Jaeger took a moment to orientate himself on the sound of the voices that drifted to him through the haze of smoke clinging to the waves.

He set off with long, powerful strokes, only his head showing above the surface. Shortly, the smoke swallowed him. He used his ears alone to navigate now. One voice in particular – the coarse but strident tones of Jones – drew him onwards.

The Sunseeker's life raft was a large inflatable contraption, hexagonal in design and enclosed within a rain cover. Jones and his three fellow survivors were inside it, the flap open, going through the craft's supplies.

Jones must have seen his shot hit Narov; seen her blasted into the sea. Not one to give up or give in, he would know he had a job to finish.

It was time for Jaeger to end this.

He had to cut the head off the snake.

The life raft was far more visible than a lone swimmer, one keeping low in the sea. When Jaeger reached its rear, he stopped and began to tread water, his eyes and nose barely above the waves. He composed himself for a second, then took a massive gulp of air and slipped beneath the surface.

He dived deep under the craft, surfacing silently at the point where the flap lay open. He could see the massive form of Jones weighing down the side of the raft. He kicked up powerfully, rising from the sea directly behind his target, and in one lightning move snaked his right arm around the man's neck in a savage chokehold, jerking his chin upwards and to the right.

Simultaneously, his left arm came around in a powerful thrust, sinking the blade of the knife down through the man's clavicle, driving it towards his black heart. Seconds later, their combined weight pulled them from the vessel, and they sank as one.

It was hard to kill a man with a knife. And with an adversary as powerful and as experienced as this one, doubly so.

As they sank into the ocean depths, the two men twisted, writhed and fought, Jones struggling to break free from Jaeger's death grip. For long seconds he clawed, elbowed and gouged, desperately trying to break free. In spite of his wound, he was immensely – unbelievably – powerful.

Jaeger couldn't believe how strong he was: it was like being tethered to a rhino. Just as Jaeger figured he could hold him no longer, a sleek, arrow-headed form flashed across his peripheral vision, its sharp V-shaped fin cutting through the water.

Shark. Drawn here by the smell of blood. Steve Jones's blood. Jaeger glanced in the shark's direction and realised with a jolt that there were a dozen or more circling them.

He gathered his strength, released his grip and kicked away from Jones as powerfully as he could. The big man spun around, muscled arms groping for Jaeger in the half-light.

But it was then that Jones must have sensed its presence. *Their presence. Sharks.*

Jaeger saw his eyes go wide with fear.

Jones's wound was pumping a cloud of blood into the water. As Jaeger kicked further away, he saw the first shark bump Jones aggressively with its nose. Jones tried to fight back, punching it in the eye, but the animal had the taste of his blood now.

As Jaeger made a desperate surge towards the surface, he lost sight of Jones's form within a sea of writhing bodies.

He was painfully short of breath now, but he knew what was waiting above: gunmen, scanning the sea. With a last burst of energy, he swam beneath the raft, using Narov's blade to slice open the entire length of its underside.

The bottom of the vessel collapsed, the three figures inside it plummeting into the water. As they fell, one of them kicked out and caught Jaeger in the head. His eyes rolled, and for a moment Jaeger felt himself black out. Moment's later his hand caught the torn edge of the craft where it was spilling air, and he pulled himself upwards.

He thrust his head and shoulders through the breech, grabbed a few lungfuls of oxygen, and dived again. As he kicked deep, he noticed that Narov's blade was gone from his grasp. He would worry about that later . . . if he ever got out of this alive.

He struck out in the direction of his own life raft. The gunmen in the water might well have seen him, but their thoughts would be all for their own survival now. There would be life vests in their stricken craft, and even now they would be trying to save themselves. Jaeger would leave them to the sea and the sharks. He was done here. He needed to get away, and get Narov safe.

Minutes later, Jaeger heaved his sodden form into the Airlander's life raft. As he lay back, panting exhaustedly, he saw Narov try to rouse herself so she could take up the oars, and he had to physically restrain her from doing so.

He got in position and began to row, heading away from the carnage and for the coastline. As he worked at the oars, he glanced at Narov. She was overcome with exhaustion, the shock kicking in big time now. He needed her to remain conscious, to keep rehydrating and to stay warm, and they would both need energy as the adrenalin began to wear off.

'See what's in the stores. The emergency rations. We've got a long row ahead and you need to keep drinking and to eat. I'll do the work, but only if you promise to live.'

'I promise,' Narov murmured, her voice sounding close to delirious. She reached to investigate with her one good arm. 'After all, you came back for me.'

Jaeger shrugged. 'You're on my crew.'

'You had your wife on that aircraft – dying. Me in the sea – dying. You came back for me.'

'My wife has got a team of medics caring for her. As for you . . . well, we're a honeymooning couple, remember?'

She smiled absent mindedly. '*Schwachkopf.*'

Jaeger needed to keep her talking and to keep her focused. 'How's the pain? The shoulder?'

Narov tried to shrug. The movement made her grimace. 'I'll live.'

Good for you, Jaeger thought. Unyielding, blunt and honest to the end.

'Better sit back and enjoy the ride then, while I row you home.'

93

Five weeks had passed since Jaeger had paddled the Airlander's life raft to shore and got Narov to the nearest hospital. It had taken him to the edge of his endurance and had seemed to age him. At least that was what Narov had said.

He reached for a surgical mask, slotting it over his mouth and nose, doing the same for the diminutive figure standing beside him. Over the past few weeks he'd spent barely a day apart from Simon Chucks Bello, and the two of them had grown close.

It was almost as if the kid who had saved the world had become like a second son to him.

Jaeger glanced up. Spotted someone. Smiled. 'Ah, great. You're here.'

The man in the white surgical suit, Dr Arman Hanedi, shrugged. 'Over the past few weeks, when have I not been here? It's been a little busy . . . I think I have forgotten what my wife and children look like.'

Jaeger smiled. He got on well with Ruth and Luke's doctor, and over time he'd learned a little of his story. Hanedi was originally from Syria. He'd come to the UK as a child in the first wave of refugees, back in the 1980s.

He'd got himself a good education and had gone on to rise through the ranks of the medical profession, which was no small achievement. He clearly loved his chosen field, which was a bonus, for during the last few weeks he'd had his work cut out, combating the world's most fearsome epidemic.

'So she's pulled through? She's conscious?' Jaeger prompted.

'She is. She came round thirty minutes ago. Your wife is made of incredibly strong stuff. That long an exposure to such a virus – to survive it . . . it's little short of a miracle.'

'And Luke? Did he sleep better last night?'

'Well, the son is rather like the father, I suspect. A born survivor.' Hanedi ruffled Simon Bello's hair. 'So, little chap, are you ready to say hello to another of the thousands that you have saved?'

The kid blushed. He'd found the media attention hard to deal with, to put it mildly. It all felt so over the top. All he'd done was donate a few drops of blood.

'Sure, but Jaeger did the hard bit. I didn't do shit.' Simon glanced at Jaeger a little sheepishly. Jaeger had been trying to get him to curtail the language, not always successfully.

They all laughed. 'Call it teamwork,' Hanedi suggested modestly.

They pushed through double doors. A figure was propped up on pillows. A mass of thick dark hair; fine, almost elfin features; plus those huge sea-green eyes, flecked with specks of gold. Were they more green than blue, or more blue than green? Jaeger never had been quite able to decide; they seemed to constantly change, both with the light and with her moods.

He was struck again by just how extraordinarily arresting his wife's appearance was. He'd spent every hour possible with her and Luke, just staring at them or holding their hands. Each time, he'd been hit by the same thought: *where the heck does love like this come from? It's the only thing that totally breaks me.*

Ruth smiled at him weakly. This was her first conscious moment since the virus had truly taken her, sucking her down into its dark and whirling vortex; since Jaeger had seen her thrust into that portable patient isolation unit aboard the Airlander.

He smiled. 'Welcome back. How're you feeling?'

'How long have I been . . . fighting it?' she replied, a little confusedly. 'It feels like a lifetime.'

'Weeks. But you're back now.' Jaeger glanced at the kid. 'And this is how. This is Simon Chucks Bello. I thought – we thought – you'd like to meet him.'

She turned her gaze on the boy. Her eyes smiled, and when they did, the world smiled with them. She'd always had this miraculous ability to light up an entire room with her laughter; her magic. It was what had first drawn Jaeger to her.

She held out a hand. 'Pleased to meet you, Simon Chucks Bello. I understand that without you, none of us would still be . . . breathing. You're one hell of a kid.'

'Thank you, ma'am. But I didn't exactly do much. Just got stuck by a needle.'

Ruth shook her head in amusement. 'That's not what I heard. I heard you got chased by the bad guys, jumped into a boat to escape, survived the sea ride from hell, not to mention an epic rescue by airship. Welcome to life with my husband – the very lovely but equally dangerous Will Jaeger.'

They laughed. That was Ruth for you, Jaeger thought. Always calm, always kind and always bloody right.

He pointed at the door leading into an adjacent room. 'Go check on Luke. Go beat him at chess. You know you want to.'

Simon Bello patted the rucksack he had slung over his shoulder. 'In here. Plus I brought him some snacks. We're good to go.'

He disappeared through the door. Luke had been conscious for a good week now, and he and Simon had developed a certain repartee.

There wasn't much in terms of electronic entertainment in the slums. Few were the households with computers or even TVs, and there was even less for orphans. Accordingly, they played a lot of board games, thought most were home-made – cobbled together from bits of cardboard and other trash.

Simon Chucks Bello was a demon at chess. Luke was using all his insider theories and trying various fancy sequences, but still Simon could defeat him within fifteen moves. It drove Luke crazy. He had inherited his father's competitive spirit. He came from a long line of bad losers.

Ruth patted the bed. Jaeger sat beside her, and they hugged as if neither ever wanted to let the other go. Jaeger could barely believe that she was back. There had been so many moments over the past few weeks when he had feared they were losing her.

'So, he's quite the kid,' Ruth murmured. She eyed Jaeger. 'And you know something – you're quite the dad.'

He held her gaze. 'What are you thinking?'

She smiled. 'Well, he did save the world. And us. And Luke has always wanted a brother . . .'

A while later Jaeger and Simon left the hospital. Once they were outside Jaeger switched on his mobile. There was the ping of an incoming message. He clicked on it.

My father took refuge in his lair beneath the mountain. Burning Angels Peak . . . I am innocent. He is a madman.

It needed no sign-off.

Finally, Falk Konig had surfaced.

It gave Jaeger just the kind of lead that he'd been looking for.

EPILOGUE

Within a matter of days of being plucked from the sea, Simon Chucks Bello had been rushed to the Centre for Disease Control and Prevention, in Atlanta, Georgia.

The source of his immunity was isolated from his blood. It was in turn synthesised into an inoculation that could be mass-produced, so that those not infected by the virus could be rendered immune.

A cure took longer to develop, but it was still ready in time to save most of those infected with the *Gottvirus*. The final death toll from the pandemic was less than thirteen hundred souls – still a huge tragedy, but nothing compared to what Hank Kammler had been intending.

At the height of the epidemic, the world had been on the verge of global meltdown. That number of people couldn't die without there being panic on the streets. But the worst of the trouble and chaos had been averted. For once world governments had been open about what exactly the virus was and where it had come from. It had taken such honesty to re-establish confidence amongst the world's peoples.

Even so, it was several months before the United Nation's World Health Organisation was able to declare the pandemic over. By then, Simon Chucks Bello had been granted British citizenship and was a part of the Jaeger family.

He'd also been given the US Presidential Medal of Freedom, America's highest civilian honour for those who have made an exceptional contribution to the security of the United States and to world peace.

However, US President Joseph Byrne did not get to present him with the medal: amidst something of an intelligence-driven scandal, he had been voted out of power. Thankfully.

Jaeger's team at Amani Beach – Raff, Alonzo, Kamishi and James – had taken a few injuries under intense fire, but they had escaped via the cover provided by the Taranis. All had survived. They still called Jaeger a glory boy and refused to let him forget leaving them to fight it out on that beach.

Irina Narov had made a full recovery – from both the virus and her injuries. But of course she blamed Jaeger for losing her precious commando dagger in the struggle with Jones.

At the time of writing, Hank Kammler – the former deputy director of the CIA – was still at large, location unknown. Unsurprisingly, he was now the world's most wanted man.

And in the meantime, Jaeger, Ruth, Luke and 'Bellows', as he'd been nicknamed, were a family again. And Jaeger had commissioned a new dagger for Narov.

He'd made a special request that the blade be razor sharp.